MORNA'S LEGACY: BOOKS 8, 8.5 & 9

SCOTTISH TIME TRAVEL ROMANCES

BETHANY CLAIRE

Editor: Dj Hendrickson
Cover Designer: Damonza

Available In eBook, Paperback, & Hardback

eBook ISBN: 978-1-947731-77-6
Paperback ISBN: 978-1-947731-78-3
Hardback ISBN: 978-1-947731-79-0

http://www.bethanyclaire.com

LOVE BEYOND REACH

BOOK 8 OF MORNA'S LEGACY SERIES

PROLOGUE

M orna's Inn—Present Day

"*S* o...what do ye think?" The question tumbled nervously from my lips. He'd taken his time reading our story. Each passing hour might as well have been a day as slowly as the minutes seemed to pass.

Spells, matchmaking, meddling—these were my talents, not writing—but my need to get our story down into a tangible form was so great that it had nearly driven me mad. My hands ached from the hours, days, and months spent working on my great project. Now that it was in front of my husband being read for the first time, I was sick with nerves.

"Did ye exaggerate for creative purposes?"

I knew without looking at the pages, without asking him, just what details in my story he questioned. I wouldn't lie to him to spare his feelings—not after so many years together. Our secrets were ours to keep but there was no room for lies between us.

"No."

"Hmm." He nodded in unison with the small noise. He may have wished for me to say otherwise, but he expected the answer I gave him. "I never knew ye loved him. I thought…"

My husband shook his head as he reached for me. Both our hands were wrinkled and weathered from time, but the feel of his touch still quickened my pulse in a way little else could. Time was powerless in dampening my desire for him.

"I thought ye stayed there to wait for me to return to ye, not because ye were happy at his side. But ye were. No matter how glad ye were to have me back, it broke yer heart to leave him. I dinna see that then. I am sorry for it. I am sorry for anything that has ever caused ye pain, but by God, I am glad that ye chose me."

"All hearts must be broken now and then." I smiled and squeezed his hand. "And I was there waiting for ye. 'Tis only that I often wondered if my waiting would do any good. But ye have to know that there was never any choice for me to make. It was always ye."

I wasn't sure my words would ease the pain I knew he must feel after reading certain parts of my story, but every word I said to him was true.

"Morna, who is this story meant for? I know that 'tis not only for us."

My husband knew me too well. Our story was meant especially for another—to lead her to the man worthy of holding her heart.

"There is a lass—the next to go back—that I intend to share my writing with. There are lessons she can learn from our story—lessons she will need before she makes a great journey of her own."

"Hmm."

My eyes were still turned toward our joined hands but I glanced up in response to his soft noise.

"What? Say whatever it is ye mean to. I canna stand it when ye beat around things so."

"Ye keep saying that 'tis our story, but 'tis not yet that. What ye have written here…'tis yer story."

He was right. It was the story of how we came to be, of all the events that led up to our life together, but there are two sides to every story, and I truly only knew my own.

"Aye, but I doona know what ye wish me to do about it. The only way for me to know all that happened in yer own life during that time is for me to spell ye, and I promised ye long ago that I wouldna do that. Unless ye finally mean to tell me everything."

Through our years together, he'd shared bits and pieces, but I never saw reason to press him on the subject. As long as we were together, I was fine with letting the past stay there. After all, I had plenty of my own secrets that I'd kept hidden until now.

"I willna tell ye a thing, but perhaps I shall try writing down my version just as ye have done. If 'tis rubbish when I finish, ye doona have to include it with what ye leave for the lass. Will ye let me try?"

Of course I would. Despite his modesty, he knew full well that whatever he wrote down wouldn't be rubbish. My husband was a closeted creative—I had a chest full of love letters and poems to prove it.

"Aye. Can ye finish it within three weeks? The lass arrives then."

He stood, still clinging to the pages he held in his hand and winked at me as he moved toward the stairs.

"I'll have it finished in half that time. The words are surfacing even now."

onall Castle—Three Weeks Later

t was odd for me to be watched so closely in the place that had once been my childhood home. I stood nervously inside the familiar walls of my old bedchamber, twisting my head at every noise or possible footstep to make certain no other tourists or castle employees were headed in our direction.

"It sure looks good, Morna. You did a really good job of making the outside look like a bunch of the other old books here. Do you have another copy? I want to read it."

A brief moment of terror filled me at the thought of Cooper opening the pages of my book and taking in the words inside. He understood far too much about everything already. The last thing he ever needed to read was every little—and sometimes scandalous—detail of my life.

"Cooper, if ye love me, ye will promise me to never, ever read what I've written. It is meant for someone else's eyes, and those are not yer own. Do ye understand?"

While young Coop usually did the exact opposite of what he was told, I could see by the concerned look in his eyes that he cared enough about my plea to listen this time.

"Fine, but I know what that means. It means there's the same stuff in this book as in the books that Mom used to read when we lived in New York. I bet you talk about kissing in there, huh?"

I could live with it if all Cooper thought was inside those pages was a little kissing. "Aye, Cooper. I'll admit there is some mention of kissing within that wee book."

"Yuck." Cooper's expression twisted into one of disgust, and he held the book away from him as if he worried the nearness of it might allow him to absorb the words. "You don't need to say anything else. I promise to never read it. But can I ask you one more thing? Why did you want me to come?"

I laughed but didn't argue the point with him. I had, in fact, not wanted him to come. If not for Cooper's unexpected arrival at our home a week ago, I would've brought the book to the castle myself but, as was customary for Cooper, he'd been quite insistent on coming with me. Apparently, now that I'd given him a job to do, he felt needed enough to forget the previous conversation.

"I suppose I just thought that mischief is more fun in the

company of others, and I know how good ye are at keeping a secret. I can trust ye to keep a secret, aye? Ye know how the others feel about my meddling. I doona wish to explain it all to them."

If Cooper felt he had an important role to play in anything, he was sure to meet it head-on.

"Of course you can. Don't you worry. How long do you think it will take for her to find it up here?"

I couldn't be certain. I would no longer spell anyone to do exactly as I wished them to, but I would always point people in the direction I knew they needed to go.

"I hope not verra long at all. She's here actually. In the castle at this verra moment."

"Really?" Cooper's voice rose several octaves in his excitement. "Can you show her to me on our way out? I promise I won't say anything to her. Let's just walk by her or something, okay?"

I was just as keen to see the woman in person myself. "Aye, fine. Now, hurry before someone finds us." I paused and pointed in the direction of the small table next to a sitting chair in the corner of the room. "Ye see there? Lay it just there as quickly as ye can. Then we must be on our way. Magic works best if ye set it and then release it to do as it should."

"Aye, aye, Morna. I am your humble servant, Pirate Cooper."

"A pirate? Have ye moved on from dinosaurs then?"

Cooper's voice, when he answered, sounded astonished and horrified.

"Move on from dinosaurs? Are you crazy? I don't think I could ever do that. But a man has to have varied interests. It makes him well-rounded."

I laughed at him and gently reached for his shoulder to steer him from the room.

"Right ye are, Cooper. Ye are a well-rounded young man, indeed."

It was my every memory—my husband's, as well—and I hoped

that when the lass found it, she would treasure every word. Only time would tell.

———————

"*I* think this one is my favorite, so far. There's just a feeling to it. I don't know what it is, really. Something magical about it, wouldn't you say?"

Laurel turned and awaited Marcus' response. She could tell by his glazed expression that her usually patient friend was losing his resolve to indulge her obsession with all things old.

"You've said that about every castle. Each one is more magical than the last, each new one is now your favorite. I'll be honest, they are all starting to look the same to me—just one big blur of stones and crumbling junk."

While many sites they'd visited over the last ten days had indeed been crumbling, Conall Castle in no way fit that description. Well-tended and magnificent, Laurel could all but see the castle's history swirling around her—could almost feel the people who lived here before.

"That's because they do keep getting more magical. I swear it. Especially this one. But you know, it may just feel that way because it seems like we are the only ones here. It's lovely to have the whole castle to ourselves rather than bumping into other tourists around every corner."

Marcus laughed and Laurel knew what he was going to say before he uttered a word. He'd complained about it for the entirety of the drive.

"It doesn't surprise me that we are the only ones here. I know lots of the places we've visited have been isolated, but this is quite literally in the middle of nowhere. If our car broke down on the way back tonight, there would be nowhere for us to stay."

Laurel found herself hoping, however wrong, that the car would break down just before dusk. She couldn't think of anything more enjoyable than being stranded amid such beauty.

"I don't think I would care too much if we got stuck out here. Surely a castle as old as this wouldn't be too hard to slip into after everyone leaves for the night. To sleep in a place like this would be pure heaven."

Marcus couldn't sound less enthused. "It probably has ghosts."

"Oh, I hope so. All of the best ones do."

Marcus' hand on her forearm drew her attention away from the tall window she stood gazing out of. "Hey, look. We're not alone, after all. Still, I agree with you that it's nice being around fewer people."

Sure enough, as Laurel turned she could see two people approaching—an older woman accompanied by a young boy who held himself very proudly as he walked.

"Let's head down toward the other end, Marcus, so that they have this area of the castle to themselves."

The woman and boy said nothing to either of them as they passed, but Laurel found herself struck by the intensity of the unabashed stare she received from both of them. She gave them a friendly smile in return, and the young boy raised his left hand and waved in greeting before they went on their way.

"Did you see the way they both stared at me? Has my blouse popped open or something?"

Laurel looked self-consciously down at herself as she tried to make sense of their wide, questioning eyes.

"No. Everything is covered as far as I can tell. Maybe they recognized you."

Laurel laughed and continued to move down the long hallway toward the last room at its end.

"Did you see how small that child was? There is no way he knows who I am. If his parents let him read one of my books at his age, then God help him. No, it definitely wasn't that. Maybe they were staring at you, and I just mistook the direction of the boy's gaze."

"Because I'm black? Come on, Laurel. Surely you think better of them than that."

Laurel couldn't tell if he was joking, but it wouldn't surprise her if he wasn't. Marcus had so many wonderful qualities. While his humility was to be admired, it drove her crazy just how incapable he seemed of recognizing his own attractiveness.

"No, Marcus. I most definitely didn't think they were staring at you because you are black. Perhaps they were staring at you because the only other human I've seen with your shape is the guy who plays Captain America."

Marcus huffed and stepped into the room to their right.

"I can already predict what you are going to say about this room."

Laurel remained just outside the doorway as she awaited his prediction.

"Oh yeah? What's that?"

"You are going to say that out of all the castles and all the rooms you've seen, this is by far your favorite."

She knew he teased her. Regardless, he was bound to be wrong. The room that lay ahead of her couldn't possibly beat the tower room they'd seen in the castle two days before.

"Let's just see about that, shall we?"

Determined to come up with a reaction opposite of what Marcus expected, Laurel stepped inside, looked around, and found herself completely unable to do so.

The room was perfect in every way. The things she loved most in all the world lined three of the four walls—books.

"It drives me crazy when you're right. This beats the tower."

"I knew you were going to say that. I knew it even before I stepped inside. I read about it in the guidebook and knew you'd love it. I can see by the happy, glazed expression on your face that you'll be in here a while. I think I'll go explore the dungeon while you do so. I'll come back for you in a bit."

Marcus nudged her playfully before leaving her alone in the room. Once he was gone, she inhaled deeply and smiled. The smell of books gave her the same kind of energy coffee did for some. She thrived off them, lived in them, made her living from them. In a room full of books, she felt at home.

She knew that the books lining the shelves didn't quite fit the historical nature of the castle—the bindings and covers were enough to tell her that none could be more than a hundred years old. Still, that knowledge did not reduce her love for what surrounded her now.

She moved to the far wall and slowly trailed her fingers along the spines moving row after row, bottom to top. It was a game she often played in libraries—letting her fingers trail the spines of many books until she felt something draw her to one in particular. As her fingers moved, she glanced to her left and took notice of a lone book sitting on a side table. Her fingers moved toward it instinctively.

She only resisted sitting on the old piece of furniture for a few seconds. As she picked up the book, she sank into the soft, empty chair, eager to read.

The chair was old and for a moment she feared it would collapse underneath her, but as she settled in more fully, it seemed to wrap her up in a way that invited her to do nothing more than read.

Marcus would occupy himself for ages while exploring the castle grounds. It wouldn't hurt anyone for her to take a moment to herself.

She opened the book gently. While it surprised her to see that the words were in English, it was the handwritten note inside that piqued her interest in a way nothing else ever had.

To whomever finds this book, you should know that it was meant just for you. Tuck it away in your bag, hide it beneath your shirt, but whatever you do, do not return it to the place it rested before. For many would read the pages contained within and dismiss my every memory and word as nothing more than fiction. But you, my first and last reader, will read these words and hear the truth in them.

Read these words. Love them, tend to them, believe them, and then once you've made peace with the truth, come and find me. By my story's end, you will know where.

Until we meet,
Morna Conall

P.S. Those who know me well know I have a terrible habit of butting in pretty much whenever I feel like it, and I'm afraid I found myself doing the same thing with my writing. As I was preparing my story, I realized that in some instances my conversational voice—sort of like this letter—was needed to show you even more. These little intrusions are scattered throughout the book. Think of them as author notes, if you will.

P.P.S. My husband has also seen fit to throw in his two cents, so you'll find parts of the book written by him, as well. It may all sound rather confusing now, but I have a keen sense of just how bright you are. You'll have no trouble at all, I'm sure. Now, get to reading. We have no time to waste.

"*D*amn." Laurel whispered the word aloud to herself, shaking her head at the book with mesmerized awe. Whatever the reason for such strange words, the author must have known that it would be impossible for the reader who stumbled upon them to do anything other than read on. She didn't know anyone whose curiosity would allow them to do differently. Smiling at the wit and the wonder of it, Laurel happily flipped to the next page and continued reading, never suspecting for a moment how such an act would change her life forever.

CHAPTER 1

Note from M.C. (Morna Conall)

I told you these would be scattered throughout the book. Here's the first one —right at the beginning.

The summer of my twelfth year was one of the most tragic and difficult seasons of my life. Looking back, those dark days marked the end of my childhood in a way that forever changed the person I was destined to become. Had my grandmother lived longer, had Grier not been forced to leave, had my father not seen fit to upend my world by telling me a truth I never really needed to know, perhaps magic would've come more easily to me, perhaps I could've saved one of my dearest friends in the world, perhaps I would've been content to live out my days healing villagers rather than pushing my way into the love lives of nearly everyone I've ever known and loved.

Perhaps, perhaps, perhaps...those questions never really get us anywhere, do they?

Still, memories have a way of sneaking into our minds when we least expect them. Most especially—in my experience—when we don't want them to. If I could tell you my story without reliving those few dreadful July days so many years ago, I certainly would. After all, this is a story of a young woman, not that of a little girl.

But the effects of this time were too far-reaching for me to exclude them from my story. So for the briefest of moments, allow me to break your heart.

I promise everything will work out in the end.

onall Castle—Summer of 1613

"What do ye mean, what do I want in a husband? I doona want a husband. Not ever."

I collapsed onto the thick blanket spread out on the ground for our lesson and looked up at Grier with confusion. Even though I was still terrible at magic, I looked forward to our daily lessons. It was the only time of day I felt like myself. While my progress was slow, my skills improved with each passing day. I saw no need to waste my precious learning time visiting about something so entirely useless.

Grier's smile didn't quite reach her eyes as she moved to sit across from me on the blanket. Her gaze looked haunted and suddenly older. For the briefest of moments, I wondered if perhaps the rumors about her were true. Maybe Grier really was much older than she appeared.

Despite the occasional weariness I sometimes saw in her eyes, Grier carried herself with an otherworldly confidence that enchanted all who knew her. I was fairly certain that everyone I'd ever known was at least halfway in love with Grier. Everyone that is, except my father. He detested my mentor. If not for Grandmother's insistence that she stay and teach me how to use my magic, he would've sent Grier away long ago.

It wasn't that Father didn't find her attractive. I knew that he did. Sometimes, I would catch him looking at her in the same way that Alasdair and every other male in the castle did. He simply hated that anyone might have more power than him. I suspected he hated me for the same reason.

"Grier...how old are ye?"

This time her smile was genuine, and my body released tension I hadn't even known it carried. That was Grier's power. In her presence, her mood quickly became your own.

"Do ye know how often I get asked that? How many times do ye imagine I've answered it?"

Grier almost always answered questions in this way. Never really answering anything, she could masterfully redirect a question.

"If it has to do with magic, ye should tell me, even if ye've never told anyone else before. Ye are the only other witch I've ever known. Ye are the only person I have to learn from."

Her eyes shifted again—back to the saddened, distant gaze of before.

"I'm verra old, though I'll never tell anyone just how old, for 'tis truly of no importance. My soul is still twenty and always shall be. Aging, or the lack thereof, is not what we are discussing today. All I will say is this, witches doona age in the same way as everyone else. One day, ye will be able to decide just how old ye wish to appear, and ye will be able to keep yerself that way for as long as ye like."

Every day the new wonders of magic astonished me. How could I have been so fortunate to be blessed with it when no one else in my family had ever had magic before? My great fortune amazed me.

"No. Ye canna mean it. If 'tis true, why canna we discuss this today? I'd much rather learn about this than discuss my getting a husband."

Grier sighed and the exhaustion in it washed over me, making my limbs heavy and tired.

"Ye needn't worry about getting a husband right now. Ye are only twelve. Even though many are wed at yer age, yer own father— bastard that he is—wouldna marry ye off so young. When ye are wed, he can no longer control ye, and he derives too much pleasure from that to rid himself of ye so soon. I only mean to make certain that the man ye do marry is the man ye wish to."

I smiled in awe. Everyone shared her sentiment about my father, but none save her would ever dare say so. She was the most fearless person I'd ever known.

"If I am not to be married, why should we concern ourselves with this now?"

"I'll tell ye after we cast the spell. We've not much time. This is far too important to leave unattended. Now, while I believe that ye doona want a husband now, someday ye shall want someone with whom to share yer life. I've already seen the sort of man yer father would choose for ye, and I willna stand for it. Sit quietly and close yer eyes."

Begrudgingly, I did as she asked.

"What am I meant to be thinking?"

"Shhh."

Grier laughed softly as she silenced me. I could sense her moving closer. While my eyes remained closed, she took my hands. Slowly, she turned them over and began to trace patterns on the soft flesh of my palms with her pointer fingers.

"Ye doona need to think a thing. 'Twill be easier for me to see what ye will need if ye quiet yer mind."

For a long while, Grier said nothing. Eventually, ever so slowly, my thoughts began to settle as I was lulled into a quiet, peaceful trance by Grier's soft touch.

When she spoke, her voice was soft and smooth. My entire body warmed through. I felt as if I could float away. I was as calm, safe, and happy as I'd ever been in my life.

"Look how lovely ye will be. I wouldna have thought it possible for yer hair to grow any thicker. Do ye feel that stubborn fire rising inside ye? Ach, I'm glad to see that it remains after what is coming for ye soon."

Something at the edge of my mind prickled uncomfortably at

Grier's warning, but I was too comfortable underneath Grier's spell to pay it any mind.

"As I feared, yer father will do everything in his power to discourage yer power. Ye will need someone who encourages ye, who is not afraid of him, who gives ye a purpose to move forward."

In my mind, I stood in front of mirrored glass, but my reflection was different. I was older, more womanly in shape, and my face was less soft and childlike. I smiled and was secretly pleased to see that my teeth hadn't twisted as I'd grown.

"Morna, each of us with magic has our own special set of gifts. Mine is to teach. A rather boring gift in the realm of what we do. Ye possess a gift that is far more interesting and, indeed, far more rare. It is within yer skill set that I've found the man who can help ye."

I wanted to call out and ask her what she meant, what my skill set was, but I couldn't move from the place inside my mind. My voice remained silent.

"I've never done it before, but I believe I can. I'll simply pull from the untapped power within ye. Allow me to stay here just a few moments more. I need to get a clear picture. I need to find him in time."

The image in the mirror swirled. Slowly my reflection was replaced with that of a man. Broad-shouldered and tan, he didn't resemble any of the men I knew. While most wore their hair long, his was cut to just below his ears though the hair on top hung long and wavy. He had no beard, but stubble lined his jaw. His eyes were kind.

The intensity of his gaze caused my breath to catch. I tried to look away, intimidated by his stare, uncomfortable with the feeling of intimacy that built between us. I couldn't move. My eyes remained locked with the stranger's as Grier spoke.

"Aye...'tis not yet time for him to come, but in a few years ye will be ready for him. A few minutes more and the spell will be complete."

I didn't want this man in my life. I could feel the chaos that his presence would bring, and it frightened me more than anything in my life ever had. I wanted to scream to stop her, but nothing would come.

Instead, everything went black as pain ripped at me from the top of my head down to the tips of my toes. I tried to breathe. When no air entered my lungs, the darkness spun.

I lost all consciousness as I faded into the nothingness that surrounded me.

I woke three days later, exhausted, confused, and totally unprepared for the hellish world that awaited me. Alasdair knelt beside my bed, both of his hands gripping mine tightly as he sobbed next to my bed.

"Morna, I'm sorry. I'm so, so sorry. Please wake up. I canna do this without ye."

He repeated the words over and over. The dread in his voice pulled me from my deep slumber too quickly. My head ached horribly, and I could only vaguely remember where I'd been before.

The meadow. My lesson. Slowly, memory came back to me. I sat up and pulled my hands from Alasdair's grip.

"The spell...what happened? Where's Grier?"

His face was red, his eyes swollen from crying. Fear lodged itself deep in my chest. In that instant, I wanted nothing more than to be sleeping again, to lose myself in the darkness of my dreamless sleep.

"She...she's gone."

My brother was a grown man sixteen years my senior, yet he looked so young and broken that terror gripped me so tightly I trembled as I struggled to speak.

"How long have I been asleep? What do ye mean she's gone?"

He rose from the floor and sat at the end of my bed, composing himself as best he could.

"Ye've been asleep for three days. I was so frightened that ye wouldna ever wake. I doona know what Grier was doing to ye, but it dinna go as she planned. Father interrupted ye both. I followed after him but I couldna stop him.

"When I reached him in the field where ye have yer lessons, Grier was standing over ye, muttering words neither of us could understand. She was pulling something from ye—a bright light poured from yer chest and ye were lifting off the ground. Grier was so lost in her spell that she dinna hear Father approach. Had she seen him, I canna imagine what she would've done to him."

He shook his head and paused, struggling for composure. In his silence, I frantically sorted through my memories of that day, searching for any recollection of what Alasdair described. I found nothing. I could remember a mirror and the hazy image of a man standing before me. Then there was only darkness.

"What did he do to her?"

"He pushed her to the ground, breaking her spell. Ye fell. Then he pulled ye up and threw ye over his horse. Ye wouldna wake. Grier screamed at him over and over, telling him to put ye down. She said that if she dinna finish the spell, 'twould damage ye, but Da dinna care. He said if it damaged ye enough to rid ye of magic, ye'd be better off for it.

"He banished Grier. Dinna even allow her to take her things. He told her that if she dinna leave his land right away, he would have her burned for witchcraft."

I swallowed. My mouth was so dry I could scarcely speak, but I couldn't allow him to continue to tell me something I knew couldn't be true. Grandmother would never allow Father to send Grier away.

"She canna be gone for long though, aye? Grandmother will see her back to the castle."

I saw it then, the deep well of grief in Alasdair's eyes. Before he could say a word, I knew what he'd been trying to tell me all along. Of course Grandmother would never allow Father to behave in such a way. If Grier was gone, Grandmother was too.

He opened his arms to me as I collapsed against him, my sobs lodging in my chest as I struggled to breathe against the shock.

"She passed in her sleep. That was why Father went to the field —to tell ye. He's been lost in his drink ever since. I havena left yer side, Morna. I've been so worried for ye. If ye'd died as well, I would've killed him. I know I would have."

I don't remember how long he held me. I eventually fell asleep again, drained from a grief so deep that I feared I would never recover. When next I woke, I found the dark, angry, bloodshot eyes of my father staring down at me.

———

"*R*ise. Ye have spent too long abed."

I couldn't move. Every time I opened my eyes, a fresh wave of grief hit me.

I said nothing. I simply couldn't bring myself to care that my inaction would anger him. My heart was too broken to feel anything other than loss.

"Do ye think ye are the only one devastated by this loss, Morna? Everyone in this castle is hurting. We must all carry on."

"I only learned of her death today. Did the rest of ye carry on the day it happened? Are ye so cruel as to not allow me even a day to grieve the loss of my grandmother?"

Father's voice was cold and slurred. He never drank, but on this night, he was so deep in his cups he could barely stand.

"Ha. 'Tis ye that's cruel. 'Tis not kind of ye to make me worry about how upset ye are over my mother's death. She is not yers to grieve over."

Between sobs, I screamed at him.

"How can ye say that? She was the only mother I've ever known."

"She was not yer mother. Nor was she yer grandmother."

For a moment, I wasn't sure I heard him correctly. He turned to leave my room, but strength I didn't know I possessed lifted me from the bed as I hurried to block him.

"What did ye say?"

Tears filled his eyes, and I gasped as he pulled me against him in a tight embrace. Father never hugged me. His breath ragged, he rested his chin on the top of my head as he spoke.

"Surely, ye've suspected it. I know ye believe I hate ye. I doona. I hate yer mother. Her dying act was to leave me with a child that dinna belong to me. Now, dress and join the rest of us for dinner. We willna wait for ye."

He pushed me away and left. As the door to my bedchamber closed, I sank to the floor and lost myself in heartbreaking sobs.

Only three days before, my world had been bright and full of hope. Now, all I could see was loss. Two of the people I loved most were gone without a goodbye, and despite my complicated feelings about my father, I'd never once suspected what he'd revealed.

Alasdair was now the only person I had left in all the world.

My childhood was over.

CHAPTER 2

*E*ight Years Later —1620

*M*uch changed at Conall Castle following my grandmother's death. At our father's insistence, no one within or around the castle ever spoke of Grier again. Within a fortnight of her banishment, all evidence of her time with us was gone. Already heartbroken and grieving over the loss of our grandmother, Alasdair and I were forced to wade through the deep loss of our friend alone.

My magic practices ceased entirely—or at least that's what Alasdair and I worked day and night to lead our father to believe. I continued to practice as much as I could, but with no one to guide me, I made little progress. My apparent lack of magic pleased my father immensely and as I grew, his treatment of me improved. My feelings toward him remained unchanged. How much can you love someone who only loves the version of you that they want you to be?

I didn't hate my father—I pitied his incurable unhappiness—but

I couldn't bring myself to love him, at least not in the way I loved my brother and friends.

Despite his confession that he wasn't actually my father, I never allowed myself to travel down the uncertain path of wallowing in that revelation. Even if what he claimed was true, it mattered little. Simply by claiming me as his own, I'd been afforded a life that most people in Scotland would only ever dream of. Even as miserable and mean as he was, I had to be grateful to him for that.

Three years after that terrible summer, Alasdair fell in love and married one of the most beautiful women I'd ever seen—Elspeth—a shy but strong woman who stole his heart the moment he laid eyes on her. At the age of thirty-one, most in Conall territory had begun to believe that Alasdair would never marry, so his nuptials with Elspeth were met with wondrous celebrations that lasted nearly a month.

Two years later, they welcomed a beautiful baby boy, Eoin, making me the happiest aunt that ever lived. Before the child's birth, I spent years roaming around the castle with no real purpose. Now three, Eoin had grown into an energetic and abnormally-tall-for-his-age child that spent every spare moment following me around. As a result, I was the closest thing that wee Eoin ever had to a nurse, and I loved every moment of it. My father, Elspeth, and even Alasdair—who usually tolerated everything I did—hated it. Childcare was a servant's work, and they all believed my role in Eoin's rearing was below my station as daughter of the laird.

It wasn't only them. Everyone I knew seemed to be deeply worried about me in one way or another.

Nearing twenty, the villagers seemed to have the same fears about me now that they'd had for Alasdair. I was quickly reaching an age where few would wish to marry me, and I knew my father well enough to know that he wouldn't let such a problem go unresolved for long. My days of freedom were bound to end soon. Until they did, I was determined to enjoy every moment with those I knew and loved. Thoughts of true adulthood could come later.

"Again, again."

I squeezed my nephew tight and grinned as his long legs bounced up and down against my thighs as he squirmed in my lap. Eoin pointed to the candles, urging me with his limited vocabulary to blow them out and relight them with my magic. For at least the eighth time that night, I flicked my wrist and watched the room go dark.

Bending in close to his ear, I whispered, "Only once more. Then ye must go to bed. Do ye avoid sleep in this manner when yer mother tucks ye in?"

Eoin simply laughed and continued to point to the candles as I re-lit the room. It was one of the few spells I could work without worry of something going dreadfully wrong, but even this must end soon. Eoin's speech improved quickly. I would have to stop doing magic in front of him before he mentioned the candles to my father.

With the room now lit, I stood and carried Eoin to his bed, tucking him gently inside. He yawned as I wrapped the blankets around him. I knew it wouldn't take long for him to fall asleep.

Most nights his mother saw him to bed, but Elspeth had appeared so weary at dinner that I insisted she go to bed early. With my brother away for the next month, I imagined that she was due a few weeks of uncrowded, peaceful sleep.

Just as Eoin began to drift, he suddenly jolted awake and reached beneath the covers for something he'd bumped against with his foot.

I watched as he pulled a large book from beneath the blanket. I took it curiously as he extended it to me.

I knew he couldn't read. Neither could Elspeth. Had Alasdair begun to read to him at night?

"Is this yer da's?"

Eoin shook his head and squirmed back until he sat up in the bed.

"No. I found it."

I held the book, flipped it over in my hands, and looked suspiciously down at him.

"Ye found it? Where did ye find it?"

Books were rarely left just lying around the castle. As far as I knew, only Father, Alasdair, and myself could read.

Eoin scooted out from beneath the blanket and crawled to the end of the bed until he could look all the way down the hallway to his right. Slowly, he lifted his finger and pointed to the room at the very end—my father's bedchamber.

I lowered my head and lifted my brows as I looked up at him questioningly.

"Ye found it or ye took it?"

The young child just smiled and returned to snuggle in beneath his blankets.

"Ye can bring it back. I doona want it."

Why the child wanted it in the first place, I couldn't guess. For the first time, I opened the book to its middle and looked inside.

A deep chill swept down the length of my body as I flipped hurriedly through the pages.

Spells in Grier's hand filled the book's entirety.

For eight long years my magic remained stagnant while assistance unknowingly lay only a hall's length away—hidden by my close-minded, controlling father.

Trembling, I tapped the book's cover as I spoke.

"Did ye see other books like this? When did ye take it?"

He nodded, and his eyelids grew heavy as he started to drift into sleep.

"Aye, in a chest. I found it this morning when I hid from ye."

His little eyes closed. I sat perfectly still until his breathing deepened enough that I knew my leaving wouldn't wake him.

Grier's spell books were still in the castle. Soon they would be mine.

I would stop at nothing to learn to harness the magic that hummed with life inside of me.

*A*n entire week passed. With each new day, I grew more frustrated at my various failed attempts to steal Grier's books away from my father. Each time I believed him far enough away from his bedchamber to risk entry, I would find him in some unexpected part of the castle. It seemed that the more I wanted access to the books, the more difficult it became to evade my father's watchful eyes.

With Alasdair still away on a secret errand for our father, I was forced to wait until the perfect opportunity presented itself. Patience came to me as naturally as obedience did—I was rubbish at both. Still, there was no one else I would put in such danger. So wait I did.

The worst Alasdair or I would receive for sneaking into Father's bedchamber was a good tongue lashing. If a servant was caught rummaging through Father's things, the most lenient punishment they would receive was banishment.

Frustrated from days of thinking up entirely useless ideas, I went in search of Mary. Two years younger than me, she'd been with our family so long that at the age of only seventeen she ran our home with a level of authority surpassed only by my father. She was my dearest friend and the only person, save Alasdair, that encouraged my magic.

I found Mary just as I expected to—in our cold and damp basement kitchen, covered in flour, ordering around half a dozen girls between the ages of twelve and fifteen with a tone that made me pity each and every one of them.

The moment she saw me standing in the doorway, she wiped her hands on the bottom of her dress and turned to address one of the youngest girls in Gaelic before joining me in the doorway.

"I doona know why I bother trying to teach them. 'Twould be less work if I sent them all away and did everything myself."

As several of the young girls looked nervously in our direction, I pulled Mary away and lowered my voice as I answered her.

"Ye teach them for ye know their families need what little they earn here. Ye care more than ye like to show."

Ignoring me, Mary quickened her steps and motioned for me to follow.

"Come with me to the village. I promised Mae I would tend the inn this evening so she may care for her father. Ye can help me. He is verra unwell. I doona believe he will live past the end of the year."

"Ach, no." It would break Mae's heart to lose her father. She knew little of life outside caring for him. "Do ye truly think he willna recover this time?"

"Every breath is a struggle. I canna see how he could improve. Mae's accepted whatever will come. The lass is stronger than I hope I ever have to be."

"What will it take for yer brother to see that Mae is in love with him? She will need someone when her father passes, and they couldna be more perfectly suited."

Turning with the speed of someone half her size, Mary spun to face me and burst out laughing. Between strangled breaths, she spoke.

"Mae...Mae doesna love Hew. What possibly led ye to believe that?"

I found the intensity of the attraction between the two of them so obvious, it was difficult for me to imagine how Mary couldn't see it.

"'Tis clear to me every time I see the two of them together, and she is not the only one who carries such feelings. Hew cares for Mae so much he can scarcely keep from trembling in front of her."

Mary laughed even more loudly as we continued the short walk to the village just beyond the castle grounds.

"'Tis true that Hew is shy, but he wouldna tremble in front of anyone, most especially Mae. Why, he's known her his whole life. Mayhap, the unused magic within ye is poisoning yer mind. Ye've never been so wrong about anything in yer life."

Unaffected by her doubt, I glanced over at the castle stables as we passed. An idea popped into my mind. If Mary had so little faith in my ability to see what was right in front of me, I would make her believe by revealing a truth about herself I knew she'd never told another before.

"Are ye so certain that I'm wrong that ye'd wager against it?"

Mary's confidence often got her into trouble. I knew she wouldn't say no.

"O'course, I am. What do ye have in mind?"

"We shall ask Mae if she cares for Hew as I believe she does when we arrive at her inn. If she either flushes blood red or says 'aye,' we will know that I am right. If I am right, which I am, ye must go and confess yer own feelings to the lad ye fancy most."

Laughing again, Mary stopped walking and doubled over as she gripped her stomach.

"Morna, ye must cease this. I havena laughed so much in weeks. I shall ache all day from it. Aye, I shall take yer wager for I canna lose."

Keeping my voice level, I smiled at Mary as she straightened.

"Lose ye will."

She shook her head and placed both her hands on her hips in defiance.

"But I canna lose, for ye know as well as I do that Mae doesna love my brother. Even if she does, I doona fancy any man around here. Thank God for it, too, for ye know how unseemly 'twould be for a woman to confess her feelings to someone she is not betrothed to."

Resuming her fast-paced trot toward the village, I ran to block her path.

"Mary, I know ye too well for ye to lie to me."

"I never lie."

"Aye, ye lie more than any good person ever should. Ye do care for a man here. Ye care for him verra much."

The amusement in her face faded, and I could see that she wondered just how I could possibly know.

"Oh? And who might that be?"

"Our stable master—Kip."

Even Mary's skin, darkened from too much time outdoors, flushed red at the mention of Kip's name. I beamed with triumph as I placed my hand on her shoulder.

"Did ye feel what yer face did? If Mae's does the same, we will know I was right."

Smiling, I turned and walked ahead of her.

My incessantly talkative friend fell silent.

CHAPTER 4

"Ye canna mean that ye truly intend to make me tell him. 'Twould be improper, and Kip wouldna care for it. 'Twill only make him uncomfortable. Please Morna, I beg ye. I'll do anything else."

Still in shock over losing the wager, Mary continued to protest as we made our way back to the castle in the dark. Upon arriving at Mae's inn, I sent word back to the castle to inform my father that Mae needed help and I would be absent from dinner, freeing Mary and me to tend to the inn until every last traveler was fed and abed for the night.

While father wouldn't approve of my helping in the inn any more than he did of my tending to Eoin, Mae's father and my own were old friends. I knew he would make no issue of my desire to help them if it was only for one night.

Of course I wouldn't force Mary to tell Kip of her feelings. I cared for my friend too much to embarrass her—not that I intended to tell her that just yet. Perhaps a few more minutes of dread would teach her to not doubt me so fiercely next time. While I wouldn't force Mary to say anything, I did intend to at least get Mary and Kip in the same room in the hopes that their feelings for one another might be strong enough to persuade one of them to take action.

"Aye, ye will tell him for I doona know if Kip will ever have the courage to do what he should without it. We will stop in at his cottage on the way to the castle."

Shaking her head in the moonlight, Mary repeated her astonishment for the tenth time since leaving the inn.

"I canna believe how easily Mae admitted it. She's never said a word about Hew before this night."

"'Tis no surprise to me that Mae answered ye honestly. Have ye ever known the lass to speak an untruth? I doona believe she's capable of it."

"Aye, I suppose 'tis true. Mae speaks her own mind too plainly to lie. Though, I must ask ye, Morna, did ye spell Mae to say what ye wished?"

An involuntary snort escaped me as I turned and looked at my friend to gauge the sincerity of her question.

"Mary, yer eye is still bruised from my attempt to send a wooden spoon across the kitchen to ye. Do ye truly believe I've the power to spell anyone to do anything?"

Rather than floating easily over to Mary's hand as intended, the spoon had flown across the kitchen with such speed that it smashed against her face and knocked her to the ground. She'd been angry with me for days.

Mary shrugged, keeping her voice low as she answered.

"I doona know what I believe about ye anymore. I still doona know how ye discerned my feelings for Kip. I've never even whispered them aloud to myself."

"'Tis a gift, not a spell. O'course I dinna spell Mae to do anything."

Kip's cottage lay just to the east of the castle's stables. His home was dark as we approached.

"Morna, he's already sleeping. We canna wake him up. I refuse to do it."

Pointing over to the stables, I grabbed her arm to prevent her from running off toward the castle.

"Look at the candlelight. He's still tending to the horses. I know he willna mind us visiting him there."

"Kip never works so late. If someone is within the stables, 'tis Rab, the newest stable hand."

Worry rolled off Mary in waves and her arm tensed beneath my grip. It was time to end her pain.

"Doona worry, Mary. I only mean to facilitate a meeting between the two of ye. Ye needn't say a thing that ye doona wish to as long as ye promise to not be so doubtful of me next time."

I smiled in the darkness as Mary sighed in relief.

"I'll never doubt ye again."

Inside, we found Kip leaning against the widest stall at the stable's far end staring intently at the mare inside. Hearing our approach, he turned to greet us. His smile was wide, and his eyes never left Mary. I wasn't even sure he knew I was there until he spoke.

"Did the two of ye come to see the birth?"

"Birth?" Mary's voice rose with excitement as she moved around me to look down into the stall.

I grinned inwardly as I slowly approached the two of them from behind. A birth would be the perfect excuse for Mary to linger. Perhaps she could offer him aid while I slipped away feigning exhaustion.

"Are ye alone, Kip? Shouldna Rab be here helping ye?"

Kip waved a dismissive hand and scooted near Mary so I could join them.

"Ach, the lad wouldna know what to do, and 'tis more trouble than 'tis worth to teach him. He said an errand—though he wouldna tell me what it was—needed his attention, and I saw no reason to keep him here."

Determined not to let this opportunity pass, I leaned forward to look across Kip at Mary.

"Kip, I canna believe our good fortune. Why, Mary was telling me only this morning that she'd never seen a mare give birth."

Eyes wide and disbelieving, Kip took over the conversation just as I'd hoped.

"No? Is this true, Mary? Surely, it canna be. Why, ye helped deliver Elspeth's baby all on yer own."

Blushing, Mary shot me a quick glance before answering him. I had no idea whether or not what I said was true, but I hoped she had enough sense to go along with it without question.

"Aye, 'tis true. Would ye mind if we stayed and watched? We'll help if we need to."

Yawning, I threw my arms above my head and stretched dramatically.

"Oh, Mary, I'm far too tired to stay, but I can see myself inside the castle if ye would like to wait for the birth."

In a gesture that surprised and filled me with hope, Kip reached out to gently touch Mary's arm as he spoke.

"Ye must stay. 'Tis a wondrous sight."

Content that my matchmaking would carry on fine without me, I bid them farewell and made my way along the short path from the stables to the castle.

I loved the castle even more in the dead of night when none but me lay awake, and I was free to roam its halls undisturbed or watched. The castle would never belong to me in the way it would someday belong to Alasdair, but in the moments when I moved through its corridors unaccompanied by watchful eyes, it felt like I was its mistress. My affection for its stone walls and elegant beauty knew no bounds.

I approached the door to my bedchamber with growing weariness as I considered just how shameful it would be to crawl into bed without changing out of my dress. As long as I woke early, none would be the wiser. It sounded delightful.

Opening the door and slipping inside, I walked through the

room's darkness picturing my impending dreams as I crawled on top of my blankets still fully clothed.

A sudden rustling sound near the window caused my head to whip in its direction. The shadowy figure of a man stood not far from my bed.

With no hesitation, no worry over what practicing magic in front of another might do, I flicked my wrist and sent the candles scattered around my room blazing with light.

At once, the man was revealed.

"Rab?"

The young man glanced around the room with horror.

"'Tis true, then. Ye really are a witch."

He held the small chest which contained the jewels I wore only on the most special of occasions in his hands.

"And ye are a thief. If ye mean to imply that my crime is worse than yer own, ye will surely find that my father would disagree. Unless ye wish me to call for him, ye will place my chest back where ye found it, and ye will sit on the ground at once."

Every last detail slipped into place inside my mind as a plan took form.

He was quiet, brave, and foolish. If Rab could so easily sneak into my room without anyone else in the castle seeing him, then surely he could do the same in my father's bedchamber.

He would either steal Grier's books for me, or my father would learn of his crime.

The choice was his.

CHAPTER 5

*T*hree glorious weeks of learning passed in a blur of sleepless nights and hazy days.

As expected, Rab eagerly agreed to steal the books to avoid whatever punishment my father would have cast upon him. Within two days of finding Rab, jewel chest in hand, every last journal was hidden away in my room. I spent every night working my way through the dozens of journals. It would take time—years even—to perfect the various spells found within, but I was willing to spend the time to have such power at my disposal.

In order to avoid suspicion, I only dared open the books once in my bedchamber for the evening. I would stay up long into the night reading and practicing until my eyes would close of their own accord. I was exhausted, happy, and terrified. The missing books wouldn't go unnoticed forever, and I knew that after having seen the learning available to me within Grier's books, I would never be able to go back to a life without them.

On the day Alasdair returned from his mysterious journey, as we sat down for our first family dinner in months, the inevitable occurred.

"Mary." Father's voice was harsh as he motioned for her to stay in the room after seeing the banquet of food she'd prepared and set before us.

"Aye, sir? Is there anything else ye wish me to bring ye?"

He shook his head and continued.

"No, there is more here than we could eat in a fortnight. Once our meal is finished, I want ye to have every servant within and around the castle brought here to the dining hall. I've a matter I wish to discuss with all of ye."

Mary hid her concern well and nodded obligingly before turning to leave.

The moment we were alone, Alasdair spoke. He looked tired and troubled. I knew something more tugged at him than what Father had just said.

"Ye've never gathered everyone together before. What's happened?"

"We've a thief amongst the servants. A great many books have gone missing from my chamber. I intend to find who took them and why. I shall see them freed of their hands."

I swallowed and glanced down at my lap in a panic as I thought of Rab. Death would be preferable to the loss of one's hands among the poor. For without hands to work with, a slow and painful death of starvation was bound to follow.

"Books? What need would a servant have of books? Most of them canna read." Alasdair's voice was disbelieving. "'Tis possible they've been misplaced. When ye sent me to yer chamber before I left, I couldna find the letter ye sent me looking for. Ye keep yer chamber in a dreadful state."

Anger flashed in Father's eyes, and his fist rattled against the table.

"I dinna misplace two dozen books. O'course I doona believe the thief stole the books to read them. They are rare and valuable— one could sell them for a high price amongst those of particular interests."

I sat in rigid silence unsure of which action would make me look more guilty—saying nothing and pretending that I couldn't hear them, or speaking up and joining in.

I glanced up and caught Alasdair's eyes and knew. My silence had already piqued his own suspicion of my involvement in this. I couldn't allow it to raise my father's.

"Particular interests? What are the books about, Father?"

He didn't bother to look at me as he answered.

"'Tis none of yer concern. Ye would all do best to take account of yer belongings. I doona believe my books can be the only stolen items."

The meal dragged on at a torturously slow pace. I couldn't eat another bite. All I wanted was to escape to my room where I could try to come up with a way to prevent my accomplice from being revealed.

Finally, when everyone else's eating slowed, Alasdair came to my rescue.

"Morna, I brought ye back a gift from my journey. If ye are finished eating, come with me so I may get it for ye."

Alasdair paused and turned to address our father.

"I'll join ye here when ye address them if ye wish it. It willna take the two of us long."

Father nodded, and I was up and out of my seat before he could change his mind. I knew I needed Alasdair's help, but all I could think of was the weariness on his face. Something had happened while he was away—something terrible.

I didn't wait until we made it to my bedchamber, instead turning toward him the moment we were a safe distance from the dining hall.

"What is it? Are ye injured?"

"No, I'm fine. What I wish to speak to ye about can wait. What have ye done, Morna? I can tell by looking in yer eyes, ye know of what Da speaks."

Nearing my room, I reached for my brother's arm and pulled him inside.

"The books father spoke of—they are Grier's spells and journals."

Alasdair's face reddened and his jaw clenched.

"I will never understand his fear of magic. 'Tis a blessing, not a curse, and 'tis dishonorable for ye to deny who ye are. How did ye learn he had them?"

I told him everything—of Eoin's discovery, of my pact with Rab, of everything I'd learned in the past weeks and of how I would run away from here before ever going without such knowledge again. When I finished, Alasdair stood in thoughtful silence for a long moment. When he finally spoke, his resolve was firm.

"Go and tell Father that Mae has sent word asking for yer help. He willna like it, but he will allow it. Tell him ye will be gone three days and that Kip will escort ye to the village. Then, go to Kip and tell him everything. Have him prepare three horses and pack enough for a three-day journey. Elspeth willna be pleased that I'm leaving again, but I doona see another way. I'll see to everything else."

"We're leaving?"

"Aye. Rab's guilt must come to light. Without someone to blame, Father will make life for the servants unbearable. Doona worry, I'll not allow Father to harm him. One way or another, we will see him safely to another territory."

"I must get the books hidden away before we leave. What if Father looks for them?"

Ahead of me, Alasdair nodded and shooed me from the room.

"I know just the place. I'll take them there myself. Go. Hurry. We've not much time. This is just the beginning of troubles we must discuss this night."

Before I could ask what he meant, Alasdair pushed me out into the hall and closed the door in my face.

"We'll stop here."

With the sun just peaking over the horizon, Alasdair abruptly pulled his horse to a stop. Rab and I quickly did the same. We remained a good distance from the nearest territory, and I wouldn't feel safe until we saw Rab away and settled from Conall land for good.

Alasdair dismounted effortlessly then moved to pull Rab from atop his horse as if he were nothing more than a small child. Confused, I called after him as he led the man away.

"What are ye doing? We should keep going. We…" I was left straddling my horse, Cadha, near an opening in the trees, staring after Alasdair as he attempted to lead Rab away from me.

Gently nudging Cadha, I moved to block their path.

"What do ye mean to do with him?"

Alasdair rarely lost his patience with me but exhaustion made him irritable.

"Even a man as foolish as him wouldna dare to step back into Conall territory after this night. There is no need to see him all the way to the next territory. I need to rest. I havena slept in days, and there is still much on my mind. We will bid farewell to Rab here."

The fear in Rab's expression was evident. Alasdair was right. Rab would never again cross over into my father's territory.

Tightening his grip on Rab's arm, Alasdair leaned in close, his voice a growl as he spoke directly to the thief.

"Had I allowed my father to do as he wished, ye would have had no hope for a future. Doona steal from another. See this as a chance to live a better life. And hear this—if word of what ye know about my sister spreads throughout this land in any way, I shall kill ye with my own two hands."

Pledging to change his ways and keep my secret, Rab ran away the moment my brother released his grip.

"Ye've more of Father in ye than ye show. Ye frightened even me."

Pulling a blanket from the top of his horse, Alasdair spread it on the ground and moved to lay on it. I could see from the weariness of his steps, he would be asleep within moments.

"Good. I meant every word. There is nothing in this world I wouldna do to protect ye, lass."

While Alasdair slept, I led each of the three horses to the small stream just beyond the forest clearing. More accustomed—thanks to my nights reading Grier's books—to being up until dawn, I wasn't as sleepy as my brother. I was, however, stiff and sore from riding through the night. Walking over to Cadha, I opened my pack to search for my own blanket in the hopes that I might spread it on the ground and rest my body for a while. My blanket was nowhere to be found.

"Are ye hiding it from me, Cadha? Or did Rab manage to take off with it?" Cadha neighed, and I took a moment to stroke her before moving over to Alasdair's horse. In the haste with which we left the castle, I assumed some of my belongings had been placed on one of the other horses.

As I reached inside Alasdair's pack, a small piece of parchment fluttered to the ground. Bending to pick it up, I struggled to make sense of the nearly unreadable hand. Slowly, I pieced the words together as my hands shook.

I found the home of the lass ye seek. I regret to inform ye of her recent death. Her home was set aflame by the laird of Kentrich territory. He believed her to be a witch. She perished in the fire.

I could think of only one person Alasdair would have gone in search of who would be accused of witchcraft. Alasdair's troubled expression suddenly made sense.

He believed Grier was dead.

I knew without doubt that she was not.

CHAPTER 6

*A*lasdair slept until midday. While I napped briefly, I spent most of my time impatiently tending to the horses. I wouldn't wake my brother—not when it was so clear how desperately he needed the rest—but it took every bit of willpower I possessed to keep from doing so. There were so many things we needed to discuss.

When at last I heard him stir, I left the horses and carried the small piece of parchment over to his blanket and plopped down in front of him, waving it in his face.

"Is Grier the lass to which this man refers?"

Still not fully awake, Alasdair stretched his exceedingly long legs and slowly pulled himself up to a seated position. His light brown hair fell in a mess of lovely waves around his shoulders. It was no wonder the female servants of the castle doted on him. Their ridiculous behavior made me hope I would never meet a man that turned me into such a fool.

After a few blinks, Alasdair seemed to realize both what I'd said and what I held in my hand. Regret etched his face as he spoke.

"Where did ye get that? 'Tis not the way I wished ye to learn of her death, lass. I'm so verra sorry."

43

I wanted to be certain before I said what I intuitively knew. I repeated my question.

"So Grier is the woman mentioned in this letter, aye?"

His eyes downward, Alasdair nodded.

"Aye, lass."

Waving the parchment excitedly, I smiled and laid it down in front of him.

"Whoever wrote this is wrong. Grier is no more dead than ye or I."

Interest piqued, my brother's brows pinched together as he leaned forward and stared at me.

"How can ye possibly know that?"

I wasn't sure, but I knew with absolute certainty that I was right.

"I still feel her somehow. 'Tis as if our shared magic bonds us in a way I doona have the knowledge to understand. Grier is still alive."

Alasdair took in breath so quickly that his lungs made a painful noise at the sudden intrusion of cold hair. Relief seemed to roll off him as I looked on in wonder.

I assumed Alasdair's distress had come from his worry over how I would handle the news of Grier's death, but I could see as I watched him that I had missed something in my assumption.

"I dinna know ye cared for Grier so much."

A half-hearted, restrained smile crossed my brother's face as he leaned back on his arms and looked across at me.

"Grier was the first woman I ever loved."

Still not understanding, I dismissed him.

"Everyone was in love with Grier."

"No, lass. Ye doona understand. I wanted to marry her. I asked her more than once but she denied me every time, never giving me an explanation that made any sense. She held my heart in a way that only Elspeth has ever surpassed."

My mind reeled. While a kinder sister would have been more

sympathetic toward her brother's heartfelt confession, I couldn't help but find it anything other than hysterically funny.

"Alasdair, I know why she wouldna marry ye."

His brows lifted again as he twisted his head in doubt.

"Do ye now? Please, do tell."

"Grier is at least four times yer age—older than our grandmother was."

I bent over and lost myself in a fit of hysterics as Alasdair's eyes all but bulged from their sockets.

"Trust me, lass. I know that canna be true. I saw more of Grier than I had right to at such a young age, and there was no part of her that was aged in any way."

I struggled to speak between bouts of laughter as I lifted from my doubled-over position to look at him.

"Aye, 'tis true. Her magic allows her to appear whatever age she pleases. She told me that I would someday be able to do the same. We doona age like the rest of ye."

I watched Alasdair's face carefully change from an expression of horror to amusement. Before long, he sat laughing even more loudly than I was.

"I hardly know what to say. While I canna rightly express how pleased I am to hear that she is alive, I doona believe I'll ever be able to think of her in the same way again."

With my own laughter finally subsiding, other obvious questions came to mind.

"Why were ye looking for her, Alasdair? We've barely spoken of her since she left."

Alasdair's face grew grim once more as he corrected me.

"She dinna leave, Morna. I doona believe she ever would have left if Father hadn't sent her away. I saw her face that day in the field. It broke something in her—not only her heart but nearly her soul—to leave us that day. Ye've need of her now. I thought it past time I saw her home."

Alasdair always believed he knew more about what I needed

than I did. Most of the time, he was right. The same age difference lay between me and Alasdair, as did between Alasdair and our father —sixteen years. Oftentimes, it seemed that while Father was Alasdair's da, Alasdair served as mine.

"Why do I have more need of her now than ever? Has something happened to me that I canna see?"

Alasdair let out a frustrated growl as he stood and paced in front of me.

"I knew he wouldna do it. He told me he would tell ye, but he's said nothing of what he's done, has he?"

"Father? No, I spoke little to him while ye were away. 'Tis usually best for me to keep my distance."

"He's sent for suitors, Morna. He expects ye to be wed by year's end. While I've no objection to ye marrying if ye wish to, and blessings to Mother for what she made him promise before her death, I doona believe men of Father's choosing should be pushed on ye."

Alasdair continued to stomp around in the field before me, speaking so quickly I had no chance to interject on any point.

"Ye are different than other women, Morna. Ye are special. Father will choose fools. There is little I can do to stop him from forcing yer hand in the direction he wishes it to go. If I was laird, I would protect ye. Ye'd be free to practice yer magic as ye wish it, and if ye never wished to marry, ye would have a home in my castle.

"I sent men in search of Grier in the hopes that she could return, and I could hide her away so that she could teach ye. That way, when ye are married, ye would at least have the aid of yer magic to ensure that ye lived yer life as ye wished it."

I thought back to that last day with Grier as Alasdair spoke. Though I spent little time thinking of marriage, I seemed far less frightened of it for myself than those around me.

When Alasdair finally exhausted himself from talking, I spoke.

"Is marriage so terrible? That day in the field—the last day we saw her—Grier warned me of the same thing."

With a reddened face and trembling hands, Alasdair joined me on the ground. Anger didn't suit him. My brother was good through and through.

"With the right partner, marriage can be a joy, but Morna, ye've been more sheltered than ye know by the life we've lived. Oftentimes marriage is a prison where women are abused and used and treated like property. And this is true for the plainest of women. For a lass like ye, for one with yer powers, the wrong sort of man would take advantage of yer abilities. If ye doona know how to control them, ye will be powerless to protect yerself from it. I suspect Grier knew that firsthand. What did she tell ye that day? And what was the spell Father interrupted? I've always wondered, though I think some part of me was too afraid to ask. While I know the goodness of Grier's soul, I always sensed a hint of darkness in her, hidden just beneath the surface of her smile."

I knew just what my brother meant. Even though I'd adored her growing up, even though I'd graciously accepted any knowledge she was willing to bestow upon me, there was a complexity of soul about her that always made me more nervous than I was willing to admit. Something about her frightened me deeply.

"I can scarcely remember, though I believe 'twas a love spell."

Alasdair's voice was incredulous.

"A love spell? At twelve?"

"No. She dinna mean for it to take place then. She was worried about who Da would choose for me later, just as ye are. I doona know what she meant to do. I canna remember her words, only a verra vague image of a man. 'Tis evident though that Father's interruption kept it from working. I've never seen the man in real life, and it seems 'tis too late if Father is inviting men of his choosing to the castle as we speak."

Alasdair nodded.

"I expect the first suitor will be there when we return. Doona allow Father to push ye toward any man ye doona love. While I can do nothing to keep him from seeing ye married, he promised

Mother long ago that the choice of whom ye marry would be yers. So wait until ye find a man worthy of holding yer heart—a man who will never misuse yer powers. Da may be many things, but he does keep his word."

I didn't wish to think or talk about suitors. I knew nothing of love. How would I know when a man was worthy of holding my heart? My sheltered life had left me ignorant of so many things. While my discernment for the attractions in others' hearts seemed engrained in my nature, I had no faith in my ability regarding my own love life. I had so much to learn.

"Alasdair, will ye continue looking for Grier now that ye know she is not dead? I would give anything to speak to her now—to have her help in learning from her journals."

My heart sank as he shook his head.

"I willna leave ye alone with Father once the suitors arrive. For now, ye must use the books and the books alone to learn."

"Where did ye put the books before we left?"

It surprised me that I'd not spent every waking moment worrying over them until now.

"I've a surprise for ye when we return. There's no more need for ye to spend yer nights toiling over Grier's spell books in yer bedchamber. I've readied a place—a safe place—where ye can learn as much as ye wish. I'll make certain that Father never learns of its existence."

I threw my arms around him in gratitude. I never wanted to live in a world without Alasdair.

If one of Father's suitors could love me half as much as he did, I would consider myself lucky.

CHAPTER 7

Note from M.C.:

There is real magic in this world and not only the sort of magic that I possess. There is a greater magic, one that works in and around all of us—connecting us in a way that we may never fully understand.

And the source of this magic—mysterious it may be—has a wondrous sense of humor. As I hugged my brother's neck silently wishing that there might be one other man who could love me as much as him, something inside me didn't believe it possible. My limited experience truly led me to believe that Alasdair was the only great man left. How foolish the naïve can be.

Never doubt the abundance that's out there for you. Our world is big, and great, and wonderful.

When I thought all that lay before me was a life of mediocrity with a man perhaps only slightly better than my father, magic was already at work, all the while laughing at my lack of faith.

While I squeezed my brother's neck, the man I wished for lay only a few dozen yards away. Which brings me to the first part of our story where my husband decided that my voice simply wasn't enough. I have to say...he was right.

I've learned so many things about him through this process. For so long, I believed he detested me. In truth, he was simply scared to death by how much he cared.

Fear makes such fools of us all.

---

 erry

Four hundred and eighty-five days is a long time for a man to remain trapped in a time other than his own. If not for my unrelenting belief that there must be a purpose to the strange happening—a reason why I was meant to visit this time—I would have lost my mind long ago. It was my faith in some sort of divine plan that kept me from giving in to the despair I knew would come if I allowed myself to believe that I would never again see my friends, my family, or my home.

With every passing minute, I inched closer to despair.

My mouth was so dry from going over twenty-four hours without even a drop of water that even breathing hurt my parched throat. For three months, I'd survived rather easily as a vagabond. With more farming knowledge than most in these parts, I was always handy enough to find short-term work that would pay me enough to see me to the next village.

Now, only one day's ride from my destination, I lay stuck in a shallow stream with one arm trapped between rocks and my other arm dislocated so horrifically that I couldn't move it at all. The pain was terrible, but it was my inability to move enough to get myself a drink of water that would kill me.

While I was nowhere near death yet, if the travelers up ahead were anything like the last to come across me, I would be soon.

They couldn't see me. While I could tell they were speaking, they were too far away for me to make out any of their conversation despite the loud volume of their dialogue with one another. I knew they wouldn't be able to hear my dry and quiet voice if I called for them. All I could do was sit, wait, and hope that one of them would venture in my direction soon.

For the longest time, everything fell silent. I worried that the strangers had gathered their belongings and left in the opposite direction. Eventually, hours later, they stirred and proceeded to talk and laugh together for another series of hours that left me reeling in frustration. Had I the ability to speak, I would've screamed obscenities at them for being so careless.

None of this was their fault, of course. I knew that. But thirst and fear makes all thought irrational. I needed help. I needed it badly. If they left here without seeing me, I would die.

I couldn't die. Not here. Not in this time. Not without knowing the reason for my sudden appearance in the seventeenth century exactly four hundred and eighty-five days ago.

Exhaustion hit me in waves as I lay propped up in my immobile position in the stream. With water lapping over both legs, I would sleep for short periods on and off throughout the day. At some point, I drifted. When I finally opened my eyes, the scene in front of me was finally different.

Rather than the same old stream, the most beautiful pair of green eyes I'd ever seen bore into my own. Her palms grasped either side of my face as she spoke in a whisper.

"I canna wait to hear how this happened to ye. Doona faint. My brother is about to move yer shoulder into place. I imagine 'twill hurt. 'Tis hanging in an ungodly position."

Before I could brace for it, an unspeakable pain rushed up and through my arm as consciousness slipped away from me once again.

I didn't care.

I was saved, and in more ways than I could have possibly known at the time.

CHAPTER 8

*J*erry, the strange disheveled man riding between my brother and me, would be fine. Thankfully, color returned quickly to his dislocated arm. Although it would be tender for weeks, it would heal. The condition of his other arm was remarkable as well. Caught in a rock fall that sent him slipping into the middle of the stream, the rock that held his right arm hadn't crushed any part of him. It had fallen in precisely the perfect position so that his arm fit snugly between two rocks. If not for the width of his hand, he would've been able to pull his arm through and free himself.

He was of average height but looked small next to my brother. His dark hair was cropped shorter than that of most men. While the length of his beard made him look older, I suspected that he was at least five years younger than my brother. He was dirty, smelled awful, and was so weary he could scarcely hold himself upright on his horse.

"Where were ye headed, lad? Were ye traveling alone? Why doona ye have any belongings with ye?"

Alasdair asked each question in such rapid succession that Jerry had no opportunity to respond. Each time the man opened his mouth to answer, my brother would send another question his way.

"Alasdair, why doona we see him to Mae's inn, allow him to rest a while and then speak to him? He canna wish to speak of any of this just now. Look at him."

Glancing over at me for the first time since we began the ride back to Conall territory, the stranger gave me a thankful, shy smile before turning to speak to Alasdair.

"Aye, forgive me, but the lass is right. My arm aches and I'm weary. If ye will see me to somewhere that I may rest for the night, I will answer anything ye wish to ask me come morning. I've little in means, but I'll find some way to repay yer kindness."

Alasdair nodded and ashamedly looked down.

"There is nothing to repay. O'course ye doona wish to talk. Forgive my rudeness. Can ye reach inside the pack to yer left? I believe there's a strong ale within that will surely help with the pain. Every drop inside is yers."

My brows lifted as I leaned forward and looked over at my brother in surprise. Alasdair hated ale. I'd only seen him drink it in front of our father. Even then, he only did so to prevent Father's teasing.

Alasdair could see what I was thinking right away.

"'Tis not mine. Rab stowed it away."

Jerry started in on the ale as if it were his first drink of water after we freed him.

He would be sick with drink by the time we reached Conall territory.

---

*A*lasdair and I returned to Mae's inn before the sun rose the next day. Wayward travelers were common in Scotland. While this wasn't the first time someone in my family had offered help to one of them, Jerry piqued my interest more than most.

It wasn't just his short hair and the oddity of the predicament we'd found him in that intrigued me—there was a familiarity about his eyes that I couldn't quite place.

Even drunk, Jerry had remained kind and courteous to us both, and I suspected that it was this that made Alasdair as eager as me to check on him the next day. Accustomed to men growing boisterous and misbehaving after drinking, the man's ability to maintain his dignity impressed my brother greatly. I'd even heard him speak to Kip about hiring the man on as the new stable hand if he was in need of work.

When we arrived at the inn, Mae was already busy at work in the kitchen, though no guests were down from their rooms yet.

"Is he awake?"

She nodded and answered my brother in a whisper.

"Aye, I believe so. I heard movement from within his room before I came down."

Following my brother, I stood back and waited while Alasdair ensured that Jerry was indeed awake and decent. When we walked inside, he looked as if he'd been expecting us for some time.

Alasdair wasted no time before asking his first question.

"Before the friendship between ye and my family continues, I must make certain that ye are not a man of ill-gotten means. Are ye a thief? Are ye on the run from anyone?"

I knew Alasdair didn't believe this man was any sort of criminal, but his question didn't surprise me. Alasdair was fiercely protective of the land that would one day be his and the people who lived on it.

"No, I survive by honest work and honest work alone. I held work at Creedrich Castle for the last year as a messenger for the laird. While I know that the circumstances in which ye found me doona speak to my talents, I know Scotland's land as if it were all my own."

"Are ye on an errand for the laird now? Were ye meant to deliver a message when ye fell?"

Jerry's beard made it difficult to discern much emotion from his expression, but I thought anger flashed in his eyes.

"No. I no longer offer my services to the laird of Creedrich territory. The man killed the...my..."

He hesitated and Alasdair pressed him.

"Yer what, lad?"

"My wife."

For the first time since meeting Jerry, I suspected him of lying. The word didn't flow from his mouth naturally. Instead his gaze dropped to the floor, and the word *wife* seemed to trip out of his mouth as if it had been pushed outward. The words hadn't been easy for him to say.

"Yer wife? Why would the laird kill yer wife?"

Jerry hesitated then stood up from the edge of the bed where he'd been sitting.

"I am sorry. I appreciate yer kindness in seeing me here, but I'm afraid 'tis not ye that I need to tell my story to. I must speak to the laird's son, for he is the only one who may be able to help me. Do ye know how I might cross his path?"

Casting me a careful glance, Alasdair crossed his arms and joined me against the wall.

"The laird's son? Do ye know him?"

Jerry shook his head.

"No, though my...my wife," again he seemed to struggle with the words, "she knew him. I have reason to believe he tried to seek her out before her death. I mean to find out why."

Every hair on my body stood on end. He couldn't possibly mean Grier. Twisting to look at my brother, I watched as he tried to mask his thoughts. Alasdair was an open book—he looked as speechless as I felt. Silently asking Alasdair to stay back, I placed my hand on his arm and stepped away from the wall as I went to stand in front of Jerry. I wanted to look in his eyes as I asked him.

"The lass ye speak of—she is not yer wife, is she?"

He stared at me for a long, silent moment, and the same strange sense of déjà vu I'd felt while on horseback yesterday evening swept over me.

"Ye can tell me. If ye lied about it, I know there must be a reason."

While I meant for my words to put him at ease, I could see in the way that his gaze hardened, I'd only aroused his suspicion. Leaning back to increase the space between us, he didn't break eye contact as he answered me.

"Lass, if ye are of the opinion that I owe ye any explanation, ye are wrong. While I'm thankful for both of ye, this here is not what I owe ye. Name yer price in regard to the work I must do for ye. As soon as strength returns in my arms, I shall complete it and call the debt I owe ye paid. Now, I would appreciate it if ye would both leave me. I shall find a way to speak to the laird's son on my own."

Laughing, Alasdair stepped away from the wall. While Jerry's response only infuriated me, I could see by my brother's expression it only endeared the man to him even more. Alasdair would've behaved in exactly the same way had their roles been reversed. Jerry didn't know that he was standing in the same room with the very man he wished to find. He only knew that the two people who'd provided him aide were questioning him as if he were their prisoner.

"Lad, ye doona owe us anything. I believe I can help ye gain access to the man ye seek. I know the laird's son verra well. Ye said before that ye no longer offer yer services to the laird of the territory from which ye came. Are ye in need of work? Not debtors work, but work in which ye may earn yer keep to stay here?"

Jerry nodded. "Aye. Any work ye can offer me, I will happily take."

Alasdair smiled, and I could sense what he meant to do. It would please him to trick the man.

"I've no work for ye, but the castle's stable is looking for a new hand. I've business I must attend to with the laird himself this evening. I shall present ye to him. If he thinks ye suitable, perhaps he will allow ye to stay on. If ye work at the castle, ye are bound to cross paths with the laird's son. Ye can then reveal everything to him that ye doona wish to reveal to us."

Jerry smiled.

"Thank ye. Yer understanding and kindness means much."

Satisfied with himself, Alasdair moved to the door.

"Ye canna come to the castle looking like that, lad. Ye must see yerself cleaned and groomed if ye wish the laird to grant ye work."

With his left shoulder still bound to his chest and his right arm bruised, he would need help.

"I doona think he can. Will it really matter?"

With a horrified expression that I knew full well was pretend, Alasdair twisted in the doorway and looked back at me.

"Aye, it matters. I willna bring any man before the laird and present him as my guest looking as he does now. What would the laird think of me?"

Shaking my head to shame him, I neared my brother and whispered, "What do ye expect him to do?"

Dismissively, Alasdair shrugged as we walked into the hallway.

"Mae can help him."

Mae constantly had more to handle than any person should ever have to. I wouldn't allow Alasdair to place one more burden on her shoulders.

"No. Say nothing to Mae. I'll see him shaved and readied for this charade of yers. Ye should be ashamed of yerself, Alasdair."

Alasdair laughed.

"Ye can tell him if ye like. Doona take long with him. Father will wish to see ye when ye return to the castle. He believes that ye've been here helping Mae, and ye know he will tell ye that he doesna care for it."

I had no wish to spend more time with the man than necessary. I wanted to return to the castle so I could see the surprise Alasdair mentioned the day before.

"Aye, I know. Go on. I'll follow ye shortly."

A few moments later, I returned to Jerry's room with a blade and bowl of water in hand. He eyed me skeptically.

"I've no desire to rid myself of my facial hair."

"Are ye in need of work? If so, I doona believe ye have a choice."

Pointing to a wooden seat in the room's corner, I waited for him to sit. He held out a hand to stop me as I approached.

"Wait. If ye mean to put a blade to my throat, I must at least know yer name first."

Setting the water bowl down on the table next to him, I reached forward to comb through the hair with my fingers. It was wiry and filthy. I couldn't wait to see what he looked like without it.

"I canna believe it dinna occur to ye to ask our names before now. 'Tis yer own fault my brother has fooled ye so. My name is Morna Conall, and the man who just offered to present ye to the laird is my brother, Alasdair—the laird's son."

Enjoying the look of embarrassed horror in his eyes, I set about my work.

CHAPTER 9

"*N*ow that ye know who I am, ye might as well tell me the truth. The lass ye spoke of before...her name was Grier, aye?"

For the first part of his grooming—while I messily sawed away at the length of hair extending from his face—Jerry said nothing to me. Eventually, I couldn't stand it. I wanted to know everything. How did he know Grier, and why was he still under the impression that she was dead?

Surprised, he glanced up at me, and I had to look away. The more I looked at his eyes, the more familiar they felt to me, and I found it difficult to maintain eye contact with him.

"Did ye know her?"

Tossing a length of hair onto the floor, I nodded. I knew I needed to be careful about what I revealed to him. While he gave the impression that he and Grier were quite close, I knew it wasn't safe to assume that he knew about her magic.

"Aye. She was one of my grandmother's dearest friends. I spent much time with Grier when I was younger."

This seemed to surprise him, and I knew that I'd been wise to say nothing of her magic.

"Friends with yer grandmother? She canna be that much older than ye are."

Twisting to clean the blade to ready it for application to his face, I smirked to myself. Grier never told men the truth about her age. If she did, she'd have a much harder time seeing them to her bed.

A flash of this man entangled with Grier flew unbidden into my mind. While I had no reason to have any feelings about such an image, I found it immensely displeasing.

Ignoring his statement about her age, I asked the same question I'd asked him earlier.

"Were ye truly married to her?"

Confirming my suspicions, he shook his head just one half motion to the right as I reached to steady his chin to clean away the first full strip of hair.

"Why did ye tell us that ye were?"

With one run of the blade completed, he seemed convinced that I didn't intend to slit his throat. He visibly relaxed.

"In truth, I canna believe yer brother left ye alone to tend to me. Had I known him to be so openminded, I might have told ye the truth. Grier and I were never married, though I lived with her for the past year."

Intrigued and far less offended than pretty much any other person in Scotland would be, I pressed further.

"My father would never stand for it, but Alasdair allows me my freedom. He believes I have a mind of my own."

Jerry surprised me by letting out a soft sigh. Under his breath, he whispered, "Aye, I doona doubt it."

"Ye dinna marry Grier, but ye loved her, aye?"

I would tell him that she lived soon enough. First, I wanted to hear his story to learn if there was a reason for Grier to purposefully make him believe she was dead.

"As a sister, aye. Grier and I were not together. Before she died, she was helping me find my way home."

The man was full of contradictions. First Grier was his wife.

Now, he cared for her as a sister. First he said he knew Scotland as if all its land belonged to him. Now he said that he needed help finding his way home.

He was a mystery—one I was intent upon solving.

Pulling my blade back across his cheek to rid it of stubble, I questioned him.

"Yer way home? I thought ye knew Scotland's lands well."

He sighed deeply and reached to grab my arm. Gently pulling it away from his face, he continued to direct the blade back to the table.

"Wait a moment. I doona wish to tell ye while ye hold the blade. 'Tis probable ye will believe me mad, and I doona wish ye to open one of my veins in fear."

Unsettled by the touch of his hand, I pulled away and set the grooming instruments down. Moving to lean against the bed, I nodded in agreement and waited for him to begin. He looked ridiculous with the length of his beard jaggedly chopped and one clean strip of face showing across his right cheek. He didn't seem to notice or care.

"I risk much by telling ye, but I know that I must. If ye knew Grier, I have to hope that ye knew of her secret. If ye did, ye might know of a way to help me. Do ye know Grier's secret?"

So he did know of her magic, and he had need of it.

"Do ye mean to ask me if I knew Grier was a witch? Aye."

Relief flooded Jerry's face as a rush of anxiety-laced air left his lungs.

"Ach, thank God for it. If yer family truly doesna share the same fear as so many in the Highlands, perhaps yer father and brother can help me as I've hoped."

Nothing he could've said would have annoyed me more. Why did he assume that they would be the ones that could help him? Did he believe all I was capable of was shaving his mangy beard? Father would be enraged if he ever learned this man had even heard Grier's name. While I knew Alasdair would be sympathetic, he would be useless. Jerry sat in the room with the only person who could possibly help him, and he dismissed me because of my age and gender.

Perhaps, he'd been right to ask me to set the blade down.

"Ye'd be wise to never mention a word of this to my father. He's gone to great lengths to ensure that no memory of Grier remains in Conall territory. If ye show him that ye were acquainted with her, the kindest ye can hope for from him is banishment."

"But I thought ye said yer family knew she was a witch? Why would yer brother send for her if yer father disapproved of it?"

"Just as I have a mind separate from that of the men in my life, so does Alasdair have a mind separate from our father's. 'Twould be foolish of ye to believe that any of my father's beliefs align with my own."

I paused, the words I so desperately wanted to say stopping at the edge of my tongue.

I could almost hear Alasdair's protective voice boom in the outer regions of my mind urging caution. There was no reason for me to trust him, no reason for me to reveal to him that I too, had magic, but as I looked across at him, no part of me worried that I would be putting myself at risk. I wanted to tell him if only to make him feel badly for dismissing my ability to help him.

"Alasdair sent for Grier because he believed I needed her help. I'm a witch, too."

Jerry's reaction was not what I expected.

Smiling so that every one of his teeth showed, Jerry doubled over and laughed.

CHAPTER 10

J erry

J laughed at the coincidence, not because I disbelieved her. After tumbling backwards through time and living with a witch for over a year, nothing should have surprised me.

I realized too late that my reaction angered Morna. With one quick flick of her wrist, the bonny lass extinguished the candles around the room, though it did little to darken the space around us. The sun was now up and shining through the small window behind her.

"Lass." I stood and reached for her, grabbing both hands. I lowered my head so she would look into my eyes. "I believe ye. I dinna laugh because I thought ye were lying. I laughed because sometimes I canna believe the oddity of my life. Now, please, finish what ye started here on my face. I must look a frightful mess."

She watched me carefully and eventually pulled away to move to the washbowl and blade. I resumed my seated position and awaited her touch. Her hands were gentle across my skin, and it took everything in me not to tremble at the light touch of her fingers.

"I canna see how ye thought it funny."

I waited until she finished one long stroke down my cheek, then spoke.

"Aye, well, if ye'd lived the past year of my life, perhaps ye would see the humor in it—dark though it may be. Can ye do more with yer magic than extinguish fire? I'm in need of great help."

I meant the question as a joke. If Grier had mentored her, the lass surely had great power, but as I watched her teeth clench, I fell silent.

"I...sometimes I can sense things that others cannot."

Astonishment in my voice, I twisted to look up at her as I spoke. "Is that all? Surely, it canna be."

Her next pull of the blade across my skin held more pressure than those before it. I could feel her anger in the way she held my chin.

"Did ye not hear me tell ye that my father sent Grier away from here? He doesna approve of magic. I've had no training in the use of my powers since I was twelve."

Shaking my head as she cleaned the blade, I reached to feel the bare half of my face. I'd not shaved since before my tumble through time.

"I doona think I care for yer father. He's allowed ye to become entirely useless."

The blade dropped against the table with a loud clank before I realized the stupidity of my words. They were thoughtless and selfish and below me. No matter how desperate I was to return home, it was unforgivable for me to behave as if anyone owed me help.

I turned toward Morna slowly, expecting to see tears fill her eyes, or at the very least for her to rear back in shock. Instead, I watched as a brief flicker of pain crossed over her eyes—pain she quickly masked with the expertise of someone well practiced at being on the receiving end of an insult. It made me dislike her father even more. My hateful words weren't the first time this lass had been made to feel useless. I couldn't remember ever feeling so despicable.

Recovering quickly, she picked up the blade. While her voice was softer, she kept it steady.

"Aye, I know. Turn yer chair around so I may reach the other side of yer face."

Unsure how to apologize without making matters worse, I silently stood and did as she asked. We remained silent for what seemed like ages as she worked on my face. Finally, as she pulled the blade across one last time, I spoke.

"I doona think ye are useless, Morna. I'm just a frustrated fool who has been away from home for far too long. I verra much wish for us to be friends. Forgive me."

She stood behind me and said nothing as she reached around to brush the last bits of hair from my face.

The smile back in her voice, she patted my shoulders as she urged me to stand.

"There is nothing to forgive. Every word ye said was true. Now stand and introduce yerself to me. Ye no longer resemble the man I met yesterday."

Brushing hair from my kilt, I stood and faced her. Her mouth fell open, and she paled.

"Do I look that bad, lass?"

While I knew I must look different, her response seemed strange. More than shock appeared in her expression. She looked deeply shaken.

Afraid she might fall, I reached forward and grabbed her hands to steady her. She pulled away immediately and backed to the other side of the room.

"Why is it that ye are always reaching for my hands? Ye are more familiar with yer touch than ye have a right to be."

Smiling inwardly at her blush, my pulse quickened. She didn't mind my touch, and the realization bothered her. While the lass was still very much a stranger, the complexity of her character intrigued me.

She carried herself with the maturity of women twice her age, yet sometimes she would do or say something that revealed how young she truly was.

"I'm sorry if I've offended ye, lass. 'Tis only that ye look quite troubled."

She pointed to the seat behind me. Understanding her silent command, I turned the chair around once again and sat. The moment I was seated, she spoke.

"I need ye to tell me everything about yer relationship with Grier. Why was she helping ye? How did ye meet her? Alasdair canna help ye with this. Useless as I am, I am yer only hope."

Her reminder of my thoughtlessness pained me, but I knew it best to say nothing else of it and answer the questions she'd asked of me. While the possibility of her being able to see me home seemed small, I knew it was the only option I now had.

"Ye may verra well not believe my story, but I beg ye to listen silently until the end."

Agreeing with one small nod of her head, I continued.

"Lass, I canna explain what happened to me. I've yet to find anyone that can, but there is truth in every word I'm about to tell ye. I was not born in this century, not even in the next. My life, my friends, my family—they all lay in the twentieth century, some three hundred years in the future."

Pausing, I searched Morna's eyes but found her gaze unreadable. I continued.

"On the eve of my twenty-eighth birthday, I went to sleep inside my old farm house, content in knowing that come morning, I would have another long day of work ahead of me. I woke in the middle of the woods, far from my home, and entirely out of my time.

"I wandered for days until I reached a village outside of Creedrich Castle. It was only then that I truly began to realize the oddity of my circumstance. I believed I'd gone mad. No modern means of transportation lined the streets. No buildings resembled the town I knew from back home. I hid silently amongst the people for the better part of a week, eating scraps where I could find them, listening in on every conversation I could. Eventually, when I came to terms with the only reality I could imagine, I made a plan to ensure my survival.

"Even out of my own time, I knew that I could navigate Scotland. So I went to the laird to offer my services as a messenger. I hoped that by traveling I could find someone who could help me home. I dinna have to look far. 'Twas at the castle, I met Grier."

For the first time since beginning my long tale, Morna spoke. "Did Grier work for the laird?"

I shook my head.

"No. The laird of Creedrich Castle, like yer father, fears magic. His wife doesna share his fear. Grier would often provide healing remedies to the lady of the castle in secret. The night I went to offer my services to the laird, Grier was sneaking away from the lady's bedchamber.

"I said nothing to her that night and was hired on as a messenger like I hoped. 'Twas only after working at the castle for some weeks that I began to hear rumors of Grier's work within the castle. Eventually, I thought it worth the risk to seek her out and tell her my story. She believed me immediately and offered to help me return home.

"In short time, Grier and I secretly moved in together as 'twas easier for us to work on possible spells and read through old spell books together. Grier worked night and day trying to find a way to send me home, but in the year I was with her, we found nothing."

"Where were ye when Grier died?"

Memory of that terrible night still caused the breath to tighten in my chest. I couldn't bear to think of my friend dying in such a horrible way, and the guilt I felt for not being there weighed on me every single day.

"I was away delivering messages for the laird. I know little of what happened. Only that I returned to find our home destroyed. When I made my way to the village, I was told that the laird found out about his wife's friendship with Grier and attempted to banish her for witchcraft. When she refused to leave, he set our home aflame. Rather than abandon her home, she allowed herself to burn inside."

It was this that made my grief easier to bear. While I missed her, I couldn't bring myself to forgive her for leaving me. Her pride sentenced me to a life out of time.

"I'm sorry."

Morna's small voice pulled me from my thoughts.

"Aye. 'Twas the darkest night of my life. In my rage, I left Creedrich territory and traveled aimlessly for months seeking work and keeping an open ear for another with magic who might help me. A fortnight ago, I crossed paths with yer brother's messenger. When I learned he sought Grier, I knew I needed to come to Conall territory. I hoped that if ye all knew Grier, ye might know of a way to help me. It seems I was right. Will ye help me, Morna?"

Slowly, Morna walked across the room, never glancing in my direction as she spoke.

"I must think, Jerry. I'll see ye this evening."

Without another word, the only other person I'd ever told my tale to walked away. Her quick retreat was enough proof of her disbelief.

She thought me mad.

Dinner with her father was now more important than ever. I needed Morna's help even if it took me years to convince her that my story was true. Work at the castle would keep me close to her.

I would stop at nothing to win the trust of Morna's bastardly father.

CHAPTER 11

M *orna*

I made the walk back to the castle in half the time it
normally took. I was still shaking by the time I entered
through the castle's main doors. While shaving the second half of
Jerry's face, he was turned away from me. The moment he stood
and faced me, I knew why I found his eyes so familiar. Every
memory of my last day with Grier returned at once.

Jerry was the man in the mirror—the man Grier intended to
find for me.

My emotions swung wildly from disbelief to fear to anger. Due
to Father's interruption that day, I assumed her spell hadn't worked.
Did Jerry's sudden presence in my life mean it had? Could his story
of being born in another time possibly be true?

There were stories in Scotland—legends of people taken by
fairies, only to be returned to a time very different from that which
they left—but this was different. Could witches manipulate time,
as well?

So much of Jerry's story made little sense. If he was indeed the man Grier intended to bring me, why did she allow him to live with her for a year after she found him? And if he truly did fall through time, it was Grier who caused him to do so. Why then, had she pretended to not know how to send him home? Furthermore, why had she led him to believe she was dead? Did she know that she could no longer pretend to be ignorant of the aid he so desperately needed and worried of his reaction once he found out she'd been lying to him?

No, that couldn't be it—Grier feared no one.

The questions in my mind only seemed to build on themselves. In my distracted state, I didn't hear my father's voice until he called to me a second time.

"Morna, dinna ye hear me? Come here, lass."

His voice caused any thought of Grier or Jerry to vanish. Any interaction with my father required my focused attention. I could never allow myself to fall behind in conversation with him. Whenever I did, it ended with me being pushed into something I didn't want.

Smiling as sweetly as I could manage, I apologized and made my way over to him.

"I'm sorry. The past days at the inn have tired me. If ye'll excuse me, I'd like to rest before dinner. Thank ye for allowing me to offer Mae aid."

My efforts to dismiss my father rarely worked, but it never stopped me from trying. I turned away as he called me back to him.

"Ye may rest shortly. What I have to tell ye willna take long."

Father's tone made me nervous—there was more patience in his voice than usual—a sure sign that he was after something. Moving to sit in the chair opposite him by the fire, I feigned concern. If Alasdair's warning the day before was correct, I already suspected what our impending conversation was about.

"What is it? Has something happened?"

"No, I've good news. 'Tis time for ye to choose a husband."

I chose my next words carefully. If I wanted him to keep the promise he'd made my mother, I couldn't anger him with my response.

"'Tis time for me to choose? Surely, ye would be better suited to choose whom I should marry?"

The words tasted like bile on my tongue.

As I knew he would, Father said nothing of his promise. Instead, he wished to make me believe allowing me a choice in my future was a show of his generosity towards me.

"Ye are to make yer own choice, though I shall invite suitors of my choice here. The first suitor is already here as my guest. He shall join us at dinner. If after meeting this man and spending time with him, ye canna see yerself wed to him, we will send for another."

He paused, and I could see by the way he looked away from me and into the fire that he wasn't finished.

"Morna, I trust ye know that what I am allowing ye is unusual. Most men wouldna allow it."

He wanted me to thank him. Doing so would cost me nothing. I could thank him and then send each and every suitor away. Eventually, perhaps he would grow tired and relinquish his quest to see me married.

It wasn't that I never wanted to marry, but like Alasdair, I wanted to understand the power within me before I relinquished my freedom to another.

Putting on the mask I always wore in front of my father, I stood, smiled, and moved to kiss his cheek.

"Thank ye, Father. Yer kindness means more to me than ye can possibly know."

Wiping my lips with the back of my hand, I went in search of the one person I knew could help me sort through all that Jerry had told me—Alasdair.

"*M*ary, just give me one wee taste. What harm will it do? I willna tell a soul ye allowed me to taste it early."

I could hear Alasdair the moment I reached the first step leading down to the castle's kitchen. Mary's banter with everyone was entertaining, but she and Alasdair shared a special bond of friendship that made it even more so.

"Alasdair, if ye doona believe I shall stick ye with this poker if ye doona step away from the fire, I shall be happy to prove ye wrong. Elspeth willna be pleased if ye wind up with an arse that's so sore ye canna walk for days."

"Mary!"

I stepped into the room, but neither of them seemed to notice me.

"Doona 'Mary' me. Yer own mouth is far more foul than my own. Ye think that ladies doona think the same foul words that ye men say every damned day. Well, we do. 'Tis only that I know ye too well to worry over what I say in front of ye."

"I know ye well, and I've never known ye to speak in such a way. Something is bothering ye."

I knew exactly what bothered her, but I said nothing as I waved when Alasdair glanced my way.

Following Alasdair's gaze, Mary ran over to hug me the moment she saw me.

"Morna, I feel I havena seen ye in years. Where were ye? I know ye were not with Mae as yer father believes."

"I'll tell ye later. Will ye allow me to speak with Alasdair alone for a moment?"

Pulling away, she crossed her arms and glared at me.

"Ye canna mean to send me from my own kitchen?"

Apologetically, I reached forward to squeeze her arm.

"Aye, I am. I'll make it up to ye. 'Twill only take a few moments."

Something about my tone must have expressed my urgency, as she left the kitchen without another word.

When we could no longer hear footsteps, Alasdair spoke.

"I came here to wait for ye. I knew ye would come to the kitchen after returning from the inn. I'm afraid I have terrible news."

"Aye, I know. I've already spoken to Father. He told me the first suitor is already here. Who is he?"

Alasdair's nose crinkled upward in disgust, which only affirmed what I already suspected. My father's opinion of me was so low he'd invited trolls into our home to woo me.

"His name is Fulton Fyfe. His father is laird of a small territory. I believe Father only summoned him here because he wishes to control that territory once Fulton's father passes. The man is weak. He would happily allow Father to run his territory. Ye willna care for him, but news of the suitor is not the terrible news I have for ye."

My already knotted stomach tightened further.

"What is?"

"I no longer have a place where ye can practice yer spells. The room I planned for ye is where Father placed the suitor. I hid the books in my own chambers until I think of another way."

Even unintentionally Father could destroy my hope. I had no time to worry over it now.

"Alasdair, I must tell ye what I learned from Jerry."

Repeating every detail of my conversation, I told my brother everything. By the time I finished, Alasdair was pacing the room while rubbing his forehead.

"By all the saints, Morna, what are we to make of it?"

"I doona know. Why would Grier pretend that she couldna send him back? Why has she allowed him to believe her dead for so long?"

Ignoring my questions, he asked one of his own.

"Did ye tell him she's not dead?"

"Mayhap I should have, but I feared 'twould hurt him. He's been through so much already."

Alasdair stopped his pacing. His voice was low and quiet when he spoke.

"I told ye of the darkness I always sensed in Grier. I worry that the lass we knew is no longer the lass she is. There is a game in this that I canna understand. Whether it be loneliness or revenge, there is a design to all of it, and Grier is its creator. Ye must tell Jerry she lives. Yer memory is proof that he is at the center of all of it. He canna remain ignorant of what ye know."

"So, ye believe I must try to help him?"

Nodding, Alasdair leaned close as if he were worried Grier was listening to us even now. Part of me wondered if she was.

"Aye, ye must. I will find another place for ye to study and learn. If Grier lives, we will see her again. I will find her and see her home. We must learn the truth."

Shivering and exhausted, I readily accepted my brother's open arms.

"Only days ago, I feared I would go mad from boredom. Now, I fear there is too much chaos. Change is coming for me, and I doona know if I'm ready."

Holding me tight, Alasdair kissed the top of my head.

"Lass, ye are ready. Ye always have been. Ye are far more ready than I. I feel that yer life—the life ye were meant to live—is just beginning. I will miss ye terribly when ye leave here."

Teasing him, I pulled away and jerked my head toward the stairs.

"'Tis time for me to begin my life with Fulton, ye mean?"

Shivering, my brother took my arm as we left the kitchen together.

"Lass, if ye marry that fool, I shall never speak to ye again."

Laughing, we walked up the stairs, right into the path of my first suitor.

CHAPTER 12

*A*lasdair included nothing of Fulton's appearance in his description. In my mind, I imagined that I would arrive at dinner to find a horrendously unattractive man twice my age. To my surprise, when I found my feet after running right into him, I looked up into the eyes of one of the most handsome men I'd ever seen in my life.

As tall as my brother, Fulton Fyfe had dark eyes, thick lashes and brows, and a full head of dark hair that made me want to reach up and run my fingers through it.

He looked as if he could command any room, but when he opened his mouth to speak, no words formed. He opened and closed his mouth three times before finally deciding to say nothing. Without a word, he turned and walked away.

"I told ye. Strangest man I've ever seen. I doona believe he's said more than five words since he arrived."

---

*U*pon sitting down to dinner, Alasdair and I were determined in our resolve to make certain that Father took to Jerry well enough to give him work in Kip's stables. I knew it would be difficult. By introducing Jerry to Father as if he were Alasdair's friend, Father would assume that Jerry was already an equal in class. To then ask Father for work would only arouse suspicion. I hoped Alasdair had something planned.

With Father at the table's end, and Alasdair, Elspeth, and Eoin lining one side, I sat awkwardly between Jerry and Fulton.

Mary prepared a banquet of food, and I found myself eating more than my stomach could possibly hold just to keep my hands and mouth busy throughout the awkwardness of our meal together. Elspeth busied herself with Eoin, Fulton said absolutely nothing, and Alasdair and I watched on with wide eyes as Jerry charmed our father as if he'd known him his entire life.

It had been months, possibly even years, since I'd seen my father get on with someone so well. It unsettled me. My father usually liked despicable people. Did the fact that Jerry got along with him so splendidly signal something about Jerry's character that I'd not seen during my limited interaction with him?

Most people, even those with strong personalities, would shrink a few inches in my father's presence. They would choose their words with care and never dared say anything that might upset him. Jerry didn't seem concerned with this at all. If anything, he sat up taller than he had at any other time I'd seen him. Not only did he say whatever came to his mind, he even dared to disagree with my father twice before the main course.

The more disagreeable and opinionated Jerry was, the more my father enjoyed him.

"Alasdair, why have ye never brought Jerry here before? I've never known ye to have such intelligent friends."

Quicker than I would've been had I been the one asked,

Alasdair took the opportunity to guide the conversation toward our desired outcome.

"He stays verra busy, Father. Until recently, he served as Laird Creedrich's most trusted messenger. He has only lived in this region for a fortnight."

Returning his attention to Jerry, Father looked surprised.

"Why did ye leave?"

As if they'd coordinated everything beforehand, Jerry picked up right where Alasdair left off.

"I much prefer the landscape here. There are too many peat bogs near Creedrich's land. I've a taste for the beautiful, and Conall territory is the loveliest in Scotland."

Picking the most beautiful area in Scotland was a lot like deciding which finger you'd like to lose—impossible. But the obvious stroke of his ego allowed Father to overlook the absurdity of Jerry's explanation.

"O'course ye do. Ye are a man of fine taste. How do ye mean to live?"

"'Tis part of the reason I invited him here tonight, Father. As ye know, Kip is now in need of a new stable hand. I thought mayhap Jerry would be a fine choice."

"A stable hand? Jerry would go to waste with such work. If he was a trusted messenger to Creedrich, he can be a trusted messenger to me. He can stay in the castle's cottage."

Choking on my food in surprise, I coughed as Jerry slyly reached to pat me on the back. He couldn't have seemed any less shocked by my father's offer. Perhaps Jerry possessed magic, as well. Father's actions were so unusual that I was beginning to wonder if he were spelled. To suggest that a man he barely knew take on such a trusted position was strange enough. To then offer the same stranger lodging on castle grounds was unheard of. With the exception of those who worked directly in the castle, such as Mary, Father never concerned himself with where his workers made their home.

Jerry continued to beat at my back while he spoke.

"Ye are too generous. A stable job will suit me just fine. I'm sure ye already have a messenger."

"Aye, but he's rubbish. I insist. I'll not take no for an answer."

Quickly adjusting his tone to one of admonishment, Father addressed me just as Jerry ceased the inappropriate thumping on my back. "Morna, compose yerself. Have ye no manners?"

As Mary brought in the last course, Father pounded one fist on the table in excitement.

"Mary, ye've outdone yerself, lass. I hope ye've saved some of everything for yerself to enjoy later."

Fulton jumped at the noise, bumping the table so that his cup of ale sloshed out on the table. The expression on my father's face made it clear that he'd forgotten Fulton was even there.

"How can a man so tall disappear so completely? Why doona ye speak, man? Have ye said two words to my daughter all evening?"

Suddenly feeling rather sorry for him, I tried to dismiss it.

"'Tis fine, Father. Yer conversation with Jerry had us all captivated."

Waving a hand to silence me, Father raised his voice in anger.

"I dinna ask ye. Speak and answer me. Have ye said a word since she sat down next to ye?"

While Father couldn't see it from so far away, I could see Fulton's hands shake as he struggled to speak. His face was so red I thought I might cry for him.

"I...I...no."

"After dinner, gather yer things and tell yer men that ye will return home come morning. There is no sense in ye being here if ye canna even speak to the lass ye wish to wed. Morna is not a quiet woman, she canna wed a mute."

Never in my life had two such completely conflicting emotions in regard to my father filled me at once. I was mortified that he didn't seem to mind the pain his words caused Fulton, but I was also pleased to see that at least some part of my father did care about my future happiness.

Unable to say a word, Fulton nodded and looked down at the table in total humiliation. Satisfied, Father resumed his conversation with Jerry.

As all attention diverted away from the devastated man next to me, I whispered an apology. Every word was forward and inappropriate, but if they helped to ease Fulton's pain, I didn't care. Only half of what I told him was a lie.

"Fulton, I think ye one of the most handsome men I've ever seen. I believe my father is wrong—I'm sure I could be verra content with ye if we were married, but ye surely doona wish to have my father ordering ye around until he dies. Be glad that he's sent ye away. Know that ye always have at least one friend here at Conall Castle."

For the first time, he smiled, and his hands stopped shaking.

"Thank ye, lass."

Quickly reaching out to squeeze his hand, I smiled then turned my attention back to the rest of the table. I could only hope getting rid of future suitors would be just as easy.

CHAPTER 13

By the time dinner ended, I was no longer sure I wanted to help Jerry. It turned my stomach to see my father so jubilant. Father was so eager to see Jerry settled that he and Alasdair left immediately after eating to see the cottage readied for Jerry's immediate use.

Despite my misgivings, I knew that Alasdair was right. We had to help him and he had to know that Grier was alive.

With Fulton away to pack up his belongings, only Jerry, Elspeth, Eoin, and myself gathered in the sitting room by the fire. With Eoin asleep in Elspeth's arms, her own eyes were slowly closing in sleep. Knowing that the time had come to tell him, I kissed my sweet nephew's forehead and moved to stand next to Jerry.

"I thought ye dinna care for my father."

One corner of his mouth pulled up into a smile, and my heart began to race. I didn't enjoy looking at him without his beard. Every time I did, my body reacted in strange, unfamiliar ways.

"I said I dinna care for him before I met him. Now that I've met him, I like him even less." He paused and leaned in close as he took a quick glance in Elspeth's direction. "But Morna, I need yer help.

Ye may not believe me now, but with time, I'll convince ye. I need to be close with yer father to get close to ye."

Leaning back to distance myself from him, I nodded.

"But, I do believe ye. 'Twas only that there was much to take in before. I'll help ye, but I dinna lie to ye before. I know little of magic. It could take me years to learn what I need to help ye."

He shrugged as if he'd expected twice that length of time.

"It could take me years to find another witch. I've faith ye will learn quickly. Though I must ask ye, how will ye learn now if ye were unable to learn before?"

It was a reasonable question, one which I myself worried over. It was precisely why I needed to tell him about Grier. Once he knew she lived, he might wish to leave here and go in search of her.

"I recently found all of Grier's old spell books and journals. Once Alasdair finds a place where I can read and work without fear of Father discovering it, I will devote everything to learning. It has been my only wish for years now. Jerry, before ye decide to stay here, I must tell ye something."

"I doona believe I have any choice in staying here anymore. I'm not certain yer father would permit it."

He said the words jokingly, but I wasn't altogether certain he was wrong.

"If ye decide to leave after I tell ye, Alasdair and I will see to it that ye are able."

"I can see no other place where I would have a greater chance of finding someone to help me. Tell me what ye must. It willna change my mind."

He needed to know, but I didn't want to tell him. Knowing would hurt him. Even as nervous as he made me, the last thing I wanted was to cause him pain.

"Grier is alive."

Jerry's teasing smile vanished, and he watched me carefully as if gauging my sincerity.

I remained expressionless as I waited for him to respond.

When he finally did, his tone was strained.

"Part of me has wondered. I never thought Grier the kind of person who would easily accept death. I canna understand it though. I...I thought her my friend. Why would she allow me to believe her dead?"

I shook my head. "I doona know. Will ye look for her?"

His voice didn't waver. "No. I will help yer brother find a place for ye to work, and together we will find a way to get me home. Thank ye for telling me."

"Alasdair believes we will see her again."

Father entered the room, and Jerry turned to walk away from me, speaking quietly over his shoulder as he went.

"I've no doubt of it, lass. Morna, do ye truly believe it a coincidence ye found her books only just before I arrived here? If ye thought Grier powerful when ye knew her, ye have no idea what she's capable of now."

I stared after him as he left, astonished that it hadn't crossed my mind before now.

Had Eoin really stumbled across the books all on his own?

CHAPTER 14

Two Months Later

With both Jerry and Alasdair eager to find a place for me to learn and work, it didn't take long for them to figure out a solution. It was much more perfect than I could've dreamed.

On the back side of the castle, hidden by years of foliage and dirt, was a door to a separate basement room in the castle. Empty for years, it was dirty and dark, but I couldn't have minded less. For despite the frigid air and damp walls, there was no reason for any of us to suspect that Father would have reason to enter it. It was private, and it was mine.

In order to allow me even more time to read through Grier's countless books, Alasdair hired a nurse for Eoin. While I missed my days spent in the child's company, I couldn't bring myself to feel guilty over being away from him. My enthusiasm allowed me to learn quickly. Within the month, I mastered dozens of spells that had been entirely out of the realm of my abilities only weeks before.

My mornings were spent in the castle, flitting around, behaving as if I were the useless ornament piece my father believed me to be. I got into the habit of sleeping late so that the mornings wouldn't seem so long.

Afternoons were my time. The moment Father left for his afternoon ride, I would slip away to my spell room and work until Alasdair came to inform me that Father had returned to the stables.

Everyone in my closest circle, save Father, knew of my work. Mary, Kip, Elspeth, Mae—each of them kept my secret.

Jerry's new position with my father provided him lodging and food, but most days he had little work to do. My father had little need of a messenger. If he wished to speak to anyone, Father preferred to meet face-to-face. So while Jerry's title offered him more esteem than the role of Kip's stable hand, most of his days were spent helping with the horses anyway. Each afternoon, he would allow me some time to work alone. Then later, he would stop in to check on my progress.

While my progress with magic was great, I'd found nothing in Grier's journals or spell books that ever mentioned time travel. I only had a few more books to work through, and I feared they would prove to be as fruitless as all the others.

"Yer hair is different."

Jerry's voice from behind caused me to jump. Even with my back toward him, I could sense that he stood close to me. I always tried to keep my distance from him. I didn't know how to handle the way my body stirred when near him.

Scooting to the side to clear him, I turned.

"Ye scared me. Aye, the wetness of the basement makes it grow to twice its normal width. Mary said if I continue to arrive to dinner appearing so disheveled, Father will begin to suspect that something is awry. I doona believe she's right. Father would have to look at me for more than the span of one breath to notice, but I suppose 'tis best to be safe." Stepping even further away, I continued, "Ye are earlier than usual. Does Kip not need ye?"

Grunting, Jerry rolled his eyes as he shook his head.

"I think I angered him. He's no older than I, but he is as impatient as a crotchety, old man. He knows everything I told him was true, but he dinna wish to hear it."

With both hands against my makeshift stone desk, I hoisted myself so that I sat upon it. It wasn't the most ladylike position, but none of that ever seemed to matter in front of Jerry. I didn't know if it was the time he came from or simply his open personality, but I suspected I could appear before him in my shift without him balking at the sight of it.

"What did ye tell him?"

He smiled and stepped closer. I immediately regretted sitting down—now there was nowhere for me to escape to. Turning so that his back leaned against the table, he lifted himself and sat down so close that our fingers brushed. I swallowed and hoped he couldn't see my skin flush in the low light of the room.

"I canna tell ye. Not yet anyway. Once he calms down and sees the sense of what I suggested, I'll share the news with ye. So." He lifted a finger and pointed to the open book on my other side. "What have ye learned today?"

I dreaded disappointing him each and every day. Even though he always responded with patience and kindness, I knew his own fears that I might not be able to help him grew with each passing day.

Leaning over with my left hand, I closed the book.

"Nothing that will help ye, I'm afraid."

Keeping his smile steady, he locked eyes with me as he leaned across me, grabbing the book beneath my hand. His nose was so close it could've brushed against my cheek had he wished it. I held my breath so it wouldn't shake.

"'Tis not what I asked. Sometimes, I believe ye think all I care about is ye helping me. 'Tis untrue. I believe I want ye to learn everything ye can about magic just as much as yer brother does. I would support anything that would give ye power over yer father's grip on ye, Morna. I'm genuinely interested. What did ye learn?"

I reached over to thumb the book open to the page I'd been working on as Jerry braced the book with his hands.

"'Tis a truth potion. Mary is gathering the necessary herbs. Would ye like me to try it on ye?"

Jerry jumped off the table so quickly he created a breeze. Laughing, he backed away and held up his hands as if to block me.

"Please doona ever slip me a potion. While I know I must use magic to get home, I've truthfully a great fear of it."

"Of magic?"

Such a confession surprised me. If he was afraid of magic, why did he come to my spell room each and every day and expose himself to it? Why had he lived with a witch far more powerful than me for over a year?

"Not of magic, per say, but of being controlled by it."

"Do ye truly believe I would do that to ye?"

His features softened.

"No, I doona believe ye would."

Slowly, he closed the distance between us, and I held my breath as his thighs bumped into my knees as he stood in front of me. Leaning in, he whispered, "Hold still, lass. Ye've a lash that is perilously close to falling into yer eye."

If not for my hands steadying me against the table, I would've trembled at the touch of his fingers across my lashes. With a soft pinch, he grabbed at something but blew it away before I could see the lash in his palm.

He stepped away as quickly as he neared me, and I held his eyes until he turned away. I could only see the shape of his eyes—the corner of the room where I sat was far too dark for him to see any of my lashes.

He said nothing else as he left.

I sat smiling long after he'd gone.

He had no real reason to touch me at all.

Jerry

For over a year, getting back to my own time was my greatest obsession. Every minute of every day, it was all I thought about. Even in my dreams, all I could see was my home. How could I relinquish my obsession so easily? Was any lass that powerful?

She couldn't see it yet—how much I cared for her. Her innocence prevented her from seeing how desperately I wanted her. I was thankful for it. For if Morna ever reciprocated my feelings, I wasn't sure I would ever be able to make myself leave this time, even if she found a way for me to return home.

And I had to return home. Of course I did. If my destiny lay in this time, I would've been born here.

Regardless, each day when I snuck down into Morna's basement, I hoped her news would be the same as the day before. Despite my better judgment, I hoped she found nothing.

It couldn't last forever. Either she would have to find the spell soon, or my willpower would betray me completely.

One way or another, I had to return. And no matter how much I wished it, I couldn't bring Morna with me.

It was torture to be near her, but it drove me mad to be away from her, even for the length of one morning.

Life at Conall Castle was miserable.

I was the happiest I'd ever been.

CHAPTER 15

"*P*sst..."

It was only mid-morning, still too early for Father to leave on his ride. So I sat in the garden watching Elspeth prune her beloved flowers as I heard the noise for the second time.

"Psst..."

Turning to look for the source of the noise, I found Jerry peeking around one of the garden's tallest bushes. He waved me toward him with one finger while he quietly called to me.

"Come here, lass. I wish to show ye something. Ye willna wish to miss it."

Making my excuses to Elspeth, I hurried after him. He latched onto my hand and quickly pulled me away from the garden the moment I reached him.

"What is it? Why are we running?"

I lifted my dress with my free hand so I could keep up with him. We ran together all the way to the small woods just opposite Kip's stables. Jerry said nothing until he pulled up short behind a wide tree.

"It may take a few moments, but we canna miss it. Lean over

and watch, but doona let Kip see ye. He willna do it if he knows he's being watched."

My curiosity was piqued. I lay my hands against the tree trunk for support and leaned far over to my left. All I could see was the side of the stables.

"What am I watching for?"

I stilled as Jerry's hands touched the trunk on either side of my waist. He leaned forward, his front pressed against my back, his cheek just a hair's width from my own as he waited and watched with me.

"Ye'll know the moment ye see it, I'm certain."

It seemed as if days passed before Kip left the stable and moved where we could see him. All the while Jerry remained with his arms around me. I was so aware of his breathing that I didn't notice how my own had escalated until I glanced down to see my bosom rise and fall with humiliating speed. Inhaling deeply, I tried to forget about how it felt to have Jerry so close and focus on the scene in front of me.

Kip paced the length of the stable, muttering something to himself that neither of us could hear. After three full lengths of pacing, I saw Mary approaching, and my heart nearly stopped.

"Do ye mean? Does Kip mean to?"

Lifting his left arm from the tree's trunk, Jerry placed his finger against my lips to silence me. The warmth of his breath against my neck caused me to shiver all over.

"Shh lass, just watch."

Mary looked shocked to find Kip standing outside the stables, but it didn't take long for her to fall into conversation with him.

I watched with joy as Kip fidgeted nervously from foot to foot. I was certain he wasn't hearing a word Mary was saying—he was too busy trying to gather his courage.

She didn't realize what he meant to do at first. Even as Kip reached for her hands, Mary continued to chatter away as if nothing were odd about his behavior.

The moment she realized what Kip was doing, her hands flew to her mouth and she started to cry.

Even unable to hear the words that passed between them, I knew her answer by the way her arms flew around his neck.

The moment they kissed, I turned away, not wanting to intrude on their private moment. Unthinking, I turned right into Jerry's wide arms.

I couldn't move without touching him, and he didn't pull away as I stood with my nose level with his chin.

Desperate to decrease the tension between us, I began to chatter away incessantly.

"Thank ye for bringing me here. I canna believe Kip finally gathered the courage. Mary will be so happy. They're suited nicely, I think. I..."

His breath still warm against my ear, Jerry spoke. "Hush, lash. They're still here. Do ye wish for us to be found out?"

Why didn't he step away? I hated how nervous I felt in front of him.

I responded in a whisper. "No, o'course I doona. Is this what ye spoke to Kip about?"

He nodded. "Aye."

"I wouldna have thought ye a romantic, Jerry."

He leaned back just far enough so that he could look down at me. His eyes lingered on my lips. I desperately wanted to duck and move away from him.

Just as I was about to run, he pulled away.

"They're gone now. I've a heart for romance when it comes to others. I've no interest in it myself."

I knew little of love, but I knew every word Jerry said was a lie. If my own discomfort hadn't been so evident, I had no doubt Jerry would've kissed me.

"Is that so? Do ye not worry that ye will be lonely?"

His voice was colder than usual when he spoke. The intimacy

between us only moments ago was gone, and that Jerry was now replaced with someone distant and dismissive.

"Do ye believe marriage means ye willna be lonely? I've known many who were far more lonely once married than they ever were before."

Although I found the notion depressing, I suspected it to be true.

"Mayhap so. Did ye know I've another suitor arriving tomorrow?"

His brows lifted in surprise. The thought of another man coming here with the intent to marry me bothered him. His jaw clenched and his hands bunched into fists as soon as I told him. His actions and words were at complete odds with one another.

"Why are ye telling me that? I doona believe yer father will wish me to dine with all of ye again. Even as much as he likes me, now that I am castle staff, there is no place for me at the table."

"I only thought ye should know so that ye willna be surprised if I doona have as much time to devote to my magic."

Huffing, Jerry turned and began the walk back to the castle.

"Lass, I'd wager ye will spend more time in yer basement once he arrives. This fool will bore ye just as much as the last."

I hurried to follow after him.

"Why would ye say that? Ye doona know him."

"I doona need to know him. I know ye. Any lad yer father picks willna suit ye."

I was inclined to agree with him.

"Jerry, if I dinna know any better, I'd say ye were jealous of me spending time with someone other than ye."

Keeping his back toward me, he increased his speed.

"'Tis good that ye know better then. I'll not be coming to the spell room today. Let me know if ye find anything."

Grinning, I went in search of Mary to congratulate her.

Whether he realized it or not, Jerry was definitely jealous.

CHAPTER 16

"*D*o ye think ye'll marry this one?"

I choked on my laughter as Mary yanked roughly at the laces on the back of my dress.

"Doona tie them so tightly, Mary. No, I know I willna marry this one. I've no desire for this lad to want me. Can ye pull my hair up so that it looks rather dreadful?"

Slipping her fingers beneath the laces, she pulled them loose.

"Ye are daft if ye think ye've any hope of dissuading him with the way ye pin yer hair. Did ye not see the way he looked at ye when he arrived?"

Shrugging, I faced her as she finished the laces.

"I suppose most would find him rather attractive, aye?"

Mary snorted and her cheeks flushed red.

"Do ye mean to say that ye doona find him handsome? Why, if not for Kip's recent proposal, I would happily tup him. Though, I'd have to fill my ears with cotton before letting him near me. The sound of his voice makes me want to weep."

Laughing until my sides hurt, I nodded in agreement. Mary didn't speak like any other lady I'd ever known. I loved her for it. And she wasn't wrong about Seumas McCabe's voice. He spoke through his nose, making every word sound breathy and thick. It made him sound ill, even though he looked anything but.

Objectively, I could see that most would find him handsome. He wasn't tall like the men in my family, but he was astonishingly muscular with long blond hair and eyes so blue they were almost white.

"I find him difficult to look at, Mary. I doona wish to sit near him at dinner. How then am I meant to get to know him?"

Astonished, Mary twisted her head to the side as she eyed me skeptically.

"Ye canna look at him? I can hardly keep from doing so."

I shivered as I moved so Mary could fix my hair.

"'Tis his eyes, I think. They unsettle me. While I've thankfully never seen a fairy, I imagine they would look much like him, only a wee bit smaller."

Chuckling, Mary combed through my mess of curls.

"I've never thought of it myself, but aye, his eyes are verra different. Does yer father like him?"

"Aye, Father's known him for a decade. He's at least fifteen years older than me, ye know. He's already laird of his own territory."

"He doesna look fifteen years older than ye. Alasdair willna like him."

Alasdair didn't like him. I already knew that with certainty. While this morning was the first time I'd met Seumas McCabe, he and Alasdair shared a history. After Grier and some time before Elspeth entered my brother's life, both men had fallen for the same woman.

It surprised me that Mary didn't know the story of what had happened between them, but I was curious as to why she assumed my brother wouldn't like him.

"Why do ye say that?"

"Morna, if Seumas looks at ye in front of Alasdair the way he looked at ye when he arrived here, I'm afraid yer brother might try to strangle him in the middle of the meal."

"'Twould at least provide wee Eoin some amusement during what is certain to be a miserably long evening."

Satisfied that my hair didn't look its best, I stood, thanked Mary, and made my way down to dinner.

Perhaps in candlelight, I wouldn't find his eyes so startling.

---

*A*lasdair didn't lunge across the table, but each time Seumas touched my arm or brushed my shoulder, he looked as if he wanted to. His face would redden, his teeth would clench, and I would watch as Elspeth quietly reached over to squeeze his hand to calm him.

It was a tense evening, but my father remained oblivious to all of it. Always an expert at conversation, he visited and laughed and seemed quite pleased with himself over his choice of suitor. When at last the meal came to an end, I stood to bid Seumas farewell, only to be stopped by Father's voice at the end of the table.

"Mayhap, ye should show Seumas Elspeth's garden?"

Before I even had a chance to glance in Aladair's direction for help, my brother stood and nudged Elspeth to do the same.

"Aye, why doona we all take a turn outdoors? 'Tis a pleasant enough evening for it."

Grateful that I wouldn't be forced to walk with Seumas alone, I took his arm as he offered it to me and followed my brother and Elspeth out into the garden.

It was a rare and beautiful Scottish evening. The air was unusually warm, and it caused all the wonderful smells from Elspeth's flowers and plants to surround us. While I did my best to stay close to Alasdair, Seumas' strength demanded that we follow the pace he set, and I watched with dread as Elsepeth and Alasdair slowly disappeared around the corner in front of us.

Once alone, I would be forced to talk to him. I didn't wish to hear his voice for anything, but as we walked down one of the garden's pathways, the silence quickly became unbearable.

"'Tis a lovely night. Yer home is north, aye? Do ye ever have evenings as warm as this?"

I looked up to see him staring down at me. Mary was right. A hunger lay in his eyes that caused my stomach to clench uncomfortably.

"Aye, 'tis north and aye, at times we've as lovely weather as ye do. I can assure ye, ye'll be quite comfortable there."

His assumption made me feel suddenly defiant, and I pulled away to face him.

"Ye seem quite certain of yerself. Ye do know that Father has agreed to let me make this choice on my own, aye?"

He nodded and smiled, and I had to resist the urge to shiver. Such unearned confidence reminded me of my father. It made me like him even less.

"Aye, he told me. 'Tis not a concern. Do ye know how many lassies would sell their soul to be where ye are, lass—to have the opportunity to marry me? I doona doubt ye'll come to see that ye willna have a better offer."

Clearing my throat, I walked past him and back toward the castle. I would tell Father come morning that Seumas could leave.

"Goodnight, Laird McCabe. Thank ye for the walk."

Before I could distance myself from him, his strong hand gripped my arm.

"I'll walk ye back to the castle."

I tried to pull away, but he held me too tightly.

"'Tis unnecessary, truly. I know my way around these grounds well."

"I'll sleep better, lass, knowing I saw ye safely inside."

I didn't believe Seumas was worried about my safety for a moment, but I allowed him to escort me toward the castle. A lifetime of living with my father made me practiced in appeasing boorish men. Often it was simply easier to allow them to believe they'd won.

Just outside the main doors, Seumas stopped, pushing me so that my back met with stone as he leaned in close.

"I'd like to kiss ye, lass. I'm certain 'twould do much to make ye want to marry me."

I would've laughed at him had his face not been so perilously close to my own. I couldn't risk the movement for fear it would cause my mouth to brush his.

As I lifted my palms to push him away, a shadow in the distance caught my eye. Standing far away, watching us, was Jerry. Suddenly all I could think about was just how much my kissing Seumas would displease him. It made me want to kiss the man all night long.

"Lass, did ye hear me? I'd like to kiss ye. Will ye allow it?"

Seumas' lips grazed my ear as he spoke, and I shivered as I pulled my gaze away from Jerry.

I reached my hands to the sides of Seumas' face and pulled his mouth to mine.

CHAPTER 17

I took four steps inside the castle before a small but strong hand reached out from the darkness and pulled me toward the kitchen.

"Mary, what are ye doing? I've had enough people grabbing me this evening."

Bending over from laughter, Mary continued to drag me down the stairs.

Still rattled from Seumas' wandering tongue, I was too dazed to fight her. As we entered the kitchen, she reached for a small, wooden stool and quickly saw me seated.

"Are ye all right, Morna? I feared ye might suffocate beneath his lips. If not for ye pulling away from him when ye did, I intended to charge ye to break his grip on ye."

Wiping my mouth with the back of my hand, my face warmed in embarrassment as I looked at her.

"Ye watched us? Was everyone in the whole castle watching?"

She smiled and hugged her waist as she laughed again.

"Ye best hope yer brother dinna see it, but aye, I did. I'm glad, too. Now, I'll be able to sleep without dreaming of the fool. Seeing the way he kissed ye cured me of any fantasies I possessed of him."

I couldn't see the humor in any of it.

"So, 'tis not always so bad then?"

"Lass, that was no kiss. Are ye sure he dinna have a twig and some chalk in his mouth? It looked as if he meant to clean yer teeth."

Relief washed over me in such a warm wave that before I could respond, I bent over and lost myself in a fit of laughter that rivaled Mary's. As long as Seumas' kiss wasn't what I would have to become accustomed to over a lifetime, I imagined I would recover.

"'Twas terrible, Mary. I doona think I even kissed him back. He dinna give me the chance."

Patting my shoulder with one hand, Mary reached up to tidy my hair with her other.

"Oh, I know, lass. It tired me to watch it. Ye best get to bed and rest. I only wanted to make certain ye were all right."

"Thank ye, Mary."

"I'll walk with ye to yer room just in case Seumas dinna go to his own bedchamber right away."

Climbing up the stairs together, we both peeked around the corners to make certain Seumas was no longer roaming around the castle. Finding the halls empty, we walked quietly to the end of the hall where my beloved bedchamber lay. I didn't know if I'd ever been so ready to hide within its walls.

My hands were at the laces on the back of my dress even before the door shut behind Mary. I was desperate to get out of my dress and into something I could breathe in. As I pulled the bottom bow loose, a hand covered my own. As I tried to scream, another hand covered my mouth.

Warm breath traveled down the length of my neck.

"As tempted as I am to let ye keep undressing, I know ye'd never forgive me if I did. Wait to undo yer laces until I leave."

Every limb of my body went limp as I recognized Jerry's voice. If not for his arms steadying me from behind, I would've fallen. I was safe. Jerry would never hurt me.

The relief of knowing it was him inside my room comforted me for only the briefest of moments before rage took hold.

As he removed his hand from my mouth, I turned and shoved him as hard as I could.

"What are ye doing? Ye scared me to death, Jerry."

"What am I doing? What the bloody hell do ye think ye were doing?"

It was the closest thing to yelling I'd ever heard come from Jerry's mouth. It was only then that I saw just how angry he really was. The muscles in his jaw bulged from clenched teeth, and his nostrils flared with every breath. He seemed to be vibrating with anger.

I'd allowed Seumas to kiss me in the hope that it would upset him, but I'd never expected it to anger him. At most, I thought it would annoy him.

"Do ye mean my kiss with Seumas?" I tried not to look disgusted as I thought back on it. "I doona think 'tis any of yer concern."

He growled as he stomped closer to me. I took a step back for every step he took forward. With Jerry more than anyone, I found distance to be important for my sanity.

"'Tis my concern when a lass as beautiful and infuriating as ye goes and wastes her verra first kiss on a bloke that wouldna know how to kiss ye properly if he spent his whole life learning to do so, just to anger me."

Every word startled me. Jerry thought me beautiful. My kiss had angered him. How did he know it had been my first kiss?

I couldn't let Jerry see how much power his words had over me —just how much his nearness caused me to shake. I crossed my arms and attempted to lean casually against the stone window ledge at my back.

"What makes ye believe 'twas my first kiss?"

He laughed slightly as he stepped toward me. Once again with him, I no longer had anywhere to go.

"Lass, do ye think me daft? Yer Father keeps watch on

everything ye do. We have to hide ye away so ye might practice magic. When in yer life would ye have had the opportunity to sneak away to kiss men in the village? And I know already that ye rarely have visitors here. Yer suitors are the first in a verra long time. Ye've had no opportunity to kiss anyone. And now, the first chance ye've had in all yer life to do so, ye waste it on that ignorant arse."

"I dinna waste it. 'Twas a lovely kiss."

Jerry's jaw clenched again, and I repressed a smile as I thought of how attractive I found him when angry. It was different than Father's anger. Jerry kept it controlled, and he wasn't angry for the sake of being angry. He was angry because he actually felt things deeply.

"Lying doesna suit ye, Morna. Ye hated every minute Seumas' hands were on ye."

Enjoying myself more than was truly proper or kind, I continued to deny his claims.

"'Tis no lie. 'Tis possible I'll end up marrying Seumas."

Jerry now stood inches away. His voice shook as he spoke. His eyes were locked with my lips.

"Is that so, lass? Ye think ye will marry him?"

My breathing escalated as I watched Jerry's expression. There was a need in it that I'd never seen before. Unlike Seumas' gaze, having Jerry want me warmed me through.

"Aye." My own voice came out on a breath, so soft that he wouldn't have been able to hear me if not for his nearness. "Mayhap, I will."

His hands lifted to my face, and I gasped at the touch of his palms against my skin. Brushing against the apples of my cheeks with his thumbs, Jerry leaned in until our noses touched.

"If 'tis true lass, I'll be damned if I let ye marry another man without ever experiencing a proper kiss."

His lips were warm and soft, and he kissed me with a gentleness that caused every sense within me to stir. I wasn't a passive partner in this kiss. We gave and took in equal measure. With each breath, our familiarity with one another grew.

He smiled against me, and slowly his tongue grazed my lips as I trembled beneath him. One hand at the small of my back pulled me closer. As my front pressed against him, his hands moved to my hair.

Jerry kissed me until every thought in my mind was of him. Every time he tried to pull away, I held him close. I'd never felt anything so intensely in my life.

"Lass." The touch of his lips against my neck caused me to moan. "Lass, I must go. 'Tis

a blessing I had ye retie yer laces. I wouldna be able to leave had ye undressed. Please doona ever let that man kiss ye again. I doona think I can bear it."

He turned without another word, leaving me shaking and wanting in a way entirely new and unfamiliar to me.

Everything seemed different now. I was finally truly awake for the first time in my life.

CHAPTER 18

J erry

J cursed myself every step of the way back toward my new home in the castle's outer cottage. I would feel her lips against mine every day until I died, but I couldn't allow my own selfishness to ruin the sweet lassie's life, and it very well could if I wasn't careful.

While I tried to cling to my desire to return home to my own time, it lessened every day. And what did that mean for me? What did it mean for her? If I stayed here, what life could I give her? Nothing like the life she deserved. Nothing like the life to which she was accustomed. If her desire for me half matched my own, there was only one thing I could do to correct what had passed between us.

I would have to break her heart and keep my distance until I could return to the time from which I came.

M orna

I didn't sleep at all after Jerry left. I spent the night lying blissfully awake, and when morning came, I felt rested and well. All I wanted to do was see him again.

I took extra time and care readying myself for the day. When I left my room mid-morning, I nearly retreated back inside as I saw Seumas standing at the end of the hall. But he saw me before I could escape so I was forced to approach him.

"Good morning, lass. Ye look beautiful. Are ye ready to tell yer father of our plans to wed?"

He offered me his arm, but I refused it. He would have to be told eventually. Now would have to do.

"I am sorry if I misled ye, but I willna marry ye. I doona think we suit each other. I know ye traveled far, and I doona doubt that Father will allow ye to stay here as long as ye wish to prepare for your journey home, but ye willna leave here betrothed to me."

I wouldn't have thought it possible for his already shockingly pale face to lose any more color, but it did. He stepped back as if I'd slapped him.

"I'll give ye the day to change yer mind. Only a fool would refuse me."

He was so much like my father. It was so impossible for him to see or relate to how anyone else might feel.

"I doona need another day, Seumas. I'm a fool."

I left him balking as I went in search of the man I really wanted to marry.

I found Jerry in the stables, stroking Father's horse, with Kip nowhere to be found.

He looked different than he had the night before. The warm glow inside me dulled as I neared him. He grew rigid as I walked the length of the stables, and he didn't smile as he looked at me.

Jerry smiled at everyone.

"Titus is a good horse. He deserves a better rider than Father."

Huffing, Jerry turned away and continued to run his hands down Titus' neck.

"I canna disagree with ye, though I believe the horse to be rather fond of him. Animals are devoted creatures. Their hearts are so much more pure."

I didn't know what I'd intended by coming to the stables. I just wanted to see him, to feel his lips against my own once again.

"Do ye enjoy the stable work? Ye wouldna have to do it, ye know? 'Tis not what Father requires of ye."

He moved to the other side of the horse. I couldn't reconcile the feeling of intimacy between us the night before with how the distance between us felt now. It was as if Jerry had built a wall of stone up between us.

"I prefer it. 'Tis possible ye could find the spell I need while I'm away for yer father, and I doona wish for that to happen. As soon as ye find the spell, I must leave here."

I don't know why it hadn't occurred to me—why his kiss had so completely obliterated all thought of Jerry leaving from my mind—but it had.

"Ye...ye still wish to leave then?"

He glanced up, locked eyes with me, and laughed.

"Aye, o'course. Ye dinna think...ye dinna think that last night changed anything, did ye, lass?"

He paused, and a bone-chilling pain swept through my body. I watched in horror as he continued, shattering something deep inside me with every new word.

"Doona feel badly if ye did, lass. 'Tis my own fault. 'Tis easy to forget when looking at ye just how young and ignorant ye are."

Despite the sudden deep ache in my chest, my pride wouldn't allow me to fall apart in front of him. If he meant to make me feel foolish, I wouldn't allow it. Inexperienced as I was, I knew he cared for me.

Opening the door to Titus' stall, I moved to corner Jerry. Smiling, I leaned in close to him. He didn't move away, and I didn't miss how his breath caught as I reached out to touch his chest.

"Do ye think ye are the only one with the ability to tell when someone is lying, Jerry? While ye may verra well return home when I find what we need to get ye there, there is no sense in pretending things are no different between us now. Aye, I am young, which is no fault of my own, but I am not ignorant. Doona be an arse, or I'll never let ye kiss these lips again. Do ye understand me?"

I didn't back away as I watched him. Slowly, as his breathing quickened, the iciness in his gaze fell way to one of hunger. I readied myself for his touch only to feel a sudden breeze as he stepped away at the sound of footsteps. From the other end of the stables, my brother's voice called to us.

"Jerry, Morna, are ye in here? I looked in the spell room and even asked Mary where ye might be. I need to speak with ye."

I remained in the stall with Titus as Jerry went out to meet my brother, and I hurriedly tried to calm my own breathing. Alasdair permitted Jerry and I to be alone together only because it had never crossed his mind that there was anything other than friendship between us. He could suspect nothing if either of us wanted to be allowed to continue our afternoons in my spell room.

"Aye, Morna is in with Titus. What is it?"

Leaning around Titus' large back end, I smiled and raised a hand in greeting to my brother as he called to me.

"Come here, lass. Anything that has to do with magic we must discuss where none can hear."

Once I made my way out into the center of the stables to stand with them, my brother excitedly gave us his news.

"I've heard news of a clan—they lay so far north that I could find none that have ever actually met them—but stories of their druid have traveled throughout Scotland for decades. I've learned that this man is known to train those with magic. I believe we should go in search of him. Surely, if he was to see what natural power ye possess, he would help ye."

I would gladly take any teaching I could get, but there was no way Father would allow me to leave here, and Alasdair would never leave Elspeth and Eoin for such a long journey. Only one of us could go—Jerry.

Without hesitation, Jerry began to ready a horse, questioning my brother as he did so.

"Aye, o'course we should find him. Do ye know precisely where they lay? I've traveled most of Scotland and have never heard of such a clan."

Pulling a piece of weathered parchment from the waist of his kilt, Alasdair extended it toward Jerry. I watched as he stared at it intensely for a long moment.

"'Twill take me months to travel there and back. We best all hope that such a long journey is successful."

Alasdair nodded, and panic rose inside me. Everything was happening too fast. Jerry couldn't leave. Not now. Not for two months or more.

"Is there such urgency that ye must leave now? Should we not discuss it further?"

"Discuss what, lass? Ye know as well as I, ye've only a few of Grier's journals left. If ye canna find the spell on yer own, we must get help."

Alasdair interrupted, and I struggled to hold back tears.

"Doona worry about Father, Jerry. I'll make an excuse for ye that he willna question. Be careful and return to us as quickly as ye can."

Desperate to have him stay, I ran to the horse as he mounted, grabbing onto his leg.

"What will ye do for food? Ye should at least wait to have Mary prepare provisions for ye."

He smiled and leaned down to rest his hand on my shoulder.

"I survived for months without Mary's meals. I shall be fine."

Bending so that Alasdair couldn't hear him, he whispered, "Lass, if ye care at all for Seumas, marry him, for I canna promise ye that I will return. Should this druid have the means to send me home, I shall beg him to do it, and then I will send him to ye to train ye. If more than two months pass without my return, doona expect to see me again."

I thought I saw tears fill his eyes, but he tore quickly away from me, nudging his horse as he called a farewell to Alasdair.

The moment both Jerry and Alasdair were gone from the stables, I dropped to the floor and wept.

ather found me crying in Elspeth's garden after returning from his daily ride. I didn't visit my spell room after Jerry left, and I spent the rest of the day avoiding everyone, content to wallow in my own self-pity.

How could he leave so easily? And his words made it plain enough that he had no intention of returning here. The sudden nature of his departure reminded me so much of Grier's banishment that old feelings of loss and abandonment dredged their way up, leaving me totally miserable.

Father joined me on the ground next to the roses without a word. Unable to acknowledge his own emotions about anything, he hadn't any idea how to deal with emotions that didn't belong to him.

Uncomfortable with the silence, I brushed a tear from my eye and looked up at him.

"Do ye need something, Father? I'll not be good company for ye tonight."

In a show of affection so strange I had to resist the urge to pull away from him, Father took my hand and gathered it between his palms.

"I sent Seumas away, lass. He told me what he said to ye. Any man that doesna want ye is a fool."

The notion that Father believed my tears had anything to do with Seumas was more proof of how little he knew me.

"Doesna want me? What did he tell ye he said to me?"

Stroking my hand as if it were a kitten, Father looked down at it as he spoke.

"Ye needn't be embarrassed, Morna. Seumas' displeasure with ye has nothing to do with ye."

Pulling my hand away, I raised my voice in confusion. "Displeasure? What are ye talking about, Father?"

"Seumas came to me and said how he told ye this morning that he doesna wish to marry ye after meeting ye."

There was nothing I could say in my shock. Every new thing I learned about Seumas made him seem more like my father. His ego was so grand that rather than have anyone know he'd been rejected, he'd rushed to make others believe the choice had been his.

"Doona worry though, lass. I swore to him that I would never provide protection to his clan again. 'Tis his mistake, and he shall pay for it if ever he needs aid from a Conall."

I could tell no one of the real reason for my tears. So, as Father leaned awkwardly over to hug me, I allowed him to believe it had everything to do with Seumas.

"Alasdair has already sent word to Henry MacNeal. Do ye remember him? He and yer brother have always been good friends. 'Twas Alasdair who suggested the match. I never would have thought of it myself, but I believe ye may find him verra pleasing. He'll be here within a fortnight."

Two Weeks Later

*M*y sadness remained as the weeks passed, and my attitude toward everyone in my life—the only exception being wee Eoin—turned to one of aggravation and hostility. As I stood at the castle's main entrance waiting to be introduced to yet another suitor, I was vibrating with irritation.

As Father left the rest of us standing inside, every bit of frustration I'd harbored toward my brother over the last two weeks exploded.

"I canna believe ye've joined him in this. Ye told me ye dinna see a need for it. Ye said I dinna need a husband until I wanted one. Now ye've gone and invited yer own choice here. It makes ye no better than him."

Looking to make certain Henry MacNeal and Father were still at the stables, Alasdair walked away, waving for me to follow. Once he entered the sitting room closest to us, he bent down to look at me at eye level.

"Is that what has been bothering ye all these days, Morna? Ye thought I'd betrayed my word to ye?"

Seeing the acknowledgement in my eyes, he stood and paced in front of me.

"Ye should have said something to me about this days ago, lass. I'd have happily explained everything to ye. I canna believe ye really thought I'd do such a thing."

"But ye did do such a thing." I couldn't withhold the venom in my voice.

"No, lass, I dinna. Do ye know who Father intended to invite here next?"

I shook my head and waited.

"Ludo Buchanan. Not only is the old fool thirty years older than ye, his temper is far worse than even Father's. I begged Father to allow me to pick the next suitor so ye wouldna be forced to be around him for a moment. I doona care if ye marry or not. If ye dislike Henry, ye can send him away just as ye've done the others, but at least I know he is a good man with no temper."

I allowed my brother's words to sink in as the anger inside me dissipated for the first time in days.

Apologizing for my behavior, I moved to wrap my arms around him.

"I should've known. There is a good reason for everything ye do. Thank ye."

Squeezing me tight, Alasdair slowly pulled away and began to lead me back to where Elspeth and Eoin stood waiting.

"I love ye, Morna. I'll always protect ye. Now, doona greet Henry with the same callousness ye've shown all of us lately. At least give the lad a chance. Ye'll like him."

I turned and stilled.

The second my eyes locked with Henry's, I knew Alasdair was right.

I would like him very much.

CHAPTER 20

Note from M.C.

Perhaps there were signs I should've seen, but I've long since forgiven myself for not. I was too young, too sheltered, too desperate to find my way to have made any better decisions than I did. If there is one amongst us that isn't at some point fooled by the charms of another, I've yet to meet them.

None of what happened in the months following Henry's arrival was Alasdair's fault. He couldn't possibly have known. Regardless, I know my brother carried undue guilt for years.

His pain is the only thing in my past I would change—my brother deserved more happiness than anyone I've ever known. Yet his life saw him bear so much sorrow.

And so much of it was entirely my fault.

ne Month Later

I watched Elspeth carefully as we readied for the most exciting event to happen in Conall territory since Elspeth and Alasdair's wedding years earlier—the impending marriage of Kip and Mary.

Elspeth's skin was glowing, but the vibrancy of her skin didn't match her behavior at all. She was so exhausted she could barely summon the strength to dress.

I'd only seen her behave in such a way once before.

"Have ye told Alasdair, yet?"

Flippantly, she glanced over her shoulder at me.

"Told him what?"

Smiling, I walked over and placed my hands on her shoulders.

"That ye are with child again. Ye are, aye?"

Spinning to face me, she grabbed my hands in a plea and stood.

"Oh, ye canna tell him, Morna, not yet. I've lost babes before, and I doona wish to put Alasdair through it again. I will say nothing to him until I can no longer hide it."

"O'course." I understood Elspeth's concern. While every miscarriage broke her heart, Alasdair took it even harder. It wasn't only his own grief that he felt—he felt Elspeth's pain just as acutely. He was always trying to carry everyone else's heartache.

I watched as she allowed herself to smile, and I leaned forward to hug her.

"Ye feel different about this one though, aye? I can see in yer eyes that ye are not as worried."

Her chin rested against my shoulder as she spoke.

"Aye, I doona know why, but I feel stronger than in the past."

She paused as she broke away from me and looked out the window. Motioning with her head, she urged me to look.

"Does he look angry to ye, as well?"

Down below, Henry stood with one of his men, his expression different from any I'd ever seen on him before. His face was red.

While we could hear nothing, he was most certainly screaming at the poor man standing across from him.

"Aye, verra angry. What do ye suppose the lad did to deserve it?"

Elspeth reached to grab my hand in the motherly way that came so naturally to her.

"The fact that ye believe any one that serves ye deserves to be yelled at rather than spoken to says much about the man who raised ye. Ye know as well as I do, Alasdair would never speak to anyone in such a way. My own father never raised his voice in all his life."

Elspeth's sudden passion on the subject surprised me. She'd read much more into the scene than I had.

"I think ye are assuming much from what we just saw, Elspeth. I've often been known to yell at people. So have ye from time to time."

"'Tis different when we yell at those we love. 'Tis love that incites our passion towards anger or disagreement. When a man yells at those who serve him—when they are not a friend or loved one—there is no passion in that, only cowardice."

Too curious to let her words lay, I pressed further as I reached the doorway.

"Are ye trying to tell me something, Elspeth?"

"Only that ye should pay close attention to everything Henry does. Take note of his habits, his words, his glances. Ye need to know someone well before ye agree to spend yer life with them."

I enjoyed Henry's company immensely. His friendship and the distraction his company provided were all that kept me from wallowing in my anger at Jerry every waking moment.

"I doona plan to marry him. I consider him a friend. I must ready myself. I'll see ye downstairs shortly."

As I stepped into the hallway, I thought I heard Elspeth say, "Ye are not his friend, ye are his target," but I couldn't be sure.

---

*M*ary and Kip's wedding was beautiful. Kip cried—something I would've never imagined possible—and Mary looked radiant and happy standing next to her new husband.

It was a perfect day, but I couldn't see Mary and Kip together without thinking of Jerry and his part in their love story. Six weeks had passed since his departure, and only a fortnight remained until I would have to resign myself to the truth that I would never see him again.

"Where are ye, lass? For 'tis not here amongst the celebration."

There was no sign of the angry man I'd seen from Elspeth's window as I stirred in my seat and looked up into Henry's deep green eyes. His dimples showed as he smiled at me, and I happily took his arm as I stood.

"'Tis nothing. Did ye enjoy dancing with Mae? 'Twas kind of ye to indulge her cause."

With each passing day, Mae grew more determined in her quest to make Hew her husband. I expected that before long she would simply lose her patience and come right out and demand it of him. While Hew had of course been at the wedding to see his sister married, he'd done a splendid job of avoiding glancing in Mae's direction. Once the celebrations had begun, Mae made certain Hew was watching and then asked Henry to dance with her. And dance he had—with an abandon that managed to make even me jealous. I was certain their time together made Hew feel the same.

Henry smiled as he slowly led me away from the crowd.

"Aye, she's a lovely dancer. Each time I saw Hew look in our direction, I would pull the lass closer. He dinna care for it a bit."

I laughed as we walked away from the festivities and back toward the castle. No one would notice our absence. Alasdair and Elspeth were too busy visiting with everyone that passed them, and Father wouldn't return to the castle until he'd successfully danced with every lass in the village.

"Let us hope yer service will irritate him enough to inspire some courage. I doubt that it will though. He is the most painfully shy man I've ever met."

There was nothing shy about Henry. He could charm anyone with his kind manners. I'd never known anyone quite as talented at conversation. He made everyone he spoke with feel like they were the only person in the room.

"Aye, I feel rather sorry for him. Morna, lass, might I ask ye something?"

When we were far enough outside the village that none could see us, I allowed my head to rest against his arm as I moved in closer and wrapped my arm more tightly around his.

"O'course ye can."

"Do ye ever intend to allow me to kiss ye?"

His question took me aback. Henry was tediously proper and polite. I'd never picked up on any sign that he wished to kiss me. It was part of the reason I was so comfortable around him. He truly made me feel as if we were friends rather than suitors. More than once I'd wondered if perhaps Alasdair brought him here knowing he wouldn't wish to marry me just to buy me some time before the next suitor was forced to come here.

"Do ye have any desire to kiss me? I dinna think ye cared for me in that way."

He stopped and untwined my arm as he stepped back and held me at arm's length.

"Whatever made ye think I doona care for ye, lass? I've spent every moment of the past four weeks trying to convince ye that I do."

"'Tis only that we get on so well together. Ye've been so kind to me."

His brows creased together forming a deep line in his forehead.

"Are ye under the impression that if a man wishes to kiss ye he will be unkind to ye?"

I thought of Seumas' persistence and then of the anger that had inspired Jerry's kiss. Until his departure, I never would've considered Jerry to be unkind. Now, I couldn't think of him any other way.

"No, I dinna mean..." I faltered, not knowing what to say. "I thought ye wanted me only as yer friend. I thought perhaps 'tis what Alasdair instructed."

He looked even more baffled the more I spoke.

"Lass, Alasdair has instructed nothing. 'Twould do him little good if he tried to do so. I've treated ye as a friend because I feel ye are one, but that does not mean that I doona also wish to make ye my lover and my wife. 'Tis my own fault if I've allowed ye to believe differently. Allow me to rectify that now."

Henry's mouth was on mine in an instant, pulling me close as his mouth explored mine with a passion that caused me to moan involuntarily. There was nothing familiar in Henry's kiss, nothing that spoke to the friendship between us. As his hands roamed down my front, I realized for the first time what it meant to feel desire so strongly you would sacrifice just about anything to have it satisfied.

Henry kissed me until I could no longer hold myself up without the support of his hand at my back. As his free hand palmed my breast and my chest filled with heat, I knew I would never be able to think of him as my friend again.

Perhaps I'd been wrong before. Perhaps this was what love really was. Perhaps at the end of the next two weeks, I would be able to look at the passing date and simply say, *Jerry who?*

CHAPTER 21

J erry

*E*ven if I rode back from the Allen territory without stopping, I would never make it back to Conall Castle in a fortnight. The date loomed in my mind with a sense of dread comparable only to that I might have if it were the date of my own death. For in a way, if I returned to find Morna married to another, most especially to the utter fool Seumas McCabe, it would be.

I considered turning back at least a dozen times in the first days after leaving Conall territory. The stupidity of my words and the unnecessary harshness of them haunted me every night and day. What sort of madness had driven me to them? Desperation? Fear? A longing for her so deep I couldn't bear it?

Whatever the reason, I knew I couldn't turn back to apologize for them. For it wasn't only my own destiny that lay in the druid's hands, it was Morna's ability to unlock the power within her, as well.

If I could find him and convince him to help her, everything would be worth it.

All of it had been for nothing.

The man I sought was not there, and no one within the territory had any inkling of when he might return. I couldn't wait. If I couldn't bring the druid back to her, I would at least return myself.

I swore to myself as I embarked on the long journey back that if Morna was unmarried when I arrived, I would never let her go again.

M orna

"*S* o...how do ye feel? Different—now that ye're married?"

Only Mary could thaw my father's icy heart enough to convince him to allow her and Kip so many days away after their wedding. Alasdair arranged a lovely cabin for them a day's ride from the castle. So she and Kip had escaped to enjoy only each other for a full seven days after their wedding.

Upon her return to the castle, I awaited her in the kitchen. I'd missed her dreadfully.

"Oh, Morna." Mary patted the top of my head as if I were a child, smiling guiltily as she did so. "While ye will surely feel verra different after yer wedding night, I have never pretended to be the well-behaved lass ye are. I feel quite the same, only more sated and rested than I've been in years. 'Tis Kip who is a different man now. Poor lad was as innocent as a wee lamb."

Eyes wide with shock, I laughed and pulled out the stool next to me so she could sit.

"No? Do ye really mean it? Kip was a...a...he..." I was the

innocent little lamb. I had so much more difficulty discussing such matters than Mary did.

"A virgin, lass. Aye, he was. I wouldna have believed it either, but the poor lad was terrified of me. Doona worry for him, though. I made certain he overcame his fear quickly enough."

I opened my mouth to ask her about their journey but stopped short when I noticed how she was watching me. Her arms were crossed and she had her head turned oddly to one side as she looked me over with just one eye.

"What is it? Is there something on me?"

She smiled, slow and wide. "Ye look different. Verra different. Is it possible ye and Henry have shared a similar experience as of late?"

Horrified at her implication, I nearly fell backwards out of my chair.

"No! O'course not. Whatever made ye think that?"

"Doona act so shocked, lass. Something happened whilst I was away. I can see by the way ye are bouncing in yer seat that ye wish to discuss it. Come on now. Out with it."

Consciously, it hadn't even been the reason why I'd gone to the kitchen, but I knew she was right. Mary was the only woman in my life with whom I could discuss absolutely anything. My mind was so muddled as of late, I feared I would grow mad from the confusion I constantly felt.

"Aye, fine. Can ye tell me why every man kisses so verra differently?"

Amused, Mary's smile remained as she scooted back in her seat and placed her hands on both my legs, effectively pinning me to my seat.

"Every man? I only know of the one ye've kissed. Have ye truly been so busy while I was away?"

"Only two others. Henry kissed me the night of yer wedding," I paused, realizing the dishonesty in my words, then finished, "and many times since. The other lad was some time ago."

Moving to cross her arms again, Mary stood and began walking in circles around the room. Mary was so used to spending every waking hour working that she could not sit still for more than a few brief moments.

"Ye canna mean Fulton, can ye? If that lad had the bravery to kiss ye, I shall be shocked. Even Hew is less shy than that poor bloke."

I'd spoken to no one of my conflicted feelings for Jerry, but it was killing me to keep them to myself.

"No, 'twas not Fulton. 'Twas Jerry."

"Ah."

She didn't look the least bit surprised.

"What do ye mean, 'ah?'"

"O'course 'twas Jerry. He's been in love with ye since the day ye found him."

My heart rallied against her words. I couldn't bear for them to be true. He wouldn't have left so easily if they were.

"No. Jerry used me in the hopes I could get him home. He doesna love me. The moment he learned of another who might be able to aid him more quickly, he left. He will never return here."

"Do ye truly believe that? 'Tis not why he left, lass. He left because his feelings frightened him. Men often run from such things. Ye doona have to believe me, but I'd wager two toes on the fact that he will return to ye. When he does, he will have realized just how foolish he was."

I couldn't spend my days hoping for his return. I thought about him enough as it was—even with the distraction Henry so willingly provided.

"Ye dinna answer my question, Mary."

She chuckled and leaned against the wall behind her.

"With the count ye've gathered over these past weeks, I'm not sure I have much more practice kissing men than ye do. Tell me what was so different about each man's kiss, and mayhap we can work through the *whys* of it together."

It amused Mary to see me so flustered over men. She was one of many who worried I would grow old alone.

"I hardly know what to say about Seumas' kiss."

Mary interrupted, laughter erupting between every word. "I saw that kiss with my own eyes. No need to say anymore. What of Jerry's kiss?"

Jerry's kiss repeated itself in my dreams. It seemed etched forever in some warm corner of my soul where all of my most precious memories remained.

"Jerry spoke to me with his kiss. 'Twas as if each touch of his lips was meant to tell me something—the way he held me stirred more than my body—it stirred something within my soul."

Mary's suspicious gaze was back. I cleared my throat in my haste to move on.

"I canna think when Henry kisses me. 'Tis as if I am consumed by him, and I disappear beneath his touch. I canna breathe nor think nor move, and I doona want to do anything other than keep kissing him when his hands are on me."

When I finished, Mary stood silently for a long time. I couldn't tell if when she spoke it would be through bursts of laughter or tears.

"Say something, Mary."

Eventually, she moved to sit next to me once again. Her voice was soft and serious when she spoke. "Have ye told Henry of yer magic?"

It had never occurred to me to tell him. "No."

"Why do ye think that is?"

I didn't know. I shrugged.

"When ye think of marrying Henry, how do ye feel?"

"I feel nothing. I doona ever think of marrying him."

She continued her inquisition as my head began to throb. "And why do ye think that is?"

Again, I shrugged.

"Lass, 'tis not a why, 'tis a whom."

His name slipped out before I could stop it. "Jerry."

"Aye. Ye already know the answer to yer own question, Morna. One man has awakened yer heart and soul, the other simply yer body. 'Tis up to ye to decide which ye desire more. Now, get out of my kitchen. The lassies who cared for it in my stead left it a fair mess."

CHAPTER 22

*F*or the following fortnight, I allowed myself to ponder the possibility that Mary might be right about my feelings toward Henry and Jerry—that perhaps my feelings for Henry were based on nothing more than physical attraction, and it was Jerry who held my heart. If Jerry returned before the end of two months, I knew where my heart would lead me.

Two months to the day that Jerry left, I made my peace in the only way I knew how. I raged and cried and went to my spell room to search for a spell that might allow me to find him. Maybe he was on his way back. Maybe the druid hadn't been able to help him. Maybe something had slowed him down along the way. There were so many possibilities, and I couldn't bring myself to give up on him without trying to find out where he was.

I'd not entered the basement since Jerry left. In many ways, the room felt as if it were as much his as mine. He'd helped create it for me, and I could see every memory of us talking and laughing in my mind as if they were only yesterday. It still smelled of him, and it made the center of my chest ache dreadfully.

I knew the book I sought—one of the first I'd read. It detailed spells for visions that I had never naturally possessed. I'd never had reason to try one of the spells until now. Such spells were tricky. So much depended upon the caster's intention—what lay in the mind of the witch as the spell was cast.

Grier's notes made it even more difficult to decide which one to use. There appeared to be multiple uses for each and every spell. I read for a long while and finally chose what I hoped would be the safest choice—a simple seer spell that was meant to show me the answer to whatever question was in my heart.

It was a simple recitation in Gaelic. As I put Jerry at the forefront of my mind, I recited the words with care. It was the strangest experience of my life. One moment, I could see the basement's stone wall in front of me, the next all I could see was a small home unlike any I'd seen before.

Its walls weren't stone, and its roof wasn't thatch. Through the window, the rooms appeared to be lit by hundreds of candles. Confused, I forced myself to glance around the scene. I gasped at the sight of a large wagon-like contraption I had no reference for.

Movement from within the home drew my attention back to the window. Tears filled my eyes as understanding sunk in. In the background, I could see a woman. Then as I continued to stare at the window, Jerry appeared, smiling widely as he reached to pull the draperies closed.

The scene confused me. It was the last thing I'd expected to see. Some desperate and hopeful part of my mind had been convinced I would find Jerry resting in the forest on his way back here. But he would never be back here again. Jerry had succeeded in finding his way home.

What I was seeing wasn't from my time, but his. The druid had helped him. Jerry was home, in his own time, happy with someone I could only assume was his wife. Oh, how she must have missed him while he was away for so long.

When the vision before me returned to my basement, I laid my head down and quietly cried myself to sleep.

*I*t was dark when I woke. The candles had long since burned away. Feeling my way to the stairs, I climbed up out of my spell room to find the moon high in the sky. Many of the castle's windows were still lit with candlelight.

What excuse would I give when I entered the castle? Father would be furious, and Alasdair would be worried. Everyone would demand to know where I'd been.

As I rounded the corner, I spotted Mary, her short legs moving so quickly she was barely able to stop herself before smashing against me.

"Morna, ye must get inside. I've made excuses for ye as long as I can. Yer father was readying himself to go into the village to retrieve ye."

"Is that where he thought I was?"

Nodding, Mary grabbed my hand and pulled me along behind her.

"Aye, when ye dinna come to dinner, I told him ye'd left to help Mae."

"Why is he angry then? I often do go to help her."

Thank God for Mary. She'd thought of the only excuse he would believe.

"I doona know, lass. Ye've not done so since Henry arrived. I believe he thought it rude of ye to leave him. Doona worry. Just doona leave Henry's side once ye enter the castle. Yer father willna yell at ye in front of him."

Reaching to adjust my hair, I pulled at Mary's hand so she would slow down.

"How did ye know where I was?"

"I know what day it is, lass. I suspected ye might have escaped to yer spell room to spend the day alone."

Hugging me tight, Mary pulled away and pointed toward the

castle. "Best get inside. Henry was in the sitting room with Alasdair when I last saw him."

---

*H*enry wasn't inside the sitting room when I entered. Neither was Alasdair. Only Father remained.

"Ah. Ye've decided to return. Come, lass. I wish to speak to ye."

"I'm sorry, Father. I wouldna have gone into the village unless I were truly needed."

Lies came too easily to me when speaking to Father.

He held up a hand to stop me. "'Tis not ye that I worry about. What will Mae do when ye leave here?"

"Leave? What do ye mean?"

Father motioned to the seat across from him. Almost every serious conversation I'd ever had with him had taken place in this room with us sitting opposite each other in just the same way.

"Doona be daft, lass. One way or another, 'tis time for ye to make a decision regarding Henry. He's shown far more patience with ye than I would have. Six weeks is a long time to make him wait."

"I doona think he's in any hurry, Father. He rarely speaks of it."

Father grunted and crossed his arms.

"As I said, the lad is patient. Ye care for him. I can see that ye do. Can ye think of one reason ye shouldna marry him?"

My only reason was now living centuries ahead of me.

"One day I may wish to marry him. I am not ready to leave here yet. I wish to see wee Eoin grow."

I said nothing of the new babe. While Elspeth would be forced to tell Alasdair soon, news of the babe was still our secret.

"Morna." Father's voice was stern, cold, distant. "Eoin will grow up fine without ye. 'Tis generous of me to allow ye to pick yer husband at all. 'Tis not up to ye to decide how long ye reside in my home."

I rarely allowed Father's words to hurt me, but with my heart still sore from learning Jerry truly had returned home, the protective wall I normally kept up between me and my father crumbled.

It was natural for daughters to marry and leave their father's home. I only wanted him to be more saddened at the thought of me leaving. Even if I wasn't truly his, had our years together not bonded him to me in some way that made him love me?

"Are ye so eager to see me gone from here? Will ye not miss me at all?"

Father's eyes softened in the same way they always did when he played with Eoin.

"O'course I'll miss ye." He paused and sighed then opened his arms and waved me toward him. "Come and sit on my knee."

I stared back at him blankly. Never in my life had my father held me. Slowly, I stood and walked toward him and lowered myself onto his lap. It felt strange and foreign, and for some reason I couldn't explain, it made me want to cry.

"I've not always treated ye as I should. I know ye wonder if I care for ye as I do Alasdair. I do, lass. I love ye so much it pains me. Do ye know how much ye remind me of yer mother? Every time I look at ye, I see her. As similar as ye are in personality, I canna believe that ye never knew her.

"No matter how things ended between us, yer mother was the love of my life. If I've distanced myself from ye, 'tis only to prevent the pain I feel when I see her reflected in ye. Ye must wed not because I doona want ye here, but because I must ensure that ye will always be cared for—even after I'm gone."

I couldn't imagine a world without him. I feared so many things about my future, but losing my father had never been one of them. He was so strong, so forceful. Although I knew it foolish, it was truly the first time losing him had crossed my mind.

Unable to stop myself, I relaxed against his chest and allowed his arms to wrap around me.

He held me there until I fell asleep. I stirred when he stood but feigned sleep when I realized what he was doing. My father—my cold, often-cruel, complicated father—was carrying me to my room as if I were a small child.

The climb up the stairs was easy for him, and he kissed my forehead as he tucked me beneath the blankets. He paused in the doorway as he left, turning back over his shoulder to whisper, "I love you" in Gaelic.

I was wide awake now—shaking and sobbing beneath the covers. It should've been healing for my father to confess such feelings to me after years of wanting to hear such words. Instead, it terrified me.

It felt so very much like goodbye.

CHAPTER 23

he next morning, I woke to Alasdair shaking my shoulders. He was trembling with excitement, and I knew before I opened my eyes that Elspeth had finally told him about the baby.

"Morna, lass, I've news to tell ye. Elspeth...she...she's with child again."

I couldn't remember a time when I'd seen him more ecstatic.

Lifting me from the bed with ease, he pulled me into a hug that left my feet dangling a good distance from the floor. He continued to speak into my ear as he spun me around.

"Ye will be an auntie again. She thinks 'tis another boy, though I doona know how she could possibly know. I doona care if the babe comes out half-horse, I shall love it. Always before, when she's lost them, 'twas earlier in the pregnancy. She has much hope that this one shall live."

Finally, he set me down. I steadied myself as I smiled at him. I didn't tell him that I already knew. It was fitting that he believe himself the first to know.

"'Tis the happiest news I've heard in some time. What do ye think wee Eoin will think of it?"

Alasdair laughed and moved to the window. Down below, Eoin was readying his pony to go out on a ride with his grandfather.

"I expect he'll be excited enough until the babe arrives. After that, I willna be surprised if years pass before he makes his peace with having less attention."

It would certainly be an adjustment for the sweet, spoiled child, but there was nothing better than having a sibling with whom to share your childhood. Alasdair had told me many times that he wished we were closer in age so that we could've grown up together. By the time I arrived, Alasdair was nearly grown.

"There will always be plenty of people around the castle to give Eoin attention, so perhaps he willna mind the child as much as ye think."

I leaned in to hug my brother once again. Alasdair's smile was contagious. His happiness pushed away the dreadful feelings I'd fallen asleep with.

"I'm happy for ye, brother. And for Elspeth. And even for myself. Being an aunt has been one of the greatest joys of my life. Have ye told Father yet?"

Alasdair shook his head and pulled away to head toward the door.

"No. I mean to join them on their ride and tell them both at once. Eoin watches Father so closely. If he shows that he is glad and happy about the news, mayhap Eoin will feel the same."

Alasdair all but skipped out of my room. I was still smiling long after he'd gone.

---

*B*y mid-day, everyone in and around the castle had heard the wonderful news, and happy chatter abounded. The sudden distraction allowed me time to roam the halls of the castle undisturbed. I spent most of the day working through my own thoughts.

I loved Jerry. I could no longer deny the truth of it to myself. I could also no longer deny that it didn't matter at all. I could never have him. I would never see him again.

What then was I to do?

I would be married by the end of the year whether I liked it or not. Was Henry the man I wished to marry?

I didn't love him—of that, I was almost certain. While I enjoyed his company well enough, my mind rarely thought of him when apart from him, and I didn't feel the same innate terror at the thought of losing him that I still felt when I thought of Jerry.

I enjoyed his company and conversation. I found him charming and attractive and perplexing in a way that piqued my interest. I was sure I would never be bored in a life with him and that at least was something.

There was also the undeniable fact that my body enjoyed his company to the point of making me feel shameful from the desire he stirred in me. While Henry had always remained semi-polite and gentlemanly, if ever the day came when he asked me to do something entirely indecent, I wasn't altogether sure I would deny him.

I think the possibility of such a request made the allure of him even greater. When in the presence of my brother or father or anyone else really, Henry was the epitome of all things proper.

When alone, he couldn't keep his hands off me. I didn't want him to.

A life with Henry would be filled with surprises, splendid conversation, and if our passion in kissing was any indication, spectacular love making. Most people would only ever dream of such a match.

Even if my heart would never love him in the way I wished it would, by the time the sun began to set over Conall Castle, I'd made my decision.

I would be a fool to send Henry away. I would tell him at dinner that I wished to be his bride.

"*D*o ye mean it, lass? Ye shall make me the happiest man alive."

I decided to tell Henry just as everyone gathered for dinner so that he could make the announcement over our meal. He appeared excited by my decision but not the least bit surprised.

I don't think he'd ever doubted that I would eventually say yes.

"Aye, I'll marry ye. I thought ye could tell everyone tonight."

"I doona wish to wait a moment. Let us tell them now."

Grabbing my hand, Henry led me into the dining hall where Father, Alasdair, Elspeth, and Eoin sat gathered around the table. Mary stood in the corner of the room, waiting for us to sit so she could summon the other servants to bring out the food.

Henry didn't waste a moment.

"Today is the happiest of days. Not only have we learned that a new child is to be welcomed into yer family, but I now know that I shall have the privilege of joining ye, as well. Morna has finally agreed to be my wife."

The reaction around the room was far more mixed than I anticipated. While Eoin began clapping in ignorant delight and Father stood to hug us both, everyone else looked as if I'd just punched them.

I heard Mary drop something in the back of the room. Elspeth glanced down at the table as if to hide her expression, and Alasdair's face gave nothing away. My brother's eyes locked with mine in a steadfast gaze that held a thousand questions.

Father carried on his congratulations with such enthusiasm that dinner was able to progress without Henry taking notice of the subdued responses from everyone else. I couldn't eat a bite. Not with the way Alasdair continued to stare at me throughout the meal. Before everyone was even finished, Alasdair stood.

"Morna, I've something of Mother's I wish to give ye. She'd want ye to have it now that ye are betrothed."

It was the perfect excuse, but I knew there was no gift awaiting me outside the room. Nerves settling deep inside me, I followed my brother outside.

"Ye've a habit of pulling me away from dinner."

Ignoring me, Alasdair turned and sat down on one of the stairwell steps. I joined him.

"Are ye sure about this, lass? Ye doona have to marry him."

I nodded.

"Aye, I do. Father has made it clear that I must marry. Ye know if I send Henry away, Ludo Buchanan will come. If he's anything like ye described him to be, I'm quite certain I'd rather die than marry him. Henry is a proper choice. I've made up my mind."

Alasdair sighed. "I want so much more for ye than a 'proper choice.' I want ye to love as I have loved."

Reaching my hand to soothe him, I patted my brother's back. "We canna all be as lucky as ye and Elspeth. Doona worry for me. I'm settled in my decision."

"Does that mean ye've told him, then? He knows of yer magic and ye trust him with it?"

My hand stilled on his back. I would never tell anyone of my magic ever again. I wanted nothing to do with it.

"No."

"Ye must tell him, Morna. I doona know what happened between ye and Jerry, but I am no fool. His departure injured ye in a way that turned ye away from magic. Ye know ye doona have that choice—magic is not something that ye can either take or leave. It will always be a part of ye.

"When ye doona practice, when ye doona continue to learn, the power builds up inside ye. Ye canna hide it from Henry forever. If ye are willing to trust yer life to him, ye must trust this secret to him, as well."

Alasdair stood, kissed the top of my head, and left me with the only ultimatum I'd ever heard escape his lips.

"'Twould be unfair to both of ye to wed and keep this a secret.

I'll give ye three days, lass. If ye doona tell him by then, I'll do it myself."

CHAPTER 24

*E*very day following Alasdair's ultimatum, I tried to tell Henry.

On the first day, I took him riding—something I rarely did. I much preferred walking, but I hoped the distance away from the castle might give me the courage to tell him.

Instead, I only ended up with a sore arse and a bad mood.

On the second day, I casually mentioned the use of magic and asked what his opinion was. His response did nothing to ease my nerves.

He said, "*I doona know what to think of those who claim to possess such magic. 'Tis much like ghosts, I believe. Until I see one myself, I canna say anything either way. Though, if I do ever see a witch, it might frighten me enough that I run them through with a sword. The very thought of another changing anything with simple words makes me uneasy.*"

So not only did the thought of magic make him uneasy, but he also considered killing witches a plausible option if seeing one. It didn't bode well.

By day three, I was resolute in my determination to tell him. I couldn't possibly let Alasdair be the one to reveal it to him.

I woke early in the morning, dressed, and after making certain that neither Father nor Alasdair were anywhere in the corridor, knocked on the door to Henry's bedchamber.

He opened it with only his kilt on—his chest entirely bare. Every muscle in my body clenched just looking at him, but I couldn't allow myself to be distracted.

"Lass, I never thought I'd see the day when ye would so brazenly knock on my door. What if someone sees ye? 'Twouldn't look good for either of us."

Undeterred, I kept my gaze on his eyes.

"No one will see me for I have no intention of stepping inside yer room. I wish to show ye something. Will ye dress and meet me downstairs?"

Intrigued, he nodded, bent to steal a quick kiss, then closed the door in my face.

$\mathcal{I}$ stood on the hidden door to my basement, staring up at Henry, completely unable to say to him what I knew I must.

"Henry, I...there is something I must tell ye, something ye must know if we are to be married."

His patience thinning, Henry reached for my hands and squeezed them gently.

"Aye, I know, lass. Ye've said that three times now. Why doona ye go ahead and tell me what ye must? There is no reason for ye to be frightened. I can think of nothing that could dissuade me from my desire to make ye my bride."

My palms were sweating, and my heart pounded painfully against my ribs.

"Doona say that until ye know what 'tis that I am."

His brows pinched together.

"What ye are, lass? What ye are is the lass I mean to marry."

Nodding, I searched for the words. Then I suddenly realized

with such clarity that it dizzied me what my problem was. I wasn't nervous to tell him. I didn't want to. I didn't feel safe.

Tears sprung up in my eyes as I looked up at him and thought of the last time I'd told someone my secret. It had been so different with Jerry. Rather than fear or apprehension, I felt desire—a desire to tell him my deepest secret with no worry that doing so would put me in danger.

I didn't feel that way with Henry. Alasdair was right. How could I possibly marry a man I couldn't trust with the most sacred parts of myself?

Henry noticed the moment something in my gaze shifted. Before I knew it, his hands were on me. It seemed to be his greatest talent—noticing when my mind would distance itself from him—realizing when doubt slipped into my mind. He used his lips as a distraction, and I always succumbed to it.

With his hands bracing my arms, his lips against mine, he moved me until my back touched the castle's outer wall. His lips were rough and demanding, and I melted against him, surrendering to the thrust of his tongue and moaning as his hands roamed my body. There was more persistence in this kiss than most. As his hand slipped beneath the top of my dress, dipping to touch my breast, I gasped and squirmed beneath him.

With each encounter, our level of intimacy grew.

Groaning, he moved his mouth to my ear.

"If ye wished to kiss me, lass, ye dinna have to create a story of some false confession to do it. I'll always touch ye if ye wish it. Ye simply could've entered my room when ye knocked. Ach, the things I could do to ye there."

I allowed my eyes to flutter closed as I relaxed against the wall, exposing my neck as he licked and bit until I was moaning in delight.

The sudden sound of a horse approaching caused my eyes to fling open as all desire left me. Henry heard it, too, and pulled himself away with incredible speed. As he stepped away, I saw the unmanned horse, and my blood ran cold.

Jerry's horse that was notorious for finding ways out of the stables to go roam on his own, slowly approached.

Without a word, I turned and ran to the stables, leaving Henry panting on top of the secret I would never share with him.

---

*T*he stables lay a good distance from my spell room. By the time I burst through its doors, I was red-faced and breathless. Bending to rest my hands on my knees, I gasped for air. I expected to find Kip, but it was my brother's voice that called to me from the opposite end.

"Morna, lass, what is the matter? Has something happened?"

Standing, I struggled to speak through gasps of air.

"Jerry's...horse..." I took a deep breath. "Did it...did it find its way back here...on its own? Did ye send someone after it?"

I couldn't make sense of any of it. Wouldn't the horse have stayed with the druid's clan?

Alasdair said nothing. He simply shook his head then bobbed it toward the space behind me.

When his hand touched my shoulder, everything grew dizzy as my mind protested against the truth. At the sound of Jerry's voice, my eyes filled with tears.

"I brought the horse back myself. The druid wasna there, and their territory lay much further away than expected."

Fury unlike any I'd ever experienced filled me. With my back still toward Jerry, I pointed to my brother and shooed him from the stables.

"Alasdair, I need ye to leave here and make certain no one else enters until I step outside these stables. I doona ever ask ye for anything. Allow me this time alone with him."

If my brother had suspected what lay between me and Jerry

before, my reaction now surely confirmed it, but I couldn't bring myself to care. Graciously, he understood the seriousness in my tone and backed out of the stables without another word.

The moment we were alone I spun, palm open, as I slapped Jerry hard across the face.

CHAPTER 25

 erry

The lass could hit with more force than most men. If I wasn't already completely in love with her, I would've fallen for her right then. It knocked me off balance, and I stumbled until I caught myself on a wooden post of one of the stalls. When I steadied myself, her eyes were as vibrantly green as I remembered them, though there was more fire in their center, and the heat of her anger was palpable.

I would allow her to scream and release her anger however she wanted. Her rage could never match the anger I felt at myself for being such a fool. As my vision cleared, I looked her over more carefully. My eyes stopped at her chest. Her gown was pulled loose, her breasts nearly exposed. I wanted to kill the man that had touched her.

She was screaming at me, and the moment I stood upright, she charged me again, her fists pounding against my chest as I moved to find support from the wall. She was sobbing, and her words came between gasping breaths.

"Ye were gone. How dare ye...how dare ye come back here? Everything ye said...the last words between us...ye made it clear I wouldna see ye again."

I grabbed her wrists and pulled her arms against me, holding her close. She looked hard into my eyes, and all I wanted to do was kiss her. Even angry and sobbing, she was the most beautiful lass in this century or any other. I refrained from doing so. I worried that in her anger, she might bite my tongue off.

My words were foolish, but my own anger rose the more I looked at her exposed chest. It made me angry at myself for encouraging her to move on.

"Do ye wish me to leave again? Ye are nearly as undressed as I found ye in yer bedchamber so many nights ago. 'Tis clear ye dinna miss me at all."

Magic slipped from her as my words filled her with more rage. Fire shot through my hands, scalding me as I released my grip on her. Astonished at how much her powers had grown in just a few weeks, I watched on with amazement as she screamed at me.

*M*orna

Only twice before had my emotions caused magic to leave me unbidden, but as Jerry accused me of callously moving on, I could no longer control the waves of power coursing through me. There was nothing conscious about the magic that left me. One moment he held me tight against him. The next moment heat soared through my hands, pushing him and pinning him away from me.

He didn't seem frightened and didn't try to move as I continued to release every feeling inside me.

"Doona ye pretend to know how I did or dinna miss ye. Ye've no idea the pain yer leaving caused me. And ye dare to chastise me for doing precisely what ye ordered me to. Eight weeks ye said...eight weeks and I should marry another.

"All I thought of for eight weeks was ye. And even then, I couldna bring myself to believe ye'd truly gone. Even if ye'd found the druid, I thought ye would return here and allow me to send ye back once I learned how.

"I held on to hope for far too long. I even found ye, Jerry. I cast a spell, and I saw ye there...at yer home...in yer own time. 'Twas only then that I truly said goodbye to ye, and it broke my heart to do so."

He started to speak but I interrupted before he could finish.

"What did..."

"No, Jerry. I'm speaking. Ye dinna allow me a word when ye left so I will speak all that I wish to now. Everything is yer fault. I couldna even bring myself to practice magic after ye left. I thought ye were my friend. I thought ye cared. I would never treat someone I cared about as ye treated me."

The more I spoke, the more my anger abated. When I was finally finished, all I felt was a deep empty ache inside.

He allowed the silence to hang between us until I released him from the spell that held him pinned. When he was free, he neared me slowly, hesitantly, as if he was afraid I would spook like an unbroken horse.

"Lass, I dinna return to my own time. I already told ye the druid was not in Allen territory. They'd not seen him in some time. What did ye see that made ye believe I was gone from here?"

The vision had been so clear that I'd never questioned it. But, of course, if Jerry was here now, it couldn't possibly have been true. What then had I seen?

I allowed him to take my hands as I thought back on the vision. I took my time in relaying every detail of it to him. When I finished, Jerry kissed both of my palms as he spoke gently.

"I doona claim to know much of magic, but I know from my time with Grier just how fickle it can be. Ye said that ye placed me at the center of yer mind. I believe that ye did, but mayhap yer question was different than ye believed it to be. Mayhap what ye saw was not where I was at that time, but where I will one day be. Mayhap it was proof that ye will find a way to see me home."

Jerry's suggestion did little to mend the ache inside me. If he was correct, then it simply meant I would be forced to lose him all over again. That even after returning here, he still wished to return to his time and leave me. It angered me and tugged at my already shredded heart. The past few days had been disastrously difficult. I no longer wanted to be near him.

If he was here, I would help him, but getting close to him would only make it more difficult once I found a way to get him home.

"Let go of me, Jerry. 'Tis unkind of ye to mislead me as ye do."

He didn't release his grip, and I did little to try and move away.

"Mislead ye, lass? How do ye think I've done that?"

I was so tired of crying. I didn't want him to see how much I cared, but my voice was choked as I answered him.

"Each time ye touch me, I feel as if ye want me. Ye are jealous of men who desire me, but ye doona want me for yerself. I am worth more than that, Jerry. Ye take advantage of my own feelings for ye, but ye still wish to return to yer own time. Ye still wish to leave me."

"No." He reached up to brush the tears from my cheeks. "Ye are wrong. For some time now, I've cared nothing about returning to my own time. I know what I said when I left. I was a damned fool for saying what I did, but I dinna go after the druid for me. I went after him because I believe just as strongly as yer brother does that ye need help growing yer powers. I went there for ye, lass, but I'll not be going anywhere without ye again."

I wanted so desperately to believe him, but his own words had already contradicted him.

"Jerry, ye just said that I must have seen yer future in the spell. Ye know then that ye still leave here. If ye truly care for me as much as ye say ye do, 'twould not be the future I would have seen."

He smiled and moved one hand through my hair so that he held the back of my neck.

"Ye also said there was a woman. I've no wife, lass. Mayhap the shadow ye saw was ye."

I would never leave my own time. I loved my brother and nephew and friends too much.

"No. I canna ever leave here, Jerry. I doona want to."

He nodded and pulled my head closer to his own.

"In my experience, 'tis best to never swear off anything. But lass, if ye stay here, so shall I. I can promise ye that. I mean to kiss ye now. 'Tis all I've dreamt of since I left. Please doona deny me."

Just as Jerry's lips neared mine, my father's voice bellowed from the end of the stables.

"Jerry, are ye in there, lad? Alasdair told me ye'd returned. We've all missed ye."

I exhaled, realizing that the shadows had prevented him from seeing us. Stepping into the light, I called to him.

"Aye, Father, he's here. I came to welcome him back myself."

Nearing Jerry, my father met him with a hug.

"Did she tell ye all of the good news, lad? So much has happened while ye were away. Mary and Kip were married. Elspeth and Eoin are expecting another child, and Morna has found herself betrothed."

Jerry looked as if he'd been stabbed as he stepped out of my father's embrace. His eyes were cold as he looked at me.

"No, she told me nothing."

Father didn't pick up on the sudden tension between us.

Slapping Jerry's back, he took my arm and began to lead me from the stables.

"Ach, well we are all glad ye've returned. I need ye and Kip to ready my and Henry's horses. We leave at sunset on a hunting trip to celebrate his betrothal to Morna."

CHAPTER 26

*E*veryone gathered to see Father and Henry off on their hunting trip. They planned to be away three days, and I found myself eager to see them gone. I needed distance from Henry to decide the best way to end things. I couldn't marry him. Even if Jerry hadn't returned, the moment with him above my spell room had sealed it. I couldn't marry someone who caused me to seize up so completely when trying to reveal one of the most important parts of myself.

Jerry cast angry glances in my direction when Henry neared me as we all joined near the stables to say our goodbyes. I ignored them each and every time. I wouldn't allow myself to feel guilty for anything that had transpired between Henry and me, and I couldn't very well behave as if we were anything other than betrothed in front of everyone.

"I'll miss ye, lass. When I return, we shall make plans to ride to my territory and for the wedding."

I wouldn't show him false enthusiasm, but I wouldn't be unkind to him. He'd done nothing to deserve it. "Doona let my father intimidate ye. He likes to behave as if he is a better hunter than he is."

He moved in to kiss me. Although I stiffened, I allowed the brief touch of his lips.

As he went to mount his horse, Jerry stomped away. I suspected it was so he wouldn't be tempted to shove Henry off the moment he got on.

Father came up to me next. The same dreadful feeling I'd had in front of him a few nights before came flooding back. I opened my arms to him and squeezed him as tightly as I could.

An urgency I couldn't explain filled me, and I hurried to return the words he'd shared with me in my bedchamber.

"I love ye, Father. Be safe. Doona venture into parts of the woods ye doona know."

He kissed the top of my head before pulling away.

"I love ye, too, lass. I'll stay to the woods I know if ye agree to stay on castle grounds while I'm away. Doona go into the village."

For the first time in my life, Father's protectiveness felt more like a gift and less like a burden. I nodded in agreement as he walked away.

We all stood huddled in a group as we waved them off. When we could no longer see them, Jerry approached. I was in no mood to speak with him.

"Stay away from me. Do ye think I wished to agree to marry him? Ye've no one to blame but yerself. Now, I must spend the day pondering how to break the engagement without causing a clash between our two clans."

"Do ye need some help, lass? I'm certain we can find a solution together. I canna bear for that man to put his lips on ye again."

I wanted to be alone—entirely alone—for the next three days.

"No. If ye come near me, I'll hit ye again."

At least Jerry had the wits to withhold his laughter until he was too far away for me to strike him.

---

*T*ime alone did little to encourage any plan that seemed worthy. I ended up spending most of my time lounging in bed, reading, and calling servants to have warm bath water brought to my chambers. If I couldn't think of a good solution, I could at least allow myself to be a little indulgent while Father was away.

On the second night of their trip, I lay soaking in a quickly-cooling tub of water when the handle to my bedchamber door turned.

"Eoin, if 'tis ye lad, I need ye to stay outside. Go and demand that yer da play with ye. I'll find ye in a while."

The door to my bedchamber opened despite my protest, and Jerry stepped casually inside.

I sloshed more than a little water out onto the floor in an effort to cover myself.

"Get out of here this instant or I'll scream. Ye canna just enter a lassie's bedchamber any time ye wish it."

He leaned against the door, crossed his arms, and stared back at me as if he were bored.

"Ye willna scream, for ye know I willna glance in the water nor touch ye unless ye wish it. Ye've avoided me for well over a day now. I decided 'twas worth risking another beating to see ye."

A beating was a rather dramatic way to describe it—his face showed no signs of my palm.

"I told ye I wished to be alone."

"Aye, I know, and why is that precisely? I have my suspicions."

Sometimes Jerry was infuriatingly sure of his ability to read me.

"Ye have suspicions?"

"Aye, I do. I think ye want me so badly that ye are frightened to be near me. I think ye know that if we were to spend time together while yer father and Henry are away, I would end up in yer bed, and ye doona wish to carry a guilty conscience for bedding one man whilst engaged to another."

I was suddenly far too aware of the nakedness of my body and

Jerry's close proximity to it. While he may not have been able to see down into the water now, only a few steps prevented him being able to see every inch of me.

"I can assure ye that no such thought has entered my mind. Please leave me so that I might dress."

"I'll leave ye, but the moment ye are dressed, I intend to step back inside this room."

Relief washed over me, and I loosened the grip on my breasts just a bit.

"Whatever for?"

"To kiss ye, lass. To kiss ye until every memory of Henry's lips on ye are washed clean from yer mind. Ye doona mind his touch. I could see it in the way ye leaned into his kiss yesterday. 'Twas not like Seumas' kiss where ye tolerated it simply to torture me. Part of ye enjoys Henry's touch. I canna sleep until I know I've changed that."

I couldn't tell if I began to tremble in anticipation or from the cooling water, but when Jerry stepped out into the hallway, I was trembling all over.

I dried myself quickly and glanced around the room with terror over what I should dress in. A full gown was foolish this late in the evening—to place on my nightgown was inviting trouble.

With Henry, I wouldn't have dreamed of it. With Jerry, it was all I wanted.

For with him, even trouble seemed relatively safe. He would protect and cherish me, and it was all I'd wanted for months.

Taking a breath for courage, I slipped on my sleeping gown and opened the door to let him inside.

CHAPTER 27

"*D*o ye wish me to leave, lass? I doona..." Jerry reluctantly pulled his hand away from my leg, allowing my nightgown to fall back toward the ground. He lay his forehead gently against my own, his breathing ragged, his voice pained. "If ye doona want this, send me away from here. I want too much from ye —things ye may not be ready to give."

He was perilously close to doing so much more than just kissing any memory of Henry from my mind. In truth, he'd already succeeded. I would never be able to kiss or look at Henry the same way again, but Jerry was holding on to his resolve to be respectful of me with so much fervor it was physically painful for him.

My mind had been made up the moment I opened the door. There was no turning back—not this night—quite possibly, not ever.

I reached up and placed my palms on his face, lifting his head up so I could look at him. Leaning forward, I whispered in his ear.

"What is it ye want, Jerry? Tell me. I want to know."

He pulled back, his face suddenly serious.

"Did ye sleep with him, lass? Ye doona seem..." He faltered, searching for the right words. "Well, ye doona seem like a nervous virgin."

I smiled and kissed him gently on the cheek before stepping away to stand across from him.

"Jerry, ye have met Mary, havena ye? I learned much about what happens in the beds of lovers at a far younger age than was proper. I know what this night can be between us. I wouldna have let ye inside this room if I dinna want it. Ye were right that night ye came into my bedchamber after I kissed Seumas. I wasted my first kiss. I doona wish to waste this."

His expression softened as he exhaled a deep, shaky breath.

"Ach, thank God, lass. I dinna know for certain. I hoped," he paused and raked his hand through his hair. "God, I hoped, but with the way the lad looks at ye, I worried ye'd bedded him."

He stepped toward me, reached for my hands, and pulled me hard against him, whispering into my ear as I allowed my front to press against his chest.

"Ye do know I love ye, doona ye, lass?"

I trembled as his lips touched my neck. When his hand cupped my breast, I moaned.

"I hoped. I dinna know."

His hand slid from my chest, up my neck, and to my face where he held me gently, his thumb sweeping soft strokes over my cheek.

"I have loved ye since I opened my eyes in that riverbed to see ye staring at me with those wide, green eyes. For so long, I wondered why this happened to me—why I was chosen to fall through time and leave everything in my old life. The moment I saw ye, I knew. We were meant for one another."

Why had I kept the truth from him? His absence was no excuse. I'd known long before that, but for so long I tried to deny it myself. Did the spell Grier and I cast so many years ago make our love for one another any less real? I worried that maybe it did. Or at the very least, that Jerry would believe it did.

Could I confess my love for him while holding this secret? Not if I wanted to sleep easily at night.

The feel of his lips across my collarbone begged me to surrender to the sensation, to relinquish my need to tell him what I knew.

"Jerry, there is something I must tell ye."

He continued to caress and kiss and hold me tight against him. His words dragged across my skin as he spoke between kisses.

"Tell me later, lass. I canna promise I will remember a word ye say to me now. I canna think with ye in my arms."

I pulled away to put some distance between us. He needed to hear me. Once he knew, it might change his feelings.

"If I doona tell ye now, I doona trust myself to ever tell ye."

"What is it, lass? Nothing can be as bad as ye are making it seem."

"Aye, 'tis." I was so much more nervous to tell him this than I was at the thought of sleeping with him. "I believe it might be my fault, Jerry. I may have spelled ye here. It might have been me that pulled ye from yer home." I couldn't keep my voice from breaking.

"Morna." Jerry moved to stand in front of me, gathered my hands in his own, and ushered me over to the bed where we sat at its edge. His eyes were kind and calm. "I doona mean to offend ye, lass, but seeing as ye havena been able to find a way to see me home yet, I doona believe ye were the one who pulled me from it."

Looking down to avoid his eyes, I spoke.

"'Twasn't my spell, though I was a willing participant. 'Twas Grier's."

I heard his breath catch and didn't dare look up to see his face.

"'Tis not possible. Grier dinna possess such knowledge. I spent a year with her while she tried to find a way to send me home. She wouldna have done that if she'd known how."

Still gazing downward, I shook my head. "I'm not so certain, Jerry. I know that 'twas she who sent ye back in time."

"How do ye know that, lass?"

I told him everything about my last day with Grier, taking care to describe the man I saw in the mirror so he would know it was him. When I finished, his hand cupped my chin and gently lifted my head so I would look at him.

"Why did ye tell me this?"

Of course I felt responsible. If only I had told Grier *no* that day, Jerry wouldn't have been pulled so suddenly from his home. His entire life wouldn't have been upended without his consent.

"How could I not tell ye? Jerry, I love ye. I've loved ye for some time now, but what if the only reason we care for one another is Grier's spell? What if 'tis magic and not truth that binds us together?"

"Magic done through love is truth, lass. I canna begin to understand why Grier lied to me for so long—why she dinna bring me straight here if she knew this was where I was meant to be. But I do know this: Grier cast that spell on the day she left because she loved ye and she wanted ye to be loved. I doona believe she found me and spelled me to love ye. I believe she looked into yer heart and saw what was destined to be."

He paused and moved in to kiss me. His lips were soft, slow, and gentle. Each moment with him holding me allowed one more ounce of anxiety to melt away. Trailing his lips toward my ear, he whispered, "I doona care how I got here, lass. I love ye. 'Tis all that truly matters. Allow me to show ye what 'tis to be bedded by a man who loves ye. Close yer eyes."

His lips touched my lids as I closed them. Slowly his hands grazed the sides of my neck, his mouth trailing quickly behind them as he continued to drag his hands down my body. The fabric of my gown was thin. As he cupped my breast, his thumb flicking the rounded tip of my nipple, I gasped and arched backward.

Eyes flickering open, I reached for his head to try and pull his mouth to mine.

He pulled away.

"I doona even have my hands on yer bare skin yet, lass. I mean to take my time with ye. If ye continue to breathe like that, I willna be able to. Close yer eyes and let all thought leave ye. Just feel my touch. Respond to it in kind."

Smiling, I closed my eyes again and lay back on the bed, my knees and feet dangling off its side. I gasped once more as his fingers brushed the uncovered skin of my leg. He swept his hand up my leg with one quick touch, and my thighs opened instinctively, welcoming the sudden sensation of his fingers trailing across my center.

"I need to see ye."

Lifting my hips, he scooted the bottom of my gown up until he could drag it underneath me. I should've felt exposed knowing he was about to see me naked. All I felt was anticipation.

"Look at me, lass."

I felt his weight on top of me, and I opened my eyes to see him straddled over me, the bottom of my gown in both hands as he worked it up and behind my back. I lifted my head to allow him to pull it off me completely.

I smiled as I followed his gaze to my breasts. I'd never seen such blatant admiration on someone's face before. It sent a flash of heat rushing through my body. Even without past experience to guide me, I felt empty without him. I wanted him inside me, claiming me. I wanted to be responsible for his pleasure.

He looked down at my breasts for a long moment. Before I could say anything, he lifted himself and went to stand at the edge of the bed.

"Sorry lass, I canna bear to have clothes on a moment more. I need to feel my skin against yer own."

Lifting myself up to my elbows, I watched him undress. He removed his kilt with little effort. As the thick fabric fell to the floor, he removed his linen shirt. I felt my cheeks warm. It was the first time in my life I'd seen a naked man.

The definition in his muscular body surprised me. I'd always known he was strong, but feeling his strength and seeing it were two very different things.

"Ye are the most beautiful man I've ever seen."

His nose scrunched up as he laughed.

"Doona call me beautiful, lass."

I smiled and motioned for him to join me on the bed. The space between us felt too vast.

"But ye are. 'Tis the only word that comes to mind. I am in awe of ye. I want ye inside me."

The noise that escaped his throat was one of pure guttural need. His eyes darkened, and he swallowed as he approached the bed.

"Lass, I already told ye, I mean to take my time with ye. When ye say things like that, ye make it verra difficult for me to hold on to my determination."

I didn't want to be bedded by someone restraining his every thought and movement. I wanted our lovemaking to be a mutually-shared moment where each of us could release everything and simply be with the other.

As he neared the bed, I sat up so I could wrap my arms around his neck. Before he could protest or push me away, I pressed my breasts against his chest and slowly kissed his neck. Feeling him melt against me, I unwound one hand and dragged it down the front of his body to touch his hardened manhood.

He gasped and went rigid.

"Morna, lass, please. I beg ye, remove yer hand. Lie back and let me take my time with ye."

I continued to hold on and gently ran my hand up and down him as he buckled slightly in front of me.

"No, Jerry. I know ye mean to be kind to me, to be gentle, but 'tis not what I want. I doona wish for ye to think about how ye must be or what ye should do. I just want ye to be here with me. Do what ye will. I'll do the same. Let us freely enjoy one another."

My words freed him, and I happily opened myself up to him as he crushed himself against me.

Every sensation was new, every touch a discovery. The pain I felt at his entry was nothing compared to the wave of pleasure that washed over me shortly after.

Our first time was rough, fast, and clumsy.

Our second time was slow and sweet.

By the early hours of the morning, I'd lost count of the number of times we sought to discover joys in the other. Each one was perfect in its uniqueness.

My world was now so very different.

I was a woman entirely in love.

CHAPTER 28

W e slept on and off through the night, waking every few hours. We would then visit before making love again. As the sun began to peek through the night sky, we both knew it was time to decide what we must do next. Our night of pretending as if we were the only two people in the world was ending.

"I wish to marry ye, lass. As soon as we can see to it, if ye'll have me. I want ye as my wife."

Laying with my head on his chest, I looked up and smiled at him.

"O'course I'll have ye. Do ye think I would have done everything we just did, if I dinna plan to marry ye?"

He laughed against my hair.

"Aye, I do. Ye wanted me that badly. What should we do? I fear when ye tell Henry he willna handle it well."

"He willna be pleased, but I've no reason to believe that he willna be gracious."

Shifting me off him, Jerry sat up in the bed.

"Ye still canna see it, can ye? I doona believe Henry is a good man. I doona say that because the thought of his hands on ye causes my blood to boil. I know ye say he's been good to ye, but all men can be good for a time if it gets them what they want. What he wants is ye, lass. Now that ye've agreed to marry him, he believes ye are his."

"Ye believe his behavior will change now that we are betrothed?"

Jerry nodded, his fingers tracing lazy circles down my arm.

"Once he has ye away from yer brother and father, once ye are at his home around his servants, aye. He yelled at Kip yesterday as we readied their horses. 'Twas the temper of a man well-practiced in cruelty."

I thought of Elspeth and the scene we'd witnessed from her bedchamber window.

"Henry can do nothing to me as long as I'm here. 'Tis Father who concerns me. He willna care for me breaking my word."

"Would he..." Jerry's voice lowered as he asked, "Would he ever permit ye to marry me?"

"No."

I hated my answer, but I knew it was true. Father saw it as his duty to see me cared for in a manner he felt acceptable. Jerry had no rank in class and no home of his own.

"Then what are we to do? I know ye willna leave here. I would never ask ye to run away with me."

He was right. I would never leave my home forever, but for a time, perhaps it would be bearable. I could think of no other way we could be together.

"We could enlist Alasdair's help. 'Twill place him in a terrible position, but I know he will help us. He cares for ye. As long as I am happy and loved, he doesna care who I marry."

I pushed myself up and twisted to face Jerry. Every inch of my body ached deliciously.

"What assistance can he provide?"

I thought for a moment, trying to work through every possible outcome in my mind. No solution was ideal, but unless I wished to leave for McCabe Castle in a matter of days, we would have to do something.

"He can help us marry in secret and see that Henry returns to his home without a dispute breaking out between our two clans. Henry is his friend. I know he can talk to him. With time, Father will have to accept what we've done. If we are married, he willna have a choice."

He did have a choice. He could always disown me and order me to never return home. But as long as Alasdair lived, I knew my brother would never allow it.

Jerry didn't seem pleased with the suggestion. His face was solemn—his eyes sad.

"I doona wish to take ye from yer family, lass. Perhaps, we shouldna marry. Perhaps, ye should send Henry away and every suitor after. 'Twill pain me to see ye in the presence of any other man, but I'd rather have ye in secret than tear apart yer family."

It was an outrageous suggestion.

"I canna bear to have suitor after suitor welcomed into this castle when I know my heart belongs to ye. We must think of another way."

We discussed various possibilities until the night was long gone and sunlight filled the room. Eventually though, with the appearance of no plausible solution, we fell asleep wrapped in each other's arms.

"*M*orna, wake up. Ye must wake up. 'Tis urgent."
I stirred to the touch of someone's hands on my shoulders and opened my eyes to find Elspeth standing next to my bed. I scrambled to cover myself and immediately flew into an attempt to explain Jerry's presence in my bed. She interrupted me before I could even start.

"It doesna matter, lass. Not now. It doesna matter. Something terrible has happened."

Jerry stirred beside me, his face turning oddly white as he looked at Elspeth.

It was only then that I could see the concern on her face.

"What is it? What's happened?"

"'Tis yer father, Morna. He's dead."

CHAPTER 29

*J*erry couldn't believe it. His reaction, once Elspeth left us, was to deny its truth. He dressed and paced around the room murmuring words meant to comfort me.

"They are not back yet. She heard this through the word of others. Perhaps he is merely injured. He'll be fine once he is home."

I knew Father was gone. I could feel it—the lack of his energy in the world. While I'd tried to deny and ignore the feeling, I knew this was coming.

I felt nothing, only a cool numbness that slowed the movement in my mind. I needed to see Alasdair. I needed to speak to him, to see if he was okay, to see what we would do now. Both our lives had always revolved around our father. What would our lives look like now? There would be much to take care of.

It surprised me how methodically my thinking became—so detached, so distant, as if I were an outsider sent here to help my family through this. I dressed slowly. I took my time pinning my hair and rinsing my face. When I was ready, I turned to Jerry and asked him to leave.

"I must find Alasdair. Go see to Mary and Kip. She will be

devastated, and she will need extra help in whatever preparations must be made."

He stared at me a long moment. I knew he was trying to gauge whether he should gather me in his arms to comfort me or do as I asked.

Crossing the room to him, I squeezed his hand like I would that of a child.

"I'm fine. We will speak of all of this later."

I went in search of my brother.

---

*M*y cold feeling of detachment vanished the moment I found Alasdair sitting by the fire in the sitting room. It was as if I simply couldn't allow the reality to set in until I was with him. It was a grief we were meant to share together.

As he stood, I ran to him, allowing him to gather me in his arms as we wept together.

I knew both of us had such complicated emotions regarding our father. But in the end, every negative thing I ever felt about him didn't seem to matter. All I felt was love for him and a deep sense of loss that seemed as if it would never end.

"He died in his sleep, just like Grandmother."

"He dinna seem ill. Though, I think mayhap he knew his death was near."

His arms still wrapped protectively around me, Alasdair rubbed my back gently. "How do ye mean, lass?"

I told him of my last conversations with Father, of the tenderness he'd shown me, of the dread I felt when he left. When Alasdair spoke, his voice was filled with emotion.

"I canna tell ye how much peace it brings me to know that. I've always worried he would leave this earth filled with regret for how he treated ye. 'Tis a blessing that in the end he shared with ye how he really felt."

I cried into my brother's chest as we clung to each other. "If it would've been less painful, I think mayhap I would've preferred for him to stay unkind. Losing him feels as if it may rip me apart."

"We shall both heal from this, lass. I will hold ye together, and yer faith in me will keep me strong, just as we have always done for one another."

"How is Eoin?"

Alasdair sighed. I could feel the burden he was already beginning to bear. He would see everyone through this, be the pillar of strength for everyone in and around the castle. He would be the best laird Conall territory had ever seen.

"I doona know how much the wee lad understands. He will miss him dearly. He was the only person whom Father softened around. He spoiled Eoin immensely."

Grief is so much more than the unbearable sense of loss. It throws you off course, makes everything seem so unsure.

"What do we do now, Alasdair?"

"First," he paused and pulled away to look down at me, "we must discuss Henry."

I felt guilty that he'd not crossed my mind before now.

"O'course. He must be dreadfully upset to have found him."

"'Twas a terrible shock for him, though 'tis not what I meant."

By the way Alasdair stared at me, I could see that he knew.

"I canna marry him."

With understanding in his gaze, he nodded. "I know, lass. Elspeth told me how she found ye this morning. Ye love him, aye? I could see it in yer eyes when ye learned he'd returned."

"Are ye angry?"

He looked confused. "Why would I be angry with ye? Jerry is a good man. If ye love him, 'tis all that matters to me."

I couldn't deny the relief I felt. Every problem Jerry and I struggled with last night was now gone. All we needed to worry about was finding a way to break my engagement to Henry. Would I take every problem back to have Father alive and well again? Of course, but that could never be.

"I do love him. Might we stay here at the castle once we are wed?"

"'Twould break my heart if ye left. Though I think it best if ye keep yer distance from Jerry until after Father's burial. Henry will insist on remaining here until then. We will speak to Henry together after that."

It wasn't Alasdair's duty to end things between Henry and me.

"I shall speak to him alone, but I will wait until afterwards." I couldn't bring myself to say burial.

Alasdair smiled in spite of his tears. "Morna, I have only one request if ye intend to live here."

There was nothing I wouldn't do for him. "Anything."

"In time, ye must return to yer magic. I shall make Conall territory a place that is safe for ye to practice openly. Ye canna continue to deny who ye are."

It seemed improper to feel such relief. I was free to marry Jerry, free to live in the home I knew and loved, free to learn and practice magic without fear of punishment. Why did the moment everything seemed to be falling into place have to be shared with such deep grief?

CHAPTER 30

We waited three days to bury Father. I spent most of that time alone, crying and working through feelings I didn't know I had for him. By the time it came for everyone to gather, I no longer had tears to shed.

Henry checked on me every day, but the state of my grief made him so uncomfortable that it never took much for me to get him to leave. Jerry kept his distance entirely, but I knew it wasn't his choice to do so. Alasdair had spoken to him and asked him to stay away until everything was settled with Henry.

When I saw him standing with Mary and Kip at Father's burial site, he looked terrible, as if he hadn't slept in days. It was the first thing I said to him.

"Are ye ill, Jerry?"

He wanted to reach for me, and I wanted nothing more than to fall into his arms, but Henry stood only steps away.

Whether he was too tired or too emotional to censor his words, I didn't know, but Mary and Kip's presence did nothing to prevent him from answering honestly.

"I canna sleep knowing I'm not there to comfort ye. Ye shouldna be alone in yer grief. I want to help ye, to hold ye, to let ye know that yer pain willna always be so great."

Mary's mouth fell visibly open, and she leaned over to whisper in my ear.

"I doona care if Henry sees ye. If ye doona hug that lad right now, I'll do it meself."

---

*A*lasdair, Elspeth, and Eoin still hadn't come down from the castle so I stood mingling with all the villagers, accepting their condolences and being smothered by hugs until Mary pulled me away from the crowd.

"Ye look as weary as I've ever seen ye. Doona exhaust yerself now. Things will only get harder as the day goes on. When ye see him, ye will likely be unable to hold back yer tears."

I knew she was right. I'd yet to see Father's body. While most had already visited him, I hadn't been able to bring myself to go to him. I wasn't sure I could bear seeing him so cold and lifeless.

"Speak to me of something else, Mary. I am weary of grief consuming my every thought."

She smiled, laced her arms with mine, and led me to the back of Mae's inn. It allowed us a view of the castle so we would know when Alasdair and Elspeth were coming. We could join the others then.

"I know precisely what I wish to speak to ye about. I can see by the way the two of ye looked at each other that ye've bedded him. Tell me everything."

For the first time in days, I genuinely smiled.

"Ye have no shame, Mary. Ye do know ye are the only lass I've ever known to speak of such matters so plainly, aye?"

She laughed and nodded. "'Tis something I pride myself on. Now, doona be coy. Ye can say nothing that will shock me."

There was far too much to tell, but there was one instance

during my evening with Jerry that I'd been curious to speak to her about for days.

"I do have something I'd like to ask ye in regards...in regards to something he did to me."

Mary's face lit up with glee. "What did he do to ye? Did he tie yer hands to the bed? Did he nip yer arse?"

I doubled over in laughter, and for a fleeting moment, I was able to forget about Father's death. Then as I remembered, guilt filled me. Mary could see it on my face and grabbed my shoulders.

"I know what grief does to ye, lass. The moment ye start to feel anything other than pain, ye worry that 'tis wrong for ye to do so. Doona ever believe guilt when it tugs at ye. Joy is always acceptable. Our misery does the dead no service. They would prefer that we cling to happiness wherever we can find it. Now..." She paused, stepped away, and smiled wide. "I can see that he dinna bite ye, which 'tis a shame if ye ask me. What did he do then?"

"Is it usual for a man to use his tongue to..." I couldn't bring myself to finish my question.

"To give ye pleasure, ye mean? I wouldna say 'tis usual, but it sure is lovely, aye? Count yerself blessed that ye have a man who cares so much about yer pleasure."

I was lucky—in every way.

"Aye, I know I am. I dread what I must do to Henry. He doesna deserve it."

Mary's nose twisted in the same way Elspeth's almost always did in Henry's company.

"I doona know if I'd say that, lass. Ye seem to be of the belief that Henry treats everyone as he does ye. I can assure ye that 'tis not true."

"Do ye think he's as unkind as Father could be?"

It was so strange for me to hear such different stories of Henry. None of them aligned with the man I'd spent so much time with.

"'Tis true that yer father could be unkind, but there was only one version of him. He would treat royalty no differently than he would treat a beggar. Authenticity is important, lass. I doona trust those that put on airs for some and show their worst to others. 'Tis my experience that such people mean to hide something, and 'tis never something good."

Perhaps she was right about Henry—perhaps they all were. It hardly mattered now. By tomorrow he would be headed back to McCabe Castle, and I would never see him again.

The crowd of villagers began to stir. As I glanced up toward the castle, I could see Alasdair, Elspeth, and Eoin riding toward the village.

Mary reached out to squeeze my hand.

"'Tis time, lass. Let us bid him farewell."

---

*I*t was a somber burial filled with tears. It was easier than I expected to see Father's body. It looked so cold, so unlike him, that I was able to detach myself from all that was happening around me in a way I hadn't expected. It was so much like the first moments right after I learned of his death.

I knew I would quietly fall apart later.

It was only at the end of the service as they lowered Father into the ground that I noticed her. Standing at the edge of the wood, cloak over her head, she remained far from the crowd. With everyone else so caught up in what was happening in front of them, I knew I was the only one that had seen her.

Grier had returned.

*A*ll I could think when I spotted Grier standing in the woods as if she'd never left all those years ago was that I couldn't let Jerry see her. Not yet—not until I'd spoken with her. I felt deeply protective of him. While I'd grieved her absence from my life once, I knew instinctively that she was not the same person I once knew.

After the burial, Grier was no longer visible. I knew she awaited me in the woods. I could feel it.

Jerry stood at the opposite side of the crowd of villagers. I made my way over to him as quickly as I could. I needed to know where he'd be so I could make certain he wouldn't run into Grier. Fortunately, I didn't have to search for an excuse to keep him busy —he already had plans.

"A lad in the village has asked Kip and me for help with a horse. I am so weary I can scarcely stand, though I think 'tis best if I stay away until Henry is gone. Do ye mean to tell him today?"

It wouldn't be as soon as I'd hoped. I would have to speak to Grier first, but I had every intention of ending things with Henry before nightfall.

"Aye."

Jerry nodded, and the line between his brows relaxed.

"Good. I'll return to my cottage later, but for now, I shall spend the day in the village and allow ye and yer brother to see Henry gone from here. He may ask ye what has caused ye to end yer engagement. If he sees me, 'twould only cause unnecessary trouble."

I nodded and turned to leave him, but his hand reached out to stop me.

"Wait, lass. I wish to give ye something. As I told ye earlier, I've not slept much these past nights. I wished to be there for ye and I couldna be, so I wrote some thoughts down for ye. I know it willna be easy for ye to hurt Henry. Ye've a kind heart, and harsh words doona come easily to ye. I hope that reading what I feel for ye will give ye strength."

I smiled at the folded parchment he extended toward me. Squeezing his hand, I slipped it into the bosom of my dress.

"I'll read it as soon as I get back to the castle. I'll see ye when everything is done."

His letter—no matter how eager I was to read it—would have to wait.

An overdue visit with a ghost from my past stood waiting just footsteps away.

She spotted me before I saw her, and her voice was as distinctive and recognizable as ever.

"Ye grew into just the woman I knew ye would—just as beautiful, just as strong, just as naïve, though the last is no fault of yer own."

She stepped from the woods with the grace of the creatures who lived within them. She could blend in anywhere. Her confidence made any place look like her home.

In the eight years since I'd seen her, she'd not aged a day.

When she opened her arms to me, I cautiously approached and allowed her to embrace me.

Her arms wrapped around me, and one hand stroked the back of my hair as she spoke. "I'm sorry about yer father, lass."

"Ye are not. Ye hated him."

She laughed and released me as she stepped away, her long hair blowing around her face wildly.

"Ye are right. I needn't lie to ye. His death is the best thing that shall ever happen to ye. 'Twas inexcusable for him to keep ye from yer magic as he did. I'm glad ye found the journals I left for ye."

As expected, she'd been watching all from afar.

"'Twas ye that led wee Eoin to the books then, aye?"

She nodded.

"O'course. Though I made sure to hide myself from him. I gently guided him with magic."

The thought of Grier's spells directing Eoin in any form filled me with unease. There was a time I would've trusted her with my life. Now, I felt suspicious of everything she said.

"What are ye doing here, Grier? Why, after all this time, have ye returned?"

"Come now, Morna. Ye must know."

I truly didn't. So little of it made sense.

I shook my head and awaited further explanation. She looked at me expectantly but quickly grew frustrated and threw up her hands in exasperation.

"'Tis all for ye, lass. Doona ye remember the spell we cast our last day together? Jerry is the man I saw in yer future."

She said it so casually as if it explained everything.

"Aye, I've known that for some time. Why then did ye keep him away from me for a year, all the while lying to him about yer ability to help him? Why did ye allow him to believe ye were dead? How did ye survive the fire, and where did ye go during that time?"

An unidentifiable expression passed over Grier's face. Distant, shaken, lonely, and most especially, embarrassed. She looked lost and unsure and very unlike herself.

By bringing up all the questions surrounding her strange behavior, I'd triggered memories she'd rather leave forgotten.

She could see by the directness of my gaze that she had little choice, and the sigh she released said so much more about her true age than her appearance ever would.

"Ye've never known what 'tis like to be truly alone, Morna. I hope ye never do. Loneliness is a slow sickness. At first painless, it eats away at ye little by little. When it starts, ye doona even realize it will change ye, but over time—over days, months, and years of having no one to love—ye change, and the person ye once were no longer exists. Ye become the pain ye hold inside ye.

"I wasna lonely the day I cast Jerry for ye, but I was an empty shell by the day he arrived in our time. I lived a full life here at Conall Castle with ye, yer grandmother, and Alasdair. Your father took everything from me the day he sent me away. For years I had nothing and no one. I dinna realize at first, lass, I truly dinna. I'd not thought of our spell in so long that when I first met Jerry, I dinna know who he was.

"When I realized, I told myself every day that I would tell him the truth, that I would bring him to ye and allow him to either live the life he was meant to with ye or send him home as he wished. But I enjoyed his company too much, and over time, the lie became too big.

"'Twas only when that bastard Creedrich set flame to our home that I saw my opportunity to free myself of Jerry. If he thought me dead, fate would see that he found ye, and it did."

She looked as sad and weary as I felt, as if all the tears she possessed had already been shed. My heart ached for her, but her story still left one blaringly large question unanswered.

"I canna tell ye how sorry I am for what my father did to ye. I missed ye for years after ye left. More than once, I thought about running away and searching for ye. But there is still one question I must ask. Forgive me if it sounds callous. If ye meant to free Jerry from ye, why are ye here now?"

"To seek forgiveness for the pain I caused him and for the time I took from the both of ye. I just need to speak to him one last time, and then I'll leave the two of ye be."

A voice deep inside me suspected the lie for what it was, but it was not my right to deny Jerry the chance to speak with her. I would have to let her see him regardless of the dread that settled in the center of my chest.

"He's in the village. He stays in the cottage that was once yer own. I will go and get him. Wait for him there."

Perhaps it was the wind, but I thought I heard her laughing as I walked away.

CHAPTER 32

 erry

Grier's arrival at Conall Castle didn't surprise me. I knew the day I learned she still lived that I would see her again, and I spent the days and months leading up to her return reflecting on my time spent with her. I said nothing to Morna, not because I wished to keep the events of that time from her, but because I saw no need to burden her with emotions that were not hers to work through. She was so much like her brother—they both felt the need to carry the pain of others.

Falling in love with Morna taught me much. Sure, I'd fancied a few lassies back in my own time, bedded more than my fair share, but I'd never loved another outside of the love one has for family or the platonic love one has for friends.

The moment I realized the depth of my feelings for Morna was the moment I could see something I should've seen from the start —Grier was in love with me. While my affection for her had been true, she'd only ever been my friend, but that had never been her feelings for me.

I'd not seen it at the time. It was clear to me now. Knowing the truth of Grier's affections allowed me to forgive the year of my life she stole from me.

After all, had it been I that held the key to sending Morna away from me, I couldn't say that I wouldn't have lied, as well. In truth, I knew I would've. There was nothing I wouldn't have done to keep her close to me.

What frightened me was the thought that perhaps Grier felt the same way—that she might still be willing to do anything to keep me close. The power of Morna's magic was pure. Everything she did or sought to do was from a place of love.

Grier had goodness within her, but her purity was buried deep, and her spells didn't always serve the greater good. Her lack of family and the loneliness I suspected she'd experienced most of her life had changed the way she thought of magic. She didn't see her magic as a duty to help. She saw it as a burden that cast her apart. If those around her couldn't accept the magic within her, she would use her powers to force the result she desired.

Grier rarely spoke of her life, but she'd said just enough in our time together to make me understand why she often didn't hesitate to force someone's hand with her magic. The evil she'd had to endure at the hands of frightened, ignorant people over and over throughout her life was enough to send anyone into madness.

I didn't know what I would say to her, but I knew there was a delicate line I would have to balance. My heart could never belong to her, and I had to make sure she understood that. Doing so put me at great risk for upsetting her. If I did—if she believed that I'd somehow betrayed her—there was no telling what Grier might do.

Every step toward my cottage was filled with a silent prayer that all would be well.

I had no confidence it would be.

*M*orna

he instant I mentioned Grier's name to him, Jerry no longer heard anything else I said. He was distracted, lost in his own thoughts, determined to make his peace with her in whatever way he could.

It pained me to let him go to her, but I knew he was deserving of my trust.

I stood at the edge of the village and watched Jerry walk toward his cottage until I could no longer see him. Once he was out of sight, I took a deep breath. It was time to proceed to the next dreadfully difficult task of the day, breaking my engagement to Henry.

I saw no one on my short walk back to the castle. Inside its walls, Henry was nowhere to be found. Alasdair was the first person I found. He sat relaxing in Father's old chair by the fire. With the room draped in the afternoon's shadow, Alasdair looked so much like Father that my chest squeezed painfully at the sight of him.

"I told everyone they needn't work today. Elspeth and Eoin are abed resting. I couldna sleep."

"Where's Henry? 'Tis time for me to speak to him."

Alasdair shook his head and yawned. Even if he couldn't sleep, he was exhausted.

"He's asleep, as well. Doona wake him just to break his heart. Ye can tell him before dinner."

I didn't argue. While I knew it needed to be done, I was in no hurry to witness his reaction.

"Mayhap, I should wait until morning. Then, he could leave right away should he wish it."

"Ach, he will wish it, lass. No man wants to stay in the home of

the lass who has jilted him. Morning then. 'Twill be best..."
Alasdair's words slowly faltered as I watched him drift to sleep, his
head slumped over against his shoulder.

I must've fallen asleep shortly after, for when my eyes flickered
open, Alasdair was gone and only a sliver of sunlight shone into
the room.

Evening was upon us, and Jerry would most certainly be wanting
to know how everything had gone with Henry.

If I left now, I could reach and return from his cottage before I
was expected for dinner.

He wouldn't be pleased, but what was one more evening of
waiting when we would have our whole lives to spend together?

If only I'd known how much could change in an evening.

CHAPTER 33

erry

Grier stood in the doorway of my cottage as I approached. While her smile was warm, her eyes were entirely unreadable.

"Did ye know this was my home for many years? 'Tis fitting it should be yer home now."

She gave no greeting and led our conversation with no apology.

"Ye are alive, then?"

"O'course I'm alive. Ye must have known such a fire couldna kill me unless I wished it."

The grief I'd felt at arriving back to see our home destroyed came rushing back to me, flooding my veins with an anger I'd not known I felt toward her.

"I knew no such thing. Do ye not care about the pain ye put me through in the months following what I believed to be yer death? I missed ye, Grier, and the guilt I felt for leaving ye was unbearable."

While my words were true, I realized the moment I said them what a mistake I'd made. Her eyes glistened with hope. My confession made her believe I cared in a way I did not.

"I only meant to help ye. I know Morna has told ye why ye are here. I know that ye know I lied to ye."

Her candor surprised me. I'd expected her to dance around the truth, to spin a tale that would leave me questioning what I knew to be true.

"Aye, I know what ye've done, and I know why."

She stepped inside the cottage as if it were still her home and not mine. I followed her inside. Once the door was closed, she faced me.

"Ye doona know why, lad. How could ye?"

"Ye love me."

Silence didn't bother Grier. She could sit in the company of others surrounded by silence and never feel uncomfortable. I settled into the silence and forced myself to relax inside it as I waited for her to decide how she wished to respond.

"I hope ye know I never intended for things to happen as they did. Ye were not meant for me, and I know it, but ye own my heart anyway."

I couldn't imagine her pain. If I could've eased it, I would have. Had Morna not returned my feelings, it would've killed me. I was doing the same thing to Grier now.

"It honors me to know that ye find me worthy of such affection. Ye are the bonniest friend I've ever known, but aye, I was meant for another, and she holds my heart completely."

The hope in Grier's expression vanished and replaced itself with a cool, collected gaze that made the hairs on the back of my neck stand on end.

"I know, Jerry. Ye needn't tell me where yer heart lies. Ye still canna see, can ye?"

She didn't wait for me to answer before continuing.

"As I told ye, I never intended for things to happen as they have, but they happened all the same. When our home was set aflame, I saw it as my path to redemption, as an opportunity to correct the wrong I did to ye. I intended to stay away, but I could not.

"I lived a life alone and 'twas misery. I canna do it again. I willna do it again. Morna will hate what I've done to her, but she willna be doomed to the same life I've lived. Now that her father is gone, her brother will protect her. He will see that her magic is tended to. He will make certain that her days are never lonely. She will have every chance of having a happy life, and in time she will forget ye."

Panic surged inside me, and I turned to run for the door, all the while knowing it would do no good. I couldn't outrun a spell. I could feel it swirling around me with every step.

"Ye may not love me in the way I wish ye to, but to ye 'twill feel as if ye do. For me, that is better than a life spent alone."

I fought against the pressure in my mind, but I was powerless against her magic. The sound of her words slurred together as my mind went eerily blank.

M orna

I heard sounds coming from Jerry's cottage—primitive, animal-like sounds—but my mind rallied against them. I didn't feel the alarm I should've felt, and I suspected nothing as I knocked on his door.

When no one answered, I pushed it open. As I looked inside, my entire world fell apart.

I should've looked away, but I could not. My brain couldn't believe the sight in front of me.

I'd expected to find Jerry alone.

Grier was still there.

They were wrapped in each other's arms.

With her back pressed against the wall of his cottage, Jerry stood naked before her, driving into her with an abandon that broke my heart. He was entirely unaware of my presence, but Grier saw me the moment I opened the door.

She locked eyes with me, smiled, and threw her head back and laughed.

CHAPTER 34

*P*erspective is everything. Seeing Jerry wrapped in Grier's arms should've broken me, but the sudden death of my father had already split me in two. Yes, I was heartbroken. Yes, I was angry. Yes, I felt betrayed, nauseated, and confused. None of it mattered.

The moment Grier laughed, I turned and walked calmly away.

Sometimes life steals the things you love. I wouldn't fight something I couldn't change. I was no match for Grier. Of course Jerry loved her. Every man I'd ever known had. Why would the man who'd spent more time with her than anyone else be any different? He'd been simply biding his time with me until she returned.

I was a fool, and I deserved this betrayal. He'd treated me exactly as I'd treated Henry.

I couldn't move past the pain here. So many horrible things over the course of my still young life held me in chains at Conall Castle. I loved my brother, Elspeth, and Eoin deeply, but the pain was too much. I couldn't stay. Not now.

I shed no tears as I walked back inside the castle. My world was chaos all around me, but inside I felt nothing. I hoped I could hold onto that nothingness forever.

I met Elspeth on the staircase on the way to my bedchamber.

"What's happened, lass? Ye are paler than I've ever seen ye."

I smiled to relieve her worry but quickly stepped into the shadows so she couldn't see my face.

"'Tis nothing. Do ye know where Henry is? I need to speak with him."

"Aye, he's in the dining room with Alasdair."

That was even better. I could tell them both at once.

---

*A*s was his habit, Alasdair dragged me out of the dining hall to discuss in private what I'd just announced.

I'd never seen him so angry. He was trembling as he held my wrist. I was certain everyone could hear him screaming.

"Have ye lost yer mind, lass? Why would ye tell him ye intend to leave with him tomorrow when we both know ye mean to end yer engagement come morning?"

My insides were like ice. All my life, there was no one who could impact the way I felt more than Alasdair. I cared about his opinion more than anyone. But tonight, his words couldn't break through the wall I'd erected inside.

"My mind is fine. I've decided to keep the engagement. I meant what I told both of ye. I will leave with Henry come morning so we may visit his home and begin preparations for our wedding."

Shaking his head, Alasdair gripped the sides of his head with both hands as he paced wildly in front of me.

"I doona understand a word ye are saying, Morna. I know ye are devastated about Da. I know what it feels like to wish ye could leave here and never step back inside these walls again. The ghost of our memories of him will stay within these walls forever, but we canna run away from this, lass. With time, 'twill get easier."

Calmly, I reached out to touch his arm to stop him.

"This has nothing to do with Father."

"What then? Has Jerry done something to ye? If he's hurt ye lass, I'll kill him."

Even Jerry's name caused me no pain. I was someone who felt everything so intensely. Now I felt nothing. I was beginning to wonder if I'd unintentionally spelled myself.

"Jerry would never hurt me. 'Tis only that he loves another. I dinna see it before, but I see it now. 'Tis time for me to move on from here and live my own life. I shall do so with Henry."

Alasdair shook his head in astonishment. He didn't believe a word I said. I didn't care.

"Love another? Jerry loves none save ye. Everyone sees the way he looks at ye. What has gotten into ye, lass? Ye have me worried."

"Grier is back, Alasdair, and Jerry loves her. I saw the two of them together."

Alasdair jerked back as if I'd slapped him.

"Grier? Why dinna ye tell me that first? We both know she is up to no good. We've known that ever since Jerry arrived here. Ye canna trust her."

"Aye, I know, and now I canna trust Jerry either. I wish to leave here. Will ye allow me to do so? Ye told me once that if ye were laird ye would let me be the woman I wished. Ye are laird now. Will ye keep yer word?"

It was a cruel way for me to persuade him to allow me to make my own decisions. Just like Father, Alasdair's word meant everything to him.

"O'course, I'll permit ye, but I doona care for it for so many reasons. Jerry aside, lass, 'tis not proper for ye to travel with a man ye are not yet wed to without an escort, and I willna leave Elspeth while she is with child. MacNeal Castle is verra far from here. If trouble came to ye, there is no guarantee I could reach ye in time."

I no longer had any concern for my own wellbeing. It was as frozen as every other emotion inside me. "No harm will befall me, and Mary and Kip can stay until we are wed. Would that suit ye?"

It was a ridiculous suggestion by societal expectations, but

Alasdair had never much cared about what anyone else thought. As long as someone he trusted was there to watch over me, that was all he cared about.

Reluctantly, he nodded.

"Aye, I suppose 'twill do. Ye do know ye doona have to marry him, lass. If ye doona love him, I wish ye would not. Ye can still send him away and live here until another ye could love crosses yer path. Ye are always welcome here. And ye needn't worry about the pain Jerry may cause ye. I shall banish the two of them from this territory come morning, and ye shall never see them again."

I knew I didn't have to marry, that Alasdair would take care of me until his dying day if I wished it, but Alasdair had his own family to tend to, and it was time for me to go out on my own.

"Aye, banish them, but it will change nothing. I've agreed to marry Henry, and I willna go back on my word."

Alasdair's arms wrapped around and lifted me into the air as he hugged me. His words were choked and broken as he spoke. Although I couldn't see his eyes, I knew he was crying.

"This is a mistake, lass. The moment ye realize it, please know ye can come home. There is nothing ye can ever do that will make that impossible. Whatever happens, know that I will protect ye here."

He clung to me desperately as I hung limply in his arms. I didn't fight his embrace, but I didn't hug him back, either.

"Do ye wish me to kill him, lass? 'Twould be a horrible sin, but I will do it if ye wish it."

What frightened me more than anything else I'd witnessed all day was how long it took me to answer him.

"No, but thank ye."

The realization that I'd even considered it told me just how much of me was truly gone—locked beneath a fortress I had no desire to unearth.

CHAPTER 35

ome morning, as we packed and loaded everything onto a dozen different horses, Jerry was absent from the stables. Without a word to end things, he'd left me for Grier.

Mary approached me tenderly, placing a hand on my back as she spoke in soft tones. She was furious at everyone—at Jerry for what he'd done, at Alasdair for letting me leave, at Kip for agreeing that they would come with me—but she was treating me with unnecessary kindness.

"Ye left the dress ye wore yesterday out of yer belongings, but I added it to yer chests, so ye needn't worry. 'Twill all get better, lass. With time, everything will be better."

"I know, Mary. I'm fine. Truly. Go and scream at Alasdair and Kip if ye wish it. Once we leave, ye willna be able to."

She looked at me with the same concerned gaze Alasdair had given me the day before, but I turned away and ignored it until she left.

There were only two people who occupied my mind—two people who even with my frozen emotions, I would be desperately sad to leave—Eoin and Elspeth.

Eoin threatened to break through my resolve most of all. The poor lad was already so saddened and confused from his grandfather's death that I worried what my sudden absence might do to him. I wanted him to be certain he would see me again.

I found him on the floor of his bedchamber stacking small stones he'd gathered from the woods into piles.

"Eoin, lad, do ye mind if I join ye?"

He smiled and waved me to the floor with his chubby little hand. As I sat next to him, he pushed a few rocks in my direction.

"Da found them."

"Oh, yer da found the rocks, did he? Did ye help him?"

He nodded, but said nothing else. He was unusually quiet.

"Eoin, did yer da tell ye that I must leave here for awhile?"

He kept his head down, fumbling with the rocks on the floor. His voice was soft and sad when he spoke.

"Will ye leave like Grand Da?"

A lump swelled in my throat, and I hurried to lift Eoin from the floor and into my lap before every emotion I was holding inside broke loose in front of him.

"No, lad. I'll never leave like Grand Da. I'll only be away for a time, and then ye will see me. I shall visit ye here. Mayhap ye can come and visit me at my new castle."

Simply knowing he would see me again seemed to relax him, and he lay his little head against my chest as I held him. With every person in the castle dealing with grief over my father's death and Elspeth dealing with the exhaustion of her pregnancy, little Eoin had been left to fend for himself more than he was accustomed.

When he began to snore, I carefully stood and carried him to his bed. Kissing his brow, I whispered a spell of protection in his ear and bid him farewell.

*E*lspeth was even more upset by my decision than Alasdair. Never one to mince words, Elspeth rained a stream of curse words down on me that I wouldn't have thought her capable of.

"Ye are a selfish wee bitch, Morna. I doona wish to see ye. I doona wish to say goodbye to ye. Ye can burn in hell for all I care."

Undeterred by her rage, I moved across the room and climbed onto the bed next to her where she sat resting.

"Ye needn't be angry with me. Ye should be pleased that I'm leaving. Ye know Alasdair worries too much for me. Ye and Eoin should be his priority."

She screamed at me between sobs. Her eyes were bloodshot, and she dabbed at her nose with a cloth.

"Do ye think Alasdair is the only one in this damned castle who cares for ye? What will Eoin do? His heart has already been broken once this week. And what of the new babe? Do ye have no desire to know it, to love it as ye have loved Eoin? And what of me, Morna? I know I am not yer closest friend, but ye know ye are mine. I doona care what Jerry has done to ye. 'Tis selfish of ye to do this, and 'tis pure lunacy for ye to marry a man like Henry MacNeal."

So what if Henry could be unkind? I could be unkind, too. So what if he hid something? I was hiding something from him, as well. Everyone seemed so much more concerned about my fiancé than I was.

"Elspeth, I canna stay here. Ye wouldna stay here if ye were me. I know ye wouldna. Ye would want yer own life, with yer own family. Is it so wrong for me to desire to have just what ye do?"

She collapsed into a hysterical fit of tears. As I moved in to comfort her, she turned her swollen eyes up toward me.

"O'course 'tisn't wrong. 'Tis only that I will miss ye so much I doona know if I can bear it. I wish ye would be here for the birth, Morna. I've not said a word to Alasdair, but I'm frightened. So verra frightened."

I pulled back to look at her more fully. Her confession alarmed me.

"What do ye mean? Do ye feel as if something is wrong with the babe?"

She continued to cry as she spoke, and I pulled her in close to stroke her hair.

"No, the babe feels strong, but I feel weak. I doona have the same strength I had when carrying Eoin."

I tried to rationalize her worry.

"Ye are older now. 'Tis no wonder that ye doona feel as strong. All will be well, I'm sure of it."

Elspeth pulled away from me and turned to grasp my hand. She squeezed my fingers so tightly I couldn't help but devote every ounce of my attention to listening to her.

"Ye must hear me, Morna. I doona believe I will survive the child's birth. Where will Alasdair and Eoin be if we both leave them?"

"What?" Horror washed over me making me dizzy at Elspeth's suggestion. It was absurd for her to even allow herself to think it. I pulled my hand away and grabbed her shoulders, shaking them gently as I yelled at her. "Doona say anything like that again, Elspeth."

"My denying it will help nothing. Yer father knew, ye know? He knew that death was coming for him."

Glimpses of him tucking me into bed flickered through my mind. I knew Elspeth was right—he'd suspected he would be gone soon, and he wanted to make his peace with me before he was.

"What does Father have to do with any of this?"

"I know how he felt because I feel it now, and ye are the only one I mean to tell. Ye must promise me not to tell Alasdair."

Just like with the news of her pregnancy, there was no reason for her to feel the need to ask me not to say anything to him. I would do anything to keep my brother from pain. There was no way Elspeth could possibly know for certain she would die in childbirth, and I wouldn't worry my brother over something that would very likely turn out to be irrelevant.

"O'course, Elspeth, but ye must not give in to this feeling ye have. Ye must try to stay strong. We all need ye."

Tears fell freely down her face. She was still so stunning that I found myself jealous of her even with her face splotched red.

"I know ye feel ye must go now, but will ye try to be back for the birth in three months' time? If I am to die, ye will need to be here for Alasdair's sake. He can bear so much, but this would test him in a way I doona believe he's prepared for."

I would go to MacNeal Castle and make preparations for my wedding, but there was no way I would possibly miss the babe's birth now.

"I'll be back in two, Elspeth, and all will be well. Ye will see."

CHAPTER 36

"*D*id ye not wish to say goodbye to Jerry, lass? I know the two of ye were verra good friends."

Henry asked the question two days into our ride, catching me off guard and forcing me out of the silence I'd enjoyed for the entirety of our trip.

I shook my head but kept my gaze ahead. "We were not so verra close."

"'Tis no matter." Henry paused, and I could see him looking at me expectantly out of the corner of my eye.

"Why is that?"

"He will be joining us in a fortnight. I heard that yer brother no longer required his services so I asked if he wished to work for me at MacNeal Castle. He agreed as long as his sister could live with him."

Mary snorted behind me. While I worked hard to remain emotionless, this sudden news nearly caused me to fall off my horse.

Whirling my head toward him, my voice gave too much away. "He what? He's coming to work as yer servant?"

Henry nodded, and I noticed that his expression was rather

furious. I wondered if he'd heard rumors about Jerry and me and my reaction had only confirmed them in his mind.

"Aye, lass. He and his sister."

I couldn't stop myself. The words ground their way through my teeth against my will.

"She is not his sister."

Henry waved a hand dismissively as if he already knew that.

"In truth, I doona care what she is to him. I see no reason to judge a man for how he lives his life in private as long as he does good work for me. I watched Jerry at yer brother's home, and he is a fair worker. I canna imagine why Alasdair saw a need to get rid of him."

His tone was accusatory. I saw no need to escalate the situation further.

"How many days until we reach home?"

I intentionally refrained from labeling MacNeal Castle as only his home. I hoped my inclusive wording of the question would cause him to relax.

"Less than a day. We shall arrive by nightfall."

There was a loud stirring in the trees to our left. Henry halted the horses as we waited for the animal within the brush to either retreat or step into the pathway in front of us. I expected a deer. Instead a tall, strapping highlander tripped his way in front of Henry's horse.

"*Pretend ye know me, lass. Otherwise, this lad will send me away, and I must speak with ye.*"

I heard the stranger's voice inside my mind as clearly as if he'd said the words aloud, but his lips never moved. The sudden intrusion inside my mind startled me so much that this time, I did fall off my horse. Before I could stand, the stranger's hands were on my arms, gently lifting me from the ground.

"Remove yer hands from my betrothed, sir." Henry's voice screamed as he dismounted and made his way over to us. "Morna, are ye all right, lass? What happened? Did ye faint?"

The stranger kept his grip on my arms and spoke quickly inside my mind once again.

"Did ye hear me? Ye must hurry. Throw yer arms around me and greet me as if ye've known me all yer life. Ye can call me Hamish. Tell him I'm a cousin and insist that I come with ye."

Too shocked and baffled to argue, I did exactly what the man asked of me. Throwing my arms around him, squeezing him with an intimacy that surprised even me, I gushed out loud about this man I'd never before seen in my life.

"Hamish! What are ye doing here? What fortune that our paths have crossed? Ye must join us. We are not far from home now, and ye look bone weary from travel."

Surprising myself more with each passing moment, I twisted with one arm still around Hamish as I turned to address Henry.

"Ye doona mind if he stays at the castle, do ye? This is my cousin, Hamish Conall, my father's brother's son."

Henry was caught off guard, but he could hardly refuse to shelter a relative of the woman he meant to marry, and I knew it. Masking his frustration, Henry nodded and extended the man his hand.

"O'course. Do ye have no horse? Where were ye headed when ye crossed our path?"

For the first time since his sudden intrusion, Hamish spoke out loud. His voice sounded exactly like it did inside my mind.

"No, I'm afraid my horse was stolen from me. 'Tis indeed great fortune that I stumbled upon ye, for 'twas my cousin's home where I was headed."

Mary's bugged-out eyes caught my attention, and I discreetly shook my head to warn her to say nothing.

"I see. Well, we've an extra horse with no baggage. Ye can ride her, though she's slower than the rest. Ye will have to take up the rear."

Hamish happily agreed. Once he saw himself mounted, our caravan of travelers continued. The moment all was quiet, Hamish's voice spoke to me in my mind once again.

"Ye can speak back to me in yer mind, lass. I'm surprised ye havena even tried."

I was too confused for it to have even crossed my mind. Hesitantly, I attempted to think what I wished to say out loud to him.

"What are ye?"

"I'm the same as ye, lass. I possess magic, and I felt yers vibrating through the forest from far away. I've been trying to meet up with ye for days."

This man wasn't the same as me. If he was powerful enough to communicate with me in such a way, he possessed more power than I'd known was possible.

"Where are ye from? And why were ye trying to meet me?"

"I make it a point to speak with everyone I meet like us, lass, though we are scattered few and far between. I'm from Allen territory, Morna. I believe yer brother sent someone after me many months ago. I'm sorry it has taken me so long to find ye."

The druid Alasdair sought, the one he believed could teach me everything I needed to know about magic, was here.

Suddenly, the darkness of the past week seemed a little bit brighter.

CHAPTER 37

M *acNeal Castle—Two Weeks Later*

*I*t took less than a day of settling into his own territory, in his own home, around his own servants for me to see exactly what everyone warned me about Henry MacNeal. The man was an arrogant brute who thought himself better than anyone below his station. He was disingenuous in everything he said, and I suspected that his tendency toward violence was something he struggled to restrain daily.

If not for Hamish's presence at the castle, I would've fled with Mary and Kip the day after we arrived. But the one positive thing about being in Henry's home was that I rarely saw him.

He never visited my room, he hadn't touched me since we arrived, and his days were spent tending to tasks left unattended while he was at Conall Castle.

It meant that I had the castle, or at least the rooms he'd given me, entirely to myself. I spent my days with Hamish. He taught me more in the span of a fortnight than I'd learned in the past decade.

The lessons were a glorious distraction from so many things I didn't want to think about. Unfortunately, Hamish didn't allow me to stay in bliss for long. On the day Jerry and Grier were set to arrive at the castle, the mysterious druid told me he was leaving.

"Must ye go? I could spend years working with ye and not learn all that I wish to."

"Aye I must, lass, though leaving ye 'twill sadden me more than ye know. If I dinna already know yer heart belonged to another, I would've spent the past fortnight trying to earn yer heart rather than improving yer spells."

I could never tell when Hamish was teasing me—he so often said things I found surprising. I'd never mentioned Jerry to him, and I suspected he knew the truth of my feelings for Henry.

"Just who do ye think my heart belongs to?"

He shrugged in a way that only accentuated the length of his arms.

"I doona know, but I know 'tis not Laird MacNeal."

I didn't want to speak about Jerry. I only wanted to beg Hamish to stay.

"Please doona leave. I need ye. I went too long without someone to teach me."

Dropping to his knees, Hamish situated himself on the floor and patted the ground so that I would join him.

"I must leave, but I will always be willing to teach ye. Ye are welcome in Allen territory any time. Those with magic are safe there, and our practice is looked at in a verra different way. Ye would like it."

Perhaps I would follow him. Once I ended my engagement for good and Elspeth's babe was safely delivered, I could go to Allen territory and devote myself to a life of learning. There were many other possible futures that seemed much worse to me.

"Do ye mean it? I will come then. There are things I must see to first, but later, I will come."

Hamish smiled and nodded.

"'Tis settled then. I shall count the days until I see ye again."

I laughed, again unsure if his small flirtations were genuine or meant in jest.

"How far is yer home from here?"

"'Tis closer from here than 'tis from Conall Castle. Though in truth, 'tis not all that far from Conall Castle either."

I thought of the months Jerry had been away while searching for him. It had to be further than Hamish realized.

"It took a man I knew weeks to reach the village when he went in search of ye. How is that not too far?"

"'Tis our magic. The forest surrounding us is spelled. Unless we know ye are coming and can clear the path for ye, anyone searching will have a verra difficult time finding us. 'Tis a wonder the lad ever found it. This lad ye speak of—is he the one who holds yer heart?"

"No one holds my heart, Hamish."

"Aye, someone does. For if not, ye would belong to me by now. Did ye know, lass, that if I were to say four simple words, I would break the spell ye've cast on yerself and ye would fall to pieces here in my arms? There is a pain inside ye that ye have buried so deep 'twill poison ye. I understand what 'tis to hurt, lass, but hiding from how ye feel only keeps ye blind."

While the thought had crossed my mind the day I found Jerry and Grier together, I'd not truly thought it possible. Had my feelings truly been so overwhelming in that moment that I'd cast a spell on myself unwittingly?

"Do ye mean I've a spell on me in a literal or figurative sense, Hamish?"

He smiled. "Literal, lass. Quite a powerful one. Do ye wish me to break it?"

Bracing for the pain I knew would come, I nodded.

Rather than the breaking of a dam, it was like a slow trickle of rain. The feelings came in a slow steady stream. As Hamish opened his arms to me, I leaned into him and told him everything.

*B*y nightfall, Hamish was gone. While a sense of misery hung over me with such intensity that I had to remind myself to breathe under the weight of it, I was grateful that I felt like myself for the first time in weeks.

I could see things clearly. I knew what I had to do.

I couldn't marry Henry. And I had to find out if Hamish was right. His last words to me would haunt me until I did.

"The lad still holds yer heart, lass. If he truly loved her, 'twould have been released back to ye. I suspect she's spelled him. The only way for ye to know for certain is to get him far away from her and see if he begins to wage a war within himself. If he is spelled, he canna do so while near her."

CHAPTER 38

*M*ary and I created a plan, albeit a faulty one, in the little time I had before dinner.

I would extend my meal with Henry for as long as possible. While he was eating and distracted, Mary and Kip would ready our horses. We both knew that once the engagement was broken, it would be in our best interest to leave MacNeal Castle with haste.

In the meantime, I simply needed to pack all of my things and have them ready to be loaded before dinner.

With everything folded, I bent to my knees to put everything away.

Jerry's letter fell to the floor from the folded clothes the moment I opened my chest. I'd not thought of it once since he'd given it to me weeks ago.

Sinking to the floor, I opened it with shaking hands.

My dearest Morna,

Oh, how I wish our first night together had not ended in such tragedy for you. There were so many things I wished to tell you that next morning, so many ways I wished to show you just how much I treasure your heart.

These past days have been a misery for me. You should not have to go through such grief alone, though I understand why your brother has asked me to stay away.

Lass, I know you worry that you are somehow responsible for pulling me from my own time. It is a waste of time. I don't care who brought me here, I am only glad to have arrived.

Do you know how many times since meeting you I've looked up into the stars and pondered how I could have been so lucky? More times than I can count.

I'm an ordinary lad who until vanishing through time lived a very ordinary life.

You have made my life spectacular. And you have done the impossible. You made me love you more than I love myself, and we both know that I love myself a great deal.

I hope you know what you've gotten yourself into, lass, for even if you were to wish it now, I'm afraid you're stuck with me. You possess my very soul—you stole it the moment I laid eyes on you.

There is naught in this world I wouldn't do for you.

All my love,

Jerry

Only someone who was exceedingly cruel would take the time to give someone such a letter if they intended to leave them the very same day. Jerry was anything but cruel.

Our plan went disastrously wrong from the start. I arrived at dinner to learn that Henry had chosen to skip it. Panicked that he might see Kip and Mary readying our things and take preventative actions to keep me from leaving, I went in search of him.

It didn't take long. Only a few steps outside the dining hall, I could hear Henry screaming at someone. His tone was angry and violent. I hurried in its direction to see what was happening. He was in one of the castle's four main towers, and I ran up the steps.

The charming, seductive man I knew was unrecognizable as he stared down at a girl younger than me who stood shaking before him.

I didn't know what she'd done to upset him, but the moment I stepped into the circular room, he slapped her. Without hesitation, I launched myself between them, pushing him away as I ushered the girl from the tower, whispering in her ear for her to run.

When I faced Henry, his face had drained of color. He preferred to lose his temper in private, when no one was watching. He believed this was the first sign of it I'd seen, and he was visibly embarrassed for being caught.

He attempted to give an explanation, but I held up a hand to interrupt him.

"No, it doesna matter what the lass did to ye, 'twas no reason to hit her."

Glancing down, he pretended to be regretful.

"Ye are right. The stress of all the work that awaited me when I returned here wears on me. I shouldna have lost my temper."

I was so angry that the sole reason for finding him was no longer at the forefront of my mind.

"From what I've heard, 'tis not the first time ye've lost yer temper with a servant."

His left brow twitched ever so slightly—a small flash of anger that he masked quickly.

"Have my servants been speaking to ye, lass? They know they are to leave ye be unless ye require them."

"'Twas not anyone here, though I suspect they are all too terrified of ye to say anything. 'Twas friends from Conall Castle. No one thought I should come here with ye."

He seemed to be searching for someone to blame—someone he could take his anger out on.

"'Twas Kip, then. Aye, I yelled at the lad once. He deserved it. I was verra clear on which stall I wished for my horse to stay in. He disobeyed me."

I could feel the magic begin to twitch within my fingertips. Even with only two weeks of training, my powers were more integrated into my being. It took little for me to call on them now, and my anger had it at the ready.

"Kip doesna take orders from ye. Not at Conall Castle and not here. I am sorry to break my word to ye Henry, but I canna marry ye."

He laughed and stepped forward to pin me against the wall.

"I've tried to be patient with ye, lass, but ye have overstepped. Ye are in my home. I shall treat my servants however I wish, and I doona allow anyone to break their word to me."

"The man I see before me now is not the man I agreed to marry. I'm under no obligation to stay here. My brother will welcome me back with open arms. My horses are ready. I plan to leave at once."

For a moment, I thought he would step away, that things would end peacefully, but as the silence stretched, I watched him change his mind. One moment, his palms braced the wall on either side of my head, the next his hands were on my waist, squeezing as he pushed me into the stones so hard that I feared my ribs would break.

He leaned in close, and the warm breath that once threatened to seduce me now made my skin crawl.

"Ye bedded him, dinna ye, lass—the stable hand? I heard talk of it and still I was willing to wed ye. Ye dare chastise me for my anger when I have treated ye with nothing but respect. I believed ye to be the kind of lass who would go to her marriage pure. Had I known ye were a whore, I would've bedded ye myself long ago. Mayhap 'tis time for me to do so now."

I had hoped to leave MacNeal Castle without revealing my

powers to a man undeserving of the knowledge, but the moment his hand grabbed at the center between my legs, I let go of any apprehension I had about spelling him.

My first instinct, however, wasn't to utter a spell. In my haste to get his hands off me, I did the only thing that came to mind. I lifted one hand in the air and jabbed two fingers so deeply into his eyes that I swore I heard one of them pop. He fell back screaming and gasping as blood poured from his eyes.

"My eyes! I canna see. I canna see."

He screamed the words over and over as I retched onto the ground.

I couldn't imagine the pain he was in, but I suspected I'd not blinded him permanently. His rage gave him the strength to stand. Just as he tried to charge me, I spoke a spell that bound him against the wall, making him unable to move anything other than his mouth.

I stood back and watched him as he realized what I was.

"Ye are a witch. I dinna believe the rumors. Had I known, I never would've agreed to marry ye."

It was oddly satisfying to watch him panic at the knowledge—knowing that he could do nothing to prevent anything I wished to do to him. I stayed silent as he rambled on.

"Do ye mean to kill me? Would ye kill a man for losing his temper?"

I wondered if perhaps I should, but I knew that I could not. While the world would most certainly be a better place without him, I couldn't live with blood on my hands.

"No, I willna kill ye, but if ye ever slap one of yer servants again or if ye ever try to bed a lass against her will, rest assured I will learn of it. When I do, I shall come and cut yer tongue out while ye sleep."

The admittance that I wouldn't kill him made him bold.

"Witchcraft is an offense punishable by death, lass. When I am free, I will let all of the Highlands know what ye are. Then even yer dear brother will be unable to help ye."

The spell wouldn't hold him forever. I wasn't even sure I would have enough time to get Jerry away from Grier before Henry was free of my spell. There was no sense in arguing with him further. I wouldn't kill him, and he knew it.

"I could always cut yer tongue out now, then ye would be unable to tell anyone anything ever again."

I hated that I wasn't as frightening as I wanted to be. He easily called my bluff.

"Ye retched after poking my eyes. Ye doona have the nerve to cut out my tongue."

Placing both hands on his shoulders, I smiled.

"Ye are right. Goodbye, Henry."

Swinging my knee far back behind me, I threw it into his groin with so much force that I knew it was he that would now be retching long after I left.

CHAPTER 39

I ran from the tower as quickly as my feet could carry me. I didn't stop until I burst into the stables, screaming for Mary and Kip to meet me.

They were ready with all of our belongings, though we'd had no opportunity to plan how best to get Jerry alone.

I'd not seen him since the day I walked in on he and Grier in his cottage. I wasn't sure my already rattled nerves could take it.

"Ye must breathe, lass. We've still much to do. We must do it quickly. Kip has a plan."

More surprised than was perhaps appropriate, I lifted my eyes to look at him. Kip was a man of few words. To think he'd been sitting around thinking of a way to help me touched me deeply.

"Ye've a plan, Kip? Whatever 'tis I'm willing to try it. I'm too shaken to think."

Kip's calm demeanor helped ease my breathing as he approached and placed a gentle hand on my shoulder.

"Ye look it, lass. How did MacNeal react?"

Still trying to catch my breath, I spoke in broken lengths.

"Not well…he…he knows I'm a witch…and I might…I might have blinded him. I canna say for sure."

"Well, lass," his voice still calm and steady, Kip continued on like there was nothing unusual about what I'd just told him, "we best get started then before he has a chance to send his men after us. Here is what I propose:

"Under no circumstance can Grier see ye. She willna trust ye and will hide Jerry away. I doona trust Mary to approach her. She's too angry and willna be able to hide it. I must be the one to lead Grier away from their new home in the village, and I know just how to do it."

*W*e approached the dimly lit home as quietly as we could, tying one horse just a short distance away while the rest remained tied in the woods for our escape. Mary and I sat on the ground on the left side of the cottage, our backs pressed against the wall.

The moment we saw Kip leave with Grier, we would enter and try to speak with Jerry. At that point, the result of our efforts was entirely dependent upon his reaction.

The cottage was in terrible condition, but its thin walls allowed us to hear every word as Kip burst inside without knocking.

"Grier, ye've arrived just in time. I need yer help most urgently."

I wanted to scream in response to the rage that built inside me at the sound of Grier's voice, but her tone echoed surprise, and it gave me hope that Kip's plan just might work.

"What's happened?"

"'Tis Laird MacNeal. He's been attacked by one of his servants and tied up in a tower. I canna stop his bleeding."

"Have ye called for a healer?"

Kip played his part wonderfully. His voice never faltered, and his story never slipped as she questioned him.

"There is no time for that, lass. Only magic will save him, and Morna doesna possess the skills to aid him. If ye are worried that someone will learn of yer magic, ye needn't be. I killed the servant that harmed him. Only Morna is with him now."

I could hear Grier gathering things inside, and Mary reached over to squeeze my hand. Whispering so quietly that it was barely above a breath, Mary spoke, "'Tis almost time. Are ye ready to see him?"

"No, but as long as ye are by my side, I will be fine."

From inside, I heard Jerry's voice for the first time. "Do ye need me to go with ye?"

"No." There was such command in the way she said it that I knew Jerry would object to her ordering him around. His silence was all the proof I needed that something was terribly wrong with him. "Which tower is he in, Kip?"

"The west tower. I'll lead ye there."

"No, ye stay here with Jerry. Ye would only slow me down if ye came. Doona leave here until I return."

I held my breath as I watched her leave. Once Kip believed it safe, he called us inside.

---

*I*t would've been so much easier if he'd looked different—if his eyes appeared spelled or if he'd not recognized me. What made it so much more painful was that he looked exactly the same, and he knew who I was immediately. He simply didn't care.

"Morna, Mary, what are ye doing here? Ye should have entered with Kip. I'm sure Grier would've loved to have seen ye."

It was such a ridiculous question—a ridiculous statement—I couldn't even bring myself to respond to him.

Fortunately, Mary found herself far less speechless than I. She marched right over to him and grabbed his head between both of her hands.

"Ye listen to me, ye damned fool. What is the matter with ye?

How can ye speak to her so plainly after what ye've done to her? Doona ye remember that ye love her?"

"Morna?"

The confusion in Jerry's voice sounded entirely genuine.

Mary shook him a little more violently than was necessary.

"Aye, Morna. O'course Morna. Do ye really mean to tell me ye doona remember loving her?"

Understandably, Jerry pulled away from her. As he approached, my entire body went still.

"What is she going on about, lass? I did love ye, but I love ye no longer. I thought everyone knew by now."

Nothing could've wounded me more. He remembered everything. She'd simply changed his feelings entirely.

Kip was in no mood to dawdle. He knew it would take Grier no time to realize she'd been tricked.

"I doona believe the castle is enough distance, lass. We must take him with us."

Before any of us could respond, Kip lifted a candlestick and struck Jerry on the back of the head.

CHAPTER 40

*J*erry was a docile captive. He didn't scream or thrash about once he gained consciousness. Instead, he told us repeatedly, as Kip secured the bindings keeping him strapped belly-down on my horse, that whatever we were trying to do to him was futile—that Grier would be along soon and would find him.

We all knew he was right. The first place Grier would go was Conall Castle. She would try to find us on the path. I couldn't go that direction with him.

"I doona know where Allen territory is, but 'twould be best if I took Jerry there. Grier knows nothing of Hamish. The two of ye should come with me, as well. I hate to think what Grier might do to ye once she catches up with ye."

Mary wasn't worried.

"We must return to Conall Castle. Alasdair must know what's happened so he may decide how to prepare for it before hearing of it elsewhere. If that bitch comes for us, I'll run her through."

Jerry started to protest at Mary's description of Grier, but Mary just slapped the top of his head to shush him.

"No, doona ye say another word about her, Jerry. I doona wish to hear it and neither does Morna." She twisted to address me. "Morna, did ye learn anything with Hamish that might give us more time—that might make us less catchable?"

It was a simple enough spell but one I doubted Grier would expect me to know. It was much like what his clan used to keep their territory hidden.

"Aye, I'll muddy yer path a bit. Ride ahead, and once I canna see ye, I'll cast it."

They didn't waste any time, and as they reached the edge of the village, Kip called back after me. "Hamish left towards the east, lass. Mayhap, if ye ride quickly enough ye can catch him."

With Jerry draped over the back of my horse like a blanket, I climbed in front of him and took off as quickly as possible in an eastwardly direction.

I didn't stop at all the first night. I cast a spell to light our path and continued through the woods, hoping with each passing second we would meet up with Hamish. He was nowhere to be found, and the mind-speak that had been available to me the day he stumbled across our path wasn't working either.

All I had was a few blankets to see us through to Allen territory.

"Lass, is there truly any reason for this? Ye are my friend, Morna, but this willna work. Ye canna force me to love ye."

He'd said little since we left. I was so concerned with trying to sense whether or not we were traveling in the right direction I'd almost forgotten about him.

"Oh, really? Ye do know that is precisely what Grier has done to ye, aye? Stolen ye from me and forced ye to love her? Yer feelings for her are not real, Jerry. She's spelled ye."

He was quick to protest. "No. Grier wouldna ever spell me."

"Doona be a fool. Even if ye feel as if ye love her now, 'tis clear enough ye still have yer mind. Ye know how ruthless and vengeful she can be. Do ye truly believe that if she were hurt enough, she wouldna spell anyone to make them do anything she wanted?"

He fell silent for a long time, and I knew he believed it possible. Just as the sun began to break along the horizon, he spoke again.

"Is it truly necessary to keep me bound this way? All my blood has run to my head. 'Tis causing me to feel rather ill, and my head aches dreadfully."

"We will stop and rest soon. As long as ye promise to cause me no trouble, I'll allow ye to ride properly when we continue."

True to my word, as soon as the sun was up, I found a place to rest.

"All right Jerry, I'm going to help ye to yer feet. Ye may be unsteady for a moment."

Untying him, I pushed him off the horse so that his feet landed first. He held onto the horse for a brief moment then took off running in the opposite direction.

Sighing, I muttered a spell to trip him and watched while his legs locked, and he fell flat on his face. He only made it a few strides away.

"Doona ye remember I'm a witch, too?"

With his head still down, it took him some effort to answer me. "Aye, but ye are not a verra good one. I thought mayhap I could get away."

Moving to stand in front of him, I nudged his shoulders so he would lift his head.

Begrudgingly, he did so. Blood was running freely down the front of his face.

"Ye cracked my skull open, lass. Do ye know of a spell that might heal it?"

*I*t looked worse than it was, but the sight of him losing so much blood had me in tears as I led him to the river to clean his wound. I knew of nothing that would heal the wound completely. As long as we held something to it, I knew it would stop bleeding soon. I was far more upset by it than Jerry was.

"'Tis all right, lass. 'Twas my own fault for trying to run."

He'd removed his shirt so I could clean the wound with it. Wetting it, I reached up to wipe more blood from his face.

"Are ye truly so eager to get away from me? Ye've said ye remember our time together. How then can ye be so callous about it?"

He closed his eyes as I pressed the cloth against his wound.

"I doona know, lass. I can only tell ye how I feel. I remember loving ye, but I canna feel the memory of it. I can only see it in my mind. I know I dinna mean to hurt ye, but when I think of Grier, all I feel is this overwhelming love and concern for her. That is why I tried to run. I know she's worried for me, and I canna stand the thought of her in pain."

"Ye felt just as strongly for me a fortnight ago. Can ye truly not see that ye might be spelled? How could yer feelings change so quickly otherwise?"

With his face now clean and the crack above his brow clotting nicely, he looked up into my eyes and stared at me in silence for a long time.

When he smiled, my heart fluttered with hope.

"Mayhap, I am, lass. Why doona ye kiss me, and we shall see how I feel?"

I'd missed the feeling of his lips so much that I threw myself into the kiss with abandon. It felt as if he were back. His hands caressed the sides of my face, his lips moved against mine willingly, his tongue slipped deftly inside. For me, it was perfect, but when it ended, Jerry leaned casually back and shrugged his shoulders.

"Nothing, lass. I felt nothing."

Just as I was about to collapse into a heap of embarrassed tears, Hamish's voice approached us from behind.

"Ach, lass. There is not a man alive that could be kissed like that and feel nothing. She's spelled him worse than I thought."

CHAPTER 41

Note from M.C.:

How are you doing, lass? I trust you are still reading and eager to hear how things turn out in the end. As I mentioned to you before, it's important for you to hear my story—it will make everything easier for you to believe once we meet.

While I know you may have your doubts about the reality of everything now, one way I can assure you my story is true is this: Were this a work of fiction, I most assuredly would not have written these next two chapters of my life.

My father's death was difficult to bear.

My own death was so much worse.

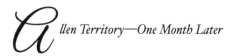

llen Territory—One Month Later

"*I* should have never told ye about this place, lass. Either way, regardless of what ye see within that pool, only pain can come from it. Please let me take ye back to the village. My uncle will continue to work with Jerry. Not a soul here will allow him to leave, and if Grier comes for him, ye know her magic is no match for what we have here. I'll come with ye to Conall Castle. We'll stay for the babe's birth and learn what shall happen as everyone is meant to. 'Tis never a good thing to know another's future."

Hamish's warning was useless. I'd made up my mind the moment he mentioned it. I couldn't stand the unknown for a moment longer. Everything in my life felt as if it were one day away from entire destruction. If the waters within Hamish's cave would allow me to know one way or the other how things would play out, then I wanted to know. I was in pain anyway. How much worse could it get?

"Just tell me how it works, Hamish. Please. If Elspeth's worry is for naught, I willna leave Jerry here. If she has truly predicted her death, we shall go and leave Jerry in yer uncle's care."

Grier's spell still held Jerry with a tight grip, and in the weeks since our arrival, he'd grown angry and cold. He hated me now. The way he looked at me sent shivers down my spine each and every time—his eyes were filled with malice.

"'Twill only show ye things that are unchangeable, which is precisely why it causes such pain. No matter what horrible things ye find inside, ye can do nothing to stop them."

I was quickly losing my patience with him. "I doona care if I canna change them. At least I will know and can make my peace with whatever is inside."

Hamish shook his head but turned to leave.

"Verra well. I'll wait for ye outside."

I don't know how long I cried on the wet stones surrounding the shallow pool, but Hamish eventually gave up waiting and came inside to collect me. He picked me up in his long, broad arms and cradled me like a child.

"What did ye see, lass?"

"Elspeth will die, and then, so will I."

Hamish's arms seized uncomfortably at my words. He dropped me to my feet and held me out away from him.

"What?"

I repeated the words slowly, terror gripping at me even as I said them. I didn't want to die. Not yet. There was still so much I wanted, so much I still needed to do.

"Elspeth...she was right. She dies giving birth to a beautiful baby boy. One month later, Alasdair will bury me, as well."

The expression on Hamish's face surprised me. He didn't look devastated by the revelation, and I started to believe that every flattering comment, every sideways glance had been in jest. If anything, he just looked confused.

"Did ye see yerself die? What killed ye?"

Sniffling between sobs, I screamed at him. "What does it matter how I die? Does it not bother ye to know I'll be dead in a few weeks?"

Hamish brushed the wet and matted hair from my face and bent forward to kiss my cheek. "Lass, ye dinna see yerself die, did ye?"

I shook my head. "No, I only saw my lifeless body being lowered into the ground."

He smiled and rubbed his hands up and down my arms to warm me.

"If ye dinna see yerself die, if ye dinna see what killed ye, then ye willna die. Did no one ever tell ye that witches doona die like everyone else? Unless harmed by the magic of another, 'tis up to us when our life ends."

I did remember Grier mentioning such a thing in regard to her aging, but I'd not remembered it at all while watching Alasdair cry over my body.

Taking a shaky breath, I relaxed just a little. "Do ye mean it?"

He nodded. "Aye, but that doesna explain the vision. I must cast deeper into yer future, and such spells are not easy. Go back to the village. I'll find ye when I know the truth of what ye saw."

Although relieved that I wasn't near death, my heart was still broken as I walked back to the village.

My brother was days away from losing the love of his life.

CHAPTER 42

When Hamish stepped into my tent late that evening, he was trembling with exhaustion. I hurried to grab his arms to usher him to a seat.

"What happened? Ye doona look well."

He half-heartedly smiled and motioned to the basin of water across from him.

"Such spells drain strength, most especially when there is much to see." He paused and drank the water I fetched for him. "I have never looked into a future so strange. Ye will not like what I found."

For half of the night, I sat and listened to his strange story, only half believing it but knowing I had no reason to doubt its truth.

"Elspeth will die, lass, there is no way around it, and there is nothing either of us can do to stop it. But yer death is a ruse to save yer brother from a violent clash with Henry's clan."

So Henry would keep his word and spread the news of my witchcraft, and my death is all that could prevent the bloodshed of others. I would gladly fake my death for such a cause.

"Has Henry already threatened action?"

Wearily, Hamish shook his head.

"Not yet, but by the time we arrive, yer brother will have

received word of the rumors about ye. His own people willna turn, but there are clans around him that will only allow Henry's claims to be ignored once they believe ye dead."

I stood, no longer worried about leaving Jerry. I couldn't help him here anyway. The spell was something only someone far more practiced in magic than I could break. Even then, Hamish's uncle didn't know if he would be successful. My clan was my priority, and it would be until I knew they were safe.

"We should leave in the morning so we have time to arrange everything with Alasdair."

He nodded. "Aye, we shall. Ye do know what this means though, aye?"

Until he asked the question, I'd not stopped to think about the ramifications of faking my own death. I would never be able to see all those I loved. For them, it would seem as if I truly were dead. It would be my last time to see my home, my nephew, my brother.

"Is there not some way for them to know of the ruse? For me to return home once things have settled?"

His gaze was apologetic.

"Yer brother is the only one who may know the truth. And ye willna return home again, at least not for a verra long time. There is more that I saw that I must tell ye."

The reality of how painful such a loss would be for me slowly sunk in. It would tear me in two to leave everyone I knew and loved. But if it kept them safe, I would gladly do it.

"What else?"

He shifted in his seat and rested his arms on his legs. "Grier tricked ye, lass."

"O'course she did. Had I known she would spell him, I would have kept Jerry from her."

"No, 'tis not what I mean. I've said nothing to ye until now because I wanted to be certain I was correct, but my spell this night confirmed it. Ye could have searched for years and never found a spell that would see Jerry home to his own time. There is no spell for such travel. The power to move through time lies with ye and ye alone."

"No." I was insistent in my denial. I knew it couldn't be true. "Grier possesses such a gift, not I. 'Twas she who pulled Jerry from his time and placed him in ours."

"Aye, she too can move others through time but only because she stole part of yer gift from ye. That is what she did to ye that day. She looked inside yer mind for yer talent and took part of it for herself."

I remembered so little from that day, but Alasdair's description came to mind.

"Alasdair said it looked as if power poured from me, as if she were pulling something from inside me."

Hamish nodded. "Aye, she was and 'twas an egregious crime for her to do so. 'Tis why the gift has not presented itself to ye before now—she weakened it. With time, I can help ye restore it."

"I thought our skills were meant to be tied to our destiny. What destiny would require me to move through time?"

Jerry was the obvious choice, but I'd learned enough from Hamish to know that magic wasn't so self-serving. My destiny would lie in aiding others.

"Every person with magic holds two responsibilities. The first is to care and protect their kin and those they love. The second is unique to their ability. That destiny has spoken to you through whispers your entire life. Think, lass, what has always come easily to you? What brings you more joy than just about anything?"

I sat with my memories for a long moment. Over and over again, I noticed a pattern. I could see inside others' hearts and match them with their mate with perfect ease. Countless villagers, Mary and Kip, Mae and Hew, even Alasdair and Elspeth wouldn't have met had it not been for my insistence. While I'd not always possessed such discernment in matters of my own heart, I was skilled at bringing others together.

"Does it have to do with love?"

Smiling, Hamish answered me. "Aye. I told ye I saw verra strange things. It seems the men in yer family are destined to prefer lassies of another century, and yer gift shall bring them together."

"And what of helping my family? Will my death be enough?"

Standing, Hamish walked to the tent's opening.

"For a time, but in several decades another evil shall threaten yer family. We shall see that all is prepared for such a time when we arrive at yer home. I'll explain everything to ye on the way tomorrow. For now, I am weary and need to rest."

I walked to the edge of the tent to see Hamish off. Just as expected, Jerry stood not too far away watching outside his own tent. It was the same every night. I would wave to him, and he would turn his back to me.

I was in no mood to be ignored. Stomping over toward him, I poked him hard in the chest.

"No one is going to be able to break this spell on ye if ye are so intent on remaining miserable. Fight for yerself, Jerry. Fight to be happy."

His jaw tight, Jerry turned away.

"I was happy with Grier, lass. Even if the spell is lifted, I shall never forgive ye for keeping me hostage. I could never love someone so damned foolish."

CHAPTER 43

The next morning, Hamish and I packed our horses and prepared to ride to Conall Castle. My heart was heavy for so many reasons, and Hamish simply couldn't stand it.

"He dinna mean it, lass. The spell is fading with time, and 'tis tearing his mind apart as it does. It canna be a pleasant thing—to feel something so strongly only to have everyone around ye telling ye that ye doona really feel the way ye do. I would resist it, as well."

"It pained me as if he meant it."

Hamish finished situating his belongings and came over to grab my hands.

"I know. 'Tis he that is the damned fool. Come with me."

Holding tightly onto my right hand, Hamish led me to Jerry's tent, pushing our way inside without a word. Jerry sat in a chair twiddling away at a piece of wood. His face showed no emotion as he looked at us.

"Stand up, lad."

Jerry didn't move. Hamish repeated himself. "Stand up or I'll pull ye from that chair and knock yer teeth in."

The corner of Jerry's mouth twitched, and I knew he wasn't frightened. He stood anyway.

"What do ye want? I thought the two of ye were leaving this morning. Ye should go. Give my best to everyone at Conall Castle."

He meant the last part. I could tell by the way his features softened. He might be angry with me, but he was still capable of caring for others.

"My uncle has been too gentle with ye. He believes time and patience will be enough to break this spell. I say to hell with it."

Releasing my hand, Hamish walked over to Jerry and grabbed the front of his linen shirt.

"Have ye not noticed how yer moods have changed, lad? When ye dinna believe ye were spelled, ye were pleasant enough. Now, ye are an arse every moment of every bloody day to everyone. Do ye know why that is?"

Jerry didn't flinch with Hamish standing so close. Calmly, without blinking, he answered him. "Mayhap because I'm being kept as a prisoner."

"Lad, if ye wish to see how prisoners are kept, I'll be happy to show ye. I'd prefer if ye were kept in the dungeons anyway. 'Tis not what upsets ye. Ye are angry because ye know ye canna trust yer feelings, and yer frustrated that ye canna find yer way back to the lass standing over there never giving up on ye."

Jerry's eyes shifted toward me for a quick uncomfortable glance. When he said nothing, Hamish continued.

"If ye need some incentive to fight harder, lad, allow me to give it to ye. I am in love with the lass ye are meant for. While I may not be her first choice, I know I could become her second. If ye doona pull out of this, I shall marry her, and we will send ye on yer merry way back to a life of false love with Grier."

Jerry's face flushed red, and my heart sped up. It was more emotion than I'd seen him elicit in response to me in weeks.

"She doesna love ye, and Morna wouldna ever marry a man she dinna love."

Releasing his grip on Jerry's shirt, Hamish turned and walked toward me, grabbing my arms and pulling me toward him. He spoke to Jerry, but his eyes were locked with mine.

"Her mind has been filled with nothing other than worry over ye and her family. She doesna know what she feels for me. Allow me to give her reason to see that her heart might be more open to me than she knows."

His lips were on mine before I could move. Unlike the last time Jerry watched on as another man kissed me, I feigned nothing as I surrendered to his touch.

CHAPTER 44

onall Castle—Six Weeks Later

I would never be ready to say goodbye to him, but I knew it was time. The spell books were in place, the plaque was painted by Hamish's expert hand, and what I knew of the story to come was ready to be told to my brother.

Hamish and I arrived at the castle on the day of Elspeth's death. While I'd kept my promise to her to be back in two months, her labor had come early, and she passed shortly after the delivery.

The weeks that followed were filled with sadness. Most of my days were spent rocking sweet little Arran and holding a heartbroken Eoin while Alasdair dealt with his grief alone.

If not for Mary, Alasdair would've remained lost in his grief for so much longer. Exactly one month after her death, Mary went to his bedchamber and spent hours inside. I suspect none of us will ever know the words she said to him, but I know her well enough to believe she treated him with the tough love he needed to get up and carry on despite the ache in his heart.

I'd told Alasdair of my plan earlier, but it had been during the deepest depths of his grief, and I knew it wouldn't fully hit him until I brought him down to the spell room.

"Ye canna do this, Morna. I canna raise them on my own. I canna bear to lose ye both."

Elspeth's plea remained a heavy weight inside my mind. She would've been so angry with me for leaving him, but I knew the future where they did not. I truly did have no choice.

"If Henry doesna believe me dead, he will gather support from other clans, and yer life here will be overturned. I'll not have blood shed over me."

"We can hide ye here, Morna. We can make them believe ye are dead. No one will ever have to see ye."

Reaching for his hand, I led him down into my spell room.

"No. Such a secret would never keep, and I willna put ye or yer boys in danger. And ye willna be raising them alone. We both know Mary has been the ruler of this castle for as long as she's worked within its walls. Ye will have her to lean on, and ye will do well."

Alasdair seemed to have an endless flow of tears at the ready. As his breath caught on a sob, I paused in the stairwell and threw my arms around him.

I wouldn't cry in front of him. It wouldn't be fair to place my own heartbreak on him, but I'd never hurt so deeply in my life. Alasdair was my best friend and the only family I had left.

"I doona want to do this without ye, lass. I doona have the strength for it."

I held him as if my life depended on it. If I could've stopped time right then, I would've.

"Ye have more strength than ye know. I know what lies ahead, and ye've been through the worst yer life has planned for ye. Ye will be happy again. I promise ye."

He wept into my shoulder. Loud sobs of heartache came from his chest. He sank onto the steps, and I held him as he cried.

"*B*y the time he is grown, Eoin willna remember the spells ye did in front of him. He willna believe any of this. He'll think me mad."

Hours later, cried out for the time being, Alasdair and I were able to discuss all of the final arrangements surrounding what would appear to be my death.

He stood, staring at my open spell books and the painted portrait of Donal MacChristy's daughter, with wide, disbelieving eyes.

"I know, and I doona care what ye decide to tell him as long as ye force him to wed the lass. It willna be Donal's daughter that he marries. The lass who arrives here is the only one who can save yer family."

"Could ye not simply come back yerself and save us? By then, ye will be in no danger. All of this will be but a distant memory."

Even if I didn't already know the destinies of Eoin and the lass from centuries ahead, I wouldn't have wanted to return. Leaving once was already killing me. I never wanted to do it again.

"No, I'm afraid 'tis destined to happen just this way. Can ye promise me ye will do what I ask ye?"

Alasdair nodded.

"Where will ye go, Morna? What will ye do if the spell over Jerry canna be broken?"

I loved Hamish. He was kind and good, and our shared magic helped us relate to one another in a way I would never relate to anyone else. But, my soul didn't long for him.

"I will return with Hamish to Allen territory where I will learn total mastery of all the magic I possess. Afterwards, we will see. Hamish wants me to marry him. I doona know if I can give up on Jerry."

Alasdair placed his hand on my back to lead me from the spell room. He knew what he had to do, and the moment the illusion of me was buried, he would seal the room.

"If 'tis Jerry ye are meant for, doona ever give up on him. Hamish's love for ye is pure, lass. He wishes for ye to be happy, even if 'tis not with him. Come lass, I've arranged for a portrait to be painted of us all. I must have some way to look at ye after ye are gone. I only wish I'd done the same with Elspeth. We will have one last evening together then I will bid ye farewell."

Tears I promised myself I wouldna cry fell as a desperate need to be near him filled me. I flung my arms around him once more.

"If there was any other way, I would never leave ye. Ye canna begin to know how much I love ye. There has never been a lass alive with a greater brother than mine."

Kissing the top of my hair, Alasdair whispered, "I know exactly how much ye love me for 'tis only a fraction of how much I love ye. Ye may be gone from here, but my love will never leave ye. Ye will feel it inside ye every day of yer life."

And I did. Until Alasdair took his last breath several decades later, he was with me every single day.

llen Territory

erry was gone when we returned to Allen territory. Hamish's uncle met us at their border with the news.

"He's been gone a fortnight. He escaped in the night. All that was left in his tent was this note."

I took the note and opened it. Inside he'd scribbled the words, *"I've gone to fight for ye. Please doona marry him."*

Hamish directed his horse nearer mine so he could read the words over my shoulder. "He's gone to Grier, lass. We must go to him."

I turned and looked into Hamish's sad, accepting eyes.

"Would ye have ever stopped trying to break the spell? Why have ye helped me when ye doona truly want him to break it?"

I knew his answer even before he said—Hamish's heart was too good.

"What I told Jerry that day was true. I am in love with ye, and love is selfless. I would have kept trying to break the spell until the day ye were ready to give up on him. I would've waited years had it taken that long. If ever the time had come when ye were ready, I would've gladly cherished ye as my wife. But, I've already lost, lass, and I know it. Let us go and get Jerry—the real Jerry—so ye can find happiness for the first time in far too many months."

*M*acNeal Territory

*M*uch to my surprise, Grier had remained in Henry's service, feigning work as an herbal healer to hide her magic from him.

She knew we were coming. She met us outside as we approached her home.

"He's not here. The spell is broken."

Gone was the mirage of a young, beautiful woman. She looked to be a hundred years old—frightened, sad, and broken.

"Where's he gone?"

"I thought ye were dead. I felt ye were dead. What sort of magic broke the bond between us?"

I'd done nothing, but I understood her confusion. I'd known she wasn't dead when Alasdair thought she was because I could still feel her magic. Hamish had done something to break our bond.

I looked at him and he nodded in confirmation before speaking. "Ye will no longer break the rules of magic, Grier. If ye steal from another, I will kill ye myself."

"Was that why we were connected? Because she stole from me?"

"Aye."

A sinking feeling settled in my gut as I realized what Jerry's absence must mean.

"Where is he?"

She smiled, and I had to hold tight to my horse's reins to keep from flying off the horse and grabbing her around the throat.

"He thinks ye are dead. I wouldna have broken the spell, otherwise. Even with ye gone, he dinna want me. He's returned to Conall Castle to seek work from yer brother."

I turned my horse around to leave. She wasn't worth another breath, but she screamed a curse at me as we left. "May ye never bear children, and may Jerry's heart be weak. May chaos follow the two of ye always."

I nudged my horse into a run. I never wanted to see her again.

I rode for a long while before I realized I was alone, and I only realized it then because of a galloping horse approaching.

I looked over my shoulder to see Hamish.

"I thought ye were behind me. Where did ye go?"

"To speak to her. I havena ever seen anyone carry such pain."

I could feel no sympathy for her.

"She deserves every bit of pain she feels. What did ye tell her?"

"Only that there was hope for her still, if only she learns to forgive herself first."

I shook my head and gave Hamish a small smile. "'Tis good that Grier's spell is broken. I would have been entirely undeserving of ye. Ye are one of the kindest men I've ever known."

onall Territory

We were much more careful as we approached Conall Castle. I'd been so sure I would never return to my home that I could scarcely believe I was back only a few days later.

We tied our horses near a stream in a secluded part of the

woods. I was to remain hidden while Hamish went to find Alasdair and Jerry.

The wait seemed like days, though I know it must've been only a few hours at most. When I heard footsteps approaching, I kept myself hidden until I heard their voices. I'd expected only Hamish and Jerry, but at the sound of my brother's voice, I pulled away from the brush and ran to him.

He caught me as I jumped toward him, my feet lifting off the ground. He pulled me into a hug as his choked voice spoke into my ear.

"I couldna not see ye again, if ye were here. Besides, Jerry and I have a plan."

I looked over Alasdair's back. Jerry's eyes were filled with tears. "Let go of yer brother, lass. I need ye in my arms this instant."

Alasdair released me, but my steps toward Jerry were much more hesitant.

"Ye told me once ye would never forgive me for keeping ye captive. Is it true?"

He shook his head. "No. There is nothing ye could do that I wouldna forgive. Can ye forgive me for all the things I said to ye? All the pain that I caused?"

Alasdair interrupted before I could answer him. "O'course she will, lad. There will be plenty of time for the two of ye to be alone. For now, we must make haste before either of ye is discovered."

"No one knows Jerry is here?"

Alasdair shook his head. "No. I knew if Mary saw him, 'twould raise too many questions. As soon as he arrived, I told him the truth of what happened. He wished to go after ye, but I knew if I kept him here, I'd get to see ye one last time." Alasdair paused and leaned in to whisper, "Ye should have seen him, lass. The thought that ye were gone...he felt the loss as acutely as I felt Elspeth's."

"Yer brother wishes to marry us."

I listened as the pair of them took turns explaining their plan, and for the first time in months, all was well.

*I*n the middle of the night, with a full moon and a blanket full of stars as our only light, Jerry and I promised to spend the rest of our lives together.

I'm not certain you could say we were ever officially married. Alasdair performed the ceremony and a druid was our only witness, but our vows were no less sacred. Ours was an unusual courtship—it seemed fitting that our wedding be unusual as well.

Once we sealed our promises with a kiss, I bid my brother one last final farewell, and we left Conall Castle for good.

*A*llen Territory—Three Months Later

*"A*ch, lass, I willna ever get tired of bedding ye. Thank God, they moved us to a proper cottage. Otherwise, the whole village would be hearing the ruckus we make every night."

I laughed as he collapsed on top of me, his lips trailing gentle, lazy kisses down my neck.

"Even when we are old and gray and our bones creak when we walk?"

"Even then."

Rolling to face him as he slid off me, I smiled in excitement as I readied myself to share my news with him. "I have something to tell ye."

"Oh?" He twisted his head and raised his brow to encourage me to get on with it.

"I've decided ye were right about something ye suggested to me long ago."

"What's that, lass? I've never known myself to be right about anything."

"Do ye remember when I told ye what I saw in the spell I cast? The home from yer time, with the lass inside it?"

He nodded but said nothing.

"I think mayhap she was me. Are ye ready to go home?"

The one thing I'd once promised myself I would never do—leave this time, my home, and my family—was now my greatest wish. I couldn't return home anyway. It was time for Jerry and me to start a life of our own—a fresh start in a fresh time.

"Are ye saying ye've learned to do it? To travel through time?"

"Aye, I have."

Jerry reached to pull me against him, devouring me with a kiss that left my head free of all thought. When he pulled away, he looked down over his nose at me.

"When can we leave?"

"In the morning, if ye wish it."

"Oh, I wish it, lass. Now, let me bed ye here one last time for memories sake."

I woke early to sneak away while Jerry still slept. There was one last thing I needed to tend to, one last goodbye I had to make.

Hamish was awake when I slipped into his tent. He sat on the edge of his bed, already dressed in his kilt, as if he were waiting for me.

"Ye are leaving then, aye?"

I went over to join him and grabbed his hands as I sat down on the bed.

"Aye. I've something I wish to give ye."

"Ye owe me nothing."

I smiled and reached up to place one hand on his cheek.

"I owe ye more than ye will ever know. I doona wish to repay ye. I wish to give ye the gift of hope."

Reaching into the bosom of my dress, I pulled out a folded piece of parchment and extended it in his direction. Smiling, I released my grip on his other hand.

"Open it."

I watched and waited as he looked down at his own piece of art. When he looked up at me, his brows were furrowed.

"This looks like my hand."

"'Tis yer hand." I paused and pointed to the various faces in the portrait. "And that there is ye, although I'll admit ye've allowed yerself to age by the time ye draw this. And there is yer wife, and yer daughter and her husband, and do ye see the wee lad on yer lap? That is little Raudrich. 'Tis yer grandson."

Hamish's eyes slowly filled with tears.

"Where did ye get this?"

"It took me most of the day yesterday to land precisely where I wished to, but I traveled to yer future to give ye hope in the now. I know ye love me, Hamish, and I love ye more than I hope Jerry ever knows, but ye yerself said I was meant for another. The love of yer life is meant only for ye. As ye can see, ye do find her."

Hamish and I visited until dawn then parted ways as the dearest of friends.

The entire village of Allen territory came to see us off. As Jerry and I disappeared into the future, I knew our adventure together was only beginning.

Note from M.C.:

Well, there you have it. I told you everything would turn out well in the end, even if there were some heartaches and times of sadness along the way.

Now that you're finished, I've no doubt you must think me completely mad. But isn't there some tiny part of you that wonders if all of this could be true?

If you wish to find out, you'll have to come and see for yourself.

We now live in that little inn I saw in my first vision of Jerry's future. While it is not visible to most, you should have no trouble finding it. Just follow the road leading to Conall Castle. We are on the right, no more than a few miles from the castle gates.

See you soon. I'll have Jerry put the kettle on straight away.

EPILOGUE

 *resent Day*

*L*aurel closed the book and looked up for the first time all day.

"Marcus, do you remember passing an inn on the way back from Conall Castle?"

"If I remember correctly, we passed at least two dozen inns. We're a good two hours from Conall Castle. Not that you would know with the way your head has been buried in that book all day. Was it really that good?"

Laurel knew that Marcus would think her request absurd, but there was no way she was waiting until morning.

"Would you like to see Scotland by dark?"

"Do you want to go to a pub?"

Smiling, she reached for his hand and tried to pull him out of his seat.

"No. I'll drive this time. I know just where we're going."

Marcus handed Laurel the keys and followed behind her. "And where is that?"

"To the inn near Conall Castle."

"Now that stretch I do remember. There was nothing in the thirty miles leading to the castle."

"There will be now, and I don't want to be late for tea."

———

MORNA'S MAGIC & MISTLETOE

BOOK 8.5 OF MORNA'S LEGACY SERIES

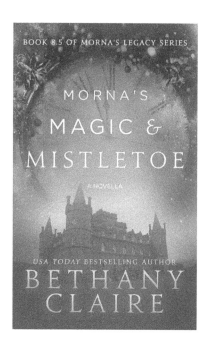

CHAPTER 1

*M*cMillan Castle, Scotland—*December of 1651*

*M*itsy is watching me again. She isn't normally awake so early, but with Baodan away for a fortnight to assist our friends at Cagair Castle, she's allowed young Rodric to sleep in her bed, and the child kicks in his sleep like an angry mule. For the past three nights she's slipped out of her bed the moment her son fell asleep and retreated to his bed. Rodric believes he's getting the special treat of snuggling with his mother while his father is away, but both of them end up getting a good night's sleep. Unlike many of my other grandchildren, I'm not certain a flock of geese flying straight through Rodric's bedchamber would wake him. Come morning, the wee babe is none the wiser to his mother's trickery.

The only complication comes in when I wake up at my usual time each morning. My bedchamber sits right next to Rodric's and as is normal for all mothers of young children, the slightest unexpected noise wakes Mitsy. Try as I might to move silently out of my room, she hears me each and every morning. So now, at least until my son returns home, I have a companion joining me for my quiet morning hours of precious solitude.

I allowed her in the sitting room under one very strict condition: that she say nothing to me during our time in the room together. She's kept her word, but I may have to be the one to break our agreement. I'm not sure I can stand to sit across from her much longer. Not knowing what she's thinking while she looks at me is driving me mad.

She thinks I'm so enthralled by the snowfall outside that I'm unaware of the look in her eyes. She's wrong. I've lived in Scotland my entire life. More specifically, I've lived in this part of Scotland —this very castle—since I was fourteen. It snows almost every day in this part of the country during winter, so I've seen my fair share of snow. While it is quite stunning with the way it falls around the pond and slowly turns the water to a frozen blanket of ice, beauty isn't the reason I sit in my favorite chair, by my favorite fireplace at the same time every day to look through the frosted window. I sit here because if I situate myself early enough, just as the sun begins to come up, I get to listen to the castle come awake. To hear my many grandchildren begin to stir, to hear their tired mothers and spoiled fathers start their day fills my heart with gratitude.

There was a time—a long time—after Niall died that I wasn't sure I would ever be capable of feeling any positive emotion ever again.

While I was now on the other side of such pain, it had been the battle of my life surviving it. The confusion and guilt I'd felt almost killed me, for how can a mother reconcile knowing that her son is a murderer? But the moment I watched another of my beloved sons leave to fight for his own life centuries ahead of me, I knew that giving in to my grief wasn't an option. There was still purpose to my life, still people that needed me, still love to be found. While Eoghanan was away, I'd barricaded myself away and fought—fought through the emotions, fought through the anger, fought through the soul-crushing grief.

Those closest to me allowed me the space I needed to rant and rage and live like a vagabond near my son's grave. I spent weeks wading through the hurt. There were days I was sure it would never end, that I would drown in a pool of my own tears, that my heart would quite literally break in two. Some days I even begged for it to, for then the pain would truly be over. But it didn't. And with time, I found peace.

There was nothing I could've done in the raising of my son or in my loving of him that could've prevented his actions. While I raised two sons that are better men than I could've ever dreamed they would be, there was never anything to be done for Niall. His actions weren't my fault. I couldn't have saved Baodan's first wife. I couldn't have saved my sister. I bore no responsibility for Niall's acts of murder.

Of course, it took me a long time to see the evil inside him. It took me even longer to acknowledge it. Mothers love their children beyond all reason—we will fight for them, die for them, and we almost always believe the best of them.

It was the darkest time of my life, but now I was truly afraid of nothing. The worst had already happened to me, and I survived. If there was a blessing to be found in anything that happened, that was it.

Mitsy coughed quietly to my left and I turned to see her still staring in my direction. I truly couldn't stand it any longer.

"Mitsy, I said ye couldna speak to me if ye sat in here, but yer eyes have been screaming at me for days. What is it?"

She blinked for what seemed like the first time in hours as her cheeks flushed a red that nearly matched the shade of her hair.

"I don't know what you mean. I wasn't staring at you—just through you. I think I was half-asleep."

Crossing my legs and pulling the blanket that lay across my lap up a little higher, I shook my head in denial.

"What is that foul phrase that ye and Jane are so fond of—bullshit? Aye, that is it. Ye are full of it, Mitsy. Ye are wide awake. What is it ye've been wishing to say to me for days?"

"You need more, Kenna."

"More?" While I always found much of what Mitsy said to be perplexing—her twenty-first century phrasing and language often conflicted with my seventeenth century language—I hadn't the slightest idea what she meant this time. "More? Lass, look around. I live in one of the finest castles in Scotland. I've not known a day of poverty in my life. I doona know what it feels like to go hungry. I know few who are as fortunate."

Mitsy said nothing as she stood and lifted her chair. Carrying it until it sat right beside my own, she returned to her seat, faced me, and reached forward to gather my hands in hers.

"You're right. Most people would be perfectly content to have the life that you do, but you're not most people. You know as well as I do that you can both be grateful for what you have and still want more. If you didn't believe that, you wouldn't constantly be encouraging everyone around you to go after the things they want. You're bored here, Kenna. You need some adventure."

"Adventure?" I laughed as imaginings of me crawling aboard a ship and sailing to new land crossed my mind. I'd be so seasick in a day that I'd want to throw myself overboard. I was too old for adventure. "Mitsy, lassies as old as me doona wish for adventure. All we want are quiet mornings, early dinners, and a good night's sleep."

Mitsy withdrew her hands and crossed her arms defiantly.

"Bullshit. Bullshit on all counts."

"There ye go with that language again. Is it truly necessary?"

"Ha. That's rich, Kenna. You've a filthier mouth than the old man who owns the tavern in the village. You just curse in Gaelic rather than English so it sounds more pleasant."

Guiltily, I glanced down. She was right. "Ach, mayhap so. It doesna matter. Get on with it."

Mitsy smiled and held up one finger. "First of all, you aren't old.

You're barely past fifty." She lifted one more finger. "Second, I feel quite sure a huge portion of people in their fifties would be quite offended by your little statement of what 'people your age' want. I know you, Kenna. You would love for your days to be a little less predictable, you would love to get to experience firsthand just a little bit of the magic so many of your family members now take for granted."

I'd never said any such thing out loud, but I couldn't deny that she was right. Magic surrounded my family. Magic had been the single force that had helped both of my sons find the women they loved—magic, and the meddling witch, Morna. I was grateful to her for all she'd done for my family, but so far I'd experienced little such magic myself. I was more than a little curious to see what it would be like to spend some time in another century.

When I said nothing, Mitsy continued.

"I think you should get out of town for a little bit—go with Cooper when he leaves at the end of the weekend. He'd love to have you along, and I'm sure Morna wouldn't mind the extra house guest."

"No." I dismissed her suggestion immediately. December was the busiest time of year at McMillan Castle. There were celebrations to prepare for, villagers to assist during the cold weather, and grandchildren that expected me to uphold our annual Christmas traditions.

"No?" The enthusiasm waned from Mitsy's voice. She'd not expected such a firm refusal. "You don't want to at least discuss the idea a little bit?"

Smiling, I softened my expression and leaned forward to pat her knee.

"I know ye mean well, Mitsy, but there's no need to discuss this. It wouldna be a good idea."

"And why exactly is that? I guarantee you that for every reason you give me as to why you shouldn't do this, I can give you ten reasons why you should. Come on then, give me your first excuse."

Aggravated, I stood and stepped closer to the fire as I reached up and placed one hand on the mantle.

"I doona need many excuses. My first is good enough. While young Cooper may be able to survive a quick dip in the freezing pond at this time of year, I would surely fall ill and die."

I could never make any sense of Morna's method of time travel here at McMillan Castle. Everyone who traveled forward or backward through time ended up splashing around in the castle pond upon arrival in their new time. It was an unnecessarily rough entry after a very long trip.

Mitsy laughed and moved to stand next to me by the fireplace.

"Nice try. You know as well as I do that she's changed that."

I was entirely unaware of the change. "I can assure ye, I've heard of no such thing."

"What? You experienced it yourself. The way we all went forward for Kamden and Harper's wedding—via the West tower of the castle—it's as simple as that now. No more rock throwing, no more swimming in the lake. Cooper's getting a little older now, and she wanted to make it easier for him to make the trip on his own."

The wedding of my twenty-first century descendent was the only time I'd traveled into the future. I'd seen many wondrous things, but much to my dismay, I'd had no time to explore them— I'd not even had the time to travel beyond the castle grounds.

"Oh. I assumed the witch only made an exception the one time since there were so many of us going forward at once."

Mitsy shook her head and smiled. "Nope. What's your next excuse?"

"I..." I hesitated. I wasn't sure, but I knew there must be some other reason I couldn't go—even as much as I might secretly want to. "I'll not deny that I'm tempted by yer suggestion, Mitsy, but I would make an awful fool of myself in yer time. I've nothing to wear, I doona know how things work, and Cooper shouldna spend his time with Morna explaining every little thing to me."

Little footsteps approached the doorway and Mitsy and I both turned to see early-riser Cooper burst through the door.

"Did you ask her yet? What'd she say?"

Winking at me, Mitsy faced Cooper.

"She's undecided. I think she needs you to convince her."

He ran toward me as quickly as his little feet would carry him, and I opened my arms to catch him as he jumped up and into my arms. He was growing quickly. I wouldn't be able to pick him up much longer. Until that sad day came, I would hold him anytime he wished me too.

"Come on, Nana. Anything that you're worried about, we've got a plan for. I promise. I know you're nervous, but it would be so much fun. I'd love for you to come with me."

Excitement like I'd not felt in years blossomed within me as I gave myself permission to do something unexpected.

"Are ye sure, Cooper? I know ye enjoy yer time with Morna. I wouldna wish to intrude."

"Are you kidding? Morna would love it. And so would I. Please, Nana. Come with me."

Mitsy reached her hand up to tussle the top of Cooper's wavy curls. She'd known all along that the moment Cooper was in on the plan, I wouldn't be able to say no.

"Kenna, if I can promise you that we'll get you everything you need, that we will prepare you in every way, will you do it?"

"If ye will make certain I willna make a fool of myself, then aye, I'll go."

Cooper squirmed out of my arms and grabbed onto Mitsy's hand to pull her out of the room. Turning to look back at me over his shoulder, he smiled at me as they left.

"Don't you worry, Nana. We've got everything under control."

That was exactly what I was worried about.

CHAPTER 2

 *hicago – Present Day*

alcolm Warren looked forward to the last day of school before Christmas break every year. It meant two full weeks with his daughter and granddaughter as they enjoyed their annual trip to Scotland to visit his brother and sister-in-law. This year would be especially festive, for at fifty-eight years young, he was an uncle for the very first time.

Rosalind was excited, too. With his window rolled down so he could wave to her from in front of the school, she started talking to him before she even got in the car.

"Will the baby be walking yet? Do you think Emilia will let me hold him?"

"Hello to you too, kiddo. Get in the car before you freeze to death. I think it's colder here in Chicago than it will be in Scotland."

Once Rosalind was safely inside the car with her seatbelt fastened, Malcolm answered his granddaughter's insistent questions.

"The baby won't be walking, though I expect he will be crawling all over the place. And of course Emilia will let you hold him. You'll be a big help to her. How was the last day of school?"

Rolling her eyes, the young girl huffed and shook her head.

"It was a total waste of time. This whole week was. It was all parties and Christmas crafts. What am I doing in school if not to do some real learning? I would've been better off just leaving for Scotland a week early."

Malcolm smiled to himself as he drove the short distance to the home they all shared.

"You know, most kids like the days when there's less school work."

She glanced over at him, giving him a smile identical to her mother's, and Malcolm's heart squeezed. His girls were his world. They would never know how much either of them meant to him.

"Pops, have I ever been like most kids?"

"No, and that's one of your best qualities. Most kids drive me crazy."

Rosalind laughed as he pulled into the driveway.

"I know you try to seem grumpier than you are, but nobody buys it. You like everybody."

It was true. While his stature might be intimidating, Malcolm knew his heart was softer than most men he knew. He was an incurable sap.

"Some people buy it. I can be grumpy when I need to be."

Rosalind ignored him as she opened the car door and stepped outside. He knew immediately from the way her eyes darted over to the tightly shut garage door she'd just noticed what he'd already seen—her mother still wasn't home.

"She's not here, Pops. I knew this was going to happen. I just knew it."

Malcolm hurried to place a reassuring hand on his granddaughter's shoulder as he guided her up the front steps to their home.

"Don't worry yet, Rosie. She could just be stuck in traffic. We don't know that she had to work late."

Shoulders slumped, head down, the young girl leaned into him as he worked to open the front door.

"She always has to work late. We're going to miss our flight."

"Don't you worry about that—we still have an hour or so before we have to be at the airport. We are not going to miss our flight. I'll call the hospital right now. Why don't you go and pack the last of your things and bring your bag downstairs? We can get the car loaded while we wait on her."

Waiting until Rosalind disappeared at the top of the stairs, Malcolm closed the door and made his way into the kitchen. Pulling out his phone, he saw the notification he dreaded might be there—a voicemail from his daughter.

Turning the volume down low so Rosie wouldn't hear it—he could hear her lingering on the stairs—he pressed play and held the phone up to his ear.

"Hey Dad. Look, I know you guys aren't going to be happy with me, and I really hate to do this, but I simply can't leave the hospital right now. Half the nursing staff is trying to take off, and I have too many patients who need me. You guys go ahead and leave for Scotland. I'll catch a flight out sometime next week. I'll definitely be there by Christmas. Tell Rosie that I love her. I love you too, Dad. Oh, and Dad. Don't call the hospital. I don't have time to discuss this with either of you. Just leave and have a great first day in Edinburgh. I'll meet you guys there soon. Bye."

Rosalind entered the kitchen before he had time to call for her.

"I guess I shouldn't bring Mom's bags down? I can tell by your face that she isn't coming."

"I'm so sorry, sweetheart. She's just too swamped..."

"No!" Rosalind's angry voice interrupted him as tears began to swell in her eyes. Her knees wobbled as she gripped the doorway. "Don't make excuses for her. Not anymore. She always acts like she has a good reason, but there's no good reason for this."

Malcolm couldn't argue with her. He knew the pain his daughter was in all too well, but it didn't give her permission to abandon her daughter. For the better part of two years, she'd closed herself off from all life outside the hospital, and it was Rosalind who suffered for it.

Moving across the room, Malcolm dropped to his knees and reached to wrap his arms around Rosie. She buried her head in his neck and cried.

"You're right. I won't. I know there have been lots of times that she hasn't been there for you since your father passed away, but this time she's gone too far. This isn't right or fair. I'm as angry with her as I've ever been. But this is Christmas, and I refuse to let her ruin it for you."

Ripping herself away from him, Rosalind picked up her bag and stormed through the front door of the house.

"She already has. Now, let's get this stupid show on the road."

Anger always caused Rosie to lash out at those around her. Only in the car for a few seconds, she began to honk the horn at him, fire in her eyes as he dragged his own bag outside and locked the front door.

The young girl was heartbroken and angry, and he would pay the price for it.

Malcolm could sense with every fiber of his being that his beloved granddaughter would give him hell during every second of their trip to Scotland.

CHAPTER 3

*M*cMillan Castle – 1651

"Y ou've no reason to be nervous, Kenna. From the first moment I met you, I knew you were a woman far ahead of your time. Much like Mitsy and Grace were born in another time but belong in this one, I've always wondered if perhaps you belonged in theirs."

I turned toward Bebop in surprise as we continued our morning walk. It was a ritual we started almost immediately after his arrival in the seventeenth century. Each morning, shortly after breakfast, we would meet in the castle's garden where, no matter the weather, we would walk for over an hour. It was good exercise for us both, and over the years we'd become the best of friends.

"Why would ye say that? I've never felt that way myself."

"Well, for starters, you don't think like most people born and raised in this time. Kenna, you are as open-minded as they come. And perhaps you've never felt that way yourself because you've never spent time in another century. I won't be surprised if you have no desire to come back after a few weeks away."

"I'll want to come back. There are far too many people here who I love to stay away."

Bebop reached over to squeeze my shoulder. "And that, my dear, is the only reason I believe you will come back."

"Do ye truly believe I'll love it so much?"

"I do. This isn't exactly related to the subject at hand, but would you like a good laugh?"

I would never say no to that.

"O'course, I do."

"We both know Cooper regularly asks interesting questions. There is nothing the young boy won't say or ask, but this question surprised even me, and I'm rarely surprised by anything."

My curiosity piqued, I took one step closer to him as we walked.

"What did he ask ye?"

"He asked when the two of us were going to get married."

"Wha...what...whatever gave him that idea?" I felt like the air had suddenly been kicked from my chest. It was the most ridiculous suggestion I'd ever heard.

Bebop shook his head as he chuckled softly.

"I haven't the slightest idea. I guess he just assumed that since we are both his grandparents now and both of our spouses are gone that we should naturally be together."

"Oh. Well, I suppose if I were seven years old, I might think as he does. What did ye say to him?"

"Firstly, I explained to him that despite my youthful appearance." He paused to chuckle at himself. "I was significantly older than you. Then, I went on to tell him that anyone who knows my real name and still calls me 'Bebop,' probably doesn't have any romantic inclinations for me."

"And do ye have them for me? I know that ye doona."

"I would be lucky to have you, Kenna, but no, you are the

dearest friend I have here, and I wouldn't want to do anything to ruin that."

"Good." I pointed up ahead where our anticipated guests were approaching the castle. "They're here."

Mitsy's closest friend, Bri, her husband, and their children, along with Bri's mother, Adelle and her husband, Hew, were coming to stay with us for Christmas. Adelle, as I'd learned shortly after Cooper's warning that they had a plan for everything, had already been assigned to help me prepare for my time in the future.

Bebop picked up his pace and reached his hand behind to wave me forward.

"We best hurry then. I've not been around Adelle too much, but I know she has a penchant for talking. You and Cooper leave this evening and I expect she will have a week's worth of information to tell you. Best you get started soon."

Nerves and excitement gathered in equal measure in my chest as I marched toward my first lesson on how to survive in the twenty-first century.

I had just fastened myself into my first-ever bra when both my daughters-in-law, Grace and Mitsy, burst into the room where Adelle and I were picking modern outfits for me to pack from her wide selection.

Mitsy gazed unabashedly at my chest for a matter of seconds and then turned to address Adelle.

"Nice. You're a little bit taller, Adelle, but other than that, you two are just about the same size."

"We are. Lucky thing, too, since much to my dismay the rest of you girls have let your collection of modern clothes dwindle over the years."

Grace laughed and passed a white button-down blouse in my direction.

"We don't really need them anymore. Why go to the hassle of keeping things that we don't wear handy?"

"You girls must be more evolved than I am. Don't get me wrong. I love my life here, but the fashion of this time doesn't suit my tastes at all. I don't really wear them anymore, but sometimes just looking at my old clothes makes me happy. I'm thrilled they will finally be getting some use."

The buttons on the blouse felt strange beneath my fingers. While the clothes were undoubtedly more comfortable, I felt uncomfortable in them—exposed and wholly unlike myself.

Grace came to stand behind me in the mirror and leaned in close while Adelle and Mitsy began discussing what they missed most about life in the twenty-first century. They were split between hot baths and microwavable popcorn.

"It will take some getting used to, but once you do, you'll love this way of dressing. And if it makes you feel any better now, you look absolutely gorgeous. How does the makeup feel? Do you think you can manage it yourself?"

"Thank ye, Grace." I reached up to gently brush at my newly blackened lashes. "It feels less odd than I expected. Aye, I think I can manage. Adelle took her time showing me how to apply it, though I refused much of what she offered me." Adelle had shoved an entire satchel full of makeup toward me, but I only ended up setting aside four items to pack—all of which were entirely new to me: a light powder, eyeliner, mascara, and a burgundy-colored lipstick.

"What you have on is perfect. You don't need much. You're stunning without anything on. I can hear my youngest screaming in the other room so I can't stay away long, but I wanted to come in here and tell you something while it was on my mind. I know that you're going *with* Cooper but I don't want you to feel like you are going to *care for* Cooper. He's stayed alone with Morna and Jerry many times. I trust them with my son completely. What I'm saying is, don't use Cooper as an excuse not to get out and explore while you're there. I want you to soak up everything there is to see, to seize every opportunity that comes your way. You deserve this. You deserve some time away. You deserve some fun. Okay? Promise me you won't feel the need to stay with Cooper every second."

Turning away from the mirror to face her, I reached my arms around Grace to hug her close.

"Thank ye. Having ye tell me that yerself will certainly make me more likely to do so. Are ye coming to see the two of us off?"

McMillan Castle's youngest babe let out an ear-piercing scream, and Grace stiffened in my arms.

"Yes, of course. I want to squeeze both of you before you go. Now, however, I must go see to that. Eoghanan is good for many, many things but comforting crying babies isn't one of them."

Grace left, followed shortly by Mitsy, leaving Adelle and me to pack up the rest of my borrowed belongings alone.

"Grace is right, you know. You need to take full advantage of your time there. With Morna involved, it's bound to be a wonderful time for you. Do you mind if I give you my own piece of advice— one grandmother to another?"

Cooper and I would leave within the hour. Everything was real now, and I could no longer hide my apprehension.

"I consider myself to be a rather strong woman, but the closer I get to leaving, the more nauseous I feel. I'll take any advice ye can give me, Adelle."

"Great. And just so you know, I'm only saying something because Grace told me how you sent her to Eoghanan's room before they were married, so I know you're secretly a modern-minded lady like myself. Otherwise, I wouldn't risk offending you."

I laughed and reached to squeeze Adelle's hand. "I canna remember the last time I was offended by anything."

"That's really good. Okay, I can tell by your complexion that it's been a really long time since you've had a good lay. If I know Morna at all, she will see to it that the opportunity arises while you are with her to fix that. Do it. Forget about all of the rules of propriety

271

that apply to things here. Things are very different in the twenty-first century. Have the sex. Eat the cake. Drink the extra glass of wine. Let your hair down a bit."

Whatever I'd expected her to say, it hadn't been that.

"Ye can tell by my complexion?" The thought horrified me.

She shrugged. "What can I say? It's always been my superpower. Now, let's get you to Cooper so the two of you can head out."

Laughing, I lifted the handle of my modern roller bag and then leaned playfully into Adelle.

"Do ye know what, Adelle? I know that I doona know ye verra well, but I already know that I like ye verra much."

Smiling, she wrapped her arm around my shoulder as we left the room.

"I like you too, Kenna. I'm totally serious, though. When you guys return in two weeks, I expect your face to be glowing. Glowing from all the sex."

"Aye, I understood what ye meant by glowing from yer first reference to my ruddy complexion."

She nodded. "Just driving the point home."

"I believe ye did. I shall endeavor to return home all aglow."

Laughing like lassies half our age, we made our way to the castle's west tower together.

CHAPTER 4

On The Road to Conall Castle, Scotland – Present Day

If Rosalind sighed any louder, the tourists in the very back of the bus would be able to hear her. It was now three days into their trip and with no word from Rosie's mother, the young girl's mood continued to decline.

Listening to the young girl cry herself to sleep had been the deciding factor for Malcolm. Staying in his brother's home where they all had so many shared memories of Christmases together only seemed to make matters worse for his granddaughter. It only reminded her that during a time of year when both of her parents should be there, neither of them were.

There was no need for them to stay in Edinburgh for the entire trip. Perhaps it would do Rosalind some good to get out of the house and explore the country a bit. They could travel for a few days and then return to Edinburgh for the real Christmas celebrations.

Unable to sleep from the soft sounds of Rosie crying inside her room, Malcolm had arranged a weekend getaway in which they would explore a bit of the Highlands. And now, only twelve hours after the decision was made, they were aboard a bus, enjoying the three-hour scenic drive from Edinburgh to the first stop on their trip—Conall Castle.

At least he was enjoying the drive. So far, the diversion wasn't working for Rosie.

"This is the castle you wanted to see, isn't it? I was almost certain this was the one you mentioned to me before."

Rosalind didn't face him as she answered. Instead, she kept her gaze focused out the bus window to her left.

"Mom and I planned to see it together. We can just add this to the long list of things she's missed."

"We can always come and visit it again when she gets here."

Rosalind turned slowly toward him, her eyes red and teary. Her eyes and nose were beginning to look raw from all the crying. Malcolm needed to find some way to make the child smile.

"Don't you know it by now, Pops? She isn't coming. Last Christmas was just too hard on her. I know she hasn't said it yet, but I know her. She won't be here for Christmas."

Malcolm worried that his granddaughter was right. Tim had loved Christmas so much. His daughter seemed incapable of celebrating the holiday now that he was gone.

"It won't always be this way, Rosie. Sometimes, grief takes a very long time to work through. She will find her way back to you."

Taking a deep breath in through her nose, Rosalind turned away from him and stared out the window once more. He could see Conall Castle in the distance through the front window of the bus. They were almost there.

"Let's not talk about your mother anymore today. Let's just try and enjoy this time together."

As the bus pulled to a stop and the castle's guide stepped aboard the bus to welcome them, Malcolm turned his attention to the tour. One by one they got off the bus and followed the perky and knowledgeable guide along the short trail leading up to the castle's main doors.

While he was certain Rosalind had followed him off the bus, he turned to whisper to her halfway through the tour and found her no longer behind him. Frantically, his gaze tore through their group. She was gone. Rosalind was nowhere to be found.

---

*M*cMillan Castle – Present Day

"*A*ch, Cooper, does it always hurt so much?" I gripped my head painfully as we slowly moved down the tower stairwell into the twenty-first century version of my home.

The method of travel was simple enough. All we needed was for Cooper to open his magical pocket watch, ask Morna to bring us forward, and in a flash we disappeared, only to reappear in the exact same location seconds later, centuries ahead of the time we left. As simple as it was, the magic's effects on my body could be felt all over. I was disoriented, and while my body ached everywhere, nothing hurt as badly as my head.

"Don't worry, Nana. Harper keeps some ibuprofen handy. She'll have it waiting for you."

I was mildly aware of modern medicines. My daughters-in-law kept several pills and tinctures hidden away for times when illness befell anyone in the castle that a simple herbal mixture wouldn't cure.

"Only for me? Does yer head not hurt?"

The young boy shrugged and bounded down the stairs ahead of me.

"Nope. The more you do it, the easier it gets. Plus, you're old so that probably has something to do with why you feel so bad."

Shaking my head, I met up with him as he waited at the bottom of the stairs for me.

"I believe we need to have a discussion about my actual age. Several instances as of late have given me reason to believe ye think me far more ancient than I am."

Cooper smiled and let out a quick giggle.

"I'm only teasing you, Nana. You're not old. You don't look it anyway."

"Thank ye. Now, where is this ibuprofen?"

"It's right here."

I looked up to see Harper, the wife of my descendent and the true leader of McMillan Castle in the twenty-first century. She was energetic, organized, and without her my home would've fallen into disrepair long ago. I gratefully accepted the pills and glass of water she extended in my direction.

"Neither of you look too worse for wear. You'll be pleased to know that Jerry is already here. He's got the car all warmed up for you."

"He's here already?" Cooper's voice couldn't have sounded any more excited. "We left our bags in the tower. Let me go and get them so we can get to Morna's."

Harper reached out a hand to stop him.

"Don't worry about that. Kamden will gather up your bags. I told Sileas you were coming this morning, and he's been wagging his tail all morning with excitement. Why don't you go and say hello to him and leave your things to my husband?"

The castle dog, Sileas, was almost taller than Cooper when standing on all fours, but the sweet beast collapsed on the ground and rolled over onto his back like a small puppy the moment Cooper neared him.

With Cooper occupied, Harper hooked her arm with my own and walked with me outside to the car.

"I'm glad you decided to come, Kenna. It will be good for you."

Still nervous, my voice was much more shaky than I wished it to be as I answered her. "That's what everyone keeps saying. I hope all of ye are right."

"We are." She leaned in to hug me and kiss my cheek as Jerry stepped out of the car to greet me. "Christmas is the most magical time of year. I can't wait to see what happens to you over the next few weeks."

*M*y first car ride was thrilling. While Cooper slept restfully in the back seat of Jerry's very tiny car, I happily sat next to Jerry in the front as I delighted in the swirl of scenery that changed every second.

"Ye are going to be fun for all of us, lass. I can tell."

I knew smiling for hours was a bit much, but I truly couldn't stop. Everything outside the car window was amazing. With all of the means of travel I was accustomed to, it would've taken days to see what we'd seen in three hours of driving.

"What do ye mean?"

"Yer excitement is contagious. 'Tis always a joy to watch another experience something for the first time. It has been far too long since we've enjoyed the company of a newbie to this time."

While I could discern the meaning of the word *newbie* by its context well enough, it was a word I'd never heard before in my life.

"How far away are we?" Cooper's sleepy voice spoke to us from behind and I twisted to look at him.

"I doona care if it takes us all night to get there. I never expected a ride in a car to be so pleasurable."

Out of the corner of my eye, I could see Jerry lift one hand from the wheel and point ahead of him.

"We are nearly there now. I'm turning onto the dirt road which leads to Conall Castle and our inn as we speak."

I faced the front to see the faint outline of the castle in the distance, but there was something else along the road ahead, a faint outline of a creature or a person walking along the road's outer edge.

"Look, guys—it's a girl!"

I leaned forward and strained to make out the form Cooper pointed at. Sure enough, a girl who couldn't be more than a few years older than Cooper, walked all alone ahead of us.

CHAPTER 5

I liked the strange girl instantly, despite her rather unfriendly demeanor. I recognized the look in her eyes—the grief and the anger that was so potently felt, she no longer tried to hide it at all. Not so long ago, I'd been there myself. She also had a defiantly independent nature that I appreciated in any woman, but most especially in someone so young. Despite having so much growth ahead of her, she already knew herself more than many women ever do.

"Look, sir, I appreciate you offering me a ride, but I don't know you. There's no way I'm getting into that car with you."

Jerry, accustomed to willful women, was unbothered by the young girl's refusal. He remained patient, calm, and insistent as he tried to reason with her. Cooper and I watched on in silence, enjoying the exchange.

"Lassie, 'twould be improper for me to leave a child stranded along a dirt road. 'Tis at least a mile back to the castle. I'll not do it. If ye willna get in this car, I shall follow along beside ye until either whoever ye are with finds ye or yer legs give out from exhaustion. 'Tis snowing and ye are near soaked through. Ye've no hat on yer head, no muffs on yer ears, and no gloves that I can see. When we do find whoever ye are with, I shall scold them for allowing ye out of doors without anything to keep ye warm."

"Watch it, old man." There was fire in the girl's tone. Something that Jerry had said made her immediately defensive. "You'll say nothing to my grandfather. It's not his fault that I ignored him."

Jerry smiled and cast me a quick glance.

"Ah. Thank ye, lass. We are finally making some progress. At least now I know who ye are with. Is yer grandfather back at the castle? If so, why doona ye get in the back with Cooper and we will drive ye to him?"

The young girl pointed to Cooper in the back seat who responded by waving at her. She rolled her eyes in response.

"How do I know that you didn't kidnap that little boy in the back and now you want to kidnap me, too?"

Cooper quickly protested by rolling down his window and sticking his head outside to speak to the girl directly.

"I am *not* that little. And Jerry hasn't kidnapped me. I'd like to see someone try to take me if I didn't want to go."

Quietly, so the girl outside couldn't hear him, Jerry leaned back and whispered over his shoulder to Cooper.

"I'm not sure if I'd be so confident about that, lad. It did already happen once before if ye doona remember?"

On impulse, I reached out and hit Jerry softly on the arm. The very memory of the old witch who'd taken Cooper from us once before made my blood boil. I tried my best to block it from my memory. I was certain Cooper tried to do the same.

The girl laughed and crossed her arms, leaning back onto her heels.

"Only someone really little would feel the need to tell me how 'not little' they are."

Cooper's face flushed red as he sank back inside the car.

Jerry laughed and attempted to divert the conversation back toward him.

"There. Cooper has told ye himself that he is not kidnapped. If ye truly doona wish to get in this car, then fine, turn yerself around and walk back toward the castle. I'll follow behind ye to make certain ye get there safely."

I could see by the flash in the young girl's eyes that she saw this as a victory. Without a word she turned and marched off in front of the car.

I leaned over and spoke softly to Jerry—not that she could hear me from outside the car anyway.

"Ye really are going to have to follow her all the way. She's strong-willed. She doesna wish to give in to ye."

Jerry nodded and pressed on the brake as he turned to address Cooper.

"Aye, I know. Cooper, what should we do? Ye know women well."

I wasn't all together sure how true that was, but I could see by the way Cooper lifted in his seat that Jerry's confidence in him was just what he needed after the girl's insult. It wouldn't hurt to let Cooper think of an idea to try.

Cooper smiled and unbuckled his seatbelt. "I know just the thing, guys. Just give me some space, okay?"

We both nodded and allowed Cooper to get out of the car. Rolling down my own window, I urged Jerry to do the same.

"Open all the windows and pull up beside them rather than behind. I wish to hear what they are saying to one another."

Jerry obeyed without question.

"What are you doing? I don't know you either, little boy. You need to get back in your car and leave me alone."

Cooper carried himself tall and didn't shrink at the girl's cold welcome. Instead, he moved to block her path and extended his hand.

"You could at least say hello to me. My name's Cooper, what's your name?"

Forced to stop, the young girl eyed him suspiciously. Cautiously, she extended her hand.

"Rosalind." She hesitated and then added, "but most people call me Rosie."

I smiled as Cooper shook her hand and moved out of her way, falling in step beside her as she continued her march back toward the castle. The name suited her. Significantly taller than Cooper, the girl was slender and pale with very short strawberry-blonde hair that fell much more in the realm of strawberry than blonde. Her eyes were jade green, and the smattering of freckles across her face would, one day when she was older, be stunning.

It was unusual in my time to see a female with such short hair, but I quite liked it. It fit the young girl's personality perfectly. Eager to see what Cooper would do next, I watched on.

"It's really cold out here, ya know?"

Rosie nodded but didn't look over at Cooper as she walked.

"Yes, I do know. Maybe you should get back in the car with the old man and the woman who keeps staring at me."

I shrunk slightly back in my seat but didn't look away at her words.

Cooper shook his head.

"Nope. As long as you're walking, I'm going to walk next to you. And, as you said, I'm little and it's very, very cold out here. I might get sick."

To emphasize this, Cooper coughed rather dramatically into his arm.

Rosalind stopped cold, crossed her arms as she'd done before and looked at him.

"You people are crazy. I don't like any of you one bit."

Cooper grinned. He could see that he was succeeding.

"We're just trying to help you."

Turning, she stomped away from him and opened the car door before crawling inside.

"I don't need anybody's help. The second we get back to the castle and I find my grandfather, I don't want to see any of you guys ever again."

Jerry laughed and sped up as we barreled toward the castle. "Verra well, lass, but see ye to yer grandfather, we shall."

*W*hen Malcolm saw the old, rickety car pull up to the front of Conall Castle, the terror that had gripped him for the better part of an hour melted away in a rush. He could see Rosalind's red hair through the window, and his knees nearly gave way as relief washed over him. While he'd known she couldn't have gone far—there was only one road leading to the castle—he'd been terrified.

Running outside to meet her, he gathered her up in his arms and dropped to his knees.

"Where on earth did you go?"

Rosalind was stiff in his grip. With a muffled voice, she spoke into the front of his shirt.

"You've got to let go of me, Pops. I can't breathe. I didn't go anywhere. I was just bored to death on the tour and thought I'd walk around a little while. I was just walking down the road."

It was only when he released her and stood that he took notice of the old man standing on the other side of the car. While it took him a moment to recognize him—it had been at least five years since he'd seen him—he knew as soon as he heard the man's voice that it was Jerry.

"Malcolm! Why, I dinna know Rosie was yer granddaughter. Had I known, I wouldna have been so patient with her. How are ye, man? 'Tis been far too long since ye visited these parts."

The snow now fell in a heavy blanket over them. As he leaned forward to hug Jerry, he could see Rosie trembling beside them from the cold. She was wet all the way through.

"I'm much better now. Thank you for picking her up."

"O'course. I was on my way back home when we spotted her. I dinna know who she belonged to, but I couldna verra well leave her out in the snow."

Noticing the castle's tour guide a few yards away, Malcolm reached for Rosie's hand.

"Jerry, it's good to see you, but I'm afraid we must both get back to the group. Rosie delayed everyone long enough by wandering off and the entire group has been searching for her. I need to let them know she's back."

Just as he began to step away, Jerry reached and grabbed his arm.

"By all means, let them know the lass is safe but then why doona the two of ye gather yer bags from the bus and come with me back to the inn for the night? Morna would never forgive me if she found out that I bumped into ye and then dinna bring ye back to the house so she could see ye."

Malcolm couldn't deny the appeal of Jerry's suggestion. Rosalind needed to get dry, and Morna and Jerry's inn was undoubtedly closer than the tour group's next stop.

"We wouldn't be intruding?"

Jerry waved a dismissive hand.

"Not at all. I promise ye, my wife would insist on it if she were here, so I must do so on her behalf. Rosie can wait in the car for ye while ye gather yer things."

Seeing his granddaughter inside the car, he leaned in close to whisper in her ear before leaving to retrieve their things.

"When we get to the inn, we will discuss this further."

*W*hile she said nothing, it was evident that Rosalind was near tears as she waited for her grandfather. Her breathing was tight, and I could see her reddened cheeks from the mirror outside my window.

Jerry and Cooper could sense the tension in the young girl, as well, and we remained quiet as we waited for the man I now knew was named Malcolm to return with their belongings.

When he began his walk back toward the car, I was able to get a clear view of him for the first time.

He was one of the most handsome men I'd ever seen. As tall as both of my sons, I would be dwarfed in size if I stood next to him. His hair was very dark and thick, slightly unruly, and much like my own, it had begun to gray in mixed places throughout. His blue eyes stood out from amongst his mass of black hair, and he had the sort of scruffy facial hair that made it look as if he were in the beginning stages of trying to grow it out. Although, I expected that with all of the fascinating tools I knew existed in the twenty-first century, that he kept it trimmed that way all the time.

I didn't realize he'd stopped walking and that we were both staring at one another until his knuckles lightly rapped on my closed window. Startled, I jerked back as my cheeks warmed in embarrassment. I was certain they were now as red as Rosie's.

"I'm so sorry to ask you this," Malcolm straightened and swept his hand downward in a motion meant to emphasize the length of his legs. "I don't think I'll fit in the back seat. Would you mind switching with me?"

There was no question that if he attempted to sit in the back, he would be forced to sit in a terribly uncomfortable position, if he could manage to fit in the back at all.

"Oh. Aye, o'course." Fumbling with the door handle, I eventually managed to clumsily step outside. When I righted myself, Malcolm extended me his hand.

"I hate to have you move. I'm Malcolm, but you can call me Mac, most people do."

He had quite possibly the largest hands I'd ever seen. I found them to be wildly attractive.

Strong yet gentle, his fingers were long and masculine. The touch of them against my own as he slid his hand around mine made my knees wobbly in a way that both shocked and horrified me.

"'Tis no trouble at all, I assure ye. I...I'm Kenna. Ye may call me Kenna." It was a ridiculous thing to say, and the smile that spread across his face at my words made me want to disappear into the snow.

"Very well. It's a pleasure to meet you, Kenna. Here, let me open the door for you."

As he ushered me into the back seat of the car next to a wet and freezing Rosie who was forced to slide over into the middle, his hand touched my back and I gasped. Thankfully, Cooper was the only one who noticed my quick intake of breath, but the oddly perceptive child immediately turned his head away from me to giggle.

The drive back to Morna and Jerry's was short, and as expected, Morna stood outside her home awaiting our arrival.

I was the first one to climb out of the car, and before I managed to say one word of greeting to her, Morna pulled me to her in a tight embrace.

"Ach, lassie. I'm so pleased ye decided to join Cooper." And then, lowering her voice so that no one save me could hear her, she pressed her lips against my ear and whispered. "Our other guests doona know about any of the magic. Best we not tell them."

Raising her voice once more, she pushed me away and moved to gather up Cooper, most assuredly to give him the same warning. Not that it was needed. Everyone who'd ever fallen prey to Morna's meddling magic quickly became accustomed to keeping secrets. Cooper would know not to say anything.

"Cooper, lad. I've missed ye more than ye know. Get yerself over here and give me a hug."

I gathered our belongings as Morna and Cooper hugged. Then I walked over to Jerry so he could direct me.

He attempted to reach for the bags, but I quickly spun them away from him.

"No, thank ye. I can manage both bags just fine, Jerry. Where would ye like me to place them?"

Smiling, Jerry pointed to the top of the stairs.

"Straight up and to yer right there are three rooms. Cooper prefers the room nearest the staircase. Why doona ye take the middle room? Rosie can have the room at the far end."

Nodding, I stepped away. "I'll just place these in our rooms then I'll come downstairs to visit. Thank ye both for letting me stay."

"We are so happy to have ye here, Kenna. We will have plenty of time for conversation. Ye must be exhausted from the journey. If ye get to yer room and feel like resting for a bit, please do so."

By the time I reached my room, my arms ached from fingertip to shoulder from the weight of Cooper's book bag.

The bed looked so inviting.

Surely, a short rest would do no harm.

CHAPTER 7

woke to the familiar sound of knuckles lightly rapping. For a few moments upon opening my eyes, I forgot where I was. It was only when I noticed the glow of electric lighting from the side table to my right and the strong smell of food from the kitchen below that everything came flooding back. I was at Morna's—some three hundred plus years ahead of the time I'd been born in.

Pulling myself from the bed, I stood and stretched then nearly fell backwards on the bed once again when I cast a glance out the window to see that the sky was now pitch black. I'd slept for the rest of the day.

The light knock returned. I ran a quick hand through my undoubtedly messy hair and moved to answer it. Expecting Cooper —although, if I were honest with myself, it would've surprised me if he'd actually knocked—I jumped back at the sight of Malcolm standing tall in the doorway.

"Did I wake you? I just saw that the light was on so I thought maybe you weren't sleeping. Forgive me, Kenna. It can wait until morning."

Still drowsy and confused at his presence, I yawned and held up a hand to keep him from leaving.

"No, no. 'Tis fine. I shouldna have slept so long. How far into evening is it?"

He pulled his lips to one side as if he were reluctant to tell me.

"It's close to midnight now. I'm the only one up. I should've assumed that you'd just fallen asleep with the light on, but I saw it and thought perhaps you'd awakened. Now that you're up, are you hungry?"

I found myself unable to remember the last time I'd eaten. The day leading up to my departure had been so filled with preparation and activity, I didn't think I'd stopped once to eat, and with all of the traveling today, I knew I'd eaten nothing.

"I'm famished."

"Good. I know I saw Morna stash some leftovers in the fridge. I'll go and warm it up."

Smiling, I nodded and reached for the door.

"Thank ye. Just give me a few moments to fully wake myself and I'll join ye downstairs."

I waited until he disappeared from view before I tip-toed from my room over to the bathroom at the end of the hall. I'd used only one modern toilet in all of my life and to my everlasting embarrassment had been forced to call Mitsy into the room to help me figure out how to work it. To avoid such mortification this time —I'd sooner die than have to call my grandson into the bathroom to educate me on twenty-first century waste removal—I had Adelle give me a thorough lesson on all the new objects I would find in Morna's home.

A mirror hung on the back of the bathroom door, and as I sat down to relieve myself, I caught a glimpse of my reflection. I'd never looked so frightening in all my life. Dark smeared circles surrounded my eyes from smeared mascara. My hair was ratted and smashed drastically to one side. And—worst of all—the top four buttons on the white blouse I was wearing had opened while I slept.

If not for the bra underneath, my breasts would have been totally exposed.

Still, even with the bra, Malcolm had just seen more of my bare chest than any man in the last fifteen years.

---

*E*ven unkempt from sleep, with eyes as dark as raccoons from her makeup, Kenna was stunning. And by God her breasts were perfect. Not that he intentionally looked at her breasts. They'd just been so there, so evident with the way her blouse lay open. He was certain she'd not known. She would be embarrassed when she noticed. Of course, he would say nothing of it. It was best to let her believe that he'd seen nothing below her chin.

The food was already warm and laid out by the time she entered the kitchen. As he expected, her face was now bare, her hair pulled back, and her blouse firmly closed.

"I haven't the slightest idea what this is, but it is delicious. Morna asked me before she went to bed to direct you to the food if you were to wake up hungry during the night."

Kenna's brows pulled together as she sat down in the chair opposite him.

"Why would she tell ye to do that? Does she not expect ye to sleep, as well?"

Malcolm realized that she must not have seen his pallet in the middle of the living room floor on her way to the kitchen.

"She only asked because I'm sleeping in the living room. I suppose she suspected I would wake if anyone came downstairs. Though, she's wrong about that. It always takes me awhile to go to sleep, but once I do, I'm out like a light."

Kenna lifted the fork he'd laid out for her, smiling as she took her first bite of food.

"'Tis shepherd's pie. Quite a delicious one." Speaking between bites of food, she continued. "Malcolm, ye needn't sleep on the floor. I can move my belongings over to Cooper's room and sleep with him."

Malcolm had seen clearly enough the young boy's desire to appear older than he was to his granddaughter. It wouldn't do to have the boy's grandmother sleep with him.

"I wouldn't dream of it. I believe Cooper has taken a bit of a fancy to Rosie. And she already wounded his confidence enough tonight. If she saw that you were sleeping in his room..." he paused and shook his head, "well, I'm not quite sure what this new version of my granddaughter would say to him, but she'd ridicule him for it. The floor suits me just fine. The mattress Morna placed there is honestly quite comfortable."

Malcolm watched as concern crossed Kenna's face. She loved the young boy dearly, and he could see why. Despite Rosie's harsh words, Cooper had been nothing but a delight during their meal. And while he knew Rosie's words must have hurt him, the child had hidden it well.

"What do ye mean? What happened?"

Standing, he went to retrieve a fork for himself before joining in on the other side of the pie.

"That's actually why I came to your room. I just wanted to apologize on behalf of Rosie. She'll be apologizing to Cooper in the morning, I've made sure of that, but I just wanted you to know that how she's behaved since you all met her...well, it's not typical."

Kenna's face softened somewhat and she surprised him by reaching forward to gently lay her hand on top of his. He stilled underneath her touch.

"'Twas Mac ye said I should call ye, aye?"

He nodded.

"Mac, I raised three children and am surrounded by grandchildren almost every day. I know all too well that to judge any child by one day's ill-tempered mood is folly. 'Twas clear to me the moment I saw Rosalind that something had upset her greatly. We all lash out when we are angry. What did she say to him?"

"She asked him if he wanted her to cut up his food since you were sleeping. That surely someone so young couldn't manage by himself."

Kenna's eyes grew wide and Malcolm noticed that he immediately missed her touch as she pulled her hand away and crossed her arms. She didn't look angry at all. If anything, she appeared amused.

"And how did he answer her?"

Malcolm smiled thinking back on the youngster's words.

"He carefully lifted his knife and cut the perfect bite of pie before placing it in his mouth like a gentleman three times his age. Then he looked directly at her and said, 'I think I can manage, but if you have any trouble with your piece, I'll be happy to help you, Rosie. And just so you know, I may look younger than I am now, but it won't be that way forever.'"

Kenna smiled wide and nodded slowly.

"That sounds like Cooper. I doona think there is need for Rosie to apologize come morning. I verra much doubt that Rosie's words wounded him at all."

If Kenna was correct, the boy was indeed much more grown-up than he appeared. Malcolm knew that at such an age, to be called small by a girl he liked would've been crushing.

"She will apologize whether Cooper needs the apology or not. No matter how upset Rosie is at her own situation, it gives her no right to intentionally try to hurt others."

Kenna resumed picking at the edges around the pie.

"Aye, fine. 'Tis o'course yer choice what ye have her do. I only meant that I doona want ye to worry for Cooper's feelings. His whole life he's dealt with people underestimating him, and he always handles it with grace. He's been a grown man trapped inside a child's body since the day I first met him."

Setting her fork to the side, Kenna pushed the pie toward him and Malcolm stood to clean up the table.

Discarding the few scraps that remained and placing the dish in the sink to wash later, Malcolm returned to his seat.

"I've no doubt of that. Since the day you met him?"

"Aye. Cooper is not my grandson by birth, though I love him no differently than those who are. His mother married my son only a few years ago."

"Ah. And how do you know Morna and Jerry? Cooper seems quite close with them."

Malcolm watched as Kenna hesitated a long moment and he couldn't help but wonder what about the question gave her pause.

"She's a distant relative of mine through marriage. My husband was her cousin. Morna and Cooper took to one another the moment they met. I suppose she and Jerry are in some way grandparents to him, as well, now. The child has many."

"He is blessed then. I'm the only grandparent Rosie has left."

The confession slipped from Malcolm without thought, and he immediately felt strange. He hated nothing more than other people's sympathy, and it took much for him to open up. Why then, had he spoken so easily of something so delicate with this stranger?

Thankfully, Kenna gave little in the way of sympathy.

"'Tis always difficult when children lose those they love at a young age. Is yer wife recently passed? Is that what wounds the girl now?"

Malcolm looked into Kenna's eyes and saw no pity. She didn't avoid his gaze, didn't smile softly to make him comfortable. It endeared her to him even more. And somehow, it made it easier to speak of things he rarely ever did.

"No. Rosie is named after her grandmother though she never knew her. My Rosalind has been gone seventeen years now. Rosie's father passed away two years ago this next week, and while she still grieves for him, her anger is now directed at her mother. She was supposed to be on this trip with us. She claims she is swamped with work, but Rosie knows better. I don't blame her for her anger. I'm angry, as well. She does not, however, have reason to make everyone else around her—most especially strangers—miserable."

"Not a one of us is miserable, Mac. Allow the girl her anger. She will come around in a few days. If I know Morna, she will see to it that Rosie's mood lifts sooner rather than later. Now," Kenna stood and stretched just slightly before turning away from him, "while I can scarcely believe it myself, I feel as if I could sleep even more. Thank ye for the food. I should go back to bed."

"You're very welcome. Sleep well." He hesitated to do so as she climbed the stairs, but couldn't keep from calling out to her once more as she reached the top. "Kenna?"

She turned toward him with a smile. "Aye?"

"Thank you."

"For what?"

"I didn't leave that conversation feeling sorry for Rosie or myself. I don't remember the last time I felt that way after speaking to anyone about our losses."

Her voice was quiet, but her tone was sad as she answered him.

"Doona thank me. My lack of sympathy wasna intentional, I assure ye. Perhaps my own dealings with grief have hardened me more than I knew. Goodnight, Mac. Rosie is lucky to have ye."

As Malcolm waited for her bedroom door to close, he knew he wouldn't sleep a wink tonight for wondering about what had pained his beautiful new friend so much.

CHAPTER 8

espite my insistence that I was indeed still sleepy after my many hours long nap, I didn't sleep a minute after returning to my room. Instead, I lay awake thinking of Malcolm—of how easy it was to speak to him, of how polite he'd been not to mention my appearance earlier in the night, of how handsome he looked dressed so casually for sleep. It was the first time in well over a decade that such thoughts of a man had occupied my mind.

Eventually, just past five when I knew Cooper would be awake. I tiptoed over to his room and slipped inside.

As expected, he sat propped up in his bed with a mound of pillows, a book on his lap. He lay his book down beside him and smiled at me as I entered.

"What are you doing up so early, Nana?"

"'Twas the nap I took last evening. I slept far longer than I should have. Cooper, I'm sorry for not tending to ye last night. I quite abandoned ye."

He shook his head and scooted over so I could sit down beside him.

"You didn't abandon me. I'm used to being with Morna and Jerry all by myself. I didn't think anything about it, I promise. Do you feel more rested?"

I suspected my sleeping patterns would be turned around for days, but for now, I did feel quite rested.

"Aye, I do. What of ye, Cooper, did ye sleep well?"

Gently laying his head against my shoulder, Cooper answered.

"Yes. I always sleep well. Maybe it's 'cause I know Morna has magic, but I always feel completely safe here. I don't worry about anything."

"Do ye not usually feel safe at home?"

"I do, but magic just sort of brings a whole other level of safety to it, ya know?"

I laughed and gently rested my own head against the top of his.

"Aye, I suppose ye are right. Cooper, Malcolm came to see me last night. He wished to apologize on behalf of Rosie."

The child lifted his head and twisted to face me. His brows pulled toward his nose in confusion.

"What for?"

"He was worried that she might have wounded yer feelings over dinner."

Cooper smiled widely. While the light was low in the room, I thought I saw a slight blush in his cheeks.

"She didn't hurt my feelings."

"No? What she said to ye wasna verra kind."

"No, it wasn't, but she's not really upset with me. I know that. I think she's *wonderful.*"

I had to swallow the giggle that rose up in my throat at the sound of complete awe in Cooper's voice as he called Rosie wonderful. It seemed that Malcolm was right—Cooper fancied the lass.

"Wonderful...how so?"

Cooper hesitated and crossed his arms as he pursed his lips.

"I wish I had a better answer, but the truth is, I just don't know her that well yet. It's just a feeling I have. Rosie is something special. Don't worry though—I'll get to know her. She may not think much of me now, but someday I'll grow. Then she will like me so much, it will drive her crazy."

The thought seemed to delight Cooper.

"So ye think ye will know Rosalind for a long time, then? Ye doona believe that once she and her grandfather leave that ye willna see her again?"

Cooper smiled and turned his head to look up under his lashes at me with an expression that was meant to tell me that I should've already known the answer.

"Nana, don't you know how Morna works by now? She hasn't admitted it yet, even though I tried to get her to, but I know Morna's magic has something to do with them being here. I have no doubt that Mac and Rosie will be in our lives for a very long time. Do you doubt it, Nana?"

It truly hadn't crossed my mind until now. Everything about the situation seemed entirely coincidental, but perhaps Cooper was right. If he was, did her plans only relate to Cooper and Rosie, or did it all have something to do with me and Mac, as well?

"I see that ye did find yer way to the kitchen after the rest of us were abed. I'm glad for it, lass. It dinna please me to go to bed without seeing ye fed, but I dinna wish to wake ye, either. Did Mac help ye heat everything?"

Entering the kitchen after my first glorious experience with a shower, I moved to where Morna worked over a flame to see what she was cooking.

"Aye, he did. Do ye need help with anything?"

Morna quickly waved me away.

"No, lass. 'Tis only eggs, and the toast and coffee are nearly ready. I've also some haggis and black pudding for ye and Jerry. No one else will eat it."

"Not even ye?" Morna was as Scottish as I. It surprised me that she would dislike food she'd undoubtedly been raised on.

"No, I've not touched either food since the age of ten when I learned what each item was made of. If my brother or father were still here, they'd think it traitorous of me to say so, but I canna stomach it."

I'd never given the making of either food much thought. I had no intention of doing so now. Eager to change the subject, I quickly peeked inside the living room to make certain that Malcolm still slept soundly on the floor.

With his soft snores audible from the bottom of the stairway, I knew it was safe to ask my question.

"Morna, how do ye and Jerry know Malcolm and Rosalind?"

Extending a mug in my direction, Morna carried her own over to the small table and motioned for me to sit next to her.

"Well, we dinna know Rosalind until last night, and it has been many a year since we've seen Malcolm. As for how we know him, in truth, 'tis his brother, Kraig, that we knew first. We met Kraig at the hospital in Edinburgh when Jerry had his knee replaced over a decade ago. He was his surgeon, and despite Jerry being the most cantankerous patient the poor doctor ever had, the two of them took to each other. We've been friends with the young lad ever since. In fact, I introduced Kraig to his wife, Emilia. We met Malcolm at their wedding."

Smiling, I shook my head.

"It shouldna surprise me to hear that, Morna, but for some reason, it does. Have ye ever met a singleton whose love life ye havena decided to meddle in?"

I knew the moment I saw her mischievous grin what I'd walked into.

"Ye are still single, Kenna. I've yet to meddle in yer life."

"Cooper is none too sure of that. He told me this morning he believes Malcolm and Rosie's appearance here is yer doing. And I'm not certain that being widowed is the same as being single."

Morna laughed and reached over to pat my hand.

"Mayhap for the first few years after such a loss, such an answer is acceptable. While ye are widowed, ye are free to love again. It has been fifteen years, Kenna. Ye are verra, verra single."

"So…" I took a sip of my coffee to listen for Malcolm's snoring. It still reverberated through the hallway. "Is Cooper right, Morna? Have ye decided to meddle in my life next?"

Morna scooted her chair right next to mine and leaned in to whisper.

"Believe it or not, lass, my magic is not the only force in this world which conspires to bring those that are meant to be together, together. While I know Cooper dinna believe me, I had no hand in this. I canna begin to tell ye how surprised I was when I saw Jerry pull up with two extra guests."

I leaned away from her. "Why are ye whispering, Morna?"

Grinning, she leaned in even closer and kept her voice low.

"Kenna, Mac has been feigning sleep since ye came down those stairs. There is no need for him to hear what I'm telling ye. Now, while I promise ye I had nothing to do with ye all finding Rosie yesterday, that doesna mean that there is no reason for his arrival. The two of ye would make a fair match, 'tis plain to see. And while I'll not use magic in this instance, I would be lying if I said I had no intention of meddling. I intend to clear the path for the two of ye just a bit, just to allow ye to see where things might lead. I would advise ye not to get in my way."

Before I could protest or even respond, Morna stood, winked at me, and then screamed out for everyone in the house to hear, "Breakfast is ready. All of ye best wake and come to the kitchen before it cools."

CHAPTER 9

By mid-morning, Morna began to execute her "light meddling." Over breakfast she all but begged Malcolm and Rosalind to stay one more day so they could help us decorate the inn for Christmas. With Rosie quite reluctant to return to Edinburgh, Malcolm agreed.

With Morna, Jerry, Cooper, and Rosie pulling down boxes from the attic, the nosy and insistent witch sent Malcolm and me out on a task to find the perfect Christmas tree from a farm a half hour away.

Knowing that Morna believed us to be a good match changed the dynamic between us. While Malcolm hadn't been able to hear our conversation, it had shifted something in my own mind, which made me nervous and awkward in his presence. I couldn't look at him without wondering "what if?", without thinking through a thousand different scenarios, without questioning whether or not my feelings were a result of actually liking him or simply the result of being on my own for so many years. Back home, I'd quickly ended any possibility of a relationship with anyone else—I'd never been interested in the slightest. Now, for some reason completely beyond me, I was.

Was it the trip? Had being away from home and in a time so unfamiliar simply overexcited me so much that I was seeing possibility, that I was seeing attraction, where it wasn't? I found this the most likely cause of my feelings and did my best to silence the endless chatter of thoughts in my mind as we pulled away from the inn.

"Don't you find it odd that the kids didn't want to come pick out a tree?"

Laughing, I remembered both children's faces when they'd told us that they wanted to stay and help Morna and Jerry get the decorations down. It was evident in their glee that Morna had somehow offered them something that appealed to them even more.

"I suspect we will return to find both of them so sick from whatever sweet treats Morna has bribed them with that 'twill be clear why they wished to stay."

"Why would she bribe them?" Malcolm's tone was genuinely curious, and I realized once more that he truly hadn't been able to hear Morna's whisperings to me.

A younger woman would've lied—would've made some excuse that kept awkwardness at bay—but sometime during my forties, my worries over what others thought of me had blessedly diminished. Being relieved of that torture was entirely worth the cost of the wrinkles such a decade had brought me. If this man was meant to like me, he would. If not, he wouldn't. Bringing up Morna's thoughts on the matter wouldn't change things one way or the other.

"Morna sent us on this errand so that we would be alone. She believes we would make a good couple."

I expected him to make light of such a statement. He did anything but.

"Does she? Well, I don't know you well enough yet to know if she's right, but I'll not go so far as to disagree with the old woman either. She said the same of my brother once, and she couldn't have been more right."

MORNA'S MAGIC & MISTLETOE

His use of the word *yet* warmed me from naval to nose. I could fool no one. While I might not care what the average stranger thought, I very much wanted this man to like me. For with each new thing he said, I found myself liking him just a little bit more.

---

*L*ord only knew how they would get the tree Kenna picked back to Morna and Jerry's. The car was small, the tree large, but Malcolm couldn't find it in himself to deny her. She was right anyway—the tree was perfect. It would fill the window in Morna and Jerry's inn, and once it was lit and decorated, it would be visible from the road to all who passed by.

"I can tell by the way ye are staring at it, ye doona think we can get it back. 'Tis fine, Mac. While this one is beautiful, I doona mind if we find one a bit smaller. No one else will mind, either."

"No, no." He reached out and placed his hand on her back to reassure her. "They will help get it situated on top of the car. We have plenty of straps to get it secured. I just...you may have to help direct me when turning corners and such. I suspect it will hang down a bit over the windshield. It's going to block part of my view."

"Oh. Well, aye, I can certainly try to do so."

"Great. Let's go pay for it."

They walked side by side to the station where they could pay for the tree and await some assistance. As they passed the car, Kenna stepped away and called back to him.

"I'll meet ye there. I left the money Morna gave us in the car."

"No need. The least I can do for her allowing Rosie and me to stay is buy them a tree. I'll pay for it myself, and I'll leave the extra money with Jerry, for I know Morna won't take it back if I try to give it to her."

Malcolm waited for Kenna to return to his side before approaching the young woman taking payment for the trees.

As he reached into his wallet for his credit card, Kenna leaned into him, her voice shy.

"What is that?"

He didn't have any idea what she referred to.

"What is what?"

She pointed to the card in his hand, and he struggled to keep confusion from etching his face.

"Oh, it's my credit card. I spent the last of my pounds at the Conall Castle gift shop. I need to find another ATM once Rosie and I return to Edinburgh. I doubt there's another one close."

Kenna continued to look at the square piece of plastic quizzically.

"'Tis money?"

He nodded and slowly handed the card to the young woman in front of them who unabashedly looked at Kenna with the confusion he was trying so hard to hide.

"Yes. In a sense. Don't you have one?"

Kenna shook her head. Malcolm had visited Scotland many, many times. The entire country was entirely modernized. Even isles that only had access to larger stores if they traveled by ferry had their own small shops that accepted credit cards. How did anyone in today's society not know what a credit card was?

"Kenna, what part of Scotland did you say you were from?"

Malcolm watched as her face changed, shielding her curiosity as she righted herself and smiled at him.

"I dinna say. Doona worry. I can see well enough what it does. I believe I'll wait in the car."

He didn't know if he'd ever been so baffled in his life. Clearly, while Kenna could see that the card had served its purpose to pay for the tree, she had no idea how it worked. And her quick dismissal of her curiosity once she realized he found it odd confused him even more.

Something was strange about this woman. He very much wanted to find out what it was.

CHAPTER 10

*T*he ease with which I was able to speak with Malcolm had lowered my guard. I was accustomed to being around twenty-first century people who knew precisely from which time I came and had no problem explaining to me all the things I didn't know. What had happened with Malcolm was exactly what I'd feared most when Mitsy had suggested such a trip. I looked like a fool, and I couldn't begin to tell him why.

I said nothing on the ride back to Morna's, save for the occasional direction I would give by leaning my head out of the car window to make sure that the road was clear. Thankfully, Malcolm said nothing of the incident at the Christmas tree farm. For the second time of me embarrassing myself in front of him, he proved himself to be a gentleman. There was at least some comfort in that.

When we returned to the inn, everyone was delighted at our choice of tree, as I knew they would be. The boxes of decorations were down, and everything was dusted and laid out for us to decorate.

We all had a wonderful time, and as the day went on and Malcolm didn't treat me like a mad woman, my worry abated. We all visited, laughed, decorated, and drank more than our fair share of hot chocolate as we worked together to make Morna and Jerry's home one of the most splendidly beautiful Christmas homes I'd ever seen.

By the time night fell, we were all exhausted and happy.

"It has been some years since Jerry and I had the energy to place so many lovely decorations out ourselves. Most years we just settle for a simple tree and a few strands of lights. This year's display makes my heart happier than any of ye can know. Thank ye for yer help. Now, let us sit down and enjoy one last meal together before Mac and Rosie leave us for Edinburgh tomorrow."

I'd known they were leaving. They weren't even supposed to be here today, but somehow through the day's festivities I'd forgotten, and the reminder that our new friends would be gone saddened me more than I wished to admit.

What would I do for the next two weeks without Malcolm here? While I'd never expected to meet him, suddenly the next days at the inn with only Cooper, Morna, and Jerry to occupy me, left me feeling rather empty.

It seemed that I wasn't the only one with such emotion, for over dinner, few words were exchanged—not until dessert was being finished and a hesitant Rosie glanced over at Morna for courage before addressing her grandfather.

"Pops, I have a question for you."

We all watched on as Malcolm lay his fork on his plate and looked over at Rosalind.

"You do? What is it?"

"Do we have to go back to Edinburgh? We always do the same things there. You visit with Uncle Kraig and Aunt Emilia, and I get stuck playing solitaire. Then you guys drag me around to fancy restaurants I don't even like until the real fun begins on Christmas Eve. Can't we stay here until then and then go back to Edinburgh in time for actual Christmas?"

If that was indeed what the young girl's Christmases in Edinburgh looked like, I didn't blame her at all for wanting to stay with Morna. Hope fluttered inside me as I watched Mac contemplate Rosie's plea.

"There's part of me that wishes we could, but I have tickets to the symphony tomorrow night. They were expensive and difficult to get. Plus, Kraig and Emilia would be very disappointed. I'm sorry, Rosie. We need to go back tomorrow."

"I have an idea."

Horrified, I looked over at Cooper and shook my head as I tried to stop him.

"No, Coop. We doona intrude on other people's business. Malcolm has given his answer. Ye doona need to suggest any ideas."

While not normally one to disobey, Cooper unabashedly argued with me.

"Why not? It's a good idea. I think Malcolm would like to hear it."

Just as I meant to speak more harshly to him, Malcolm stepped in to rescue Cooper.

"It's okay, Kenna. What's your idea, Cooper?"

Now that he was allowed to speak, Cooper hesitated.

"What...what if Rosie stayed here and you went to Edinburgh with Nana? I know she would like to see the city at Christmastime, and I doubt that we would make the trip there on our own. She's more likely to enjoy the stuff that Rosie wouldn't."

Before I had a moment to object or Malcolm had a moment to answer, Morna smiled and stood from the table as she started to gather dishes.

"Why Cooper, 'tis a splendid idea. Malcolm, ye know we would take great care of Rosie. The lassie expressed a desire to learn how to bake this afternoon while ye and Kenna were away. If I had a few days with her, I could teach her much."

Rosie quickly chimed in, her voice filled with anticipation.

"Oh, please let me, Pops. This school break has been rotten so far. If Mom's not going to be here for Christmas, you could at least let me do something I want to do for a few days. Please let me stay.

Go and do the things you have to do in Edinburgh and then come back and get me in a few days. Please. I would love you forever, Pops, if you'd let me."

I saw the exact moment Malcolm surrendered. Smiling, he nodded.

"Okay, okay. Fine. If you want to stay here a few days, that's fine, Rosie. I have no doubt you'd have more fun here with Cooper than you would in Edinburgh. But you've all made quite the assumption by assuming that Kenna would even want to accompany me."

Speaking with as much enthusiasm as the children, I interrupted him as Grace's insistence that I not concern myself with Cooper while here crossed my mind.

"I do want to. I really, really do."

There was an excitement in Malcolm's eyes as he looked at me that caused the hairs on the back of my neck to stand on end.

"I'm pleased to hear it. We'll leave first thing in the morning."

CHAPTER 11

The drive to Edinburgh the following morning in the car Morna had "delivered" for us during the night, was long, but nowhere near the length of time it would've taken me to travel there in my own time. I was in a constant state of amazement in this century, but I promised myself before leaving the inn with Malcolm that I would not make the same mistake I'd made the day before. If something confused or surprised me, I would keep my reaction to myself and make a special note to ask Cooper about whatever I saw once I returned to get him in three days' time.

Pulling into the city required me to stifle all sorts of emotions. While Edinburgh's grand castle still sat on top of the city center, so much else had changed. The lights, the cars, the noise—I wasn't sure I was a good enough actress to hide my utter amazement.

"I called my brother last night after everything was decided. They're expecting you. No need to be nervous."

Perhaps that's how my excitement looked to him with the way I was all but bouncing in my seat with my eyes peeled outside the window, but in truth, I wasn't nervous at all. I was delighted at the opportunity to explore this time period. While I'd listened to everyone's insistence that I enjoy this time and see as much as I could while here, I'd not really expected such an opportunity to arise.

The city was beautiful at Christmas—covered in snow, with garland and lights strung up over many buildings and doorways.

I didn't realize I'd not replied to him until Malcolm spoke up again.

"Are you all right, Kenna? You've hardly said anything since we left Morna and Jerry's."

Reluctant to look away from the window on the chance that I might miss something wonderful, I turned my head and smiled at him. He was right—I'd been quite rude.

"Ach, I'm sorry, Malcolm. 'Tis only that I canna remember the last time I was so excited about anything. I've simply been enjoying the view."

He smiled a crooked smile, and my heart sped up in response. The view outside was wonderful, but I couldn't have been missing anything that looked better than looking at him.

"You don't get to Edinburgh very often, then?"

I answered honestly. "The last time I was in Edinburgh, I was fifteen years old."

He looked as if he didn't believe me.

"Truly? Have you lived in Scotland all your life, or did you leave here for a while?"

"Aye, and all of my life."

Malcolm slowed the car and turned the corner onto a street lined with tall, connected buildings with doorways lining the front and steps leading up to each one. They looked like homes, though I'd never known homes to be connected in such a way.

"In what part of Scotland do you live, Kenna? I still haven't gotten an answer from you."

I wasn't sure how to answer him. I didn't know just how familiar he was with Scotland's geography. If he was familiar at all, it wouldn't be difficult for him to catch me in a lie. Most especially since I had no way of knowing if areas that were once remote, still were today. I decided it best to lie as little as possible.

"I live with my...my nephew at McMillan Castle. McMillan is my last name. He and his wife run the castle and keep it open to visitors. I assist in managing the staff."

It was an answer that was only about halfway true, but I saw no way for him to be able to discern that I lied.

His face lit up, as if my words had suddenly solved a great mystery.

"Ah! Well, that explains it, then. I'm sure you have people that bring whatever you need to the castle. If so, there wouldn't be much need for you to leave the area or to do your own shopping."

While I didn't quite appreciate the insinuation that others did everything for me, I couldn't argue the point. In truth, there was much that was taken care of for me. I was a remarkably blessed woman in any century.

Slightly embarrassed, I nodded.

"Aye. Though 'tis not as if I couldna do any of those things myself if I needed to."

His hand reached across the space between us and squeezed my hand as the car slowed to a stop in front of one of the doorways.

"I wasn't suggesting that you couldn't. That just explains your reaction to my credit card at the Christmas tree farm yesterday. Hey, McMillan Castle is the one with all of the extraordinary Christmas decorations, isn't it? Rosie has wanted to see it for years. Perhaps, you could arrange a special tour for us?"

I nodded and then pointed to the woman who had just appeared in the doorway closest to the car.

"Aye. O'course I can. Is that Emilia?"

I knew her name from Rosie's mention of them yesterday. The moment a man cradling a baby appeared next to her, I knew I was right.

"Yes, it is. She will be thrilled to meet you. Don't worry about your bag. I'll get them after we say hello."

The moment I stepped outside the car, the woman called to me.

"Kenna, lass, if ye wish to see Edinburgh at Christmas, ye have come to the right place. While he may not be Scottish himself, Malcolm knows the city better than even I do. 'Tis a shame, but it seems that it often happens in such a way. Locals doona appreciate the uniqueness of a city the same way that visitors do, so we doona get out and see as much."

Emilia talked quickly and without end as she wrapped one arm around my shoulder and led me inside their home.

While quite small, the home was beautiful and welcoming. I'd been unable to keep up with Emilia's chattering. Just as I worried that I wouldn't be able to answer her should she ask me a question, I was rescued by a hand at my back and turned to greet Malcolm's brother.

The man, while shorter than Malcolm, still stood far above the top of my head. He strongly resembled his brother with the same thick dark hair and brows. But where Malcolm had blue eyes, Kraig had brown, and his face was clean-shaven. He also had no gray in his hair. As I examined his face, I looked over his smooth unweathered skin and saw a man not much older than my sons. Kraig Warren looked all of twenty years younger than his elder brother.

"Welcome to Edinburgh. You must be Rosie's new favorite person. By agreeing to come with Malcolm, she got to stay away. I know we were boring her to tears."

Kraig pulled me in tight with one arm while still holding the baby in his other arm. Once he released me, I reached out and placed my palm gently on top of the babe's head.

"And this must be Robbie, aye?"

Kraig nodded, and the glimmer in his eyes as he looked at his son nearly brought tears to my eyes.

"Yes. I don't imagine he will sleep too much longer, though. Soon he will bid you a proper hello by screaming at the top of his lungs."

I grinned as he walked away and Malcolm came up behind me.

He must've read my mind for he leaned in close to answer the question I'd not yet asked him.

"Kraig was the surprise of my mother's life. She had him when I was twenty-eight years old, at the age of forty-four. Our father was forty-eight. My mother and my wife were pregnant at the same time." He laughed. "It was a very strange time in my life."

Eyes wide, I looked up at him.

"Ach, God bless her. Kraig would've been seven years old when yer mother was my age. I canna imagine it. My grandchildren are work enough. Did she..." I hesitated. "Did she live long enough to raise him?"

Malcolm smiled and pointed to a photo on the small table to my left.

"Oh, yes. She's still very much alive. You'd never guess she's as old as she is. She lives in Scotland now, just across the street actually. I'm sure you will meet her either tonight or tomorrow." He paused and his brows pulled in. "Which I suppose means that I lied to you before, though I didn't mean to. My mother is technically a grandparent to Rosie, but she's lived in Scotland since Rosie was born. They're not very close."

I'd thought nothing of it.

"It takes more than blood to form a bond, Malcolm. Look at wee Cooper. I am not his blood, but I am no less his grandmother for it. In the same way, blood doesna necessarily make someone a grandparent. Ye dinna lie."

"Oh, look at the two of ye. Look where ye are standing."

Emilia stood in the kitchen but pointed to us. She looked thrilled. We both looked blankly back at her.

"Ye are under the mistletoe. Come now, Malcolm. Ye must kiss her. 'Tis bad luck if ye doona do so."

I'd not been kissed in fifteen years. My entire body seized up with nerves at the thought of being kissed now. Surely, I'd forgotten how. Surely, I would do it all wrong.

I had little time to think on it as Malcolm's hand slipped to my lower back and he pulled me gently against him, his head quickly bending to my ear.

"You heard her. We can't have bad luck following you around."

I'd always thought the notion of women swooning in response to a man's touch lacking in realism. I was a level-headed woman—ahead of my time is what my daughters-in-law always called me—but as Malcolm's lips brushed against my own, I knew that if not for his steady hand holding me tight, I would've dropped to the floor like a sack of flour.

It was that wonderfully, deliciously good.

"*A*re you awake? I was surprised to see the fire still burning when I woke to relieve Emilia for a little while."

Malcolm stood from his makeshift bed on the couch and waved his brother downstairs to join him.

"Yes, wide awake. Here, why don't you hand me Robbie. I'll bounce him until he goes back to sleep. You can go back to bed if you wish."

While his brother didn't hesitate to hand him the baby, he didn't turn around and head back upstairs.

"I'm awake now, too. I'll stay up and visit with you. I haven't had a chance to visit with you alone yet."

Malcolm knew well enough what his brother would ask him, and he had no answers to give him.

Whether it was the touch of someone new or just the fact that Malcolm was so warm from laying near the fire, young Robbie relaxed instantly as Malcolm cradled him in his arms. He continued to bounce the child gently as he walked around the room.

"It's been a long time since I've held a baby—not since Rosie was one."

Kicking Malcolm's pillow onto the floor, his brother collapsed onto the couch and propped his feet up on the coffee table.

"You've always been good with them, but I don't want to talk to you about babies."

Keeping his voice low so Robbie would continue to drift to sleep, Malcolm walked over behind the couch.

"I know what you want to talk about, but there's not anything for me to say."

"Sure there is. You didn't tell me anything on the phone yesterday when you called to tell me she was coming with you. Who is she?"

Malcolm still knew so little about her. Just as he'd begun to believe that her strange behavior at the Christmas tree farm had been explained away, her behavior at the symphony had raised new questions in his mind.

He couldn't recall a single melody the symphony played. He'd spent the entire two hours watching her take in the spectacle.

She looked on with the wonder of a small child. As the lights changed around the stage, her eyes darted around to watch them as if looking for the source. When the conductor stepped up to the microphone and his voice boomed out over the audience, she'd nearly fallen out of her chair. It was the strangest thing he'd ever seen. It was incredibly enchanting. Wonder was something he'd not felt in decades. That Kenna could still be so surprised and fascinated by anything at their age was one of her many attractive qualities, but it still made no sense.

"I've only known her a few days. She's related to Morna and Jerry. She and her grandson were visiting them when Rosie and I intruded on their trip. The rest is exactly what you've heard. Rosie wanted to stay and Kenna wanted to see Edinburgh at Christmas. So here we are."

His brother twisted in his seat on the couch and looked back at him.

"And that's it then. She's just your friend?"

Kenna had given him no indication that she was interested in anything more than his friendship. While he hoped that would change, he couldn't claim that they were more than that now.

He nodded and his brother stood from the chair and reached for Robbie as he shook his head.

"I wonder what Emilia would say if I kissed one of my female friends under the mistletoe like that? I can't imagine that she would be very pleased."

J woke sometime in the early hours of the morning, just past midnight, with my bladder so full I thought it might burst. While I knew it probable that there was a restroom somewhere on the top floor, I had no desire to start opening doors in the dark, and I knew with certainty that there was one just past the front door on the bottom floor.

With Malcolm sleeping on the living room couch, I opened the bedroom door quietly, intending to sneak through the house unnoticed. Instead, as I opened it, I could hear voices from down below, and the staircase was illuminated by the fire that still burned.

"And that's it then. She's just your friend?"

It was Kraig's voice. I knew I should back up into the room and close the door and hold it until morning—Malcolm's answer to his brother's question was not something he intended me to hear, but I desperately wanted to know his answer. Instead, I moved just a little closer to the staircase and listened.

Nothing. Malcolm gave no answer. Before I could move away, Kraig was moving toward the staircase with the baby in his arms, calling back over his shoulder something about kissing his friends under the mistletoe.

Knowing that I could do nothing to keep from being seen, I spoke out to try and avoid the uncomfortable interaction that was headed my way.

"Kraig, is the baby awake? I was just going down to the restroom but if ye'd like me to take him for ye, I'd be happy to."

Kraig smiled at me and reached a hand out to gently squeeze my arm in thanks.

"No need now. Malcolm got him to sleep. I hope we didn't wake you."

Perhaps too dramatically, I dismissed him with a wave of my hand.

"No, ye dinna at all. I dinna even know ye were down here until I saw ye coming toward me on the stairs. Goodnight, Kraig."

Hopeful that I'd covered up my eavesdropping well enough, I made my way downstairs to where Malcolm stood behind the couch.

"Ye should be asleep, Mac. Ye promised me a full day of sightseeing tomorrow, and I'll not let ye out of it even if ye are tired."

He laughed and looked down at me. I suddenly felt very self-conscious in Adelle's robe.

"I think my anticipation for tomorrow is precisely why I can't sleep. Don't worry. I won't back out on you."

Leaving him to return to bed, I went to the restroom and came out with every intention of sneaking back upstairs. Instead, I walked past the living room to find Malcolm sitting on the couch as he faced the fire.

"Do ye not wish to at least attempt some sleep?"

Using his head to wave me over, he didn't face me as he spoke.

"Why don't you come and sit by me a minute? Maybe after some conversation, I'll feel like sleeping."

I knew he'd not meant anything unkind, but I didn't hesitate to point out what his words had suggested.

"Well, thank ye. I'm so pleased to hear that speaking with me is an effective way to put ye to sleep."

He laughed, his voice deep. Knowing that I would now sleep little myself, I went to join him. He sat at one end of the couch with both the middle and its other end unoccupied. I began to retreat to the couch's other end, but the warmth of him was too alluring. Cautiously, I slid closer toward the middle.

"You know I didn't mean it that way. Kenna..." he hesitated as I turned to look at him. The glow from the fire made his eyes look even more blue than usual. With the memory of his lips against mine still fresh in my mind, I couldn't keep my eyes from drifting toward his mouth.

"Aye?"

"May I ask you a question?"

"Ye may."

He reached for my hands. I adored how strong and warm his grip was. His hands completely enveloped my own.

"What are we doing? I'm past the age where games suit me. Shall we be friends or is it possible that we might be something more?"

I could hear my heart beating in my ears. There was only one thing I wanted to do in answer to his question.

With my hands still clasped in his, I closed the space between us and leaned in to kiss him.

The urging of all the twenty-first century women in my life sounding in my mind, I allowed myself to stop thinking as I moved against him, opening to his tongue as his hands pulled away and moved to the sides of my face. We kissed until my body shook all over from need. Recognizing where this would lead if I didn't stop soon, I pulled away.

"Was that your answer? If so, I'm very much in agreement with it."

Malcolm's own breath was shaky, and the need in his eyes made it difficult for me to breathe. I scooted away to give myself the space to gather my composure.

"In a way, though 'twas not all of my answer. I wish to tell ye something."

While I was here, I wanted Malcolm. I wanted to feel alive, to dust off some of the neglected parts of my soul and body, but I needed him to understand that I could promise nothing beyond the next few days. It wouldn't be fair to either of us to enter into something that was bound to cause us eventual pain without knowing exactly what would come.

"Tell me. I would listen to you say anything."

Hesitantly, my voice unsteady as the effects of his kiss continued to course through me, I told him everything that was on my mind.

"Mac, I was fourteen when I married my husband—still a child. And while I did love him in my own way—I never would've chosen him for myself. He was two verra different people, and I kept my distance from him because of it. He was a remarkable father to his children—fair and gentle with them all his life. But William was far too serious and harsh with me. He never laughed when we were together, and I only saw him smile in the presence of his sons. Our marriage cost me much of my childhood, but for him, our marriage cost him the woman he truly wanted to marry. While I played no hand in our betrothal, I doona think he ever forgave me for it."

I could see the question in Malcolm's eyes and paused to give him time to ask it.

"It was an arranged marriage? At fourteen? That's outrageous, Kenna."

Ignoring most of his questions, I continued.

"Aye, 'twas arranged from the time of my birth. If there is a blessing to come from it, 'tis that William vowed to never force his own children into such an agreement. Despite our lack of passion for one another, we lived easily together as husband and wife.

"William has been gone for fifteen years now, and there's been no one since then. I only tell ye this so that ye may understand why I'm about to propose something that may not be acceptable to ye. If 'tis not, I willna blame ye for it."

I waited for him to say something, but instead he just nodded, urging me onward.

"I've never known what 'tis like to explore a relationship of my wanting. If I were wiser, I would stifle what I feel for ye now and accept yer friendship. But Malcolm, for once in my life, I wish to be selfish. I wish to be selfish even knowing that in a few days, we will go back to Morna and Jerry's where ye will collect Rosie and I will most likely never see ye again. We live in verra different worlds, we canna pretend otherwise. So..." I was shaking all over again, but no longer from need. I'd never felt so vulnerable, so open to rejection. "To answer yer question after a verra long explanation—aye—I wish to be more than friends with ye, but I canna promise ye that anything shall last past the next few days. Can ye accept that and not think me the most selfish of women?"

Malcolm looked at me for a long moment, the need still evident in his gaze. He smiled slowly. As he pulled me against him, he whispered in my ear.

"Kenna, I will take you any way I can get you for as long as you'll allow me. I've never been one to worry too much about the future. All we have is now."

As his lips began to nip at the length of my neck, I allowed myself to drown in the sensation of his touch, quickly silencing the small voice in my mind that insisted I'd just asked him to agree to something I would never be able to uphold myself.

CHAPTER 13

*M*alcolm stayed true to his promise. Despite the fact that we both were sleep deprived after spending most of the night visiting, cuddling, and aye, occasionally kissing by the fire, he was up and ready for our day in the city before I was.

I found twenty-first century clothing so much more difficult to assemble. In my own time, I owned only four dresses save for the two I reserved for only the most special of occasions. There was nothing to think about when getting dressed—no decisions to make and no make-up to fuss with. With the assortment of items Adelle packed for me, I was left confused each and every morning as I tried to piece together items of clothing that would look nice together.

Since it was freezing outside and snowing on and off almost every day, I chose a pair of tight jeans, boots that went over them almost up to my knee, and a thick wine-colored sweater. After throwing on a hat, a scarf, some gloves, and my coat, I was ready to go.

I was determined not to apologize for making him wait on me. It was known across all time periods and countries that women take longer.

"So, what do ye have planned for the day?"

Seeing that I was already bundled up for outside, Malcolm reached for his own coat and scarf, donning them as he spoke to me.

"Lots. I'll drive us closer to the city center. Then I thought we could get a ticket for the double-decker buses. I'm sure being Scottish, you'll find them very touristy, but they really aren't a bad way to get from place to place, and it helps you get a layout of the whole city."

I was only familiar with the word *bus* because of the bus Malcolm and Rosie had been on at Conall Castle. I hadn't the slightest idea what a double-decker bus could be.

"I will find nothing too touristy, Mac, I assure ye. I've never been on a double-decker bus."

Surprise framed his features. It was an expression he wore often around me, and try as I might to not give away how out of sorts I was in this time, it was impossible to always say just the right thing.

"Well, good. Then you won't mind it. Here's a summary of the itinerary I have planned for us. If there's anything you don't want to do, just tell me, and we'll find something else."

When I nodded, he looked down at his list and began to read.

"First, after taking the whole bus loop, I thought we could grab breakfast at Emilia's favorite café. She used to work there as a teenager. They have the best coffee in Edinburgh."

I smiled as I glanced over to see Emilia nodding enthusiastically. "Sounds perfect."

"Next, I thought we would go over to the German Christmas Market. They have some of the prettiest trinkets and toys you've ever seen, and there's a big ferris wheel that will give us a spectacular view of the city."

Again, I had no idea what a ferris wheel was, but I said nothing.

"Afterwards, I thought we could go to The Dome for lunch in the tea room and to see their unbelievable decorations."

He paused and looked up at me and I knew he was wanting some sort of confirmation that all his plans were okay with me.

"I canna wait, Malcolm."

He let out a big breath of relief and grinned with pride as he looked back down at the list. The gesture made him look two decades younger—slightly nervous and even a little shy.

"Okay, after lunch, I thought we could explore the Scottish Market for a bit and then go on a tour of Edinburgh Castle."

"Oh, aye, let's. I would love to see the castle." Edinburgh Castle was the one thing he'd mentioned that I knew. I'd been there once as a child. It was where I'd first been introduced to William. It would be fascinating to see how much had changed.

"Then we most certainly shall. And lastly, I have us booked for an early dinner reservation at The Witchery. It's an Edinburgh tradition, and I know you'll enjoy it. Is there anything you want to change?"

I wished to do everything he mentioned, but I hated the idea of him repeating activities he'd already experienced many times for my sake.

"No, though I do have a question for ye. Have ye done all of these things before?"

He nodded and stuffed the list into his pocket before buttoning up his coat.

"Yes, but I enjoy doing them every year, so don't worry about that."

"There must be something ye wish to do in Edinburgh that ye havena done before. Whatever 'tis, let's do it after dinner."

"I know exactly what he needs to do." Emilia's voice interrupted as she made her way over to me. "Malcolm desperately needs an education in real Scotch. I've taught Kraig everything I know, but I've never had the opportunity to do the same with Malcolm. I know just the place the two of ye can go. They stay open late, and they offer tours that give ye more to taste than the wee sips most distilleries do. He'd love it."

I didn't even look up at Malcolm as I answered her.

"Aye, 'tis perfect. Every foreigner needs a proper introduction to Scottish whisky. Can ye arrange it for us?"

She gave me a quick nod and turned to address her brother-in-law.

"Malcolm, I'll text ye the address and time I've booked ye for in a while. Now, get out of here and have a grand time. I'm sure the two of ye will be out late. We will see ye tomorrow morning."

*W*ith his head already starting to ache and his feet far less steady than he liked, Malcolm had only two questions. First—why couldn't they have gone on a basic whisky tasting tour—one where they only got to taste the smallest sip of each whisky? Such a tour would've sufficed just fine. Second—how the hell was Kenna still standing? She'd drunk just as much as he had and showed no signs of intoxication. She was one of the daintiest women he'd ever seen. Short of stature, slender, all of her features were petite. How then, was she drinking him under the table?

Thankfully, as their host reached for their glasses to pour yet another dram of whisky, Kenna reached out a hand to stop him. Malcolm simply couldn't drink another drop.

"Thank ye, sir, but I believe my companion here has had all he can manage." She leaned over the counter playfully and whispered below her breath as she giggled. "He's American."

Perhaps, she was more affected by the tasting than he originally thought. Still, she was holding her liquor far better than he was.

"Kenna." He spoke slowly and with intention. He'd be damned before he slurred his words in front of her. He was a grown man and one that didn't drink often. He'd not have himself looking like a lush. "We can't drive back. The car is safe where I parked it this morning. Do you want to step outside and hail us a taxi while I pay for the bottle we are bringing back to Emilia and Kraig?"

Confusion and something resembling panic crossed Kenna's rosy cheeks, but before he could inquire into her concern, their tour host stepped in.

"No need. We've cars waiting out front. 'Tis customary on this specific tour. Rarely do we have a guest that is fit to drive afterwards."

Had this been Emilia's intention? Malcolm couldn't help but think that it must've been.

Kenna held tightly onto his arm as she stood from the barstool and waited for him.

"Shall we go then? Ye doona look so good, Malcolm."

He didn't feel so good.

"Yes, I think we should."

Just as their guide had promised, a car awaited them outside the distillery. With Kenna snuggled warmly into him on the ride back to his brother's house, he found it difficult to stay awake. Just as the car pulled up to the front of the house, Kenna leaned up to kiss his cheek.

"I had the best time tonight, Mac. Truly, I dinna ever want today to end."

Paying the driver, he stepped outside and took Kenna's hand. Emilia had left the outside light on for them. Walking up to the front door, he paused and leaned in to kiss her. She melted against him instantly. It was all he could do to remain of sound mind. He wanted to be with her more than he'd wanted anything in his life— but not tonight, not when both of them were exhausted from their day in the city and more than a little tipsy.

"I'm not sure I've ever had more fun with anyone, Kenna. Now..." Pulling away while he still had the wits to do so, he turned to insert the key into the lock. "I must bid you goodnight the moment we step inside. Otherwise, I'll ask you to come to bed with me."

He expected her to reprimand him. Instead, as they stepped

inside, she took his hand and led him over to the couch where his bed was all set up.

"I doona mean to offend ye, Mac, but even if I did join ye here this evening, I believe ye would be asleep before ye could undress me."

Perhaps she was right. His lids did feel very heavy. Gently, she guided him down to the couch, pushing his shoulders back until he was lying down. She moved to pull off his shoes. He didn't want to fall asleep until she was gone. He wanted to see her every moment he could.

"Kenna, what surprised you most about today?"

Setting his shoes next to the couch, she moved to sit next to him, gently brushing the hair from his face as she leaned in to gently kiss him goodnight. After a quick peck on his lips, she stood and answered him as she made her way upstairs.

"Besides learning that ye canna hold yer whisky, ye mean? I think perhaps 'twas Edinburgh Castle. It truly hasna changed all that much in the last three hundred some odd years."

By the time her words made their way through his whisky-doused brain and he realized the oddity of them, she was gone.

He fell asleep dreaming of the castle and what Kenna could've possibly meant by such a strange statement.

CHAPTER 14

*S*everal nights of sleep deprivation and a day filled with a flurry of activity seemed to have caught up with Malcolm when I woke the next morning. I slept pretty late myself and took my time getting ready before wandering downstairs. When I finally did make my way downstairs, Malcolm still slept soundly on the couch, despite the noise from Kraig, Emilia, and little Robbie in the kitchen.

It made me feel better to see him sleeping. The foolish mistake I'd made came to me in the middle of the night, causing me to sit up in bed in such a panic that it had taken well over an hour for me to calm myself and go back to sleep. My last words to Malcolm before going to bed—while clearly a result of too much whisky—could've been disastrous had he not been so altered by drink himself. The fact that he still slept gave me some hope that he wouldn't remember my words when he did wake.

"Good morning, Kenna. Ye look better than I expected ye to. I doona believe I'll be able to say the same for Mac when he wakes."

I gratefully took the cup of tea Emilia extended in my direction and moved to sit by Robbie who was strapped into the most ingenious invention—a seat and a table in one that kept him upright and able to sit at the kitchen table with everyone else without being held.

"I believe ye are right. The poor man doesna drink often, 'twas plain to see." I paused as I reached out to take little Robbie's hand, smiling as his chubby fingers wrapped around mine. "Why, Robbie looks fine and happy this morning in his...his..." I stalled on purpose, hoping that Emilia would simply believe that I'd forgotten the word and would answer my question that way. She didn't disappoint me.

"His highchair."

"Aye, highchair. The word slipped my mind for a moment."

She laughed and set a plate of breakfast down in front of me. "Whisky will do that to ye. Did the two of ye have a good time yesterday?"

I waited until she and Kraig were both seated with their food before I began to eat.

"Aye, there wasna a single activity that I dinna love. He couldna have planned a better day out."

"I'm so glad the two of ye had a good time. I canna remember the last time Kraig and I had a day out just the two of us. I wouldna trade Robbie for the world, but he has changed my life in every way. Sometimes, I canna remember the woman that I was before him."

Emilia sighed in a dreamy way that caused me to really study her for the first time. While fatigue couldn't fade the young woman's beauty, the sleep deprivation that comes to any parent of a small child had left its mark. Small bags hung under her eyes. I doubted she'd taken any time for herself in months.

I had an idea, although I knew I couldn't manage it by myself. "Emilia, do ye have a phone I could borrow and perhaps a computer I could use? I'd like to check on some things and call my grandson."

I only knew what a computer was from seeing it at Morna's and only knew how to operate a phone because of the detailed instructions Cooper had given me before I left, including the number to Morna's so I could reach him.

Emilia stood without hesitation, and I momentarily regretted interrupting her meal.

"O'course. I'm sure the lad will be glad to hear from ye. Follow me into Kraig's office. 'Tis just off the kitchen. There is a phone in there, and ye can use the computer for whatever ye like. Ye can even bring yer breakfast with ye if ye wish. Kraig eats in there all the time."

Lifting my plate with one hand and holding my tea with the other, I followed her, the surprise taking form in my mind as we went.

"*F*or the love of God, Emilia, please tell me you have some aspirin."

Squinting, Malcolm trudged into the kitchen. He couldn't remember the last time he'd slept so late or felt so rotten.

"Look there."

His gaze traveled to the place on the table where his sister-in-law pointed.

"I've already set some aspirin next to yer breakfast. Along with some coffee and a secret mixture that will taste awful but will have ye feeling just like yerself by lunch."

Malcolm sat at the table, popped the painkillers, and looked squeamishly at the glass of gray liquid sitting next to his coffee.

"What's in it?"

"Dinna ye hear what I said? 'Tis a secret. Just drink it. I promise, ye will be glad ye did."

Pinching his nose to keep from smelling the vile concoction, he chugged it in two swift gulps. As soon as it was down, he reached for his coffee and drank. He didn't care if it was hot enough to burn him, he needed the taste of the previous liquid out of his mouth immediately.

"That was the worst thing I've ever tasted. Where's Kenna? Did you make her drink that?"

Emilia laughed and leaned against the kitchen island.

"Kenna dinna need it. And she's in Kraig's office. She said she wished to call her grandson and needed to take care of a few things on the computer."

Hoping that Kenna would still be on the phone and that perhaps he would be able to say hello to Rosie, Malcolm scarfed down his food and stood to head to the office.

He knocked lightly, but when there was no answer he stepped quietly inside, standing back while Kenna spoke.

"What is the name of the place that Jane always says she misses, Cooper?"

There was a short pause, and then Kenna answered the boy, excitement in her voice.

"Aye, a spa. And how do I find and plan a spa?"

Another short pause as Malcolm watched on in amazement. Could she really not know about all of the things Cooper was explaining to her?

"What is a 'google'? Can I call this google? Oh...I must type it on the computer."

He continued to watch with amusement as Kenna typed one finger at a time on the keyboard.

"Cooper, if I arrange this, should I just give Emilia the cash to pay for it?"

Malcolm could barely hear the boy's voice, but it was just mumbling from so far away.

"Oh, I see. I need one of those credit cards. I doona have one."

He couldn't keep quiet any longer. She was clearly struggling, and he could see by the way she held one hand up to the side of her face that overwhelm was setting in. With the mention of a credit card, he saw his opening.

"I have one. What is it that you're trying to do, Kenna?"

Turning toward him, Kenna smiled. The relief on her face was evident.

"Ah, Cooper, never mind, lad. Mac is awake now. I believe I can get him to help me."

Now that he stood right next to her, he could hear the boy clearly.

"Oh, good. I was about to have to hand the phone to Morna. You were getting into stuff I don't know anything about."

Kenna laughed and held the phone away from her so he could hear better.

"Aye, well ye needn't bother Morna now. Are ye having a good time, Cooper? How is Rosie doing?"

"Oh, I'm having the best time, though I still haven't been able to get Rosie to warm to me. Not to worry though, she'll crack eventually. And Rosie's having a good time, too, I think. She and Morna have been spending so much time in the kitchen baking up all sorts of yummy goodies. I think by the time you and Malcolm get back, Jerry might be as fat as Santa Claus."

Malcolm always loved the way Kenna laughed, but when laughing in response to her grandson, there was a special joy in her voice that caused his heart to skip just a little. He knew the kind of love she felt when speaking to him. The love of a grandparent for a grandchild surpassed anything he'd felt in his life.

"I'm so glad, Cooper. Is Rosie around? I'm sure Mac would like to speak to her."

"Actually..." Cooper's voice sounded regretful. "She and Morna went into town to get some more baking stuff. There's no telling what they will make next."

Malcolm lowered his head and spoke into the phone to calm Cooper's worries.

"It's okay, Cooper, I'm sure Rosie is enjoying having some space away from me for a bit. I'll see her tomorrow when we return."

"Sounds good. I miss both of you guys. Good luck planning your surprise."

Malcolm waited to speak again until Kenna said her goodbyes and hung up the phone.

"So...what is it you are trying to do? Why would you need to give Emilia cash?"

Malcolm listened to Kenna intently. As she laid out her plan to give Kraig and Emilia a day and evening away, he knew that what he'd been trying to silence inside of himself for the better part of two days was true. He was in love with Kenna McMillan. He might not know her well, but he knew enough. She was kind, funny, and thoughtful. She loved her grandson deeply and said whatever was on her mind. He knew what he'd told her before, but it was no longer true. He was fairly certain that it hadn't been true then. He wouldn't be able to let her go tomorrow. He wasn't sure that he would ever be able to.

"Did ye...did ye hear me? Ye doona look as if ye heard a word I said. Will ye help me? Do ye mind if we stay here this evening and watch the babe for them?"

Shaking himself from his thoughts, he smiled and bent to kiss her.

"I heard every word. Of course, I'll help you. I can't think of anything else Emilia would want more this Christmas. Scoot over. I'll get everything set while you go and tell them to pack a bag for the night."

Kenna stood without a word and all but skipped away from him in excitement.

He called out to her just before she left the room.

"And Kenna...don't let Emilia turn this offer down. She will try to."

"Oh, doona ye worry about that, Malcolm. I always get my way. I doona know what 'tis exactly, but people have always had a difficult time telling me no."

He knew precisely what it was. The woman contained magic, surely, and he was entirely under her spell.

CHAPTER 15

$\mathcal{W}$hile I hadn't noticed the black dress until after I arrived in the twenty-first century—for I surely would've had Adelle remove it immediately if I had—I was grateful it was there as I readied myself for the evening while Malcolm worked at preparing dinner for the two of us in the kitchen.

I felt naked in the dress with the bottom hem hitting just at my knees. I'd never worn anything that showed so much of my legs. And the cut at the top was even more scandalous. I was now showing even more than I'd revealed to Malcolm the day my blouse had burst open during my nap. Still, I thought I looked quite beautiful in the dress. I hoped Malcolm would think so, too.

If I didn't wake with the dewy skin Adelle was so sure I needed after wearing this tonight, there was nothing that would get Malcolm to sleep with me.

Slipping on the pair of heels, which were another twenty-first century invention I could see no sense in, I reached for the lipstick I'd yet to wear and carefully applied it before heading downstairs.

I spent the better part of two hours feeding, changing, and bouncing the child before he finally fell asleep. I very much hoped he would at least give us a handful of hours of alone time before he woke up in need of some attention.

"Kenna..." Malcolm's tone was nearly breathless. "You are the most beautiful woman I've ever seen."

I felt almost ill at how quickly my body warmed in response to his words. He looked rather handsome himself, though he wasn't dressed up as I was.

"That canna be true, but I'll accept the compliment. Thank ye. What are ye making?"

"Braised beef in a cherry sauce with crisped onions and asparagus. It's the only dish I know how to make well."

"I'm sure 'twill be delicious."

I walked over to wrap my arms around him, but he quickly stepped out of my way.

"It's nearly ready. Let me step into the bathroom and change. You look so nice. I don't want to look like a slob next to you."

I grabbed his hand and pulled him back toward me.

"No, doona change. No one will see us. I only wore this for ye and I think ye look handsome dressed just as ye are."

His response was immediate. A low, guttural noise escaped from deep within his throat. Pulling me against him, he kissed me greedily, allowing his hands to roam my body in a way he never had before.

I gasped and moaned in response, pressing one of my breasts into his palm as his hand slipped down my chest while his other hand roamed down to cup my bottom.

"Mom?"

Thinking that I'd just found the fault in him I'd been waiting for, I stilled and pulled away. I should've realized by the inflection in his tone, but it took me far too long to catch on.

"Malcolm, while I am a mother, I am not yer mother and the thought of ye referring to me as 'Mom' makes my skin crawl all over. Perhaps we should cease this and just eat."

Malcolm's expression looked horrified.

"God, no, Kenna. I would sooner die than call you Mom. It's my actual mother. She's here."

An unsettling mixture of relief and embarrassment rushed over me as I turned to see an astonishingly beautiful elderly woman standing no more than ten steps from us. As I locked eyes with her, she lifted her hand and waved before giving me the biggest smile I'd ever seen in my life.

CHAPTER 16

"*E*xcuse me. I believe I hear Robbie upstairs. I best go and check on him."

Malcolm waited until Kenna was out of view to address his mother. The moment he turned toward her, his mother pursed her lips guiltily.

"I am so sorry, Malcolm. Kraig told me that you had a lady friend here tonight, but it truly never crossed my mind that she was anything more than a friend."

He'd known that Kenna was bound to meet his mother sometime during her stay in Edinburgh. He only wished his mother's timing was better.

"Why would you assume that?"

She lifted her eyebrows and looked up at him knowingly.

"Well, it's been a very long time, son. Forgive me if that isn't where my mind went right away. I am sorry for intruding though. If there's anything I can do to make it up to you, just say the word."

As if on cue, Robbie let out a bloodcurdling scream that reverberated down the stairway. He didn't even have to ask the question before his mother stood and brushed off her lap.

"Absolutely. It's been months since Emilia has allowed me to take Robbie overnight. I believe she feels guilty asking me because she knows that I raised babies much later in life than most. As if that is her fault, of all things. I'll go and take the child from Kenna now. Start cleaning the kitchen. It will increase your chances greatly. Nothing turns a woman on more than the sight of a man doing dishes."

Thankful that his mother's shocking remarks had lost their effect on him ages ago, he did as instructed. He loved his mother, but he'd never been so ready for her to be out of his sight.

I'd rocked and bounced my fair share of babies, but never had I seen one so upset. Robbie screamed endlessly. With each new wail, I knew my hopes for what this night could be were now squandered.

"There is nothing wrong with his lungs, is there?"

I half-smiled, half-grimaced as Malcolm's mother, Nel, stepped into the nursery and closed the door behind her.

"Aye, I doona believe the wee lad is accustomed to being away from his mother."

"Oh no, not at all. It won't last forever, of course. I think it's something that most first-time mothers go through, but Emilia rarely wants to be separated from him for more than a few hours. The fact that she agreed to let you and Malcolm watch him overnight is proof of just how exhausted she must be."

"I've not heard her complain once since I've been here, but aye, I do believe fatigue was beginning to take its toll."

I stood from my seat and cradled the baby as I began to swing him side to side. Slowly, his wails began to subside.

"How many grandchildren do you have?"

I couldn't help but smile when thinking about each and every one of them.

"Five."

"And how many children do you have?"

"Three." The sharp, familiar pang that always coursed through me at the thought of Niall ran its way up and down my body. "But one of my sons passed away a few years ago."

Nel's expression was immediately sympathetic. "I'm so sorry."

She glanced down in the way that people often did at hearing such news and shifted from foot to foot for a moment as she looked for a way to transition to a more pleasant conversation. Eventually, she spoke again.

"I am sorry for interrupting your evening. To make up for the intrusion, I've decided to take Robbie with me back to my place across the street. I believe you two probably need some alone time."

The embarrassment I felt at knowing that Malcolm's mother knew what we were up to caused me to immediately regret every instant I'd been so straightforward about such matters with my own sons' significant others. I was always so blunt with them—it couldn't have been very comfortable for them to hear me speak of such things. I certainly wasn't comfortable now.

I fumbled over my words as I tried to respond to her.

"Oh...um...that 'tisn't necessary. Truly."

She reached forward and pulled Robbie from my arms, sending him into a fit of screams, once again.

"I believe it is. Kenna, it was wonderful to meet you. I haven't seen my son so happy in a very long time. Please don't hurt him."

My heart squeezed familiarly in response to her plea. I knew precisely what it felt like to worry over the well being of a child's heart.

"I doona wish to hurt him." I paused, unsure of why I felt compelled to explain anything to her. "But, we are from verra different worlds. I'm not sure there is anything either of us can do about that."

"There is always something to be done. You only have to decide whether or not you want to put forth the effort."

Turning before I could respond, she fled the room, leaving me to think on all she'd said.

I wanted to be with Malcolm this night—I wouldn't deny myself that—but deep down I knew sleeping with him could only have two possible results. Tomorrow I would either wake happy and full of clarity, or I would wake utterly and completely miserable with confusion.

CHAPTER 17

I took my time before joining Malcolm downstairs. I needed a few moments to reset my mood—to open myself up to the possibility of intimacy once again. After taking a quick glance in the mirror, I nervously made my way to the staircase. Malcolm stood in the living room, in front of the fireplace as he stoked away at the logs he'd just added to the fire.

"I wasn't sure at first, but it turns out her surprise visit wasn't such a terrible thing after all, was it?"

He must've heard my footsteps for he didn't turn and look at me as I approached. Hesitantly, I wrapped my arms around him from behind and pressed myself against him for warmth.

He sighed, hung the fire poker back on its hook, and turned into me, winding his hands through my hair as he did so.

"It must be near morning now. It felt as if she was here forever."

Laughing, I leaned back to bare my neck to him as he bent to kiss it.

"I doona believe she even stayed an hour. We still have the whole night."

Malcolm ceased his soft touches up and down my neck as he pulled away and regarded me sternly.

"Thank God for that. For, Kenna, I plan to spend the rest of the night exploring and tasting every last inch of you. That is..." He hesitated, and I didn't miss how his lower lip trembled just slightly. "If you'll allow me."

I wanted to be with him in every way that I possibly could.

Smiling, I nodded and reached for the collar of his shirt.

"I want ye to make love to me, Malcolm. Over and over again until I am too blissfully weary to do anything other than sleep."

In answer, he gently spun me away from him, and gently pulled down the zipper at the back of my dress. It hung loosely at my shoulders, and he moved his lips to my cheek kissing it softly before dragging his tongue down the arch of my neck. I shivered at the sensation as his hands slipped through the opening in the back of my dress, sliding against my bare skin.

I gasped as his hands cupped my breasts. When he moved to gently tug at my nipple with his fingers, I moaned and leaned into him.

He shifted and my dress began to slip. Instinctively, my arms jerked upward to prevent its fall.

"Wait."

Malcolm stilled immediately, quickly withdrawing his hands before stepping away from me.

"What is it? Do you want me to stop?"

With arms crossed over my front to keep the dress up, I faced him.

"No. The verra last thing I want ye to do is stop. 'Tis only that I'm frightened, Mac. I havena...'tis been a verra long time since anyone saw me naked."

Relief washed over Malcolm's face as he smiled and stepped close to me, wrapping his arms around me in an embrace that helped to melt away my fears.

"Come here, Kenna."

He turned and walked to the couch, leaving me to follow him as I continued to cling to the front of my dress.

Once I was seated next to him, he placed his hands on the sides of my face and kissed me until I was warm and tingling all over. When he pulled away, his voice was strained with need. "I don't think any man enjoys vulnerability, Kenna, but for you I will lay myself bare. I am frightened, too. So frightened that if I weren't pressing my legs into the ground right this second, I'm afraid my legs might tremble. It's been a very long time for both of us. There is no need for us to rush tonight. I will take as much time as you wish me to."

Knowing that I wasn't alone in my nerves was all I needed to hear. Rising, I allowed the dress to fall down to my waist as I crawled into his lap and began to kiss him.

True to his word, and ever the gentleman, he did take his time, undressing himself before pulling the dress off me completely and laying me backwards on the makeshift bed. We explored and tasted one another slowly. When we finally did come together, it was all I could do to keep from weeping at the pleasure that rolled over and through me as we rocked together in unison.

I'd heard whisperings of what lovemaking could be between a man and a woman—the feelings one could experience when two people came together as one.

Until now, I'd never experienced it for myself.

I would never, ever be the same.

---

*T*horoughly sated, deliriously happy, and now rather hungry, Malcolm sat across from Kenna by the fire where they both sat draped in sheets as they munched on a bag of microwave popcorn and sipped on glasses of wine. While he didn't believe that either of them had ever held much back from another, their shared intimacy had opened them both up in a way that had them sharing with each other like never before. He could scarcely believe his ears now.

"You can't be serious. Ever?"

Kenna smiled, laughed, and popped a handful of kernels in her mouth. He loved that she didn't wait to finish eating to answer him. She spoke as she munched, and it made him feel even closer to her.

"Aye, I am verra serious. I always knew it was supposed to be possible, but my late husband was never overly concerned with how pleasurable the experience might be for me. Sex was for creating our children, little more."

Malcolm shook his head in disbelief. What sort of a fool could show her such little care?

"The man sounds like a damned moron."

Kenna reached for a log behind her and tossed it into the fire as she laughed.

"I'll not speak ill of my sons' father, but I willna disagree with ye, either. Do ye know, Malcolm, thinking on the young girl I'd once been, I believe I know the sort of man I would've chosen for myself had I been given the choice. I believe it would've been someone like ye—someone who knew how to show strength and gentleness in equal measure, someone who showed kindness in all things, and who knew how to laugh. Someone who made me feel wanted."

He was certain he'd never been given such a kind compliment. He hardly saw himself in such a good light.

"I wish I had known you then, Kenna. Or, at the very least, I wish I'd met you ten years ago, when we were both far enough past the loss of our spouses to be open to new love. It would've given us so much more time than we can ever have now."

A sadness crossed Kenna's face, and the melancholy feeling quickly spread through Malcolm, as well.

"Kenna..." He paused, not wanting to ruin the evening but knowing they couldn't avoid the conversation forever. "Did you mean what you told me before? Do you really intend for this to end when I drop you off at Morna and Jerry's tomorrow?"

She scooted near him and leaned into his chest.

"I doona want it to be over, but I must see first. There is someone I must speak to, to see what might be possible."

Who besides the two of them would need to have any say in how things progressed? Malcolm couldn't imagine, but he knew better than to question her too much.

"I want you to know, Kenna, I will want you for as long as you want me. Whatever happens from here on out is entirely up to you."

And he meant it. If she would have him, he was hers. He would do anything he needed to do to make it work.

He only hoped she would give him the chance.

CHAPTER 18

The drive from Edinburgh to Morna and Jerry's the next morning was an awkward one. We were both exhausted, and the great joy of the night before seemed to put a damper on our feelings of today. Neither of us knew for sure where our relationship would go from here and the uncertainty had us both out of sorts.

I'd already decided that I wanted Malcolm in my life for much longer than the end of today, but until I spoke with Morna, I couldn't know for sure if my hopes were foolish. How many families could Morna safely expose her magic to? Our relationship would put her most at risk. I would say nothing to Malcolm until I spoke to her.

I rode for the first hour thinking about all of the possibilities— all of the ways Morna might respond to my request. Thankfully, Malcolm eventually spoke, breaking the silence and providing me with a distraction from my nervous thoughts.

"Kenna, do you remember how when we got to Edinburgh, you mentioned that you could arrange a tour of McMillan Castle for Rosie and me?"

I'd forgotten, but I'd most assuredly meant every word. Kamden and Harper would both be thrilled to show them around.

"Aye, were ye thinking about taking Rosie there on yer way back? 'Tis out of the way, but 'tis worth the trip."

He smiled at me and reached over to squeeze my hand. The simple contact seemed to ease the tension inside the car—as if his touch broke through an invisible barrier between us.

"Yes, that's what I was thinking. I know she won't be happy to leave. I hoped that if I could tempt her with the promise of something I know she's wanted to see for a while, she might make it a little easier on me."

"Aye, I think it could be just the thing to make leaving easier for her. I'll call them as soon as we get to Morna's."

"Thank you." He lifted my left hand and kissed it. I leaned toward him as much as the barrier in between our seats would allow.

"'Tis no trouble at all."

"Kenna..." He paused the way he often did before asking me a question. It seemed to be a habit of his. I found it rather endearing.

"Aye?"

"There's a question that has been on my mind since the first night I met you, but there hasn't really been an appropriate time to ask it. I'm afraid it will make you sad, but I'd very much like to know."

He had to know that after such a statement, any female would be too curious to discourage whatever his question might be. Whatever could he ask me that would make me sad?

"Being sad shall hardly kill me. Ask whatever 'tis."

"That first night we met, when I thanked you for not showing me pity, you said you'd experienced your own share of grief. I know you lost your husband, but after all you've said of him, I think you must've meant something more."

Knowing that I intended to share more of my life with him meant that I wanted him to truly know me—to know and understand my wounds as well as my joys.

"Aye, I did. The grief I referred to...a few years ago I lost a son."

I'd never spoken of Niall to anyone outside of my family, and I hardly knew how to do so now.

"My son wasna a good man. He had an evil in him that I was blind to for far too long. While I refuse to take responsibility for his actions, I do sometimes wonder." My voice caught as the inevitable lump rose in the back of my throat. Turning away, I allowed the tears to fall as I continued. "I...I sometimes wonder if I had I seen who he really was sooner, perhaps I could have done something to prevent everything that happened."

Without a word, the car slowed as Malcolm pulled to a stop on the side of the road. He waited until I faced him to speak.

"I will show you the same courtesy that you showed me. I will give you no pity, but I don't believe this is the sort of discussion one should have while driving. I want you to know that I hear you and that I recognize the strength it must've taken for you to get through something so horrible. I am sorry, Kenna. You only have to tell me what you wish to."

It was right of him to recognize that I would be as reluctant to someone's pity as he was, and I appreciated the space he created for me to tell him the story. I did so for the better part of an hour. Sobbing, I told him things that I didn't even know I needed to say out loud—things I could never say to my family, for they were too intimately connected to all that had happened. Having someone outside of the situation made it so much easier.

"I think what pains me the most is the undeniable truth that I still love him. I shouldna love such a monster. But even years since his passing, even knowing that he murdered my first daughter-in-law, knowing that he murdered my sister and tried to kill his brother and me, I still love him fiercely. 'Tis why it took me so long to see the truth—we mothers always believe the best of our children. Perhaps, 'tis what it means to be a mother—no matter the joy it can bring, it can also be the most painful thing in the world."

Malcolm had tears in his eyes, too, but not tears of pity—his gaze made that clear. They were the tears of empathy. While one separates, the other binds. I'd not thought it possible for me to feel closer to him than I had last night, but in some way this story was even more personal than sharing my body with him. I'd never felt so close to anyone.

"Of course you still love him. Love, once truly given, doesn't ever go away. And there is no truer love than that of a parent for their child."

He brushed the hair from my face and stroked my cheek as I drew in shaky breaths.

I knew I needed no one's permission to love Niall, but just hearing Malcolm acknowledge that it was okay made me feel so much less alone. I felt free for the first time in years, as if some poison within me had finally been flushed away.

"I've never cried in front of anyone the way I just cried in front of ye, but now I'm quite ready to stop. Do ye know any good jokes, Malcolm?"

He chuckled just a little and raised his brows mischievously.

"Not a one, but I think I know of something that might put a smile back on that beautiful face of yours."

I was open to anything.

"What?"

He grinned and reached to open the door on his side of the car.

"Get out for a minute. I'll show you."

No sooner did I step out of the vehicle than I was smacked directly in the middle of my chest with a giant snowball.

Chaos ensued as we played and wrestled in a giant field of snow just off the road in the middle of nowhere.

We arrived at Morna and Jerry's two hours later than expected, soaked through, looking utterly a mess, and blissfully happy by each other's side.

CHAPTER 19

Our late arrival at the inn changed everyone's plans—not that anyone minded. Rather than head to McMillan Castle for their tour today, Malcolm and Rosie would leave tomorrow. The extra time together gave me hope that I would be able to speak with Morna before they left, and one way or another I would be able to tell Malcolm how things could move forward.

While the days spent together had made Cooper tolerable to Rosie, it was evident that it would still take much convincing for her to consider him a friend. Ever the determined young lad, Cooper wasn't worried in the least.

"Nana, I think I'm in love."

"Really?" Smiling at him as he entered my room, I patted the bed so he would come and sit down. I'd just finished drying my hair from the snow fight and was carefully applying just a little bit of make-up so I would look presentable for dinner. "What makes you think so?"

"Do you remember when Dad was falling in love with Kathleen?"

I nodded, laid the lipstick down, and faced my grandson.

"Aye."

"He was so grumpy and strange, but he still wanted to be around her. That's how I feel now, Nana. I shouldn't want to be around someone that dislikes me so much, but..." he held up both palms and shrugged as he shook his head, "for some reason, I kinda like it that she's so mean to me."

Laughing, I moved to pull him into a hug.

"'Tis something I will never understand, but it seems to be common amongst men, Cooper. Perhaps, ye are right. Ye may have gotten yer first taste of love."

He pulled away and grinned up at me with excited eyes.

"Should I tell her?"

Panic ran through me as I dropped to my knees to discourage him.

"Ach, no lad, I wouldna do that if I were ye. I doona think Rosie would take to it well, and while those first feelings of love can be verra powerful and they come on verra fast, they also often pass just as quickly."

Thankfully, Cooper didn't seem bothered by my dissuasion. He nodded as if he understood and moved toward the doorway.

"Okay, good thinkin', Nana. I'll wait."

"Good, I truly think that best, Cooper. Are ye headed downstairs?"

He nodded and reached for the doorknob.

"If Morna isna busy, will you ask her to come up here? I'd really like to speak to her."

"Sure thing, Nana. She's not busy. She's just watching Rosie cook. She's gonna make the whole thing by herself tonight."

There was such admiration in Cooper's voice when he spoke of Rosie. There was no question—my grandson had found his very first crush.

———

*T*he smells coming from the kitchen were wonderful. Situating his bag next to his pallet on the living room floor, a freshly showered and dry Malcolm called out to Morna to see if he could offer some help.

"Morna, that smells fantastic. Is there anything I can do to help you?"

Rosie's voice answered him.

"It's me, Pops. Morna's not in here."

He stepped into the kitchen to see his granddaughter smiling the first true smile he'd seen on her since arriving in Scotland. Standing proud in front of the stove, she wore an apron that hung just a little too long. It didn't matter that she had to stand on her tiptoes to look down at the food, she appeared to know exactly what she was doing.

"Are you making all of this yourself?"

She reached for a spoon, dipped it into the pot she worked over, then carefully balanced it over her hand as she walked over to him.

"Yes. Morna watched me for a little while just to make sure I didn't have any questions, but when she saw I had it mastered, she went to go see Kenna. She's letting me do everything on my own tonight. Here, taste it."

Taking a brief second to blow on the stew, he placed the spoonful in his mouth.

"It's delicious."

Rosie regarded him skeptically.

"Really? You don't have to lie to me."

"Really, Rosie. It's wonderful. I can't believe you learned so much in just a few days."

Malcolm would be forever grateful to Morna for the way she'd turned this holiday around for his granddaughter. It seemed the old woman had known just what Rosie needed.

"Morna is a great teacher, Pops. She even taught me how to read UK recipes. They use measurements that are pretty different than how we do things back home, but it didn't take me long to get the hang of it. It actually makes more sense than what we use. Pops..." Rosie laid down the spoon and surprised him by wrapping her arms around his waist. "Thank you for letting me stay. I know I wasn't very nice to you. I'm sorry. I was just...I was just sad."

He bent to kiss the top of her head. If he loved the child any more than he already did, he worried his heart would burst from it.

"I know, kiddo. It's okay to be sad. Just a few more days and then your Mom should be here."

"I hope so, Pops. I really, really do. But even if she doesn't come, this has already been one of my favorite Christmases ever."

"Well, it sounds like you need to thank Morna for that, Rosie."

"No, Pops. It's not Morna that made this great. It was you. If you hadn't tried to cheer me up by booking that tour to Conall Castle, we would've never stayed here."

The decision had been so last minute. All he'd wanted was to get Rosie out of the house in the hopes of making her smile. How could he have possibly known that such an outing would change so much for both of them?

Even if things didn't turn out how he hoped, he would treasure his time spent with Kenna for the rest of his life.

"You know what, Rosie? This has already been one of my favorite Christmases, too."

CHAPTER 20

"*D*id ye really believe for a moment that I would say ye couldna tell him, Kenna?"

I didn't know Morna as well as many of the members of my family. While I knew she often allowed matters of the heart to direct her decisions, in my mind, it was still entirely possible that she could reject my suggestion.

"I dinna know."

Morna patted my knee in a motherly fashion.

"Lass, 'twas I who encouraged ye to see if the two of ye had something together. It pleases me more than ye know that ye do. I thought on this quite a lot while ye were in Edinburgh. As ye know, there have been many I've had to share my magic with over the years, and if one thing is for certain, 'tis rarely knowledge they accept easily. I think I know of a way that might make him more accepting."

I'd seen first hand what a difficult time Grace's sister, Jane, in particular, had with learning of time travel and the magic that surrounded pretty much all who knew Morna. If the old witch had any idea as to how to make it easier for Malcolm to accept, I would allow her to direct our next steps.

"Morna, ye have done this many more times than I. Whatever ye wish me to do, I shall do it."

"Good. Pack yer bags and tell Cooper to do the same. When Malcolm and Rosie leave in the morning, we are going to McMillan Castle with them."

"Are ye so ready to be rid of us, Morna? Ye do know that Cooper and I were meant to stay with ye for another week, aye?"

"Aye, I know 'twas the original plan, but it no longer fits with what needs to be done. Ye need to be at McMillan Castle with Malcolm. If ye and Cooper will be headed there anyway, ye may as well go home afterward."

While Cooper was normally very sympathetic to the needs of others, he wouldn't be so forgiving of anyone who shortened his time with Morna.

"I canna do that to Cooper, Morna. He's looked forward to his time here for so long."

Morna stood, quickly dismissing my concern.

"Doona worry about that, lass. Much as I loathe to admit it, I lost a bet with the lad, and my loss has caused me to do something that I've sworn more than once I wouldna do again."

I knew from experience that it was never a good idea to make bets with Cooper. He never forgave a debt, and I knew of only one thing that Morna had vocally promised to never do again.

"Ye canna mean...?"

"Aye. I hope the wee lad knows how much I love him, for he is the only one that could get me to agree to go back once again. It seems Jerry and I will be spending Christmas in the year 1651."

"Oh, Morna!" I stood and threw my arms around her as she laughed. "I've not heard such good news in a verra long time. Everyone at the castle will be so excited. We must send word to everyone—all of the relatives—and have them come stay, too. It will be a grand reunion. We are long overdue for one anyway."

Morna sniffled, and I pulled back with shock to see that she was crying.

"Well, if I shall be there anyway, then I would verra much love to see everyone."

Gripping her shoulders, I gave them a reassuring squeeze.

"Then we shall make certain that ye do. Now, tell me. Just how should I explain everything to Malcolm once we get to McMillan Castle?"

*T*he nerves I felt standing nearly naked before Malcolm were nothing compared to the nerves I felt walking into the grand room of McMillan Castle. Morna was right—it was the perfect place to tell him the truth. My likeness hung in the room, right in line with the dozens of portraits of my ancestors and the descendants that would come after me. It would be a sure way to get him curious, for the portrait looked exactly like me. Only in the McMillan Castle of today, the woman in the portrait should've been dead for hundreds of years.

While it would help raise the question in his mind, he would still believe me mad. Any sane person would. Thankfully, McMillan Castle provided quick access back to my own time where I could show him in person. Morna, Kamden, and Harper were in on the plan, too. They would keep Cooper and Rosie occupied and away from this part of the castle for the next few hours—plenty of time for me to tell him what I must and also to take a quick trip back into the past to prove that all I said was true.

After that, it would be up to him. If it turned out to be too much, he and Rosie could leave, and I would officially let go of the dream of being with Malcolm.

"Where did everyone else run off to?"

"I believe they are ice skating on the pond. Then they plan to go on a carriage ride through the grounds."

His expression was quizzical.

"Are we not joining them?"

"No, Malcolm. I need to speak with ye."

"Do you intend to put me out of my misery? Please say that you are. I don't think I can stand another moment of wondering. Rosie and I leave this afternoon. I made myself very clear to you in Edinburgh. I want you. I want to be with you, and if all continues to go as well as it has the past few days, I want to enjoy the next forty years of my life with you at my side. But I need to know, Kenna...do you want me, too? Did you find whatever answers you needed—speak to whomever you needed to speak to?"

"Aye, Malcolm." I hurried to his side, reaching up to kiss him as his nearness helped my fears fade. "I want ye. I want ye more than anything I've wanted in my entire life. And aye, I spoke to whom I needed to. But there is something I must tell ye. It may change the way ye feel about our future together."

Reassuringly, he took my hands and kissed them.

"I don't think there is anything you could tell me that would do that."

Pulling one of my hands from his grip, I pointed to my portrait behind him.

"I want ye to look at that painting, Malcolm."

He turned and stared at my likeness for a long moment before speaking.

"Wow. I knew you were a McMillan, but you're a McMillan by marriage, correct? How could a McMillan ancestor resemble you so much?"

"'Tis not an ancestor. The woman in that painting is me."

Malcolm's brows pulled together in confusion, and his mouth opened and closed several times without a word.

Just as he started to speak, his phone rang.

Instinctively, I knew the call was not good news.

cMillan Castle – December of 1651
Three Days Later

I didn't cry upon returning home to my own century. It wasn't as if Malcolm had broken my heart or disbelieved my story. In truth, I'd not given him the chance to do either of those things. Malcolm's phone call from his daughter had made the absurdity of my dream for us clear.

The lives of his daughter and granddaughter were in America. Even if he loved me—which I knew he did—he would no sooner ask them to uproot their lives than I would ask my family to uproot theirs. Even if I told him about the magic, it would bring our worlds no closer together.

"Your skin looks better, but other than that, you look worse than I've ever seen you. It's been three days, Kenna. I know that you and I aren't very close, but you have to tell someone what happened while you were away. I'm nosy enough to hound you about it even though I can see you're hurting, so it might as well be me. Now spill."

It didn't surprise me in the least that Adelle would enter my room without knocking. She wouldn't leave me alone until I told her something. I would tell her only what was absolutely true. Not a word more.

"I fell in love. As foolish as it sounds, I fell in love with a great man in a matter of only a few days, but it couldna ever work. I'll not upend his world by telling him the where and how I live when our love is doomed from the start. He's gone. Back to America with his granddaughter, which is exactly where he should be. I'll not speak of this again. 'Tis too painful, and I'll not be sad at Christmas for 'twould only spoil the season for everyone else. Please leave me, Adelle, and doona ask me anything else."

She must've recognized just how much my heart was aching, for in a move quite out of character for her, she turned and left me without another word.

I did cry then. It was well into the night before I fell asleep, my pillow soaked with tears.

Chicago

Malcolm was angry—angrier than he'd ever been. It made no sense. None of it. Just minutes after telling him that she wanted him more than anything she'd wanted in her life, Kenna ended things with a coldness that nearly knocked him over.

All he'd done was announce that he and Rosie would have to fly back to America before Christmas. It had been Madeline on the phone with the news he'd hoped wouldn't come, but expected anyway. She'd decided not to come to Edinburgh for Christmas, after all. Despite the fact that his daughter had insisted that he and Rosie stay to enjoy Christmas in Scotland, he knew in that instant what they must do. For his daughter to believe it was acceptable for her to choose not to spend Christmas with Rosie, well, that was a line he simply wouldn't allow her to cross. His daughter needed a reality check. If that meant he would have to cut their trip short to give it to her, he would gladly do so.

He never expected such an announcement to incite such a shocking reaction from Kenna. She had children—children she loved more than life itself. He'd been so certain she would understand.

Instead, even as he tried to explain to her, to tell her that while he must go back to Chicago now, he would come back to Edinburgh for the new year so they could work things out and decide best how to make their relationship work, she'd had none of it. She ended things quickly, bidding him farewell as if he were little more than a stranger.

He still couldn't wrap his mind around the fact that it was truly over. What had happened to change her mind? And what had she been about to tell him? Her nonsense about the portrait was still a mystery. It was almost as perplexing as what she'd said to him about Edinburgh Castle on the night of the whisky tasting.

There'd been so much anticipation, so much excitement, and then in seconds, it was all gone. His heart hurt in a way he didn't know was possible.

"Dad?" His daughter's voice stirred him from his thoughts as she spoke to him from the chair next to his in the living room of their home. "Where are you? It's definitely not here."

He answered her unthinkingly. "You of all people have no right to speak to me of being away."

His daughter jerked back as if he'd slapped her. "What is that supposed to mean?

While Malcolm regretted the abrupt nature of his words, such a conversation with his daughter was long overdue. While it was always best to speak when not angry, he doubted he would feel a sense of calm ever again. And what he needed to say to Madeline was too important. If she didn't wake up from her selfishness soon, her relationship with Rosie would be irreparable.

"Madeline, you know exactly what I mean. I know that losing Tim was difficult for you, and I have tried to give you the space you needed to grieve, but this has gone far beyond that. You're punishing your daughter for something that isn't her fault—you're avoiding her because she looks like him. She sees you pulling away. And as much as it breaks her heart to do so, she's pulling away from you, too. She knows that she must in order to protect herself."

Madeline's face was red and angry and tears pooled in her eyes as she answered him, her voice shaky.

"You don't know what you're talking about. I'm not punishing her. It's just...it's too hard, Dad."

His own voice rose with his anger.

"Tough. Life's hard. If you think you're the only one that has ever gone through something, then you need to pull your head out of your ass. You lost your mother when you were Rosie's age. What would it have done to you if I'd treated you the way you treat Rosie? You'd think you'd see that. It's exactly the same thing. You look just like your mother. It was hard for me, too, but I wasn't as selfish. I'm not sure I've ever known anyone as selfish as you, and I won't put up with it anymore."

"Put up with it?"

Madeline was screaming at him now, and Malcolm knew Rosie would hear them. Maybe that was okay. He wanted his granddaughter to know that he was willing to fight for her.

"Yes, Madeline. I won't put up with it."

"Put up with it?" His daughter repeated herself, the octave of her voice high and filled with venom. She was shaking all over. "This is my house, Dad. Did I ask you to move in here? No, I did not. You did it after Tim died because you insisted that I needed you.

Perhaps for a time, you were right, but I don't need you anymore. Pack your things and get out. You are no longer welcome in my home."

For the second time in the span of a week, Malcolm's world collapsed.

CHAPTER 22

hristmas Day

a knock on his hotel room door woke him just past nine in the morning, Christmas Day. He hoped to spend the day sleeping. Perhaps then, he would pass the holiday without reflecting on the fact that it was his first Christmas spent alone.

Losing Kenna was difficult enough, but being away from his granddaughter on her favorite day of the year was unbearable.

"Room service. I've got your breakfast here."

The voice was strange, oddly high for anyone old enough to be working in a hotel.

Flipping the lamp on next to the bed, he called out in answer. "I didn't order any room service. You must have the wrong room."

There was a slight pause, and then, "It...It's free on Christmas Day."

Hope coursed through Malcolm's body. It almost sounded like Rosie, but of course, that couldn't be so.

"I'm not hungry."

"Oh, come on, Pops. You're really making it hard for me to surprise you. I've been up since five waiting to come and get you, but Mom made me wait until the sun was up."

Tears filled Malcolm's eyes as he stood from the bed, threw on his sweats and a shirt and ran to the door to pull his granddaughter into a hug.

"What are you doing here?"

She squirmed until he released her.

"I already told you, Pops. Mom and I have a big surprise for you. She's in the car downstairs. You gotta hurry."

Reaching for his coat, he left his other belongings in the room. Everything that he needed was right in front of him.

---

*I*nside Madeline and Rosie's home—he was no longer sure he could call it his own—Malcolm walked into a living room filled with wrapping paper. Open packages lay sprawled out all over the floor. Only one unwrapped present remained under the tree.

"What can the surprise be? You two already did the fun part without me."

"Oh, no we didn't. This wasn't nearly as exciting as your present. Mom just let me open these so I would stop bugging her about going to get you so early."

He didn't think he'd ever seen Rosie so excited about anything.

"Ah. Well, I can't imagine what it could be. Do you want me to sit?"

"You better, Pops. Otherwise, I think you might fall over."

Madeline walked up behind him and wrapped one arm around his waist, pulling him into a hug.

"Rosie, you're going to give it away if you're not careful. Why don't you grab it and bring it over here?"

As Rosie walked to the tree, Madeline turned to look up at him.

"I'm so sorry. You were right about everything. That's the only reason I got so mad. I knew you were right even as I was screaming at you. I just couldn't stand what I'd done. I love you, Dad. "

"Oh, Madeline." He kissed the top of her head as if she were a small child. To him, she always would be. "I love you more than you will ever know. I'm sorry for how harsh I was. I should've gone about it another way."

"No, Dad. I don't think I would've been able to really hear it if you had. It was the first time in my life I think I saw you really, truly angry, and I believe it may have saved my life. It woke me from a fog I was in for far too long."

Rosie was back by their side, pulling at his arm to try to get him to the couch. "Come on, come on. You gotta open it now."

As soon as he sat down, Rosie placed the package in his lap. He carefully began to unwrap the paper. Rosie was bouncing up and down in her seat as he opened the box. As he looked down at the contents, all he could feel was confusion.

Packing tape, labels, and a business card for a Chicago realtor lay inside.

"Is this a polite way of telling me that you've found me a house of my own?"

Rosie leaned across him to shoot her mother a disapproving look.

"I told Mom that it wasn't nice to trick you that way. Lift that stuff up, there's something else underneath."

At the bottom of the box were two envelopes.

"Open the one on the left first, Dad."

Following his daughter's directive, he picked up the envelope on the left and carefully broke its seal. Pulling its contents free, he unfolded the papers, and read aloud, "Dear Mr. Kilmer, I would like to inform you that I am resigning my position at Mercy General Hospital effective January 7th."

He stopped and looked over at his daughter in bewilderment.

"Madeline, is this real or another part of the joke?"

Rosie answered. "It's real, Pops. I went with her when she delivered it. Now, open the other one. It's the best one."

His curiosity caused him to be less careful with the opening of the second letter. Turning the contents over so they would spill onto his lap, he stared at the tickets as he struggled to comprehend what all of this could mean.

"It's three one-way tickets to Scotland, Pops!"

"I see that, Rosie. You were right. I'm glad you told me to sit down. Now will the two of you please tell me what's going on before I lose my mind?"

Rosie pointed at her mother. "Take it away, Mom. This part's all you."

Twisting, Malcolm directed all of his attention to Madeline, his confusion giving way to curiosity and a glimmer of hope that frightened him more than he wished to admit.

"Come on, Madeline. What is this?"

"I didn't sleep for the first twenty-four hours after you left. I want you to know that I've thought through all of this. It isn't some knee-jerk decision. Rosie and I have discussed this extensively, and she is one hundred percent on board."

"I sure am!"

Malcolm turned to wink at Rosie before waving his hand toward Madeline so she would continue.

"Chicago has too many memories—too much pain—for all of us. We all need a fresh start. All of our family is in Scotland now anyway. It's the only place that makes sense for us to move to. Plus, I need a slower pace of life, and the job that I've been offered sounds like just the thing that will give me that."

Malcolm could scarcely believe how quickly his worst nightmare was turning into his greatest joy.

"You already have a job?"

"Yes. As you know, Emilia's mother is the director of a home health agency that oversees a large portion of Scotland. They have need of a new nurse on the Isle of Skye, and she's offered me the job. Grandma Nel has agreed to let us all live with her in Edinburgh until Rosie and I can find the perfect place."

"Just you and Rosie?"

"Yes, Dad, just me and Rosie. Skye isn't that close to Edinburgh, but it's not all that far from McMillan Castle. Rosie told me about Kenna. That's where you need to be. It's time that I learn to stand on my own two feet. You'll still be able to see us all the time."

Sadness filled him at the mention of Kenna's name.

"Kenna doesn't want me. She made that very clear."

Rosie rose from the couch and moved to stand in front of him, blocking the space between him and Madeline.

"Don't be stupid, Pops. Of course she wants you. She just got scared is all. You gave up on that *way* too easy."

Madeline's head appeared beside Rosie's as she leaned over to speak to him.

"I don't know this Kenna, but I bet Rosie is right, so here's the plan, Dad. We will enjoy Christmas Day here together. I have a breakfast casserole and some coffee cake in the oven now. Then, you'll start packing, because your flight leaves tomorrow. Rosie and I will meet you over there after the New Year. Go and get her, Dad. It's way past time for you to be happy again."

CHAPTER 23

*M*cMillan Castle – *1651*

*C*hristmas Day was over, but the celebrations at McMillan Castle would last until after New Year's Day. With Morna and Jerry visiting us in the seventeenth century, it had taken no convincing to get all of our distant family and friends from all over Scotland to join us at the castle. The Conalls—those who had remained at their home when Bri and Adelle came—made the trip over, and all of those at Cagair Castle made the journey, as well. McMillan Castle was bursting at the seams with guests, but not one person complained. We were all thrilled to spend the holidays with those we loved most in the world.

The one downside to the large number of guests, however, was that it was nearly impossible to find a single blessed moment for one's self. I was a woman who required solitude more than just about anything. It was why my early morning hours were so precious. Even those were no longer possible—guests were staying in the room in which I always lit my morning fires.

The day after Christmas, in the late afternoon while all of the children were occupied or sleeping and their parents were outside enjoying a sleigh ride around the castle grounds, I saw my opportunity to escape to my bedchamber for just a little while.

I'd looked forward to the quiet all day, but rather than finding my room empty, I stepped inside to see what could only possibly be a ghost or a delusion.

Malcolm, dressed in clothing not suited to this time, stood a few arm lengths away.

"Wha...How?"

I stuttered as he faced me.

"Morna led me to your room. Kenna, this has been one of the longest days of my life. My head aches, and it isn't just from the time travel. Please get over here and kiss me so I will know I wasn't a fool to come all this way for you."

I nearly fell over from the shock of seeing him here. Even as I crossed the short distance between us and allowed him to take me in his arms, I couldn't make sense of it. I allowed the kiss to go on until he pulled away.

"Is this why you panicked, Kenna? You didn't want to tell me about all of this?"

I answered with my arms still wrapped around him and my face pressed against his chest. I didn't want to be away from him ever again.

"I did want to tell ye. I tried to the day ye left. 'Tis only that when yer daughter called, I knew if I told ye, 'twould be the most selfish thing I could ever do. I couldna bring myself to do it. Yer family is in America, Malcolm, and I wouldna ever ask ye to leave them. And no matter how much I love ye, ye must know that I canna ever leave my family, either. 'Tis more than just distance that separates us—time does as well."

Malcolm's hands found their way to my shoulders as he pulled me away from him so he could look straight at me.

"Do you love me, Kenna?"

The question surprised me. I thought we'd both made that abundantly clear in Edinburgh.

"Ye know that I do."

"I suspected, I hoped, but I don't believe you've ever said the words before now."

Moving my hands to his face, I stood on my tiptoes and kissed him once more.

"Well, let there be no question about it. I love ye, Malcolm, and I always shall."

Stepping away from him, reality began to set in once more.

"And while I canna tell ye just how glad I am that ye are here and that ye know of Morna's magic, it solves nothing between us. What is it that ye are doing back in Scotland, and how did ye come to know all that ye do? Ye must feel verra out of sorts."

Malcolm laughed and moved to sit on the end of the bed. He looked beyond weary. I knew how exhausting the time travel could be, and I'd not experienced it the first time just seconds after learning that something I always thought impossible was very much real. Once he did fall asleep tonight, I expected he would sleep for a whole day, at least.

"I'm not sure that describes the half of it. The flight from Chicago was bad enough. My long legs are not made for eight hours on today's airplanes, and the moment I landed, I rented a car and made the long drive to McMillan Castle. I was so ready to see you, Kenna. But then I arrived only to be told that you weren't there."

"Was it Kamden and Harper that told ye the truth?"

"Yes, and I believe I owe them both an apology. I lost my patience with them. I thought they were simply making an excuse for you. I didn't believe a word until they all but forced me into the tower. Once you actually make the travel, it's rather hard to continue denying it. Kenna, how is this possible?"

I shrugged. There were so many things in life that seemed rather impossible to me.

"I doona know, but 'tis the reality of our lives around here, and if ye wish to be with me, 'twill be one of yers, as well. Do ye wish that ye dinna know?"

He still looked rather dazed. It would take days for him to fully adapt to his new perception of reality, but I was still relieved when he shook his head.

"Not at all. It explains a lot actually—your reaction to my credit card, your fascination with the lights at the symphony. Many things are beginning to click into place. I can't believe I'm in love with someone who was born over three hundred years before I was."

I didn't like the way that sounded at all.

"For the love o'God, Malcolm, doona ever say that again. Ye are older than me, in truth. Doona ye ever forget that."

He laughed then gripped his head.

"Doona worry. We do have some modern medicines here that should help that." I hesitated, but I knew that no matter how much I didn't want to hear his answer, it was a question that had to be asked. "Malcolm, what about yer family?"

"That's the thing, Kenna. It's not the issue you think it is. We're moving to Scotland—all of us. I'm already here, and Madeline and Rosie are coming just after the New Year. They will be living on Skye, which isn't all that far from here, so even with this strange business of time travel, we should be able to see them often. There's only one problem."

"Oh?" If we could be together and still be with our families, there was no other problem that was insurmountable. "What might that be?"

He stood and began to pace nervously in front of me.

"Kenna, I had a very different idea of what I was going to ask you this morning, but now after knowing what I do, I'm not sure it would be appropriate. Will you stand for a minute?"

Completely confused, I did as he asked. The moment he dropped to one knee, I jumped away from him in horror.

"Malcolm, what are ye doing? Stand up this instant."

Brows furrowed, he stood and gripped onto my bedpost for support.

"You...you don't want to marry me?"

I was suddenly getting a headache, as well. I pinched the bridge of my nose as I answered him.

"No. I love ye, Malcolm, but no. Not yet anyway. Why would ye ask that now?"

An expression I'd never seen on him before—one of pure embarrassment—crossed his face. He quickly looked down at the floor to avoid my gaze.

"I...you're right. I wasn't thinking. What I was going to ask you, what I planned to tell you before I learned that you were from the seventeenth century, was that I am currently rather homeless. I was going to ask if I could live with you for a little while. But then..." He started pacing again. "Then, when I learned that you were from the seventeenth century, I got to thinking, and it would hardly be appropriate here, would it?"

Laughing, I walked over and grabbed his hands so he would cease his wandering.

"Malcolm, there is nothing about my family that is customary or appropriate for the times. Even if it were, I've never given much concern to anyone else's opinion of how I live my life. Ye are welcome to live here as long as ye promise not to ask me to marry ye for at least another six months. And even then, I canna promise ye that I will say aye. I might find that living in sin is preferable."

His lips found mine quickly, and his aching head didn't prevent him from loving me in a way that made our night in Edinburgh seem only mediocre. If it was true that some things only got better with age, I couldn't imagine the sort of pleasure we would be able to find with one another in a decade.

It was the happiest holiday season of my whole life.

ne Year Later
Edinburgh – Present Day

ix months to the day that Malcolm arrived in the seventeenth century, he risked rejection once again by dropping to one knee. Much to his excitement and everlasting relief, I gave him the answer he hoped for. I very much wanted to be his wife.

We wed in the prettiest little chapel either of us had ever seen, right in the center of Edinburgh. I wore a simple gold gown and Malcolm wore slacks and the sweater I first saw him in. It was intimate, with only those who knew us during our time in Edinburgh in attendance. Cooper stood at my side, while Madeline and Rosie stood at his. Morna, Jerry, Kraig, Emilia, Nel, and the toddler-terror, Robbie, watched on.

It was perfect.

At a certain age, I'd stopped hoping for much more than I had.

But there is so much more magic in the world than we can see.

Sometimes, life can surprise you in the very best possible way.

LOVE BEYOND WORDS

BOOK 9 OF MORNA'S LEGACY SERIES

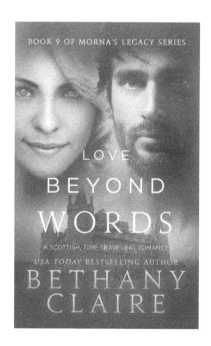

CHAPTER 1

*B*oston, Massachusetts—*Present Day*

"*Y*ou're going to be late if you don't hurry up and leave, Laurel. Please don't sabotage this date before it even begins."

"This *date*," I placed as much snark into my tone as I possibly could as I answered her, "wasn't my idea. I can't pretend to be excited about it."

Kate didn't seem at all bothered by my bad attitude.

"Are you seriously still mad at me about the dating profile? You have to admit that I did a fantastic job writing it. I picked only the best photos of you, and..." She waited, leaving a pregnant pause while I stared at her. "It's taken someone who had previously gone three years without a single date and turned her into someone who has gone on ten dates in the last three months."

"Ten first dates in the last three months and every single one of them was awful. I'm not sure we can call that a win."

Scooting herself from her seated position on the couch so she could look back at me, she smiled.

"Okay, I'll admit that none of them were stellar and there were definitely a few weirdos in the mix, but that doesn't mean this date will be bad."

"It's just a feeling I have."

"You always have that feeling. Tell me, how does someone who writes romance novels for a living have such a blatant dislike for all men? It seems to me that would be counterproductive to what you do."

I didn't want to admit that she was right, but since my fallout with the one man I'd thought hung the moon since elementary school, I certainly hadn't seen many examples of great men.

"I don't dislike *all* men. It's just that I seem to come across more rotten men than good ones. And it's called compartmentalizing. People across all professions practice it every single day. If we all had to believe in what we do for a living, the workforce would cease to exist."

My sister's smile dropped as she closed her eyes and shook her head at me.

"Jesus, Laurel, that's the most depressing thing you've ever said. Have you ever considered that your attitude may be the reason why you never seem to stumble across any good men? The law of attraction is real, big sis. Maybe your attitude is just scaring them off. Your vibes are toxic."

She lifted both arms and flailed them around as if to clear the air of my toxicity. The stump on her right arm and the burns over her left hand caused my heart to squeeze painfully in my chest, and in an instant I gained a perspective that riddled me with guilt for what a complete and ungrateful snob I was.

All my sister wanted was for me to have something that she believed she could no longer ever have. And while I knew she was wrong—her beauty could hardly be marred by injury—I understood her need to fill her empty schedule with something that made her feel useful. She would happily trade me each of these terrible dates, if she felt she could.

Blushing in embarrassment and shame, I walked around to the front of the couch and sat down next to her.

"You're right. It's not fair of me to judge each of these guys before I even meet them. I promise that I'll give him a chance."

"Thank you. Now, you better go. It's eight o'clock now and you've still got a ten minute walk to the restaurant."

Leaning to kiss Kate on the cheek, I stood and reached for my purse. The moment I reached the front door of my apartment, I heard my phone ding from inside my bag. Unzipping the bag, I retrieved my phone and looked down at the photo message in horror.

"And...I'm out."

Dropping my bag, I kicked off my shoes, hung up my jacket, and began to undress as I tossed my phone onto the couch with my sister and made my way to the bathroom to draw up a nice hot bath.

"What's wrong?"

Unable to form a proper sentence in response, I simply said, "Just look."

Stunned silence was quickly followed by uncontrollable laughter as Kate read the message and then looked at the photo that would be forever ingrained in my mind.

"Hurry up, babe. The bread basket is getting cold. Here's a taste of what you can have for dessert."

Ignoring her cackles, I turned on the hot water all the way. I generously poured bubble bath into the tub and all but dove into the water. When I looked up, Kate stood in the doorway, still laughing hysterically.

"I mean...you gotta give him some credit. Most men lacking in that way wouldn't feel confident enough to send you a dick pick. Do you want me to text him back for you?"

I rested my forehead against my palm as I shook my head.

"No. There are so many things wrong with that message. It

doesn't even deserve a response. First of all, I don't know this man. I don't know where the hell he gets off calling me 'babe.' Second of all..." The shockingly tiny appendage flashed through my mind and I started to laugh, as well. "Second of all...ew. Just block his number for me."

Giggling, Kate turned and left as I disappeared beneath the bubbles.

I stayed in the tub until I was thoroughly warmed and wrinkled, and I saw Mr. Crinkles' paw swipe underneath the closed bathroom door as he tried to get inside. The solid black cat was my sister's baby and the reason she'd not escaped the fire unmarred that had destroyed her home. Not that I could blame her. The cat was ornery, lovable, and incredibly cuddly. After the past six months of having him live under my roof, I was completely in love with him. I would've done exactly as my sister had done if the situation had been reversed.

"Hang on just a second, mister. I'll let you in."

Slipping on my robe and slippers, I opened the bathroom door to allow the cat to slink inside. He immediately dragged his body against my leg before flopping over onto his side between my legs as he purred and begged for me to touch him.

My sister wasn't the only one who lost something in the fire that had pulled me away from my once-in-a-lifetime trip to Scotland so many months ago. Mr. Crinkles—injured by the same beam that had fallen on my sister's right arm—had lost his eye. While it must have been an adjustment for the cat, I quite liked the way he looked with just the one eye—it gave him character and added a little bit of edge to his otherwise friendly disposition.

"Hey, Laurel, if you're out of the tub, come here for a second. I want to show you something."

"You heard her. We've been summoned."

Mr. Crinkles meowed as I lifted him from the floor and carried him into the living room where Kate sat with her eyes glued to the television screen.

"Have you heard of this castle before? Maybe it will provide you some inspiration for your next book."

My next book, which was months past due, didn't exist. I'd been unable to write anything in over a year. I seriously doubted that some television documentary would give me the inspiration I needed to dive back in. Inspiration was the reason I'd left for Scotland, with Marcus in tow as my sidekick, in the first place. I needed an idea, needed to see the sights and the people in the flesh to know which direction my new stories needed to go. I'd almost found it in Scotland, thanks to a mysterious book and an even more mysterious message inside, but just as I'd been about to go in search of answers to the questions the book had posed, we received word of the fire back home, and my trip had come to an immediate end.

"I don't know. What castle is it?"

Lifting her legs, I scooted underneath them as I snuggled into the couch next to her.

"The Castle of Eight Lairds is what it is known as now. I'm sure at one time it had another name, but the documentary hasn't mentioned what it was. Just watch. There's a really fascinating legend behind it."

Something about the name of the castle sounded familiar, but I couldn't recall why. As the commercial ended and the program resumed, I turned my attention to the screen and listened in.

Kate was right. It certainly was an interesting legend, and one, surprisingly, I'd never heard before. If anything was capable of stirring my imagination enough to make me write again, it was this. For the first time in many, many months, an idea began to bud in my mind.

An isle off the mainland of Scotland—much like the name of its castle—was known as The Isle of Eight Lairds, and the story surrounding its legend went back over four hundred years.

The legend went that eight druids must always pledge their magic to the territory and its castle to prevent a hidden darkness from re-emerging and destroying the people of the village. Each generation of eight must pick a new eight to follow them, for if ever one of the eight passes and they are left with just seven, the evil within the castle will rise again and destroy the isle until it is but a blip in Scotland's memory.

The story, as depicted by below-average actors and the narrator's deep baritone voice, weaved a tale of heartbreak, magic, and lore. Of ghosts and banshees and witches. The general consensus now was that little of the legend was true, but I couldn't help but think of the parallels between this story and the one I'd discovered inside Conall Castle so many months ago—of Morna's strange tale of magic and love, and her insistence from the notes inside that all of it was true.

I'd felt the magic throughout Scotland every day I'd been there. I couldn't so easily dismiss the stories, for all stories have some basis in truth. I desperately wanted to know just how much of it was real.

Just as the documentary ended, there was a crash to our left and we both turned to see Mr. Crinkles causing a ruckus on the shelf of one of my bookcases. As I watched one of the books drop to the floor, I realized why the name of the castle had sounded so familiar. Just two weeks earlier, I'd found a book in the middle of the street just a few blocks from my apartment—it was a book about The Castle of Eight Lairds. I'd yet to open it. At the time, the only thing that had been on my mind was how I couldn't bear to see any book left abandoned in the street, so I brought it home. Now, I couldn't wait to look inside.

"Kate, that book that your cat just shoved onto the floor is the one I found the other day. I didn't make the connection until now, but look at what it's called."

Standing, I moved across the room to grab the book. After glancing at the title, I extended it toward Kate's remaining hand.

With eyes wide, she stared down at the cover as her jaw slowly opened in surprise.

"Wow, what are the chances of that? This is a sign, Laurel. This castle is what you're supposed to write about."

My sister was a bit of a wannabe mystic. She ate up horoscopes, signs, and all things whimsical like candy. But in this instance, I couldn't deny that the coincidence did indeed feel like a sign.

"Maybe so. It definitely has sparked more ideas than I've had in a very long time."

My sister was no longer listening. She'd flipped the book open to a double-spread portrait towards the middle of the book and was staring at the image intensely.

"Laurel, look at this. This guy looks just like Marcus. I mean, just like him."

Leaning over her shoulder, I looked down to see what she was talking about.

Across the page was a group portrait of eight men. Sure enough, the man on the far right did bear a startling resemblance to my best friend.

Kate twisted to look up at me.

"You should call him, Laurel."

"What for? To tell him that I found a portrait of someone who looks like him? He wouldn't care."

Kate reached up and grabbed my arm to pull me around to the sofa.

"No, of course not for that. It's a strange coincidence—another sign that is perhaps telling you that you need to reach out to him— but I hardly see why Marcus needs to know. You need to call him for you. He's been calling every two weeks for months now. I don't know what happened between the two of you since you've refused to tell me, but I know Marcus, and it couldn't have been anything bad enough to warrant you cutting him out of your life. He's too important to you. You haven't been yourself since the fire. You mope around here pretending to tend to me, which we both know you refuse to do."

She winked at me, and I knew she meant to reassure me that she wasn't angry with how stern I'd been with her. During the first two months following the fire, our mother had stayed in Boston to help me care for Kate. It had been an unmitigated disaster. Heartbroken for her daughter, Mom had doted on Kate in a fashion that only furthered her new difficulties. She would do anything and everything for her. It did nothing but slow her recovery. Eventually, fed up and eager to have my house under my control again, I sent Mom back home to Florida. Kate healed more in the three weeks following our mother's departure than she had in the two months prior, simply because I wasn't as sympathetic. Even when she cried, even when she begged me to do simple tasks that were easy for me to take for granted but were now incredibly difficult for her, I made her do it herself. Each new victory increased her confidence and slowly, she healed.

Seeing how much Kate had improved was the only thing that helped Mother forgive me for how I'd treated her.

"Don't get me wrong. I'm glad you've been such a hard ass. I'm just saying, you always pretend that I need you, but you don't really do anything for me when you're here anyway. It's an excuse. I'm tired of being your excuse. It's time for you to get your life back. You need your best friend. You need to start writing again. You're not the one who lost everything in a fire, Laurel, yet you walk around here like you are. Whatever you need to do to get back to the life you had before I moved in here with you, you need to do it."

Someone's words had never had such a profound effect on me. I reeled back on the sofa as if she'd slapped me. She was right, but I didn't know how to begin. Everything felt so completely off course.

"I don't know how, Kate. I don't know what to do. I'm not blaming you. I don't ever want you to think that, but before the fire, I felt like things were just beginning for me, like I was on the verge of some big shift in my life. Then just like that, with one phone call, everything stopped. I floundered, and then I got comfortable in the floundering. Now, I can't see how to pull myself out of it."

Kate leaned forward to pull me into a hug.

"I know you don't blame me, but I've upended your life all the same. And don't worry about what you need to do. Signs always come in threes. You've another one due anytime. Just watch for it. You'll know what to do."

Squeezing her tight, I laughed at her confidence.

"Is this what you intend to do for your next career? Are you going to start predicting people's futures?"

Gently pushing me away, Kate stood and reached for Mr. Crinkles.

"It's not fortune telling, Laurel. It's common knowledge. As a writer, I'd think you would know that. Anything important always comes in threes."

I smiled at her as she made her way to her bedroom. It took all of three minutes for me to fall asleep on the sofa.

A loud banging on the front door woke me up from a dead sleep at three a.m.

CHAPTER 2

A llen Castle—Scotland—1651

T he lass was persistent. It was the tenth letter he'd received from her in as many months. He'd yet to open a single one. He knew what he would find—a series of blurred letters to taunt him. Simply more proof that he was losing his sight. And even if he could make out Sydney's words to him, what would he say in return? There was so much he couldn't tell her. Until his land was securely deeded to another, he couldn't tell her the truth of where he lived, or what he did, or even truly, who he was. Until he returned home to the rest of The Eight, he couldn't know if the damage to his eyes was permanent. Even if it was, Sydney was the last person he would want to know. She was one of the few who knew his heart. If he truly lost his vision, he wanted her to remember him as he was before.

As much as it pained him, he would have to let his friendship with her die.

"Thank ye, Madge. Please take this to my bedchamber and leave it with the others."

The old woman nodded but leaned in to quietly whisper in his ear.

"Aye, o'course, sir. If ye'd like to have someone read it to ye, I can have my son come to ye when ye retire this evening. I could assure his discretion."

Raudrich reached out and grabbed her arm as she stepped away to leave him.

"Ye do know that I can read, doona ye, Madge?"

Her voice still low, she answered him.

"Aye sir, but ye canna see the words, can ye?"

His heart sank at Madge's observation. His position as laird was already precarious enough.

"Do others know?"

"I doona believe so. Not many spend as much time with ye as I do. Though ye willna be able to hide it forever."

"Thank ye, Madge. Just leave the letter with the others."

He waited until she was gone from his view before standing from his seat. Music surrounded him as his clansmen danced and drank with merriment. He wished he could enjoy the evening with them, but a strong sense of foreboding made him uneasy. Two tragedies in the span of two months. First, the unexpected death of the man set to replace him as laird, followed shortly by the sudden and swiftly progressing loss of his eyesight. A third tragedy couldn't be far behind—they always came in threes.

He could still see at a distance, though the edges of things were slightly blurred. He hoped it would hold steady until he could find another man to replace him. He'd been away from the eight for far too long, and having his powers stretched over such a great distance and for so long was costing him his vision. Never before had one of the eight stayed away from their magic for so long. Even those who had left for a short while had suffered much, and he'd been away for two and a half years.

He could just make out Silva standing at the end of the hall, hiding under a castle archway as she waved him toward her.

He waited until he neared her to speak. "What is it?"

"A messenger arrived from yer home, Raudrich."

Panic set in at Silva's words. Everything seemed to be falling apart so quickly. She hurried to reassure him by placing a hand on his arm.

"Doona worry. 'Twas I who greeted him. No one else saw the rider arrive or leave. Ye needn't worry."

Silva, the widow of the man set to replace him tonight, knew nothing of the truth about him, but she knew him well enough to see that something was wrong. Otherwise, she wouldn't have hurried to calm his nerves.

There were few among his clansmen that he trusted fully, but he would have to trust Silva with the truth this night. This was a letter he couldn't put off opening.

"Will ye come with me to my bedchamber, Silva? I need ye to read the letter out loud to me, and it must be read in private."

He didn't need to see her face clearly to know that her expression was confused, but she said nothing as he turned to make sure that she followed along behind him.

The moment they were safely inside his room, she spoke.

"Why do ye need me to read this? Surely, there is no need for me to know what is inside."

"I canna see it. A fortnight after yer husband passed, my vision began to decline. Each day it grows a little worse."

Silva's voice was filled with concern.

"What would cause this? Have ye seen the healer about it? Mayhap there is something she can do to help."

"No. I know the cause well enough. All that I doona know is whether or not the vision is restorable. Please read the letter."

He moved to sit as Silva opened the letter. He knew what would be inside.

The third tragedy. He knew there was no other reason for

someone from The Land of Eight Lairds to ride here. They all knew how dangerous such a message would be for him.

As Silva began to read, his worst suspicions were confirmed.

Timothy, the oldest of The Eight had lost his long battle with illness. The Eight were now seven, and it was more important than ever that he make preparations to leave Allen territory for good.

Once Silva finished reading the letter, she moved to bend in front of him, gathering his hands in hers.

"Who is this man that ye've lost? Who is so urgently calling ye away from here?"

An unprecedented idea came to mind as he looked at Silva. There was only one thing he could do. With one of The Eight now dead, he couldn't remain here another day.

He took his time explaining everything to her, sparing her no truth.

"When my brother passed, this land became mine, but it is not mine by right. Since the age of thirteen, my loyalty has been pledged to another clan, which, as ye know, voids me of my inheritance. There is a land verra far from here that requires the magic of eight druids to keep the evil that resides within it at bay. Like my grandfather before me, I possess magic. I am one of The Eight. The man that passed was one of The Eight, as well. With The Eight now broken, the evil back at home will begin to look for a way to rise. It is imperative that I return home so we can search for a worthy man to replace Timothy.

"I came here after my brother's death to see the village settled, to make certain that I found a just man to take my brother's stead as laird. It has always been my intention to return to the isle that is now my home. No one else in the clan can ever know of this. If they do, they willna accept the decision I know is right."

"And what decision is that?"

"I must leave here tonight, but first we must find a witness. I shall deed all of my land to ye, Silva. Ye shall be the first female laird of Allen territory."

CHAPTER 3

Present Day

I stumbled over to the front door as I called out to my sister to tell her to stay in her room until I found out who was at the door. She replied with a snore. She could sleep through just about anything—even a fire.

"Who's there? Don't you know what time it is?" I stood an arm's length away from the door handle as I called out.

"It's me. Open up." The moment I heard Marcus' voice on the other side, I went limp with relief. Hands shaking, I unlocked the door and threw it open as I stepped aside to let him enter.

"What the hell is wrong with you? You should've called first. You scared me to death banging on the door like that.

He looked around the room with undisguised disgust. He'd not been inside my apartment since Kate moved in. Since then, my aptitude for tidiness, much like my aptitude for just about everything, had slipped significantly.

"You wouldn't have answered if I called. I've been trying to get ahold of you for months."

He moved to shuffle through the pile of mail on my entry table. I quickly moved to block him as I threw my hands down over the stack and glared up at him.

"You can't just go through my mail. What are you doing here?"

"Are you not paying your bills now? Have you turned on a vacuum cleaner in the last three weeks? It smells in here, Laurel."

I was most certainly paying my bills. It was just any other business that I allowed to slip through the cracks.

"It's the cat." I wasn't altogether sure that was true. Kate was a stickler for making certain that Mr. Crinkles' litter box stayed immaculate, but at least the cat was an easy scapegoat. He couldn't argue with me. "And not a single thing on that table is a bill. Of course, I'm paying my bills. I'll ask you one more time, Marcus, what are you doing here?"

"This has gone on long enough, Laurel. I messed up. I know that. I've known it since the words slipped out of my mouth. You're not crazy. I never should have said that you were. I've been trying to apologize to you for months now, but you wouldn't hear it, which frankly, isn't fair. We've been friends for twenty-five years. I should be allowed one mess up. I've certainly forgiven you your fair share of stupidity."

I hardly knew what to say to him. I was still so angry with him, but as he stood before me now, I couldn't recall exactly why. What he'd said had wounded my feelings to be sure, but was it really all that cruel? From his perspective, he believed he was helping me. Perhaps, he was. Was it really myself I was angry at?

"I..." I said the one thing I felt most strongly as I stared back at him. "I've missed you."

I expected him to hug me or at least soften a little at my confession. He did no such thing.

"Have you? Well, I can't really say the same. The longer this has gone on, the angrier I've become at you for pushing me away. But guess what, we are about to fix that. We're going back to Scotland—back to the place where all this fell apart. And we aren't leaving the country until two things happen."

He paused and lifted one finger, followed quickly by a second as he continued.

"One, everything is fixed between us. And two, we know once and for all whether you're mad for believing that old woman's story and her letter to you."

Marcus was the last person I wanted to go looking for Morna's inn with. He didn't for a moment believe that it was there.

"You don't have to do that, Marcus. We don't need to go to Scotland to heal things between us. I forgive you, and I'm sorry for acting like such a child. I think I was angry with myself for hoping, angry for believing that something impossible just might be possible. When you confronted me that day, you made me kill a dream, and it made me resent myself for being so foolish."

He did hug me then—a big bear of a hug that draped me in more comfort than I'd felt in months. I collapsed into him and began to cry.

"Oh, Laurel." He held me tightly and kissed the top of my head. "I'm a shit friend. Even if I did believe you were mad, I should've just supported you. I've done many things I know you thought were crazy, but you never let me know that. I'm so sorry."

It shouldn't have been the thing I noticed in his apology, but one thing stood out amongst all the rest.

"You just said that you *did* believe I was mad. As if you don't anymore."

He pulled away, but kept both hands on my arms as he held me away from him.

"About that...something very strange happened last week that may have changed my mind."

I raised my brows and turned my head like a confused puppy dog.

"Oh, yeah? What's that?"

"I received a letter last week. There was no address, but the country of origin was Scotland, and it was signed by someone named Morna."

A chill swept over my entire body. I didn't believe I'd ever been so surprised in my entire life.

"Morna was the name of the woman who wrote the book I found in Conall Castle."

Marcus nodded.

"I know. The entire letter was just her giving me a thorough lashing for encouraging you to cancel your plans to return to Scotland. How could she possibly know that I'd done that? How could she even know who we are?"

I stared back at Marcus, saying nothing until he broke the silence.

"What are you thinking, Laurel?"

"I shut my mind to the possibility of any of this being real months ago. Now, I don't know what to think. Why did she wait so long to reach out? If she has the ability to know so much about both of us, why not contact me when I was searching for her? And why would she send you a letter? Why not just reach out to me directly?"

Marcus shook his head. He looked as confused as I felt.

"I don't know. But my own curiosity is now piqued enough that I know I won't be able to get anything done until we both find out. I've booked us both on a flight that leaves tomorrow afternoon. If the inn really does exist, we'll find it."

Perhaps, my sister was right and signs really did come in threes.

I couldn't see Marcus' sudden arrival here any other way.

CHAPTER 4

"*W*ell, this is a pleasant surprise."

Dreary-eyed and still a bit wobbly from sleep, Kate entered the kitchen where Marcus and I sat at the table, a road map of Scotland spread across the top. It was just past nine in the morning. We'd spent the rest of the night catching up while he helped me pack.

Marcus stood the moment he saw Kate and moved to wrap his arms around her just as he'd done me the night before. He really did give the very best hugs.

"You look wonderful, Kate. I'm glad to see you getting on so well."

She smiled, but the smile didn't quite reach her eyes. She always tried so hard to stay positive, but every once in a while she couldn't hide her pain.

"Thank you, Marcus. I'm glad, too. It's been a long few months, but I'm feeling a little more like my old self every day. When did you get here?"

He chuckled lightly and bared his teeth in embarrassment.

"About three a.m. actually. I'm afraid I gave Laurel quite the scare. I think I'll run home and get my own bag ready. I'll let Laurel tell you what's going on."

He bent to give her a quick kiss on the cheek before pointing to me.

"I'll be back to pick you up at two. See you in a few hours."

Kate waited until he was gone to say anything.

"Well, that was some night, wasn't it? I went to bed wondering if you two would ever speak again, and I wake up to find the two of you as chummy as ever. What's going on?"

Setting a cup of coffee down on the table for her, I waited for her to sit down to answer. The moment she was seated, Mr. Crinkles jumped up into the empty chair between us and purred so that I would pet him.

"You know how yesterday you were begging me to get my life back and to leave you be for a while since I don't do anything for you anyway? Well, you're about to get your wish. Marcus and I are going back to Scotland this afternoon."

Kate's face lit up with excitement. "To visit the castle in the documentary? I really do think it could be just the place to get you writing again. Oh, Laurel, this is wonderful."

I'd almost forgotten about the castle, but Kate was right. If I was going to be in Scotland anyway, I should definitely pay it a visit to see if it could spark some writing inspiration.

"Well, that castle isn't actually the main reason for our visit, but I do want to get over to it while I'm there."

Kate's smile fell. "Oh. Then, what are you going there for?"

I'd said nothing to anyone about what had happened to me in Scotland, and Kate had been so overwhelmed with her own recovery after the fire that she'd not noticed the hours I'd spent digging for information. It was hardly the sort of story you could tell someone without coming across as insane, but I could see no way to leave without telling her now.

"Would you like to know what happened between me and Marcus all those months ago?"

She nodded and leaned back to sip her coffee.

"So, we had a fantastic trip, but there was something that happened not long before the fire that I haven't told you about. At one of the castles we visited, I came across this book. You know how I am with books—if there's an interesting one just lying around, I can't really keep myself from picking it up. It was the strangest book I'd ever seen. There was a note inside addressed to whoever found it, and it made the point of telling the reader that the story inside was true. Within the first twenty pages, any rational person would realize that the woman's story couldn't possibly be true. It was filled with witches and magic and love, and most surprisingly, time travel. I didn't put the book down until I finished. And then...at the end, there was another note imploring the reader to come and find the woman who wrote it at the inn where her story ended."

I stopped and looked nervously at my sister. Her expression was entirely unreadable.

She waited a long moment before saying anything. I could see by the way she kept pursing her lips that she was thinking through everything I'd just said.

"Well, did you go and visit with the author?"

"That's the thing. The inn she mentioned was along a road that Marcus and I had passed many times. It wasn't there, but the story implied that maybe the inn wasn't always visible. That when we were meant to find it, we would."

"Was it there?"

"I don't know. I got the phone call from Mom about the fire on our way to see. When I got home, I looked for information about this woman, but all I could find was the historical info about a Morna who died back in the seventeenth century. While that would fit with the woman's story, it couldn't possibly be the same woman who wrote the book."

She nodded in agreement.

"Obviously, but you still have to get in touch with her. It's just all

407

too curious to let sit. I'm sure it's been driving you crazy all these months—wondering what that conversation would've been like had you found her."

"It has. The thing is..." I hesitated. It embarrassed me to even say the words out loud. "I sort of believed her story. I know it's impossible, but it just...it felt so real. I don't know. If you'd read it, perhaps you would be able to say the same thing. Anyway, Marcus knew I believed it, and it worried him. When he saw how much time I was investing trying to get to the bottom of this after we got home, he confronted me. He called me crazy and told me I should drop my plan to return to Scotland to search for the woman once you were well. I think what upset me the most is that I was starting to feel a little crazy myself. I lashed out and pushed him away. I haven't looked into the woman any further. But then Marcus showed up last night with some very interesting news."

Kate leaned forward in her seat as her voice lifted with curiosity.

"Which was?"

"He received a letter from someone named Morna, and she somehow knew that he talked me out of returning to Scotland to look for her."

Kate's eyes opened wide.

"What? Are you serious?"

"Completely. And it must've really gotten to him because he showed up here last night already having booked us on a flight out today. Which brings me to you. I know you can take care of yourself, but that doesn't mean you should have to. Will you be okay here? I'm not sure how long we will be gone. If you want, I can call Mom. You know she'd be here by this evening if you wanted her to."

She reached out her hand and placed it on mine as if to stop me.

"Oh God, no. Don't call her. I'll be fine. I promise. I'll call Maggie and she can come and stay with me a few days. Some time alone will be good for me. I miss my independence. It's time I start practicing doing even more by myself. Just promise me one thing."

I smiled and leaned forward to hug her.

"Anything. What is it?"

"If all this does indeed turn out to be true...if the woman is some centuries old witch who travels through time, just give me a call and let me know before you go hurtling through to the past."

I laughed and pulled back assuming she was joking, but there was no humor in her eyes as I stared back at her.

"You don't actually believe that it could be possible, do you?"

She shrugged. "I haven't any idea, Laurel, but isn't it more fun to live in a world where it just might be? Most of what any of us believe about the world is delusional anyway. We might as well believe in delusions that make us smile. The thought of you getting to travel back and get a glimpse of all those wonderful things you write about makes me smile. So...like I said, if it is real, just promise you'll call me."

It was the most ridiculous promise I'd ever made, but I couldn't deny my little sister anything.

"Okay. I promise to call you before I allow a witch to send me into the past."

She smiled as Mr. Crinkles crawled into her lap.

"Good. I can't wait to get that phone call."

CHAPTER 5

*O*ver the *Atlantic Ocean*

*T*he downside of our last-minute flights—besides the exorbitant price that Marcus paid for them—was that we were unable to sit together for the journey. Sandwiched in the middle section, in a middle seat, it was the longest and most miserable travel experience of my life.

The woman to my right smelled of dust bunnies and cheese, and the man to my left liked to spit when he talked. He really liked talking. He was a native Scot, and I wasn't sure I'd ever seen anyone as excited to get home.

"I tell ye, lass, eight weeks is far too long to be away from yer own bed and yer own coffee maker. America is fine in most respects, but none of ye know how to make a proper cup of coffee, and yer breakfasts are terrible. I doona want cereal in skim milk for breakfast. Or worse, a couple of soggy waffles from the hotel buffet. Give me meat and eggs or nothing at all."

I wasn't in an appeasing mood.

"I quite like cereal with skim milk."

The man, who'd yet to introduce himself, threw up both hands to cover his heart, accidentally elbowing me in the side of my arm hard enough to make me wince.

"Ach, doona wound me so. I thought ye were a lass with better taste."

"Nope. I'm afraid I have very bad taste indeed. Now, if you'll excuse me, I think I better try to get some sleep. I've got quite a long car drive once we land."

It was the absolute wrong thing to say. It gave him the perfect opening to question me.

"Oh, is that so? Whereabouts are ye headed? I know Scotland like the back of my hand. I could tell ye some bonny places to stop along the way."

I could hardly say anything to him about the inn, so I decided to stick to the closest thing to it.

"Conall Castle, actually. I've always wanted to see it."

This man didn't need to know that I'd visited before.

"Ach, aye, 'tis a lovely castle. There is actually not much to stop and see along yer way there, though the drive is quite beautiful. Where else in Scotland are ye planning to go?"

"The Isle of Eight Lairds."

"Best be careful over there, lass. 'Tis cursed land. Only a few still reside there."

I'd heard this much from the documentary I'd watched with Kate, but I was fairly certain the castle was still open to visitors, and there was a ferry that went out to the isle twice a day.

"I don't believe in curses. Besides, wasn't the original curse from the legend broken at some point? It must have been for the land to have been ruled by one laird at a time rather than eight for the last four hundred years."

The stranger clucked his tongue disapprovingly at me.

"I know nothing of the legend, lass. I only know what I've heard all my life. My own grandfather wouldna step foot on the isle, and there are many in Scotland who feel just as he did. 'Tis mainly foolish tourists like yerself that do."

"You do know that your insistence that this place is cursed has just increased my desire to go there tenfold?"

He shook his head.

"As I said lass...foolish tourists."

---

*M*arcus was several rows in front of me, so by the time I deplaned, he was waiting for me just outside the gate. He looked rested and annoyingly fresh.

"Were you on an entirely different flight than I was? You look great."

He winked and reached for my bag.

"Well, thanks. I'll take it. Rough night, huh?"

"You could say that. I hope you're willing to drive because I'm completely useless. I plan on being asleep five minutes after we pull away from the car rental."

"That's absolutely fine. It's not as if you haven't seen the landscape before. Do you need to stop in at the restroom before we head out?"

His question sounded much more like a suggestion, and by the look in his eye, I could tell that I was right.

"Do I have something on me?"

"No. I just thought..." He squirmed, as if he wasn't quite sure how to say what he wanted to. "I just thought you might want to splash some water on your face, freshen up a little bit. If the inn is there, I assume we will stop before we find a place to stay for the night."

"If it's really an inn, I assume we'll stay there."

He nodded. "Precisely. I know you. I doubt you want to show up looking so tired."

From most people, such a statement would've pissed me off, but

I was close enough to Marcus to not take offense to him very politely telling me I looked like crap. I was tired. Of course, I looked that way.

"Okay. You're right. I'll be right back."

I took my time in front of the mirror as I applied a bit of makeup and brushed my hair.

It was always a bit of a strange experience for me to see myself in makeup. In truth, if I was really honest with myself, it was equally strange for me to see myself in real clothes. As a writer, most of my days were spent makeup free, and yoga pants were my work uniform of choice.

Satisfied that I wouldn't frighten anyone, I returned to Marcus and we made our way towards baggage claim.

It took less time than either of us expected for our bags to arrive on the conveyor belt, and as he lugged them along behind us and we made our way out of the airport towards the rental car area, I noticed an old man waving at me from the corner of my eye.

Unthinkingly, I waved back. It was then that I noticed the sign he was holding. Both of our names were written on the small piece of cardboard.

Slapping Marcus' arm a little harder than necessary, I gripped at his arm in my confusion.

"He couldn't possibly mean us, could he?"

I watched Marcus' face as he squinted to make out the names.

"Of course not. No one knew we were coming. It's just…it's just a coincidence." He didn't sound all that convinced. "Let's go."

Just as we turned to walk away from him, the old man called out to us.

"Oy, ye two. Get yerselves over here before I freeze to death."

I stopped and turned toward the voice and pointed at the center of my chest in confusion.

"Do you mean us?"

The man nodded and waved us toward him with his free hand.

"Aye, o'course I do. Laurel is not that common of a name, is it?

Get over here so I might introduce myself. Ye willna be needing a car."

Baffled beyond comprehension, Marcus and I both looked at each other for a moment then obediently walked over to the stranger. Placing the sign between his knobby legs, he extended his right hand.

"I'm Jerry, Morna's husband. She dinna wanna risk either of ye not making it to our home this time, so she sent me to fetch ye. Come on now. We best get on. She's not a woman known for her patience."

I took his hand and gripped at Marcus with my left hand to keep myself steady. It wasn't possible that this man was the same one from the story I'd read, but his description matched that of the Jerry in Morna's story exactly.

Realizing that I was shaking his hand for an awkwardly long time, I quickly pulled it away.

"Pick yer chin up, lass. This is only the first of many surprising things ye will learn this day."

I had absolutely no doubt about that.

CHAPTER 6

An Unnamed Village in Scotland—1651

He couldn't make the rest of the journey home alone. His horse knew the path well, but not well enough to lead him home unguided, and he couldn't see well enough to distinguish the paths in front of him. He would stop for the night and spend some time in the local alehouse. In any village, there were people looking for work. Anyone willing to guide him for the rest of the journey would be well paid.

The tavern was boisterous and filled to capacity with both locals and travelers. It took some time for him to get the barkeep's attention once he made his way to the counter.

"Excuse me, sir. Might I ask ye a question?"

Even with bleary eyes, Raudrich could see how weathered the man was. A ragged scar sliced down one side of his face, and the man kept his hair long and disheveled. He was one of the broadest men he'd ever seen.

"Are ye a paying customer? If ye have no intention of drinking or eating here, I'll not be answering anything."

Pulling the small bag from his kilt, he plopped three coins down in front of the man.

"I'll be doing both."

Quickly sliding the coins toward him, the barkeep twisted and hollered to someone in the back room to bring him some food.

"Then I'm pleased to make yer acquaintance. Name's Pinkie. What can I do for ye?"

Raudrich had never heard such a strange name before. He couldn't help but ask.

"Is that yer real name?"

"O'course it isna my real name, but 'tis the name I gave ye."

Raudrich liked the man already. He was as rough around the edges as many of the other eight.

"Verra well." He extended his hand. "I'm Raudrich, and I'm in need of a hired hand to lead me home. Do ye know of anyone in the village who is trustworthy, knows the country well, and is in need of work?"

"Ye need a guide to take ye home? Are ye lost? Do ye not know the way yerself?"

Pinkie's questions were valid. He only wished he didn't have to answer them. He was weakened in his current state. It wasn't something that he believed he would ever grow accustomed to.

"I'm not lost. I know the way verra well. 'Tis only that my eyes are failing me. They grow worse each day. I canna see the path to lead my horse."

The brief silence before the man's response was filled with the one thing he loathed most in the world—pity. It was what he dreaded most about losing his sight—knowing that others would pity him.

"I see. And where is yer home?"

"The Isle of Eight Lairds."

The man's reaction was exactly as expected.

"'Tis a far journey. Ye shall have to pay someone much for them to agree to be away from their own home so long."

"Aye, I know. I would prefer to hire someone without family. If it is someone without work, they can set their own wage. If ye have someone in mind who already has work, I will double whatever they make now for as long as the journey takes."

The man who must've been in the back taking Pinkie's orders suddenly slipped in next to him and placed a steaming plate of food down on the counter. He looked up to thank him.

"Thank ye, sir. It smells delicious."

Pinkie leaned in close and whispered in his ear as he bent down to eat.

"Ye best eat quickly. Old man Stuart will have ye thrown out on yer arse just as quick as ye can say gypsie the moment I tell him that ye've just hired me away from him. I'll meet ye outside just as soon as I tell him the news."

Raudrich turned to look at the man and spoke below his breath as he watched Stuart return to the kitchen out of the corner of his eye.

"Pinkie, I dinna mean ye. I was asking if ye knew of someone who would be good for the job."

His new friend laughed and clasped him on the shoulders.

"Too bad. 'Tis me that ye've got. Ye just said ye would be doubling my wages, and I'll get to leave this hellhole for the foreseeable future. I'd sooner pull out my one good tooth before I let ye hire someone else."

"Verra well. Eating quickly shouldna be a problem. I'm starving. I'll see ye outside shortly."

At least he knew the remainder of his journey home wouldn't be a dull one.

CHAPTER 7

*M*orna's Inn—Present Day

*W*riters live in stories. We spend most of our days vividly imagining the worlds we are creating when we write. It's sometimes even worse when we read. With our imaginations already overactive and without the pressure of having to create the world ourselves, we read and are truly taken away to the world the writer has created for us. Pulling up in front of the inn in the same car as a man I'd read so very much about felt like stepping right into a storybook.

It looked exactly as I imagined it would. With the unbelievable act of Jerry awaiting us in the airport, I felt the old hope and dreaming rise up inside me again. That little voice that whispered *"what if"* so many months ago when I'd read Morna's story in one of the bedrooms of Conall Castle crept back into my mind.

Marcus appeared bug-eyed with shock. Even with the letter, he'd been certain someone was playing tricks on us. He never believed for a moment that the inn would actually be here. The fact that it was had him more than a little rattled.

As soon as Jerry parked the car out front and exited the vehicle, I turned to him.

"Are you okay? You look like you might be ill."

"This inn was not here before. You know that, right?"

I nodded. "Yes. I do know that."

"Then how is it here now? How do you explain this?"

"I don't know. I can't explain any of it any more than you can." I reached out to squeeze his hand gently. "I don't mean to sound harsh, but I have a feeling you better strap in. Everything so far is exactly how she described it. If this trend continues, we're in for a bunch more unexplainable things."

Knuckles rapped against the window, and I twisted to see Jerry smiling, his face all but plastered against the glass.

"Just what are the two of ye doing? I told ye that my wife is not a patient woman. Leave yer bags and come on inside. We can get those in a bit."

I didn't wait for Marcus to exit the car. I was now too excited to worry too much about his psychological wellbeing. I wanted to see the inside of Morna's home. Even more than that, I wanted to see Morna, worse than just about anything I'd ever wanted in my whole life.

She stood just inside the doorway, her graying hair framing a face that was still just as beautiful as I'd known it would be. Looking at her, there was no doubt in my mind that she was the same Morna from the story. The only question was how much of her novel was true.

"Laurel, lass, it certainly has taken ye long enough to get here, though o'course I understand why. 'Tis terrible what happened to yer sister, though I can promise ye it will all work out just fine for her in the end. Come here and give me a hug."

Of course she knew about Kate. I doubted there was anything I could tell her about myself that would surprise her.

"I…" I faltered as I walked toward her with open arms. "It's lovely to finally meet you. I have to tell you, I feel as if I know you after reading your book."

"Why, surely ye hear the same thing from yer own readers often, do ye not?"

I laughed as her arms wrapped around me. She was significantly shorter than me, and I had to crouch to bring myself down to her level.

"Not really. Though, my stories aren't about me. They're about the characters that choose to tell their own stories through me."

"Ah. Well, I suppose 'tis true."

Releasing me, she grabbed my hand and led me to a cozy living room just off the main entry.

"Come, dear. I know ye must have lots of questions for me."

"You have no idea."

She turned to wink as she laughed.

"Oh, I bet I do. Though, let's wait until yer friend recovers from his shock and comes to join us. 'Twill be easiest to explain everything to the both of ye once."

As if summoned, Marcus appeared in the doorway. I took a seat on the couch as Morna stood to greet him. After simple niceties were exchanged, Marcus joined me. After a short moment of awkward silence, Morna spoke.

"All right ye two, should I go first, or would ye like to?"

I had a list of questions I'd been waiting to ask her for months. I raised my hand as if I were in school.

"I'll go."

She nodded and lifted her palm from her lap to tell me to begin.

"How much of the story was true? Obviously, the love story was, but the rest of it—the time travel, the magic—it can't be real, right?"

She seemed surprised by my question.

"I have to say, lass, 'tis not what I expected ye to ask me. If it wasna true, how could ye be here right now? How could I have written to Marcus? How could I have known ye were returning to Scotland? If the magic wasna real, why would I have needed to see ye?"

I smiled and shook my head as I shrugged.

"I don't have the slightest idea on any of it. For argument's sake, let's say everything in your story was true—that you are a witch born centuries before now—that still doesn't explain why you needed to see me at all. You don't know me. Why would you want me, of all people, to read your story?"

"I doona choose who I'm meant to help, lass. The names and faces come to me at all times of day, and yers came through clear as a bell."

I didn't feel as if I was in need of any help whatsoever.

"And just how are you meant to help me? Do you plan on sending me into the past?"

She smiled and nodded excitedly.

"Aye, precisely."

Marcus spoke up for the first time since sitting.

"Not that I believe any of this, but why? Why would Laurel need to go into the past?"

A small piece of Morna's story entered my mind, and a nagging nervousness lodged itself in my stomach as I whispered the answer under my breath.

"She's a matchmaker."

Jerry spoke up from across the room.

"What's that, love? I canna hear as well as I once could."

I straightened in my seat as I looked directly into Morna's eyes.

"You're a matchmaker, right? If that's what you're trying to do with me, let me just bid you good day now. I'm so not even remotely interested."

Marcus chuckled, and I had to press my palms into my legs to keep from shoving him off the couch.

"Why not? Lord knows you need a man in your life, Laurel. You might as well be a nun as empty as your love life is."

Morna laughed and Jerry quickly joined in. I glared back at all of them.

"Doona worry, lass. 'Tis true that I've been known to make a few matches now and again, but 'tis not how I intend to help ye."

I relaxed noticeably in my seat.

"Okay. Well, then why exactly do I need your help?"

She raised her brows as if I should already know the answer.

"How long has it been since ye've written?"

I knew the answer by heart.

"Thirteen months and sixteen days."

"That is how I shall help ye, lass. I will send ye back for inspiration. So that ye may find the exact story ye were meant to tell."

That appealed to me much more than I wanted her to know.

"And in what century does my inspiration lie and where in Scotland?"

"The year 1651 on The Isle of Eight Lairds."

A familiar chill swept over me—the same I'd felt when glancing at the book that Mr. Crinkles pushed from my shelf.

"The book?"

"Aye, the book and the documentary, o'course. I intended for ye to see them both." In response to my open mouth, she chuckled and continued. "Do ye really believe that coincidences are ever truly that? Let me assure ye, 'tis not the way this world works. People are so unwilling to see the tiny miracles, the tiny pieces of magic, that happen in their lives almost every day. 'Tis a shame really."

I smiled as Kate sprung up in my mind.

"You sound like my sister."

Standing, Morna motioned for us to do the same.

"Yer sister is wiser than most people give her credit for. Now, come. Let's get a bite of food in the both of ye. I've much to explain and prepare ye for. Ye are due in the village on The Isle of Eight Lairds tomorrow at noon."

"We?" Marcus sounded horrified. "I'm not going into the past."

Laughing, Morna placed her hand gently on his back as she guided him out into the hallway.

"Aye, ye are. 'Tis the only way ye will ever truly believe any of this."

"You're right about that, but it still doesn't mean that I want to go."

Morna wasn't interested in arguing with him at all.

"Tough. Ye are going, and that is the end of it. Yer destiny is more tied to the isle than Laurel's."

Before Marcus could ask what she meant, Jerry, who'd walked on ahead of us, hollered after his wife from inside the kitchen.

All I could think of as I followed after them was the portrait inside the book. At the time, I'd simply thought the man resembled Marcus. Was it possible that it actually had been him?

Was Marcus destined to be one of the legendary eight?

CHAPTER 8

"*D*on't tell me that you're becoming a time traveler already?"

Kate answered on the second ring. I had no doubt she was awaiting my call.

"Actually...I think I just might be."

"What?" Her voice was a high-pitched screech that caused me to hold the phone away from my ear. "Are you serious? I truly had been sort of joking."

"I know you were. I mean, let's be realistic, every logical part of me tells me that come noon tomorrow that when this supposed witch casts her spell, Marcus and I will look around to find ourselves totally unmoved. I know that. And that's totally okay with me. I just made you a promise that I would call should the need arise, and according to Morna, it has."

"How will I know if it is real?"

"Well, I'm quite sure that this woman is harmless, so you needn't be worried about her harming us. If her spell does nothing, I'll call you the moment Marcus and I leave here. If you don't hear from me tomorrow, then I guess you can assume that it worked."

Kate sighed, and the sadness in her breath made me hurt all over.

"What's wrong? Do you need me? If you do, I'll head back home right now, Kate."

"No, nothing's wrong. I'm a little jealous, is all. An adventure like that sounds amazing. Also, you should know. Mom called me this afternoon, and I made the very stupid mistake of telling her where you'd gone. She's booked on the next flight out here tomorrow."

That went a very long way to explaining the sigh.

"Oh, Kate. I'm sorry. Whatever you do, don't let her do everything for you. The last thing you need is to have her coddling delay your progress."

"I know. I won't."

I immediately felt guilty for ordering her around. She wasn't a child. She knew better than I what was best.

"I'm sorry. I just worry about you."

"I know you do. How long will you be gone? You'll be able to come back right?"

"Of course, I will. I could never leave you and Mr. Crinkles. I've become quite attached to that damn cat. Morna says whenever I'm ready to leave all I need to do is place a letter to her in the fireplace, and she will return us to her inn. Sounds simple enough."

"Sounds a little too simple."

Kate's tone was suspicious. I understood why. I'd had the same foreboding feeling when Morna had explained everything to me.

"It does, doesn't it? But, I can hardly argue with her."

"Where are you going?"

When I told her where, she repeated the shriek she'd let out earlier.

"I told you that book was a sign! The documentary too! You know, Laurel, I've never been jealous of you. Not once in our whole lives. I always thought I'd lose my mind if I had a life as isolated as yours, but right now I'm so green with envy I could burst."

"I suppose if Mom starts to drive you too crazy, you could always come. Morna knows who you are, and I'm pretty sure she already likes you. Just have her send you back, too."

The words slipped out unthinkingly, and I regretted them right away. It wasn't right of me to assume that Morna would be willing to do any such thing, and I knew Kate well enough to know that before the fire, it would've been just the sort of thing she would jump on.

"Mmm...if only, big sis. This century has enough difficulties for me now. I imagine several hundred years in the past would be even far less accessible for someone with my challenges. If you can though, if there's any way, please let me know what's going on with you. And promise me you won't stay too long."

"I promise."

The door to the bedroom Morna had placed me in opened and Marcus stepped quietly inside before gently closing the door. He looked frightened. Covering the speaker so Kate couldn't hear, I mouthed to him,

"What's wrong?"

"Laurel, I'm scared. I think we need to get out of here right now."

I held up a hand to stop him and hurriedly bid my sister farewell. The moment I ended the call, I stood up and walked over to him.

"Why? What are you talking about?"

"I was in the bathroom just about to brush my teeth when I heard voices from what I assume is their bedroom. It was coming through the vent. Jerry seemed to be trying to keep his voice low, but with his bad hearing, he speaks more loudly than he realizes."

Marcus was shaking he was so worked up.

"Okay, and what did they say?"

"He was scolding Morna, telling her she shouldn't have lied to us, but if we believed her we were daft fools. He said we had a right to know what we were getting ourselves into. That it wasn't right for her send us back without us knowing there was no way to return."

"What?" I dropped to the edge of the bed. He might as well have kicked me straight in the stomach for as ill as I suddenly felt. "Are you certain that's what he said?"

"I'm sure. Laurel, I have a life back home. People I love. A job I love. I don't want to be here. Not for even a minute more."

I nodded in agreement and stood as I began to pace. My bag was still packed.

"Where's your bag?"

"I packed it before I came in here. We need to go. Now."

Reaching for my bag, our biggest obstacle came rushing to the forefront of my mind, and I had to reach for the edge of the bed for support.

"We don't have a car, Marcus"

"I saw Jerry's keys laying on the entranceway table. We're stealing the car. I'd rather end up in a Scottish prison than trapped in another century for the rest of my life. Let's go."

I was inclined to agree with him.

We exited the room as quietly as we could, and Marcus lifted his bag from the top of the staircase before we made our way downstairs.

I could see the keys glistening under the lamp on the table right by the front door. Marcus moved ahead of me to grab them and hurriedly opened the door. As I moved toward it, the handle swung out of his hand and the door slammed shut in my face.

I'd never experienced such overwhelming fear in my life.

We faced the stairway together and stared into Morna's rather surprisingly sympathetic eyes.

"I really am sorry about this. I'd hoped for the journey to be consensual, but I'm afraid I canna allow ye to leave. Neither of ye know just how important 'tis that ye go."

Marcus stepped forward with rage in his eyes, but just as he opened his mouth to speak, the room began to spin. I reached for him, and as I latched onto his arm, everything went black.

CHAPTER 9

he Castle of Eight Lairds—1651

here was hay everywhere. It stuck out the top of my shirt, poked me in the bum, and I suspected it would take me hours to get all of it out of my hair. I was disoriented and I hurt all over. I blinked slowly as I strained to try and focus my vision. Large, beautiful brown eyes stared down at me. As I tried to push myself up and out of the giant mound of hay, the horse to my right neighed happily. If I didn't know any better, I would've said he looked rather amused. I was sure it wasn't every day that strange women fell from the sky and into his hay.

"Marcus?"

He grunted in response. Reaching for the stable door, I pulled myself up and looked over at the other side where Marcus lay balled up on the floor.

"Are you okay?"

He lifted his head to look at me.

"I'm alive."

"Well, get up and get in here with me. If someone comes in, at least we can hide in here. We need to figure out what to do."

Marcus was angry. I could tell from the way the muscles in his jaw were bulging as he ground his teeth.

"My head is splitting, Laurel. What did that damned witch do to us?"

My head hurt, as well, but I had too much on my mind to pay the pain any mind.

"She did exactly what she told us she was going to do. She sent us back in time."

Lifting the latch on the stall, Marcus opened the door and stepped inside with me and the horse.

"We're stuck here, Laurel. I heard what Jerry said to her. He said there was no way for us to get back."

I couldn't allow myself to believe that was true. I knew Morna through the story she'd shared with me. She wasn't evil. She wouldn't upend someone's life so completely without a reason. I would say nothing to Marcus about the book and his portrait inside, but I suspected the reason we were here had everything to do with him. If I had to guess, I assumed I was here for moral support and maybe—as she'd said—to regain some inspiration for my writing.

"I don't believe that. And you can't allow yourself to wallow in that hole, either. She said that we were meant to be here. Maybe there is something we are supposed to do, some role we are meant to play, and when we've completed it, we will be able to return home."

Marcus didn't appear to be convinced.

"And what role is that? We know no one here. We will both stand out like sore thumbs. We have nowhere to stay, no way to earn money. Heck, I don't even know how money works in this time. We will be lucky if we survive a week here."

"I don't know."

As if she'd heard his worries from centuries ahead, there was a loud, sudden thump on the other side of the stall wall where I'd found Marcus. I leaned over to find a pile of folded clothes with a letter on top.

"You've got to be kidding me."

Marcus retrieved the items and ripped open the letter as he leaned against the side of the stall. I reached out to stroke our new equine friend as he read the letter aloud.

Laurel and Marcus,

I am truly sorry for the scare I've given you. While I've been known to surprise others with the travel, never before have I sent someone through when they believed me capable of ill intent. I promise that I mean you no harm. I know you must have many questions. Firstly, put on these clothes straight away. Unless ye wish to be burned for witchcraft, doona let anyone see you dressed as you are now.

Laurel, you are in the stables of the castle you wish to visit. Had you traveled back tomorrow, I would've placed you on their front steps, but since you made me send you in the middle of the night, I thought it best you hide out until morning. Some of The Eight travel down to the village every third day to check on their tenants and to see to the needs of their people. Tomorrow is just such a day. Best be out of their stables by sunlight lest you wish to be accused of trying to steal their horses.

When you approach the castle, tell whomever greets you that you are here to see Laird Allen. He's familiar with me. He'll know what to do with you.

Marcus, I've never been one to mince words, so I'll not dance around something I'm sure you already know. Things may not be easy for you here. The color of your skin may subject you to unfair prejudice, and I am sorry for it. What I can promise you is that the men within this castle are different. While you are among them, they will protect you and treat you as the equal that you are. When Laurel gains entry to the castle, insist that you would never allow Laurel to enter without an escort. They will expect to know what you are to her, and a friend simply won't do. Say you are adoptive siblings. They should allow you to stay at the castle, as well.

Once there, try to relax and enjoy. Get to know the men. Get to know the castle. It won't take long for the reason I've sent you here to be clear.

I'll be watching. If you ever truly need me, I'll be there.

Much love,

Morna

P.S. If it makes you feel any better, Jerry is very cross with me. He wanted you to know that. He tried to talk me out of all this many, many times.

When Marcus finished reading the letter, he crumpled it up and threw it as hard as he could across the stables.

"This is madness, Laurel. What are we supposed to do until tomorrow?"

I patted my new friend as the horse leaned his large head into my hands. I could see that Marcus was angry, worried, and grappling with how any of this could be real. I was worried for him, too.

"Hey." I walked across the stall and reached for his hands. "Are you okay? I believe what Morna says. I don't think she would allow anything to happen to you. If she says that these men are different, I'm certain they are. And as for what we do, I guess we hang out with this big fellow." I patted the horse as if Marcus didn't already know who I meant. "At least we are safe in here, and it will be far warmer than camping outside."

Marcus' angry expression softened as he pulled one of his hands away from mine to gently cup the side of my face.

"Laurel, as angry as I am with the witch, I'm glad she didn't bullshit me. Of course, things will be trickier for me here. Although, I imagine things will be more difficult for you here, as well. I'll be fine. Anything that is said to me, I doubt it will be anything I haven't heard before. And I agree, if there is any real danger posed to me, surely if Morna has the power to send us here, she has the power to help me out of a bind. I want you to promise me something, Laurel."

"What?"

"When ignorance rears its ugly head—which it's bound to— please keep your mouth shut. I know you mean well, but sometimes you tend to make things worse. I can handle myself, okay?"

I knew he was right. Marcus might as well have been my brother for as protective as I was of him.

"I'll do my best."

He smiled and threw me the dress he'd draped over the side of the stall and closed his eyes tight.

"That's all I ask. Now, let's get changed. The next time I see Morna, I'm going to kill her."

Laughing, I began to undress. Marcus was the gentlest man I knew. "Says the man who called me when a mouse got into his apartment."

"All right. Maybe I won't kill her, but I'm definitely going to give her a piece of my mind."

"I'm sure you will. Now, help me tie this up, and can you please just try and enjoy this a little bit? We've stepped into a world most people have never seen."

It took a few hours of visiting and me making every possible effort to make him laugh, but as the night wore on, Marcus relaxed.

By the time we stopped talking and decided to try and get some sleep, he was as curious about what the next day would bring as I was.

Our excitement was replaced with fear as we were both startled awake at dawn.

CHAPTER 10

The Castle of Eight Lairds

*L*ifted up by my arms in the middle of a deep sleep, I struggled fruitlessly against the hands that gripped at me as I woke.

A giant of a man with curly red hair and a frizzy red beard held me away from him as I found my footing. He smiled widely but shook his head and clucked his tongue before speaking.

"Ye two are the worst thieves I've ever seen. Ye fell asleep in the middle of yer jobs."

"We're not...we're not thieves."

I glanced over to see Marcus who was being held back by a tall but slender man with dark hair that was cropped short and eyes that were a startling blue. His face was grim. He looked remarkably serious.

Marcus said nothing. He still looked half-asleep.

The man in front of me—seemingly deciding that I was no

threat—released his grip on me as he crossed his arms across his chest.

"Oh, really? Then how and why did ye climb our gates in the dead of night, and why are ye asleep in the stall with our finest horse?"

"We were on our way to see Laird," I completely drew a blank on the name Morna mentioned in her letter. "Laird...Laird Aldridge. He's expecting us."

Marcus groaned, and I knew that I'd said the wrong name.

The man in front of me laughed. "Laird Aldridge? There is no such man here."

"I...I mean Laird Albert."

I knew the second I uttered the name that it was wrong, as well. In an attempt to save me, Marcus spoke up for the first time. It was a struggle to refrain from literally facepalming myself on the forehead. I felt like a total idiot.

"Laird Allen. We are here to see Laird Allen."

The man turned to face Marcus.

"And ye say he's expecting ye? Ye think I should believe that when this lassie," he paused and pointed his thumb at me, "doesna even know his name? Do ye know him?"

I tried to recover.

"I do know his name. You just startled me, is all. And we do know him. As I said, he's expecting us."

He swiveled back toward me.

"This shall be fun, lass. Okay, if ye truly do know him, pray tell me what he looks like."

I was an imbecile. I glanced back and forth between the two men and pleaded with Marcus with my eyes for help. He simply shrugged.

"It's been a very long time since I last saw him. I would've been a small child, really. Although, I do remember that he is very tall."

"Just how tall would that be, lass?"

I pursed my lips and attempted to look like I was trying to remember. "I would say just a little bit shorter than you."

For the first time since our exchange began, the man holding Marcus' arms released him and cracked a silent smile.

The red-haired man shook his head and smiled even more widely.

"Ye've managed to make Calder smile. He doesna smile for anyone. I suppose that means that thief or not, we canna kill ye. 'Twould break his heart."

My eyes must have widened with worry for the man hurried to reassure me.

"Doona fash, lass, I only speak in jest. We wouldna ever kill ye. Now, do ye have any idea what ye said that might've made Calder smile so?"

I shook my head. I didn't have any idea.

"Lass, Laird Allen canna be more than a few years older than ye are. I doona believe that he was my height at the age of ten."

"Damnit."

The redhead's eyes widened.

"'Tis unladylike to curse, lass."

"Ha." Marcus seemed to be enjoying the spectacle I was making of myself. His smile was as wide as Calder's. "There's nothing ladylike about Laurel."

The redhead raised his brows at me in question.

"Is that so, lass? Ye look like quite the proper lady."

I shot Marcus a frown. I was low-maintenance to be sure. I didn't fuss with fashionable clothes, and I never paid more than twenty dollars for a tube of mascara, but I'd never considered myself unladylike. Perhaps, I did need to start trying just a little harder. I didn't like the thought of anyone thinking of me as a manly slob.

"I...I am too ladylike." My answer sounded ridiculously childish.

The redhead gave me a sympathetic look. "O'course ye are. Laurel, was it?"

I nodded.

441

"'Tis a bonny name." He extended his hand to me, and I gladly took it. His grip was firm and his handshake was a little over exuberant, but it made me like him immediately. "I'm Harry."

"It's nice to meet you, Harry." I pointed to Marcus once my hand was free. "This is my brother, Marcus."

As expected, Harry's brows lifted as his trademark smile spread across his face once again. He was looking at the obvious difference in our skin colors and not buying it for a second.

Harry extended his hand toward Marcus and spoke as they shook. "Yer brother? Are ye sure ye dinna mean to say friend or mayhap, lover?"

Marcus spoke and the lie sounded remarkably believable even to me. "Her parents took me in when I was young. I'm her brother in every way that matters."

Understanding spread across Harry's face, and I could see right away that Morna had been truthful. There was no malice in the man's doubt, only curiosity. "Neither of ye are from here, aye? Not that I rightly care, to be sure. 'Tis only that I've never heard such speech in my life. I've already told ye Calder's name. He's a shy one. Ye willna get much out of him. Now." He clasped his palms together and rubbed them back and forth excitedly. "Calder and I are expected in the village shortly. 'Tis time we decide what to do with ye."

"What to do with us? Are you not going to let us speak to Laird Allen?"

"Laird Allen isna here. He hasna been in two and a half years. I doona expect he will be here for another fortnight, at least. While I doona believe for a moment that ye know him or that ye even have business with him, I like ye well enough that I'm willing to host ye until he returns. I'm verra curious to see how he responds to ye."

For the first time, Calder spoke up, his tone filled with warning.

"She's a lassie, Harry. She canna stay in the castle. 'Tis not allowed."

Harry waved a dismissive hand.

LOVE BEYOND WORDS

"Calder, 'tis a foolish superstition—one we should've tested long ago. She tries to control us through fear. 'Tis likely that much of what she says is untrue. I hardly believe that having one lass inside these walls will cause us trouble."

"Let us at least have them stay in the village, Harry. 'Twill be safer for everyone."

Harry gestured toward the stable doors with a small nod of his head. Together, we all began to move toward the exit.

"Ach, doona be such a worrier, Calder. 'Twill send ye to an early grave. 'Twill lift everyone's spirits to have a lass about—even yers, I reckon."

As Harry pushed the large doors open, we stepped out into the fresh air, and Marcus and I got our first look at The Castle of Eight Lairds. It was even more gothic and intimidating than it appeared in the documentary. Dark, dead vines creeped up the front, and the forest surrounding it dropped off steeply on each side.

Marcus muttered under his breath, "Wow."

Harry clasped Marcus on the shoulder. "'Tis even more impressive in the daytime, aye?"

Marcus nodded as Calder stepped over near Harry. "I doona think this a good idea."

Harry's tone dropped and I noticed that his face—when he wasn't smiling—made him appear very unfriendly.

"I doona care what ye think, Calder. See them settled inside while I ready our horses. Place Marcus in Timothy's old room. Place Laurel in the castle's finest bedchamber."

"But that's Raudrich's room."

Harry nodded. "Precisely. Raudrich has always had a soft place in his heart for the lassies. He willna have the heart to remove her once he arrives, and it will keep the rest of us from being unsettled. He can sleep elsewhere."

Without another word, Harry turned to leave us. Desperate to see the inside of the castle, I all but chased after Calder as he walked inside.

CHAPTER 11

*T*he rest of the day passed rather strangely. After Calder showed us to our individual rooms, he informed us that the other men of the castle were out in the forest working and that the master of the castle—whatever that meant—was already in the village for the day. He told us to make ourselves at home, to explore as we wished, and to be in the dining hall for dinner at sundown.

It was all very strange. While Calder was polite, he did nothing to hide his disapproval of Harry's order. I couldn't blame him.

It was one thing to allow us to stay here until Laird Allen returned. It was another thing entirely to leave us unattended in a massive castle that was undoubtedly filled with all sorts of valuable items.

I loved it. I couldn't remember a time when I'd been more excited about anything. I'd thought touring Scottish castles long after their prime was the peak of excitement. I was wrong. Touring them in this time, as a guest, was something I would be able to live off of for years.

It was unlike any other Scottish castle I'd ever seen. Gothic and exaggerated, each new wing was creepier than the last. And it was blatantly obvious that men lived and ruled here. It lacked anything feminine or fancy. Everything was for function, nothing for fuss.

Marcus and I spent the day familiarizing ourselves with the castle. About an hour before sunset, we each went to our room to freshen up.

I was ready way before Marcus. He was notorious for taking forever to get ready for anything. I waited inside my borrowed room until he came for me.

"You ready?" He called to me through the door just as the sun dipped below the bedchamber's tall window, and I threw the door open with way too much force.

"So ready."

He smiled at me and offered his arm.

"You look good, Laurel. More like yourself. As angry as I am at that witch, I'm pleased that you're enjoying this so much. You needed something to bring you back to life."

---

*T*he ruckus from the dining hall could be heard as soon as we descended the castle's grand stairway, but the moment Marcus and I stepped into the room, it fell completely silent.

"Hi." It was literally the only thing I could think to say as seven men who were even more impressive in stature than Marcus rose from their seats around the table.

Harry was the first to speak.

"Laurel, lass, ye look even lovelier than ye did this morning. Ye and yer brother come around here so I may introduce ye to everyone."

Nodding, we made our way to the side of the long table where there were two empty seats waiting for us.

He wasted no time in making introductions. I paid special attention as I was determined to do a better job of remembering each of their names than I was usually capable of doing.

"Calder, o'course."

He pointed briefly to the man we'd already met and then moved his finger to the next man around the table.

The man had solid gray hair that fell just below his chin. He had kind but sad green eyes and stubble along his cheeks that was a slightly darker shade of grey. He was easily the oldest man at the table. He was also the shortest. He looked like he hadn't slept in weeks.

"This is Nicol. He is the master of the castle and the man whom we all serve."

Nicol dipped his head in recognition and gave us both a smile that made my heart ache. He looked heartbroken and pained.

"Greetings to ye both. Ye are welcome here as long as ye wish. Any friend of Raudrich's is a friend of mine."

Out of the corner of my eye, I noticed Calder begin to open his mouth, but before he could say anything, Harry elbowed him straight in the ribs and gave him a look that made it clear he'd not told the rest of the men the truth about who we were.

I muttered a quick greeting and a thank you to him before Harry continued his introductions.

The next, a man named Quinn, had brilliantly blond hair that fell to his waist. His eyes were dark brown. He was striking in the most unusual way.

Next to Quinn sat Ludo. Ludo had the coolest curls I'd ever seen. They framed his face in a way that would make any girl envious, and his honey-colored eyes matched the shade of his hair. I was certain he had no trouble wooing ladies.

At the table's end was Paton. He was easily the youngest. I couldn't imagine that he was much older than twenty. He had jet black hair that he kept pinned at the nape. His brown eyes were kind and soft.

Finally, Harry ended his introductions with the man directly to Marcus' right—Maddock. He had broad shoulders and strong arms— a trait every man around the table shared. Maddock kept his hair cut short, although it was slightly longer on top. His hair was a dirty blond and he had green-gold eyes. His nose was slightly large, with a knot in the middle which was a sure giveaway that at some point he'd broken it. His cheeks were smattered with freckles. I couldn't explain why, but I felt an immediate kinship with this man. He reminded me of someone I'd known before, but I couldn't recall who.

When all introductions were made, we sat down to enjoy our meal.

"Who did the cooking?"

Ludo answered with pride in his eyes, straight away.

"Tonight, 'twas I, but we share all duties equally. Tomorrow is Quinn's turn so if ye are wise ye will fill yer belly tonight. Quinn is a rubbish cook."

Quinn tried to protest but was quickly silenced by the chorus of voices who chimed in to agree with Ludo.

Once their teasing ended, Ludo spoke up once again.

"We doona have help here at the castle, so we must all do our part. 'Tis why it is time for Raudrich to return home. We've all been doing his share of the work for far too long. He has much to make up for. If ye doona mind me asking, how exactly is it that ye know him?"

I felt the light tap of Harry's foot on top of my own. A slightly more gentle warning than he'd given Calder.

I winked at him to let him know I understood while I scrambled for a believable explanation.

Morna was a Conall and she'd claimed that Raudrich knew of her. Perhaps I could claim relation to them.

"I'm a distant cousin to the laird of Conall territory. As you know, Laird Allen is friends with the Conalls. We met while we were both staying at the castle many years ago—when we were children."

Paton chimed in from the table's end.

"And why do ye need to see him now? I'm surprised that ye

knew he was here. To the people of this territory, Raudrich has another name. He's had to keep his identity a secret to protect his familial clan."

He might as well have been speaking gibberish. There was so much about this time, about their customs and the rules among clans that I didn't know. I would have to tread carefully.

Marcus didn't allow me the time to formulate an answer. "She's in love with him."

The blood drained from my face as I shrank in my chair in horror.

Every man around the table looked as shocked as I felt.

I could see that Harry was struggling to suppress his laughter. "In love with him, ye say? Promise us that ye will wait to tell him that until we are all around to see it."

Meekly, I tried to respond with something reasonable. "I think that's something best expressed in private."

"Right ye are, lass." Harry stood and the rest of the men followed suit. "I think it best we all retire early. Ye two must be tired after yer journey."

Clearly the rest of them didn't know about our night in their stables. Although, I couldn't disagree with him. I was exhausted and I couldn't wait to sleep on a seventeenth century bed. I had no idea what to expect.

"I can't speak for Marcus, but I am rather tired. Thank you all so much for your hospitality."

"'Tis our pleasure, lass. Mayhap tomorrow I can get ye to help me with something?"

"Of course. I'd be happy to help you all in any way I can."

"Good."

It was evident from the way every man stood around the table unmoving that they were waiting to disband until we made our leave. Glancing at Marcus to make sure he was on the same page, we stood and left the dining hall.

Baring my teeth, I whispered to him through my clenched jaw. "You are so dead."

He barely made it out of the dining hall before he burst into laughter.

CHAPTER 12

I watched Paton's every move carefully as he worked to light the fire in my bedchamber. I wanted to be able to do it myself if I ever needed to. He built the fire carefully, placing only two logs to burn so I'd have enough light and heat to get safely into bed, but not so much that it would keep burning well into the night.

"Thank you so much. I'm sure I could've managed it myself." It was a complete lie, but as this was surely a task anyone from this time could do in their sleep, I thought it best to pretend that I was equally as familiar with the process.

Righting himself as the flames grew, Paton turned to smile at me as he brushed away my thanks.

"No need, miss. Tonight 'twas my job. Tomorrow, Nicol will see the castle lit at night."

I smiled at his use of *miss* when all of the other men would've said *lass*. It confirmed what I already suspected. Paton was the baby of the group.

"Well, thank you all the same. Have a good night."

"Ye, as well. If ye need anything, I willna mind if ye wake me. 'Twould be better for ye to do that than go traipsing around the castle in the dark. There are far too many corridors for ye to get lost in unless ye are verra familiar with the castle. My room is at the bottom of the stairs, to the right."

As he closed the door behind him, I placed both hands on my hips and turned to look at the room and started to laugh. There was no way for me to brush my teeth or my hair—only a basin of cold water to splash over my face. While the thought of going to bed without brushing my teeth did ick me out a little, it was no bother to me that I would have to forgo my nightly ritual of proper skincare. A few days—or even weeks, for that matter—of a good water cleansing wouldn't kill me. What made me laugh was thinking of Marcus and the reaction I knew he must be having in his own room.

He was remarkably high-maintenance for someone with so little hair, and I knew having to pee in a small basin would horrify him.

Smiling to myself at the thought of Marcus stomping around his own room cursing everything and everyone in this castle, I washed my face as best I could, used the less-than-ideal facilities, and crawled into bed in my dress.

The bed was surprisingly soft and with the number of warm blankets spread on top, I found that while it was significantly lumpier than my modern memory foam bed, it wasn't uncomfortable in the least. What *was* uncomfortable was the binding of my dress. I knew I wouldn't be able to sleep with it on.

If every one of the men within the castle walls hadn't been perfectly respectable at dinner, I might have hesitated to strip down and sleep in the nude when there was no way to lock my door, but I knew Morna in a way that Marcus never would, thanks to the story she'd gifted me so many months ago, and I knew she wouldn't have placed me here if I was in any real danger.

Sighing with relief as I loosened the laces and allowed my breasts to spring free, I shimmied out of the dress and crawled happily into bed.

I was lulled to sleep by the slowly dying fire.

*R*audrich could see nothing in the darkness of night. All he could make out was the faint glow of the moon. He couldn't see the road ahead or spot any branches that might be hanging down in his way on the forest path. He only knew they were drawing close from Pinkie's descriptions of what surrounded them.

Daylight was difficult enough, but once the sun went down, he caught glimpses of the fate he would face if the rest of The Eight were unable to heal him. The one hope he had was that his vision had not grown worse since leaving Allen territory, which meant that the progression of his blindness was indeed somehow connected to his time away from the castle and the fact that their spell of binding on the faerie buried below them was pulling more strength from him now that Timothy was gone.

Pinkie was a talented navigator, which more than made up for his bawdy language and incessant chattering. The man had as much stamina for riding as he did, which allowed them to ride more quickly and for longer stretches than he'd expected. He was worth more than the amount he'd paid him. The journey would've been entirely impossible without him.

"I believe we are here. I've never seen such gates in my life. Just who is it that ye are trying to keep out of here?"

Pulling his horse to a stop, Raudrich dismounted and, with his arms in front of him, carefully made his way over to the gate.

"These gates are not intended to keep others out. They are intended to keep a great evil in."

Pinkie laughed.

"Is it a three-eyed monster, then?"

Raudrich placed both palms on the gate as he felt around for the delicately hidden latch. "'Tis far worse. Surely, ye have heard the stories of this place?"

Pinkie's tone was surprised and more somber when he answered.

"Aye, o'course, but not many such stories are true."

Grasping the small lift that only The Eight knew was there, he felt the gate give way enough for him to push it open.

He was more certain of his steps on his way back to his horse. He knew the land around this castle like the back of his hand. He could make the remainder of the journey alone.

"Aye, well, the stories of this place are true."

Pinkie spoke quietly and Raudrich thought he detected fear in his tone.

"Ye are a druid, then? One of the mysterious Eight?"

Raudrich mounted his horse with ease.

"Aye, and here is where I must bid ye farewell. I've been away too long, and I doona know whether or not 'tis safe for ye beyond these gates." He reached for his bag of coins and tossed it toward Pinkie. "'Tis all that I owe ye, along with enough to see ye settled and fed in the village tonight."

Raudrich extended his hand and waited for Pinkie to shake his hand in farewell.

"Thank ye for this. It has been my pleasure to ride with ye these last days. If ye ever need my assistance again, ye know where to find me."

He waited until he could no longer hear the hooves of Pinkie's horse retreating back down the hill before pushing his way through the gate. After making sure it was securely closed behind him, Raudrich rode the rest of the way up to the castle.

The others wouldn't be expecting him for at least another three days, which was exactly as he preferred it. This way, he could slip quietly inside, retreat to his bedchamber, and get a thorough night's sleep before having to face the endless questions he knew they would all have for him.

Raudrich sighed as he dismounted once more and guided his horse into the stables. This was the only place in the world where he felt truly like himself. There were many troubles ahead of him, he knew. With Timothy gone, they all faced the arduous task of finding another druid worthy of replacing him, and he could already feel the power of the fae they kept locked away rising again. But all of that could be dealt with in a few day's time. For now, he had a long-awaited appointment with his sorely-missed bed.

He could feel the warmth of his blankets, could sense the sweet dreams he would have just thinking about it. He couldn't wait to crawl inside.

CHAPTER 13

There was a residual feeling of warmth lingering in his bedchamber as he slipped inside and quietly closed the door—almost as if a fire had been lit inside not long ago.

Raudrich walked over to the fireplace and hovered his hands over the ashes. They were still warm.

Paton. It had to be Paton. He was the only one with reason to want to steal his bed. He couldn't even bring himself to blame him. The poor lad's own room was barely larger than a cupboard.

He held his breath and listened carefully. Within seconds, the soft rise and fall of someone breathing from under the covers reached his ears.

If he woke him, Paton would wake the rest of the men and the night of precious sleep he'd spent weeks longing for would be ruined. He'd be damned if he would be denied his own bed the first night after returning home in years.

Groaning, Raudrich walked over to the bed. Placing his hands on top of the blankets, he pushed the lad from the center of the bed over to one side so there would be room for him, as well.

The lad felt lighter than he expected. Perhaps, the pudgy

adolescent he'd known before he left had grown more slender in the past two years.

Paton let out a soft whimper as Raudrich moved him, and Raudrich couldn't suppress a laugh at the unusually high pitch of the sound.

Kicking off his shoes, Raudrich removed his riding shirt. With his riding breeches still on, he crawled inside and fell quickly to sleep.

I dreamt I was sleeping. The dream was spotty, and dark, and sexy as hell. I was in the arms of a man with my head snuggled against his broad, firm chest. He was warm and I was more comfortable in his hold than I could remember ever being in another's. I loved the way the stranger's hand—which came protectively around my back—cupped at my breast as we slept.

My head lifted and lowered with his chest as he breathed and his breath would lightly tickle my nose as he exhaled. Smiling, I slowly wound my right leg in between his broad thighs, pulling us even closer together.

My hand lay gently below his chest, and I allowed my thumb to swirl small circles on the tender side of his stomach.

His muscles tightened as he groaned.

It was a deep, sexy noise and my knee seemed to slide gently up and down the space between his legs on its own.

The slow rise and fall of his breath quickened as I felt him harden beneath the light touch of my knee.

My own breath came more quickly. As I breathed in, the smell of him—sweat and earth—reached my nostrils, and something at the edge of my mind began to tickle uncomfortably.

A thought was trying to break through, to break into my dream, but I fought against it. It was one of those dreams you never wanted to end, and as you feel morning coming, your conscious mind quietly urges your unconscious mind to just stay sleeping a little bit longer.

The man shifted beneath me, as his left hand came around and began to roam over my body. I moaned in response to his touch, and then the thought I'd been trying so desperately to ignore came soaring into my blissful dream.

This was *too* real—the warmth, the rise and fall of my head with his breath, the smell of him. It all slowly fell into place in my mind as I woke. I had no choice but to open my eyes.

It was still completely dark in the room and it took a long moment for me to wake enough for panic and terror to set in.

There was a man in my bed, and I was naked.

Shrieking, I raised and scooted to the edge of the bed, bringing my knees back until I kicked him in the side with so much force that he landed on the floor with a loud thud.

I continued to scream, then remembering that Marcus was only a room away, I began to call for him as I scuttled off the bed and pulled the mound of blankets onto the floor with me to cover myself.

The man I'd pushed to the floor began to scream, too. Not the same loud, panicked scream I was emitting, but a deep cry of pain and confusion.

The door to the bedchamber burst open. As I heard Marcus call out to me, I stopped screaming. If he was here, I was safe. I trusted Marcus with my life.

"Laurel! What's happening? Are you okay?"

Shaking, I stood and wrapped the blankets around me and held them tight with my arms.

"I woke to find one of them," I paused and pointed to the stranger who was now lifting himself off the floor, "in my bed."

In between groans, my assailant spoke.

"Paton, ye sound like a lassie. Why in God's name did ye kick me? Ye've broken at least one rib, I'm sure of it. And ye woke me from the bonniest dream."

Completely baffled, I walked around the edge of the bed to look down at him. His voice didn't match that of any of the men we'd met at dinner, and I couldn't deny that he sounded genuinely confused.

Just as he tried to stand, Marcus moved from the doorway and shoved him back to the ground.

"You stay right there, you son of a bitch, or I'll kill you."

I'd never heard Marcus so angry.

"Broken rib or not, I'd like to see ye try, lad." Pushing Marcus back with surprisingly little effort, the man did manage to stand. "Who the hell are ye, and what in the name of God is going on?"

Marcus held a lantern in his left hand and shoved it toward me just as he threw his right fist into the man's nose. The crack of it made my own nose hurt. There was no way it wasn't broken.

The impact sent the man tumbling backwards as the back of his head cracked against the stone wall a few feet behind him.

Just as the man crumpled to the ground, Harry, Ludo, and Quinn appeared in the doorway, each with a candle in hand.

Harry took one look at me and then at the man lying unconscious on the floor and quickly turned toward Marcus.

"Lad, I doona know what happened here, but I'm certain 'tis not how it appears. Take Laurel to yer room and tend to her. My men and I will tend to Raudrich, and I assure ye we will get to the truth of what happened here. If I am wrong about his character—if he did intend the lassie harm—ye can rest assured that we will see him duly punished for his crime."

Marcus was trembling with rage.

"Of course he meant her harm. He crawled into bed with her while she was sleeping. What else could he have meant?"

Harry's tone was sympathetic but he remained calm as he pointed to the unconscious man Quinn and Ludo were now lifting off the floor.

"He dinna know the two of ye were here, and 'tis his room that

Laurel was sleeping in. Perhaps, he dinna know she was inside when he crawled in bed."

With the adrenaline slowing wearing off, I was able to think more clearly. I wasn't all that hard of a sleeper. If he'd tried to hurt me, I would've woken much sooner. And as loathe as I was to admit it, I could recall the beginning of my "dream," where I'd rolled toward him and slipped into the space between his arm and chest.

Gently, I stepped between Marcus and Harry and placed a light hand on Marcus' arm.

"I think he's right, Marcus. He didn't hurt me. It just scared me to death when I woke up and saw him. I thought...I thought I was dreaming. I truly do think this was just all a big mistake."

Marcus let out a breath that made me throw my arms around him in comfort. I knew what it felt like to be so worried for someone that when you learn they're okay, breath that you didn't even know you were holding comes out so quickly that it's hard to stay standing. It was the same way I'd felt when Mom had told me that Kate had woken from her coma.

His arms came around me quickly, holding the blankets up around me.

"Are you certain, Laurel? He didn't touch you? Didn't put his hands on you?"

There was no need for anyone else save me and this stranger to know the truth about just exactly how much touching had gone on.

"No. When I woke, I was on one side of the bed. He was on the other. It just scared me is all. I'm so sorry for causing this whole mess."

Harry placed a light hand on my back.

"This is my doing, lass. Calder was right when he said I shouldna have put ye in his room. I shall pay for it when Raudrich wakes. This is hardly the welcome he expected."

Marcus' voice was shaky but I knew he was satisfied that I was okay. He took one look at the blood pouring out of Raudrich's nose as Ludo and Quinn struggled to get him situated on the bed and winced.

"I'm sorry for hitting him."

Harry laughed and slowly ushered us out into the hallway.

"Doona be sorry, lad. Ye did what any good brother would do. Ye both need to rest after such a scare. We will see all of this settled come morning."

Marcus nodded and turned to lead me away.

We both knew we were done sleeping for the night.

CHAPTER 14

*R*audrich didn't know if he'd ever been in such pain before. There was no part of him that didn't ache dreadfully. He didn't care at all. He would gladly accept such pain forever for the blessing it had brought him.

He could see. Not as well as he once had, but so much better than the day before. The man to his left was more than a blurry blob. If he strained and looked past the swollen knob between his eyes, he could see that it was Maddock.

"What are ye smiling for? Ye really dinna need anything to make ye any uglier. Yer nose was large to begin with. It will be even larger when this heals."

Raudrich laughed but stopped abruptly at the sharp pain that shot through his side in response.

"I can see ye. Ye canna know how happy that makes me."

Maddock's brows pulled together in confusion and Raudrich delighted in the fact that he could see the gesture.

"What do ye mean? Marcus hit ye in the nose, he dinna poke yer eyes out."

"I'll tell ye all about it in a bit. First, I need one of ye to explain to me what happened last night. Who is the man that did this to me, and why did he wish to kill me?"

The entire night was a blur to him. It had been one of the happiest night's sleep of his life. He rarely dreamt of anything, but last night—on his first night home in far too long—he'd dreamt of a woman. Naked and pressed against him, he held her warm breast in his hand as her silky leg rubbed against his manhood, stirring him to arousal. It had all ended much too abruptly as Paton kicked him from the bed. The next thing he knew there was an angry voice in his ear and a fist flying toward his face. Then, everything went dark again.

Maddock shrugged.

"I doona have any idea. Harry willna tell me anything. I doona believe Nicol, Calder, or Paton even know ye are back yet. Harry woke me..."

Raudrich held his hand up to stop him.

"What do ye mean Paton doesna know I'm back yet? Was it not he that I found in my room last night?"

Maddock's eyes widened in understanding.

"Ach, no wonder he broke yer nose. Ye thought Paton was in yer bed?"

An uncomfortable sense of dread began to creep up his spine.

"Aye, 'tis what I said. 'Twas it not?"

Maddock started to grin.

"And ye crawled in bed with him?"

Raudrich nodded, his frustration growing.

"Aye. I was exhausted from the journey. I knew if I woke him, he'd wake the rest of ye and then I wouldna get to sleep until dawn."

Maddock shook his head and Raudrich could see he was suppressing laughter.

"Paton wasna in yer room last night."

"Then who the hell was?"

"Laurel."

Raudrich's body flooded with heat and horror. Was it possible that he'd not been dreaming? Had there truly been a lassie in his bed? Surely all that he'd felt—her skin, her breasts—it couldn't have been real? But if it was...had it been his doing or hers?

"Who is Laurel?"

"What do ye mean, who is Laurel? Ye've known her since ye were a child. She came all this way to see ye, though I doona believe she expected the greeting ye gave her."

He knew no one by the name of Laurel, but there were greater things on his mind.

"Is this Marcus her husband? Is that why he attacked me? He entered to find us asleep next to each other in the bed? I swear I thought 'twas Paton."

"Marcus is her brother, though not by blood."

The door to his room slowly creaked open as Harry stepped inside.

"Thank God, Harry. Ye were here last night, were ye not? Tell me what happened. Doona spare me anything."

Harry leaned over the bed and gave his leg a quick pat.

"Doona worry, Raudrich. All is well. The lass understands what happened and she isna angry with ye. She says that ye dinna touch her. She woke in the night to see ye lying on the other side of the bed and it gave her quite the fright. Ye can thank her for yer broken ribs. I just had Quinn ready a bath for her, but she'd like to speak to ye a bit later if ye doona mind. She's worried ye might be angry with her."

Angry with her? Her assumption made no sense to him. It was he who had crawled into bed with a naked woman and given her what must've been one of the greatest frights of her life. Accident or not, he owed the lass an apology.

"O'course I doona mind, but tell the lass I'm not angry with her. How could I be?"

Harry shrugged and turned to leave.

"I know. I told her that 'twas she who should be angry, but more than anything, I believe she is embarrassed."

"And she told ye that she knows me?"

Before answering him, Harry asked Maddock to bring him up some breakfast. The moment Maddock was gone, he leaned in close.

"Aye, though 'tis not true. Calder and I could tell straight away the moment we found her and Marcus out in our stables. She called ye the wrong name twice. She knows of ye, but I doona believe the two of ye have ever met. I thought it best to let the other men believe otherwise. Ye know most of them believe women to be a curse in this castle. If they thought her a stranger, they wouldna let her stay here. Because they believe she knows ye, they permitted it without question."

His curiosity for this woman grew with each new thing he learned about her.

"Ye found her in the stables? How did she get past the gate?"

"I doona know. It confounds me, though I doona believe she brings ill will. I quite like the lass, actually. Though, she has her secrets to be sure. I thought I would have time to try and learn them, but 'twas only yesterday morning that I found her."

"And what of Calder? He canna be pleased with this."

"He's not. But he willna say anything to the other men. He has his own secret that I keep for him."

Raudrich knew better than to ask.

"How bad does my face look, Harry?"

"I willna lie to ye. Ye look foul."

Harry turned to leave but called back to him as he left.

"I canna believe ye had a naked woman in yer bed and dinna know it. That must have been some journey. I doona believe I could ever be so tired."

CHAPTER 15

"Marcus..."

"Yes, Laurel?"

Marcus was sitting on the floor, his back against the side of the bed so that I was entirely shielded from his view as I bathed. He didn't want to be forced to answer questions about last night alone and I didn't want to be alone. I had to spill my secret shame to someone or I feared I would burst.

"I did a bad thing. A very bad thing."

"What could you have possibly done?"

He didn't sound like he believed me at all.

"You remember how I said that when I woke up, Raudrich and I were both on separate sides of the bed?"

"Yes. What about it?"

Thoroughly clean and freezing—the water had cooled quickly—I stepped out of the tub, dried myself off, and slipped back into my dress.

"Well, it wasn't exactly true."

"What?" Marcus flew off the floor and I had to run to block him from charging out the door.

"Hang on. Let me explain."

He was shaking again.

"What's there to explain? He either touched you or he didn't. Last night, you said he didn't. Now, you say he did. I'm back to wanting to kill him."

"Don't jump to a conclusion. There's a lot to explain, actually. You see," I couldn't even look at him while I said it. I stared down at my bare feet. "When I woke up, I was in his arms, my head on his chest, my legs intertwined with his. It was...intimate."

I glanced up at Marcus to gauge his reaction. He looked like he was about to blow a gasket. I held up a hand to stop him.

"Hang on. Let me finish. You see, I had a very interesting dream last night. At least, I thought it was a dream until I woke up in Raudrich's arms. Initially, I freaked out, which you already know. But what you don't know is that as I stood there watching you and Harry hash this out, I remembered something from the beginning of what I thought was a dream. Raudrich didn't initiate contact with me. I was the one who rolled over in the bed and snuggled into him. I touched him. He didn't touch me."

Marcus stepped back and moved to sit on the edge of the bed.

"Seriously?"

"Yes." I threw my hands up to cover my face. "I know I was sleeping, but still...I shamelessly felt him up. I even..." I hesitated and then lowered my voice as if I were worried the stone walls wouldn't keep my voice inside, "aroused him. Then I freaked out and broke his ribs."

A smile slowly spread across Marcus' face as he silently crossed his arms and stared at me.

I dramatically slid down to the floor. "Why are you smiling?"

"You think this man will be angry about this?"

"Of course, he is."

Marcus shook his head.

"I'll admit that I'm sure he's not too pleased about the cracked ribs, but if you think he's upset you rubbed yourself against him, you know nothing about men. Besides, he was asleep until you kicked him off the bed. He may not even remember that you touched him."

That was true. Perhaps, I could get away with pretending nothing happened.

"You think?"

"Just go talk to him and say nothing to him about your sleep-induced fondling. Do you mean to apologize to him?"

An apology had never crossed my mind. I was embarrassed and felt guilty for what I'd done to him in my sleep, but I wasn't sorry. Accident or not, my reaction had been perfectly reasonable. What woman wouldn't have reacted in much the same way?

"No. I'm not going to apologize for kicking a man that crawled into bed with me while I was sleeping. I just need to talk to him. We both do, really, but I think it best if I visit with him alone first. I'm going to tell him what Morna told us to. And then we'll just," I shrugged, "see how he responds."

---

*I*t was midday before the string of men stopped entering and exiting Raudrich's room on an endless rotation. Each of the men seemed anxious to visit with their friend who had been away for so long. I was also sure they all wanted to know exactly what happened last night. It was fine with me if they visited with him all day. I wasn't really looking forward to the awkward conversation.

After more than an hour of creepily hanging out in the hallway outside of his room, I finally worked up the nerve to knock. His response was immediate.

"Come in."

His voice sounded weary, and for a moment, I wondered if perhaps I should wait until another day to speak with him. He had to be exhausted, and there was no question that he was in pain.

Hesitantly, I stepped inside and said nothing for a few seconds as I looked him over. Even with his swollen nose and face, I could see that he was handsome. He sat propped up on the bed, with fabric wrapped tightly around his chest to help stabilize his ribs.

"Hi." I gave him a little wave, but stayed standing in the doorway. "I know you've had visitors all morning. I can come back later, or even tomorrow, if you'd rather."

He shook his head and waved me toward him.

"Nonsense, lass. I've been waiting for ye all morning. Do ye mind coming a little closer so I might tell ye how sorry I am, and so that I can properly see ye. Ye look like little more than a ghost from there."

I cocked my head to the side in confusion. The distance between us wasn't far at all. It couldn't be more than ten feet. Had Marcus truly hit him so hard, or was the man's vision naturally weak?

"Of course. It...it's not the injury that is making it difficult for you to see, is it?"

A chair sat right next to his bed, left there by the last man to visit with him. Following his gesture toward it, I took my seat next to him.

"No, though my nose is swollen enough that I do see more of it than anything else at the moment. I've been nearly blind for many weeks now. 'Tis healing though, now that I'm home."

That made absolutely no sense to me. I'd never heard of someone's vision improving based on location, but I said nothing of it. There were lots of things about the last few days that defied reasonable logic.

I decided it was best to start off with a proper introduction. I extended my hand.

"I'm Laurel."

He took it, and as he gripped my hand, I couldn't help but remember the way that same hand had felt cupped around my breast. My cheeks warmed at the thought, and I was certain my cheeks blushed. Thankfully, by the way he was squinting at me, I didn't think he could see it.

"I'm Raudrich." Releasing my hand, he began to apologize as I relaxed into the seat.

"Lass, I canna begin to tell ye how sorry I am for frightening ye last night. I promise ye, had I known that a lass was in my bed, I wouldna have entered it uninvited. As I told ye before, my vision is poor and at night, I canna see a thing. I did hear someone inside when I entered, but I truly thought it was Paton. I've been away from here for sometime. I thought perhaps he had decided to make himself at home in my chambers while I was away. If ye knew what his own room looks like, ye would understand why. In hindsight, I know that I should've awakened him to check, but we doona ever have lassies here. 'Tis a shock to me that Harry allowed ye entry. Ye must have charmed him more than ye know. I never dreamed that the person in my bed was someone I dinna know. I am sorry, lass."

His tone was remorseful, and I knew looking into his eyes that he meant every word. If I hadn't already been convinced of his innocence, his speech would've done the job.

"I know. There's no reason for you to be sorry."

He started to interrupt me, but as he leaned forward, the muscles across his chest tightened and he groaned at the sharp pain that ran through him. Taking in a pained breath, he leaned back into the pillows before speaking.

"There is much reason for me to be sorry. 'Tis bad enough that I entered the bed as ye slept. 'Tis another wrong entirely that I pulled ye against me. I swear to ye, I did so unconsciously in my sleep."

My breath caught uncomfortably. He did remember, then. Asleep or not, he was aware of the way we'd touched. In an uncomfortable panic, I set out to make him think otherwise.

"I don't know what you're talking about. You didn't pull me against you."

He smiled sympathetically.

"Lass, ye owe me nothing. Ye doona need to attempt to make me feel less guilty. I know I held ye in my arms."

"I'm not trying to make you feel anything. Our handshake was the first time we ever touched. When I woke up, I was on one side of the bed and you were on the other."

He didn't appear to believe me, but I could see by the way he started to speak but then bit his lower lip that he'd decided not to argue with me.

"If that is the way ye remember last night, I am glad of it, for I dinna care for the way I felt about myself this morning. The thought that I frightened ye or made ye feel unsafe wounded me greatly. I'm glad that we may put all that happened last night behind us."

I smiled and crossed my arms as I leaned back in the chair. With that discussion out of the way, I felt much more comfortable.

"Me, too."

He nodded in agreement and then took a deep breath before speaking once more. His tone this time was more direct, and far less friendly.

"Now, lass, forgive me for being so blunt, but why did ye lie to Harry? I doona know ye. I know with certainty I've never seen ye before in my life. So what are ye doing here, and how do ye know my real name?"

So much for being comfortable.

CHAPTER 16

*R*audrich watched Laurel closely as she shifted in the seat. She was beautiful. With blonde hair that fell just past her shoulders and thick, dark brows that framed icy blue eyes—even blurry—she was more attractive than he imagined she would be. It made his dreamlike memories of the night before come to life in a way that made it impossible to deny what had happened.

He'd not been dreaming. When the lass had woken, she'd not been on the other side of the bed. Why then, did she wish to pretend that nothing had happened? He believed her when she said she wasn't trying to ease his guilt. What then wasn't she telling him?

There were so many things he wanted to ask her, but he thought it best to start with the most pertinent question. They all needed to know why she was here.

"Why...why am I here? Would you believe me if I told you that I'm not quite sure?"

He shifted and then cried out as the pain in his side ricocheted down his body. His damn ribs were going to be a problem. He didn't have time to lay in bed while they healed. He would have to call on the other men to use power they truly didn't have to spare to heal him. There was so much they all needed to do to protect their home and people now that Timothy was gone.

Before he knew it, Laurel's hands were on him. Gently she leaned toward him, placing her arms underneath his. Her movement was so intuitive, so natural, that he didn't question it as she spoke gently near his ear. The feel of her breath against his neck sent shivers down his spine.

"Here." She lifted him off the pillows, as she reached behind him to adjust them. "That doesn't look like the best position for those ribs." After a few moments of maneuvering, she released her grip and encouraged him to relax. "See if that is any better."

It was. He sighed as he relaxed into the greater support that was now built up behind his back.

"Aye, thank ye."

Smiling, she resumed her seat next to him.

"You're welcome. I'm sure you were about to tell me no—that you wouldn't believe me."

She was right. He didn't.

"Ye are not from this village. To come to our territory requires not only a long journey by horse, but also the short distance between this isle and the mainland by boat. Why would ye make such a journey if ye dinna know yer reason for doing so?"

Laurel sighed and leaned forward to rest her elbows on her knees as she spoke to him. It was a casual position and one he'd never seen a woman rest in. He found it rather endearing.

"You're going to think I'm crazy."

Laurel's accent was one he'd heard before. He sensed that if he could simply place it, so many answers about the strange woman would fall into place.

"Where are ye from, lass? Yer speech is uncommon, but I'm sure that I've heard it somewhere before."

Laurel's expression lifted, as if his acknowledgment gave her hope.

"Boston." She hesitated and then continued. "In...in the colonies."

"Ah."

It came to him in an instant. Sydney. Laurel's accent was much like Sydney's. In truth, she was like Sydney in many ways. They shared the same speech, the same casual mannerisms so different from most women he knew. He expected that if he was given a chance to know this woman more, he would find that she was as loose with her speech as Sydney was, as well.

Smiling, he thought of Harry's claim that they'd found her in the stables. The assumption that was forming in his mind truly was the only explanation.

"Are ye one of Morna's lassies?"

Laurel straightened and smiled as she pointed to him in her relief.

"Yes. Yes, Morna. That's what I was working up to, although I had no idea how you'd react. So you know her?"

Even before Sydney entered his life, he'd known of Morna. From the way his grandfather had always spoken of her, he wondered if perhaps he'd been in love with the witch. Though, for the sake of his grandmother, he'd never asked him outright.

"I've never met her, but she was a dear friend of my grandfather, and I know another lass she sent back."

Laurel looked immensely relieved.

"Oh, good. That must be why she left instructions to ask for you. So, you will believe me when I tell you that she sent Marcus and me two nights ago? We landed in your stables."

"Aye, lass, I believe ye." He chuckled as he thought of Sydney and all the other tales he'd heard of Morna's time-traveling lassies. "Are ye being truthful when ye tell me ye doona know why ye are here? I've only ever known of one reason for Morna to send lassies through time. She means to see ye matched with another."

He wondered if perhaps it might be him, and it shocked him to realize that the idea wasn't unappealing. God knew it had been too long since he'd taken a real fancy to any woman.

"Nope. That's not it this time."

He didn't quite care for the disappointment he felt at her quick dismissal.

"I know that's her usual thing, but she assured me that it wasn't this time. In all honesty, we didn't have time to get much explanation from her. She sort of sent us back against our will. She used some excuse that I might be able to get some ideas for my next book."

Curious, he interrupted her.

"Yer book, lass?"

Her cheeks blushed bright enough that he could see it through the fog of his vision.

"Yeah. I'm a writer. Or at least I used to be. It's been a while since I've been able to get myself to write anything."

He'd never known of a female to write before. Most didn't even know how to read. With so many opportunities for women in the time these lassies came from, he couldn't imagine how difficult it must be for each of them to wind up here.

"'Tis impressive, lass. What do ye write?"

She smiled and shook her head.

"It doesn't matter. In truth, I don't believe that's the real reason Morna sent us back here. I think it has something to do with my frie..." She hesitated and changed her wording. "With my brother, Marcus."

Raudrich had yet to meet this Marcus, though he already knew what the receiving end of his fist felt like, and he didn't wish to anger the man ever again.

"Why do ye say that?"

"Before I tell you, will you explain to me what the deal is with this place? I'd like to know how much of the legend is true."

He knew there were stories about him and the rest of The Eight throughout Scotland now, but it shocked him to hear that this woman—born centuries after all of them would be dead—knew anything about them at all.

"Do ye mean to say that in yer time—whenever that is—ye knew of us before ye came here?"

She nodded. "Yes. There are books written about you, even a documentary."

He had no idea what a documentary was.

"A documentary?"

"Nothing. I just want to know the real story, then I'll tell you my suspicions about Marcus."

It was such a long story—one that would take him far more energy to tell than he had now. And it would be easier to show her anyway. He needed sleep and to speak to all of the men alone. They'd yet to grieve Timothy together, and they needed to form a plan on how they would begin the search for the next druid.

"I'll happily tell ye, lass, but not just now. Might I find ye later? I promise ye I'll tell ye all of it then."

She stood and smiled. She had the prettiest smile—warm and friendly—and it had a slightly mischievous look to it that made her even more alluring.

"Okay. I'll hold you to that. You need to rest anyway. It was lovely to meet you, Raudrich."

As she left him, he couldn't help but think about how unexpectedly lovely it was to meet her, as well.

His life suddenly felt very different, like with one simple introduction, things would never be the same.

Good or bad, he didn't yet know.

CHAPTER 17

I'd wanted to speak to Raudrich alone in the hopes of getting the real story about this castle and the interesting men within it without Marcus being present. If even part of the story I'd watched with Kate was true, if the book was to be believed, Marcus' reason for being here would have a lasting impact on the history of this castle and territory. I knew Marcus well enough to know that he wouldn't be receptive to such news.

He loved his life back in Boston—even with the recent downturn in his freelance photography business. While I was his best friend, he had many others, as well. And he was even closer to his family than I was to Kate. He was a modern man. He didn't share my same passion for all things old. Scotland didn't seem to call to his soul like it did mine.

Was it possible that Marcus was indeed a druid? Did he have powers just waiting to be brought to life inside of him? If so, I knew he was entirely unaware of it.

I found myself wishing that I'd taken the time to actually read the book that had fallen from my shelf. In the surprising turn of events that occurred that night, I'd not thought much of the book as we packed to leave. I regretted being so thoughtless now.

At some point in history, the supposed curse on this land must have been broken. For if not, I imagined the Eight Lairds would still split the land equally in my own time. From what I'd read online about visiting the castle in modern times, this wasn't the case. What I didn't know was at what point in history the curse was broken. Was it soon—as in the following weeks while Marcus and I would be here? If so, perhaps it was possible that Marcus could become one of The Eight, help to break the curse, and then return home. But, what if the curse was to live on in this land for another generation or two? If that was the case, and Marcus was destined to be one of The Eight, did that mean he would have to stay here forever?

I'd said nothing to Marcus about any of it, and I had no plans to until I had more information at my disposal. To do so would only make him more eager to find a way to return home. Something I seriously doubted would be possible until we'd fulfilled whatever Morna believed we were meant to.

Besides, so far I'd seen no indication that any of The Eight were capable of magic. I knew it was very likely that once Raudrich was rested enough to tell me the truth, I would learn that much of what had become legend in my own time was untrue.

Since I knew I would be waiting around impatiently for Raudrich unless I found something to occupy my mind and time, I decided to go in search of some writing materials. While no clear story was yet in mind, I could at least start taking some notes and see where my brainstorming might lead.

Most of the castle corridors were quiet, much like the day before. The men of this castle worked hard, and it didn't surprise me that I had difficulty finding one of them about.

After searching most of the second floor, I made my way downstairs where I could hear the faint sound of voices from a dark corridor I'd yet to explore.

Remembering Harry's directive that we were free to roam as we pleased, I followed the noise to the top of another stairwell. Two voices—one I recognized as Calder's—were speaking down below.

Not wishing to eavesdrop, I called out to them right away.

"Hello? Is it all right if I come down?"

The voice that wasn't Calder's answered back. "Aye, o'course. Calder and I were just trying to find the source of the foul smell down here. Mayhap ye could help us?"

I could smell nothing from where I stood, but as I made my way down into the dank storage room, the scent of rot reached me. I pinched my nostrils closed to block it.

"Wow. That is rather bad, isn't it?"

Maddock stood at the entryway to the small storage room and held up the lantern so I would have some light as I descended the last few steps.

"Aye, lass. I keep telling Calder 'tis likely that moisture got into one of our barrels and ruined food, but his imagination has run away from him. He believes something more nefarious is at work."

I looked over at Calder to see him staring at Maddock with annoyance before turning angry eyes toward me.

"This is yer fault, lass. Ye have no business here. 'Twas clear enough from the moment I met ye that ye were a liar. Now ye have placed us all in danger. Ye and yer brother—if he truly is that—need to leave. Now."

Stunned, I stepped back against the cold wall behind me. I knew Calder was wary of our presence here, but until now, he'd at least been cordial. Something in his eyes was different now, and I didn't like his gaze at all.

Before I could say a word, Maddock stepped between me and Calder.

"Shut yer mouth, ye rude bastard. We doona even know what the source of the smell down here is. 'Tis a natural occurrence, I'm certain. Doona place this on her. Time away from polite society has ruined yer manners."

Calder stepped very close to Maddock, and his tone was filled with venom as he spoke. "Look around, Maddock. Open every storage barrel. Ye will find the same as I did. I spent all morning searching. Nothing is rotting. 'Tis Machara's anger rising from her tomb. Ye know as well as I that it willna be long before she begins to act out. Timothy's death was enough to strengthen her. A lassie's presence will give her even more power. I doona care if the rest of ye are so lust-crazed that ye are willing to damn us all just so ye can stare at a woman for a few days. She's not worth it, Maddock. I might understand if she were pretty, but ye all know she is not. She's got more padding on her than half our pigs. Ye are all ignorant fools, and I willna placate a one of ye."

If he'd said such insulting words directly to me it would've been bad enough, but the fact that he was saying it about me—right in front of me—somehow made it worse.

I'd never been small or particularly slender. I was tall for a woman, and my stature would never be described as delicate. I was undoubtedly thicker—curvier—than what modern-day media would have people believe was "beautiful," but in truth, I was no larger than the average woman. For much of my life, it had been my greatest source of insecurity, especially since Kate's perfect figure had been the envy of every girl we knew growing up.

For me, those thirty extra pounds were something that ate at my confidence and led me to believe that I deserved less of everything than I did. Less money, fewer friends, less love, fewer experiences. It took me most of my twenties to get to a place where I could see that every self-depreciating belief I held about myself was a lie.

Perhaps someday I would lose the weight. Perhaps not. Either way, my size fourteen jeans were still the least interesting thing about me.

At least, I thought I'd evolved enough for such words not to hurt me. Calder's words made me think differently. With his few thoughtless sentences, it felt like high school all over again—like standing in the locker room hearing the jeers and whispers of anorexic-looking brats. I had half a mind to tap him on the shoulder and then shove his balls halfway up his ass with my knee for being such an asshole, but while I was still reeling from his words, Maddock grabbed Calder by the throat and threw him up against the wall with so much force that I wouldn't have been surprised if his head was now cracked and bleeding in the back.

Unfortunately, it wasn't.

"I doona know what has gotten into ye, but fear has made ye someone I'm ashamed to know. Get out of my face before I break yer neck. If I see ye anywhere near Laurel or Marcus for the rest of the time they are here with us, I shall see ye sent away from this castle for good."

I could see by the look in Calder's eyes as Maddock stepped away that he knew his threat wasn't an empty one. Leaving Calder trembling against the wall, Maddock took my hand and quickly ushered me back upstairs.

The moment we were in the light-filled grand corridor of the castle, Maddock looked at me. Whether it was intuition or my quickly-reddening face, he knew I was about to cry.

"Come here, lass."

Even once we're grown, we all carry wounds that when poked cause us pain.

In a few hours, I would be fine, but for now, I couldn't deny how hurt I felt.

I allowed Maddock to pull me into his arms as I wept.

"What do ye mean Calder is gone? Do ye mean to the village? When will he be back? He knows 'twill require all of ye to heal me."

Maddock's jaw was clenched, his eyes narrow. Raudrich was half-surprised that steam wasn't coming out of his ears. Maddock was one of the most calm and centered men among them. Raudrich had never seen him so angry.

"No, I doona mean to the village. His horse and satchel and every personal item he had are no longer in the castle. I followed him to see if he would truly go through with it, and he has. He loaded himself and his horse on a boat and left the isle completely. He has abandoned his post here and us along with it."

Raudrich couldn't believe what he was hearing. They couldn't afford to lose another man.

"And why dinna ye stop him?"

Maddock's tone was entirely without remorse. "If that arse of a man wants to leave us, then good riddance to him. I thought I knew him. 'Twas clear to me earlier today that I dinna know him at all. He is not the sort of man we need here with us. If ye'd heard what I heard, ye would've not only let him leave, ye would've taken him down to the shore and thrown him in a boat yerself."

"What did ye hear?"

Just as Maddock opened his mouth to answer him, Harry, Ludo, Quinn, and Paton entered his bedchamber. Nicol was still sleeping, as he did every day until dinner.

"Maddock, we hoped ye were already in here. Where is Calder? We've much to discuss while Quinn's stew cooks away in the kitchen."

Raudrich barely listened as Maddock told the rest of them what he'd just told him. His mind was now too busy wondering what this would mean. Was it even possible for one of The Eight to leave, to break their bond of their own accord? It had never been something they'd had to worry about before now. If there was a way for Calder to remove his magic from its bind to the isle, what would happen when The Eight became Six?

He was deep in thought when Quinn reached out and grabbed his arm.

"Are ye here, Raudrich? Did ye hear a word we said?"

"No." He shook his head as he shifted in his bed. It was impossible to get comfortable with the ache in his ribs. "I dinna. I'm sorry. Calder's departure means bad things for all of us."

Quinn nodded as they all gathered around his bed.

"Aye, there is no question about that, but we doona have the luxury of dwelling on it. Nor do we have the time to mourn Timothy's death with ye as we wished to. As ye know, we saw him buried shortly after his death. Ye must say goodbye to him on yer own time now."

He'd hoped they would all have a chance to reminisce about their old friend, to bid him farewell properly, but Raudrich understood Quinn's urgency. With each new event at the castle, their time became all the more precious.

"Aye, I shall visit his grave as soon as I can walk without crying out in pain, which I'm afraid may be weeks now that Calder is gone."

"No."

Harry's sure voice surprised him. Healing magic was exhausting. With his magic too weakened by the frail state of his body, they couldn't risk the strain that such an act would place on the remaining five.

"What do ye mean, no? I'll heal as quickly as I can, but I doona know how I can rush it."

Harry sat down on the edge of the bed. Raudrich could see by the stern gaze in his eyes that his mind was already made up.

"We canna wait weeks for ye to heal. If Calder truly means to leave, he will begin to look for a way to break his bind with us. Should he succeed before ye are healed, none of us can know the strength it would give Machara. 'Tis better for us to all let our magic be weakened for a day or two now than for us to be without the magic of three of the eight in a few week's time. Ye willna be able to wield all of yer own power until yer body is healed. We shall pool our energy now and make tomorrow a day of rest for all of us so we might regain our strength before we determine what must be done next."

Raudrich couldn't deny that such a plan appealed to him. He wanted his body back, and if they could, his sight, as well.

"If ye all wish to do this, I willna fight ye on it. With my eyes, and now this, I havena felt like myself for far too long. Timothy's death has placed a strain on all our magic. It willna take long for Calder to begin to feel the ill-effects of being away from the castle."

Maddock's angry voice spoke beside him.

"Then may he lose his sight completely and much more quickly than ye lost yers."

All of the men looked at Maddock in question, but before he could say more, Harry stood.

"Then, let us begin, lads. Should this work, Raudrich, ye may have to be the one to finish dinner for I doona know if the rest of us will be able to stay standing afterwards."

Raudrich laughed as the men formed the necessary circle around him.

"If ye succeed at healing my ribs, my nose, and my sight, I shall wait on ye all hand and foot for a fortnight, at least."

Ludo laughed and Raudrich shifted so he could lie down completely on the bed. The healing was bound to be unpleasant, and he needed to prepare himself for the pain.

"Doona make promises ye have no intention of keeping. We all know that by this time tomorrow, ye will be ordering us about. Ye will have no sympathy for our exhaustion."

Ludo was probably right about that. Serving as laird for the past two years in Allen territory had made him bossy. It would take time for him to grow used to an equal partnership with the other men again.

Energy built in the room as they started to chant. It didn't take long for the pain to begin to sear through his body. Try as he might to swallow his screams, they wouldn't stay inside him.

It was horrific. No matter how much he screamed at them to stop, they continued their chant.

He wished he would pass out, but as the pain raged on, he remained awake, feeling the shift of every bone and every pull of his skin.

Only as his vision cleared and he was able to make out the beams across the ceiling was he able to relax into the pain.

As soon as they were finished, it would all be worth it.

CHAPTER 19

rue to his word, Raudrich worked in the kitchen finishing their meal while the rest of the men rested. He had more energy than he'd had in months.

His ribs were still sore—a garish bruise spread all the way down his left side—but blessedly, they were no longer broken. His nose was as straight as it ever had been, and his vision was completely healed.

The only thing putting a damper on his mood was the anticipation of the hard time the men would give him over the quality of their meal. He'd not had cooking duty in over two years, and it showed.

The bread was edible, but chewy. The stew was too salty and the meat within it too tough. His hope was that they would all be too tired to care about what a poor job he'd done finishing Quinn's stew.

"I willna be surprised if Harry sleeps through dinner. I could hear his snores from the other side of the castle."

Raudrich looked up to see Maddock enter the kitchen. The man looked dead on his feet, wobbly and unsteady as he walked toward him.

"Take a seat, man. Ye should be in bed yerself. I told ye all I would come to fetch ye when 'twas ready."

"Ach." Maddock waved a dismissive hand but took a seat on the wooden stool that sat beside the large wooden preparation table. "I'm still too angry to sleep."

So relieved at his recovery, Raudrich had been able to put thoughts of Calder aside for a short while. Maddock's words immediately brought the questions he'd had before the healing session back to him.

"Ye never did tell me. What did he do? What did ye hear him say?"

Maddock leaned into the table for support as he spoke.

"I'll not tell the other men. 'Twould embarrass Laurel if she heard of it, and I doona wish to betray her trust. But seeing as ye've known her so long, I thought it best ye hear what was done to her."

Raudrich didn't bother correcting Maddock. It was fine with him if all save Harry believed he and Laurel had a history. It would allow him to spend more time with her without questions arising from the other men. He barely knew the lass, none of them did, but he very much wanted to know more about her.

Whatever he'd expected, it had never crossed his mind that what had happened with Calder had anything to do with Laurel. The sense of protectiveness he felt come over him at knowing Calder had wronged her surprised him immensely.

"Laurel? What does she have to do with this?"

"It has everything to do with Laurel. He all but attacked her, and when I stepped in to chide him for it, he said things about her that I wouldna say to a dog. I wanted to kill him. Truly, I did."

"What did he say?"

Maddock shook his head and exhaled sadly.

"Ach, Raudrich, ye should've seen her face. She looked like a child her expression was so wounded. I doona think I shall ever be able to forget it. Not that I blame her for being hurt. His tone was so cruel and his words unjust in every way."

Raudrich quickly grew impatient.

"For the love o'God, man, what did he say to her?"

"He dinna say it to her, which, if ye ask me, made it even more unkind. He spoke to me, though he knew good and well she could hear every word. She was standing right next to us."

Raudrich dropped the knife in his hand dramatically and crossed his arms as he stared at Maddock, silently urging him to continue.

"He said that 'twas bad luck that she was here, that only bad things would come from it, and that the only reason we permitted her being here was because we were filled with lust and enjoyed having a lassie about. Then he said she was too full-figured to be pretty and that we were damned fools. He said that half our pigs were less pudgy. 'Twas unnecessary and cruel. Most men would've simply decked him, but ye know as well as I how such words would wound a woman. She did nothing to deserve his cruelty."

Raudrich knew he should've felt angry, but confusion was pushing any other emotion away.

"What the hell is he talking about? I doona believe I've ever seen a woman whose appearance I fancied more than Laurel's."

The confession slipped out of him, and he immediately regretted his honesty as he saw Maddock smile.

"Well, I'm certain she will be glad to hear it. Her brother claims she's in love with ye. But I..."

Stunned, he interrupted Maddock.

"In love with me?"

Maddock, wide-eyed and smiling, nodded.

"Aye. She hasna yet told ye, then? Well, pretend ye are surprised when she does. I wouldna want her thinking I spoiled her admission."

Maddock was clearly under a false assumption, but he could see no reason to correct him.

"I dinna mean to interrupt ye, ye just surprised me, is all. What were ye about to say?"

He sat quietly for a moment as if he were trying to remember.

Then he shook his head as it came back to him.

"Oh, I was just going to agree with ye. While I suppose such a scrawny, unfortunate looking bastard like Calder would prefer a lass small enough to make him feel like more of a man, I doona mind a lassie with more meat on her bones. I find Laurel verra bonny, as well. I believe ye would be hard pressed to find a man who shares Calder's opinion of her."

Even Maddock's suggestion surprised him. While he knew his vision had still been impaired when he visited with Laurel, her size had never crossed his mind. More than that, he could still remember what it felt like to hold her in his arms. He'd never found the feel of someone against him more pleasing.

"Calder is an imbecile and I am glad we are rid of him." Raudrich paused and brushed his hands on his pants. "Now, let us put all of this nastiness behind us, for I doona like such talk of Laurel even between us. She deserves more respect than to be whispered about amongst men."

Maddock stood and nodded in agreement.

"Aye, 'tis precisely why I will say nothing of this to the other men. 'Tis only that I willna be surprised if she still seems rattled by the whole ordeal over dinner. I dinna want ye asking her what was wrong in front of everyone else, so I thought I should tell ye."

If Laurel's belief in her own beauty was in any way damaged by Calder's idiocy, he would make certain that her confidence was restored.

"I'm glad ye did. Do ye have the strength to go and gather the others for dinner, or should I?"

Maddock sank bank down onto the stool.

"If I walk back up those stairs again, I willna have the strength to come back down them for dinner. Best ye go."

Raudrich smiled. He expected his friend was milking the situation just a little.

"Aye, fine. Go and rest yerself at the table. I'll gather everyone now."

CHAPTER 20

"*I* can wait if you want, Laurel. It's really not a big deal."

Marcus was eyeing me skeptically. He could see that something was wrong. While he knew better than to ask, I could see that it annoyed him that I'd yet to tell him what was up with me.

I didn't want to talk about it. Not with Marcus. Not with anyone.

It had taken an hour-long walk, three failed attempts at meditation, and some serious positive self-talk to gain my composure. I'd actually been thankful for the screaming—terrifying as the sound was with the way it echoed down every hallway in the castle—when it began. It helped me block out my own self-pity-filled thoughts. By the time the mysterious screaming finished, I was in a much better mood.

"No, it's okay. Go ahead and go down. I'm just going to finish braiding my hair. I'll be down in just a minute."

I wanted a few minutes to myself before dinner. I needed to take a few deep breaths and figure out how I was going to manage to sit across from Calder without lunging across the table at him or collapsing into tears again.

Maddock had been nothing but the perfect gentlemen—understanding and tender as he'd held me and allowed me to cry. He'd also hit on me in the absolute kindest way I'd ever been hit on in my life, but I'd not read into that overmuch. It was a pity come-on, but I still appreciated it, all the same.

Marcus hesitated as he reached the doorway.

"Do you think it's safe? What do you think that screaming was?"

While part of me hoped the screaming was a result of Maddock hooking Calder up to some horrifying torture device, I knew his rude words weren't enough to deserve such pain.

"I'm not sure, but I suspect maybe they came from Raudrich. I don't know how medical stuff works around here, but if they were trying to set his ribs or his nose or something, that must have hurt like a son of a bitch."

Marcus bared his teeth sympathetically.

"Ouch. I really do need to apologize to the guy. Can't say I'm looking forward to that interaction."

If Raudrich's interaction with me was any indicator of his true character—which I had a feeling it was—he would be perfectly receptive to Marcus' apology.

"Maybe after dinner you can go and see him. He'll be kind to you, I'm sure. You'll feel better once you get it out of the way."

He nodded and opened the door to leave me.

"You're right. Don't take too long. I don't want to field dinnertime questions from everyone without you."

Once the door closed behind him, I quickly finished the loose braid at the nape of my neck and allowed it to drape over my left shoulder.

I never braided my hair back home, but something about it felt century-appropriate regardless of whether or not that was actually true.

Taking a glimpse of myself in the mirror, I felt a little bit better than I had all day. Calder was entitled to his opinion. It didn't make it true. My breasts looked awesome in this dress, and my extra "padding" as Calder had said, gave me a comely shape that I quite liked. I had a pretty face and smile, and as far as I was concerned, Calder had the face of a constipated pug. I was certain I had far less trouble picking up men than he did women.

"Screw him."

I whispered the words under my breath just as someone began to knock on the door to the bedchamber. Dread filled me. If it was Calder, I didn't want to answer. I didn't need his apology. I didn't need to ever speak to him again. Smoothing my dress and straightening my shoulders, I cautiously walked over to the door.

"Who is it?"

"'Tis Raudrich, lass. I came to fetch ye for dinner."

"Raudrich?"

I was so surprised to hear his voice on the other side of the door that I flung the door open so quickly, it nearly hit me in the head. As I looked back at him, I reeled back in shock.

"Wha…Wha…How? You look great."

It was nearly as baffling to me as the time travel. Raudrich had looked absolutely awful only a few hours earlier, now he looked unnervingly hot.

His bloodied and swollen nose was healed, and from the way he stood, I didn't believe his ribs were hurting him any longer.

He also was no longer squinting, almost as if he could see perfectly well.

He smiled at what I knew had to be my bug-eyed expression.

"Ye do know that we are druids, lass? Dinna ye hear me screaming? They healed me."

So that part of the legend was true. I could mark one question off of my very long list.

"Um, yes, yes I definitely did hear you screaming, but I never imagined that they were doing all of that." I motioned up and down his body with my hand, and he laughed.

"Ye approve then? I look fair better than I did before, aye?"

"You still looked pretty good before, too, but now you look...wow."

The moment I heard the words leave my mouth, I nearly fell back in shock. What the freaking hell had gotten into me? I could feel the blood rush to my face as I warmed into a horrifyingly embarrassing blush.

Thankfully, he said nothing to embarrass me further and gracefully moved on to another topic of conversation.

"I hope ye are not overly hungry. The lads are all rather tired after the spell they did for me so I was forced to finish the meal. It has been some time since I cooked. 'Tis rubbish."

I was famished, but I wouldn't tell him that.

"I'm sure it will be fine. Is everyone else already down there? I'm sorry if you all were waiting on me. You really should have just gone on ahead."

"All save Calder are on their way downstairs now."

At the mention of Calder's name, my smile fell. I hoped that Raudrich didn't know about what happened. I tried to keep my tone as congenial as possible as I asked about him.

"Why isn't Calder going to dinner?"

"He's gone, lass."

"Gone?"

I couldn't tell from his expression whether he knew about what had happened or not. He was totally unreadable.

"Aye. We doona expect that he will return."

"Oh." It felt as if a weight had lifted from my chest. I was beyond glad that I wouldn't have to see him again.

He offered me his arm and I took it as we made our way downstairs.

"Do ye still wish to know the truth of this place?"

I nodded as I looked up into his dark brown eyes.

"Of course, I do."

"After dinner, come and wait for me on the stairs. I must make certain that Nicol is out of the castle before I show ye. Once he is gone, I'll come to get ye."

I couldn't wait for dinner to be over.

CHAPTER 21

Seeing her now, laughing at one of Ludo's very unfunny jokes, her blue eyes twinkling in the candlelight, he knew one thing with certainty: he wasn't the one with unwell eyes, Calder was as blind as a bat.

Raudrich already knew he thought her beautiful, but with his sight fully restored, Laurel truly did take his breath away.

She seemed to be having a similar effect on Maddock, and Raudrich didn't care for it at all. The man stared at her with doe-like eyes as he laughed and smiled right along with her. For a group of men who were supposedly so weak from using their magic on him, not a one of them was having a problem conversing with her.

He and Marcus seemed to be the only one's not enjoying dinner with the same joyous abandon as the rest of them. They sat awkwardly next to one another, neither of them saying a word until Marcus finally leaned over to speak halfway through dinner.

"Uh...I suppose it's time that I introduce myself to you. I'm Marcus."

Raudrich gladly took the man's hand. He needed a distraction from watching the other men fawn all over Laurel.

"Raudrich. I am sorry I was not here to greet the two of ye when ye arrived."

Marcus snorted and withdrew his hand.

"I'm sorry you weren't here, too. If you had been, I wouldn't have had reason to punch you in the nose. By the way, I really am sorry about that. I mean, if it had been how it appeared, I wouldn't be sorry at all, but seeing that it wasn't, I do regret breaking your nose."

Raudrich pointed to his nose and smiled. "No worries, lad. As ye can see, 'tis fixed well enough now."

Marcus nodded. "Good. I'm glad there are no hard feelings."

"None at all. Ye were right to defend Laurel in such a way." He looked across the table and glared as Maddock reached out to touch Laurel's hand as he spoke to her. "I can assure ye, I would do the same if I saw anyone place an unwanted hand on her."

He was tempted to smash Maddock's nose in right this second.

Marcus followed his gaze and laughed.

"She's oblivious to it, you know. She knows so much about love in her writing and so little about it in real life. I've watched grown men trip over themselves trying to get her attention, and she doesn't notice."

Marcus' insight into Laurel was enough to pull his attention away from the soon-to-be-sorry Maddock.

"Love in her writing? Does she write poetry?"

"No. She writes romance novels."

He'd never heard of such a thing.

"Romance novels?"

Understanding moved across Marcus' face as he lowered his voice.

"Did Laurel tell you...do you know where or more precisely, when we are from?"

Raudrich responded in kind by leaning closer to Marcus. None of the other men knew.

"Aye, lad, I know all about Morna and her penchant for sending lassies through time."

"Good. Anyway, I'm pretty certain romance novels don't exist in this time. It will take quite a long time before women start really owning their sexuality."

Raudrich liked the sound of that very much. He thought perhaps he would like the future.

When he said nothing, Marcus continued.

"She writes love stories. You know, stories about men and women falling in love."

"But ye say that she knows little of this herself?"

The man snorted again. He wondered if perhaps it was a nervous habit, although nothing about the way the man held himself indicated that he was intimidated, and he'd certainly not behaved that way last night

"Laurel? God, no. She dates because her sister forces her to, but I've never known Laurel to be with a man for more than a few months. She's very distrusting of men, and she's a bit of a heartbreaker, but like I said, she doesn't see it. I'd say nearly all of the men she's ever dated have fallen for her by date three. But as soon as she sees them start to invest, she flees. I know her better than anyone, and I've never been able to determine exactly why."

Each new thing he learned about her made him even more curious to get to know her. It was time for their dinner to come to an end.

Standing, he pushed back from the table and addressed the group.

"It has been a long day for us all. If everyone is finished, I believe it best we all find our way to bed."

Even as riveted as the men seemed to be in their conversation, all of them agreed that they were indeed tired. As the men stood, he winked at Laurel to acknowledge their upcoming meeting.

Turning, he left to head for the castle's highest tower where he could watch for Nicol's nightly exit.

*T*ry as I might to convince Maddock that it really would be fine for me to bunk with Marcus, my new friend wouldn't hear of it. So, rather than wait on the stairs like I promised Raudrich I would do, I was forced to follow Maddock up to his bedchamber, while he chatted away about why this was the best solution for everyone.

"I promise ye, lass, 'tis no trouble at all. I willna place ye in Calder's room on the off chance that he might return, but I've no problem confronting him if he does, so I will stay in there. Even more, my bedchamber is one of only two that has a lock that ye may bolt from the inside. I've been known to walk about in my sleep, ye see. So I lock it before bed to keep myself inside. Doona want to go tumbling down the stairs in the night, aye?"

While I appreciated his kindness, it was ridiculous for so many people to be unsettled due to our invasive arrival into their lives. Marcus and I had shared rooms on countless trips and sleepovers.

"Maddock, I truly do appreciate your thoughtfulness, but I wouldn't be able to live with myself if I woke to hear that you'd walked out of Calder's room in the middle of the night and broken your leg by doing what you just told me you feared."

Just as we turned the corner down the long corridor leading to Maddock's bedchamber, Raudrich appeared from a set of stairs to my right. He stopped short when he saw us and slowly glanced back and forth between us.

"What are ye doing, Maddock?"

I couldn't understand the frustrated glint in Raudrich's eyes.

"I'm seeing Laurel to my bedchamber."

Frustration turned to anger in a flash, and before I knew it, Raudrich had stepped between us as he shoved Maddock with one hand and grabbed my arm with another.

"Like hell ye are, Maddock."

Raudrich turned his angry eyes on me, and I pulled out of his grasp as he spoke.

"Lass, I know Maddock can be verra convincing with his words, but ye doona want to do this. Ye barely know him. He is not the man for ye."

Maddock burst into laughter.

"Careful, Raudrich, yer envy is showing. I wasna leading her to my bedchamber to bed her, ye daft fool. I thought mayhap since my room has a lock, she could stay there while I move to Calder's. Laurel and I shall be bonny friends, I'm sure of it, but I doona think we shall ever be more. Right, lass?"

A blush blossomed underneath Raudrich's rather tan and weathered skin, and I couldn't help but grin at how boyish he looked when embarrassed. It made me feel better about the idiotic compliment I'd given him earlier.

I nodded emphatically. I liked Maddock immensely, but I wasn't interested in him in the least.

"Right. All the same though, as I was saying to you before, I don't need to stay in your room. I'll stay with Marcus."

"No." Raudrich recovered quickly from his embarrassment and turned to look me straight on.

"Ye willna stay with Marcus, nor will ye stay in Maddock's room, for Maddock will kill himself traipsing around in the night if he isna locked up inside. Ye will stay in my room for 'tis the nicest and is precisely where a lady like ye should be. I'll put a bolt on it before bed. I shall move to Calder's room."

I had rather liked Raudrich's room a lot.

"Okay, great. Thanks anyway, Maddock. Now, let me go and tell Marcus where I'll be staying. I'll meet up with you in a bit."

I turned and left both men to finish their arguing alone.

CHAPTER 22

*R*audrich was waiting for me on the stairs by the time I finished explaining to Marcus what I was doing and where I would be staying tonight. He wanted to come with me, but I talked him out of it by claiming that I thought I would be more likely to get more information out of him alone. It wasn't true. I had no doubt that Raudrich would be just as willing to tell Marcus everything as he was me, but I wanted the opportunity to learn the truth on my own, so I could know just what it meant for my very best friend and the rest of his life.

"I'm sorry for earlier, lass. 'Tis not my place to tell ye who ye should spend yer time with. 'Tis only that it was a shock for me to see ye heading to Maddock's room with him. He's not good enough for ye."

I smiled and accepted his apology with a wave of my hand.

"It's fine. Although, I have to disagree with you on behalf of Maddock. I'm a hard sell when it comes to most men. Maddock is one of the good ones."

Raudrich raised his brows but nodded in agreement.

"Mayhap so, lass. It doesna mean ye should be with him."

505

I'd blown off Maddock's mocking of Raudrich earlier, but just now I couldn't deny that his tone did sound slightly jealous. Of what exactly, I couldn't imagine. He didn't know me well enough to be jealous of anything.

"You're right. Now, enough talk about me. I've had questions stirring inside me all day. Where does Nicol go at night, and why did we have to wait until he was gone to discuss this?"

Raudrich bent so that his face was right next to mine. Quietly, he whispered in my ear, and I had to reach for the handrail to stay steady. His breath against my neck brought up memories of the night before.

"Do ye trust me, lass? It will be easier for me to show ye than tell ye, but to do so requires that we travel somewhere ye willna like at all."

It surprised me to realize that I did trust him. While I had no real reason, I just intuitively felt that I would be safe with him.

"I think so. Show me and we'll find out."

He extended his hand. The moment I latched on, he turned and walked back up the stairs. I had to move quickly to keep up with him.

"I doona wish ye to think that I am doing anything Nicol would disapprove of. He wouldna mind me showing ye. 'Tis only that I prefer to do so without his knowledge for I know how much it pains him to speak of it."

With the castle already down for the night, no flames were lit along the hallways. I didn't realize until we turned down a dark corridor around the corner from Raudrich's bedroom that neither of us had any lighting. The hallway was lined with windows, which allowed for some moonlight to stream in, but it was still very dark.

"Should we go back and get a light?"

He chuckled quietly beneath his breath.

"I doona need it to find my way around this castle, and we willna need it once we get where I'm taking ye."

At the end of the hallway, we reached a door, and Raudrich released my hand as he opened it and stepped inside. I followed after him.

It was a bedchamber I'd yet to see, and this one was even larger and nicer than Raudrich's.

"I thought you said your bedchamber was the nicest."

"'Tis the nicest among The Eight. I doona include Nicol's room for this castle truly belongs to him. 'Tis only fitting that he should have the fairest room."

This bedchamber was a corner room and was unlike any room I'd seen in any castle I'd ever been in. The two outside walls were solid glass. They filled the room with a blue cast of moonlight that made it easy to see.

"Nicol had us spell these walls for him shortly after he gathered us here under his command. He is terrified of the darkness, though that is only a small reason why he sleeps during the day."

I'd thought earlier that it was odd that I'd not seen Nicol anywhere about until dinner. Now I knew why.

"What's the other reason?"

He reached for my arm and gently led me over to a large painted portrait that hung above Nicol's bed. It was the likeness of Nicol, though he was significantly younger in the painting. He stood behind a beautiful young woman. Her dark hair cascaded all the way down to her waist, and her eyes were so alarmingly black that I thought they might haunt me in my sleep.

"Who is that?"

Something about the portrait brought tears to my eyes. It had a heavy feeling to it, almost as if it might come alive if you looked away. It was creepy in a way that broke my heart.

"'Tis his wife, Freya."

"Is she..." It seemed slightly rude to ask such a blunt question, but it was the only assumption I could come to since I knew women weren't supposed to be inside the castle. "Is she dead?"

Raudrich shook his head. As I looked up into his eyes, I could see that he was saddened by this story, as well.

"'Tis far worse than that, lass. Nicol prays for her death, her true death, every day."

The insinuation that Freya was undead chilled me all over. Still staring at her portrait, I unconsciously took a step backwards and felt my back press against Raudrich's chest. He didn't step away from me. Instead, he placed his hands on my arms and began to rub me.

"The fright of it has chilled ye, aye? It does so to me every time I think of it, as well. Doona be scared. She canna harm ye. Would ye..." He hesitated and it only caused my fear to grow. "Would ye like to see her?"

"See her?" My voice was soft and unsteady as I twisted to look up at him. "Is she dead or not? If she's dead, I'm gonna be honest with you, I'd rather not."

He laughed and the warmth that radiated from his chest allowed me to relax just a little.

"Her body turned to dust long ago, but her spirit remains locked on this isle until the faerie below us either dies or releases Nicol and Freya from her grip."

"Huh?" He might as well have been speaking German.

"As I said, lass, 'twill be easier if ye allow me to show ye."

I was intrigued to be sure. It didn't mean that I wasn't also scared shitless.

"Don't move away from me, okay?"

In one swift motion, his hands moved from my arms and wrapped protectively around my front as he bent down and pressed his cheek flat against mine.

"I'll not go anywhere, lass."

Slowly, with his arms still wound around me, he moved me over so that we stood right in front of the large glass pane on the far side of the room. The view below was of a small garden that had been invisible to Marcus and me from the front of the castle.

Every plant and flower was withered and dead.

Nicol sat on a stone bench in the garden's center. The translucent figure of his wife—a ghost if I'd ever seen one—sat next to him.

CHAPTER 23

*A*ctually seeing a ghost was far less frightening than thinking about seeing one. As Raudrich and I looked down at Nicol and his wife, I felt no fear, only sadness.

"She's a ghost, then?"

"Not exactly." Raudrich kept his voice low. While I knew they couldn't hear us, I understood why he did. There was something intrusive about us staring down at their shared moment. "Ghosts rarely speak and they often repeat the same motions or move down the same paths over and over again. Freya is still who she was while living. She has thoughts and feelings and expresses them freely."

"But she's trapped there?" It was perhaps the most horrifying fate I could think of.

His voice was sad and reluctant.

"Aye. As I said, her fate is worse than death. If Nicol ever lives to see the day that she is released from this hell and she is able to once and for all truly die, he shall rejoice in it. We all will.

"During the day, she simply doesna exist, but each night she appears in her garden, cursed to see the man she loves but unable to feel his touch on her skin, doomed to never feel warmth again or to travel past the outskirts of her long-since wilted prison."

"Who would do that to her? Who would do that to anyone?"

I could think of no one I hated so much that I would wish them such a fate. No wonder Nicol looked so weary and sad. To spend his nights haunted by the love of his life, unable to help or save her, and to spend his days sleeping like a nocturnal animal—his existence had to be just as painful as her death.

"Are ye familiar with the fae, lass?"

I shook my head and had to keep from shivering at the way my cheek felt brushing back and forth against his stubble. It was dangerous for me to be this close to him. All I wanted to do was face him and repeat what I'd done to him last night.

"Only vaguely—a story here and there, perhaps. It's not something anyone really believes in or speaks of in America."

"Here." He released his hold on me and I immediately felt cold from the space that now lay between us. He moved toward Nicol's bed and quickly pulled a blanket off the top before sinking to the ground in front of the window. Gently he spread his legs out in front of him and motioned to the space in between. "Sit down, Laurel. Ye can lean against me while I tell ye the story. Ye are shivering where ye stand. I'll keep ye warm."

There was something mischievous in his voice. I kind of liked it. Smiling knowingly at him, I joined him on the floor. I sighed as I leaned back into his chest, and he draped the blanket over us. Once we were situated, he returned his arms to their place around my waist.

It was an intimate position for two strangers, but somehow I knew that our unacknowledged memories of the night before had us both feeling more comfortable around one another than we would have under normal circumstances. Sitting in his arms now, I felt rather silly for having denied any contact with him so ardently earlier in the day.

"Now, lass. Are ye ready to hear the true tale? Then, once I'm done ye can tell me just how right or wrong history has written it."

"Deal. I'm ready."

"This Isle has not always been known as The Isle of The Eight. Twenty years ago, 'twas The Isle of Whispers, and this castle was known as Murray Castle after Nicol's family and ancestors. He is one in a long line of Murrays that have tended to the people of this isle. For centuries, this land knew peace. When he was only five and thirty, his life became something other than his own.

"Ye see, fae are often spoken of in folktales as ways to frighten children into behaving as ye wish them to. But in truth, sightings of them and interactions with them are far less common than Scottish grannies throughout the country would have ye believe. Most doona truly believe they exist. Until my arrival on this isle as a child, I doona think I would've believed in them, either.

"Nicol was much the same. When one child from the village went missing, he thought it an accident, despite the insistence of the child's mother that a faerie had lured her son into the faerie land. Children often played too close to the water's edge or among rivers. He believed the child had been pulled away and drowned.

"But soon after, two more went missing, and their parents believed the same as the first. In an effort to stop the rising panic amongst the people of this village, Nicol went in search of the fae, and much to his misfortune, he found them."

I shivered as another chill swept through me. Acknowledging that magic time travel existed was one thing. Learning that ghosts and fairies existed was another. It seemed the world I'd spent most of my life living in was more sheltered than I'd realized.

"He found them here? On the isle?"

Raudrich nodded and pulled me in a little closer.

"Aye. All faeries are manipulative and selfish creatures. Ye canna trust a one of them, but Machara is worse than most. She yearned for a child—a half-human child—of her own. She captured the children of this village to lure Nicol away from the castle so she could strike a bargain with him: the safe return of the children she took for a night in his arms so she could have his child. It was a mistake he made in a moment and one that has placed a darkness over his entire life."

I twisted to look at Raudrich.

"She broke her bargain?"

"'Tis the way of faeries. They only keep their word to a degree. Machara returned the children, but they were not as they were. When they returned to their parents' doorsteps, they were older than their parents. For time doesna work the same in the land of the fae, and ye never know just how it shall ruin ye. Some men return to find they've stayed the same, but hundreds of years have passed. For the stolen children of this isle, their childhood was taken from them in the week they were gone."

"Oh, my God. Their poor parents."

"Aye. Many families fled here in response. They feared the same fate for their own children, and Nicol couldna blame them."

It was one of the saddest stories I'd ever heard, but it still didn't explain Freya's fate.

"And where does Freya come in?"

"Freya wouldna enter Nicol's life for another five years. Ye see, Machara loved the child she had with Nicol, and each year she would return to lie with him again. There are many tales of faerie lying with mortal men, but more often than not, 'tis the mortal that would be ruined with unquenchable lust and yearning for what they wished they could have but couldna—the love of the fae who used them.

"As with most things, Machara was different. She has never followed the patterns of most fae. Nicol stayed indifferent to her, and slowly over the years as Machara bore more of his children—children he's never seen nor loved—she fell in love with him.

"Despite his annual obligations to Machara, Nicol believed himself a free man. During a short journey off the isle, he met and fell in love with Freya. Unaware of the doom it would bring them both, he married her before returning home. When Machara learned of Nicol's new wife, she went mad with jealousy.

"She confessed her love to Nicol and promised to forgive his trespass if he sent Freya away, but Nicol's love for Freya knew no bounds. He defied Machara and fled the isle with her.

"They spent five years away. They were the only happy years of Nicol's life. It was through his travels and his studies that he discovered a way to defeat Machara—it was how he came to form The Eight.

"Fae magic is stronger than that of any one witch or druid. Nicol learned that it would take many—the magic of eight—to cast the spell that would bind Machara for eternity. He and Freya traveled throughout Scotland gathering druid men young and old who were willing to pledge their loyalty and magic to him. I was among the first as were Harry, Maddock, Timothy, and Quinn. Ludo, Calder, and Paton joined us later after three of the original eight passed away.

"We practiced the spell for months before returning with him to the isle, for we all knew the spell would have to be cast almost immediately if we were to avoid Machara's wrath. We all urged him to leave Freya on the mainland until Machara was safely bound in her cell below the castle, but he couldna bear to leave her. He regrets that decision every single day."

I could no longer peel my eyes away from Nicol and Freya down below us. Their story was unlike anything I'd ever heard in my life.

"So what happened when you got here?"

"Machara saw us coming and waited on the front steps of the castle, the lifeless bodies of each child she bore with Nicol laid out beside her. She hoped their death would riddle Nicol with guilt for abandoning her, but the children were inhuman things, beings he'd never known nor wanted. He felt nothing save relief that they'd not grow up to turn into beings as evil as their mother.

"His lack of emotion sent Machara into a rage, giving us just enough time to cast the spell as she lost her mind in a fit of screams and roars unlike anything I'd ever seen in my life. The spell worked, but not before Machara had time to do one last act of violence upon

Nicol's life. She killed Freya by running her through with the sword she drew from Nicol's sheath. Just as Freya breathed her last breath, Machara cursed her to endure the state she is in now. It was the last thing Machara was able to do before our spell was finished and bound."

Raudrich drew in a sad, deep breath. It was clear that even telling the story exhausted him.

"For the past twenty years, Machara has remained locked away deep below this castle. As long as there are eight druids with their magic bound here, she canna escape. 'Tis why it is so urgent that we find another to replace Timothy, and why it is even more distressing that Calder has left us. Our magic is stretched until Timothy is replaced. If Calder finds a way to sever his tie with this isle, Machara may find the strength to break free."

Just as Raudrich finished his story, the sound of laughter, dark and sinister, traveled up through the floor beneath us.

"'Tis her, lass. 'Tis her dungeon that I meant when I said I must take ye somewhere ye willna wish to go. If ye want to know the truth of all of it, 'tis time for ye to meet Machara."

CHAPTER 24

*C*alder had been right about the smell in the storage room. I knew it the moment Raudrich opened the secret passageway in Nicol's room and we stepped into the dimly lit stairwell. It hadn't been the smell of rotten food. It was the smell of very angry faerie.

Lit candles lined the steps downward, but they cast an otherworldly green glow that should've been impossible through normal fire.

"Best ye breathe it in, lass. Ye will grow accustomed to it sooner that way. While I know 'tis foul, it willna harm ye."

I could scarcely bring my feet to move. Terror gripped at my every limb. I couldn't see her, and despite the fact that she was no longer laughing, I could feel her hatred in every nerve ending in my body. I grabbed at Raudrich as he stepped away and down one step.

"Wait. Raudrich, I don't think this is a good idea. She doesn't like women here, right? That's what Calder told Harry when he invited Marcus and me inside. Won't her seeing me make her even angrier?"

Raudrich's gaze was sympathetic as he turned toward me, but I could tell by the firm set of his feet that he had no intention of returning to Nicol's room.

"I should've been honest with ye, lass. I doona only wish to bring ye down here so ye might believe me. There is another reason, as well."

"Which is?"

He leaned in to whisper into my ear so quietly, even I had to strain to hear him.

"There is a reason Machara doesna wish for another woman to enter Nicol's home. Even in her anger, even in her rage, she pines for him still. She knows he can no longer touch Freya, no longer hold her and make love to her, so Freya is no longer a threat to her. But another woman, one that is still alive, just might be. If we can convince Machara that ye are not Nicol's and never shall be, perhaps we can prevent her from trying to harm ye while ye are here."

Even as frightened as I was, it hadn't occurred to me that she could actually cause me any real harm.

"Can she do that? Doesn't your magic keep her from doing harm to anyone?"

He took a deep breath. It did nothing to ease my worry.

"Until this morning, I would've said no. I would've been certain that she couldna do anything from her cell, but everything is different now that The Eight is no longer complete." He hesitated and looked regretful. "Lass, Maddock told me what happened today with Calder. While I'll make no excuses for what he said, he was right that the odor ye smelled was not from food."

I interrupted him. I didn't want to think on that moment a second longer.

"I know. The smell down here is the same."

He nodded. "Aye, and 'tis the first time such an incident has occurred. It means that her power has strengthened, and there is no way for us to know just how much."

I suddenly felt very willing to go along with whatever Raudrich needed me to do. I had no desire to be the target of an evil faerie's ill will.

"So how do we convince her that I have no interest in Nicol?"

He smiled. By the glint in his eye, I knew what he would say even before he said it.

"By convincing her ye belong to another."

* * *

*I*t was a rotten thing to put the lass through, but it truly was the only thing he could think of to keep her safe, and he was determined to do anything to do just that.

"Stay behind me, lass."

He knew it was an unnecessary directive. Laurel was plastered against him, and he knew she was doing everything she could to keep from shaking all over.

He'd not seen Machara in years, but the moment he lay eyes on her, all his hatred for her came rushing back.

She slinked toward the front of her cell, her silver hair dragging on the floor behind her, her long nails drumming against the rail as she smiled at him.

"Yer absence was good for me, Raudrich. 'Tis been more than a decade since I have felt this strong."

"Enjoy yer strength while ye can, Machara, for it willna last long. Timothy's body was weak for years before he died. The next druid will be stronger and with it, so will his magic."

She laughed, and the sound of it caused the hairs on his arms to rise.

"We shall see. Let me see the bitch behind ye, Raudrich. Let me see the whore that has come to try and seduce Nicol."

He'd known Machara would try to rile him up. He couldn't allow himself to give in to the anger he felt at hearing Laurel referred to in such a way. He needed his composure to keep his powers in check.

It was even more important, with Laurel down here, that he not allow Machara to weaken him through rage.

"She is no threat to yer love for him, Machara. 'Tis why I thought ye should meet her."

Stepping away from the bars of her cell, Raudrich watched as Machara crossed her arms.

Carefully, he stepped away to clear the path between Laurel and Machara. He'd expected Laurel to hesitate, but she did no such thing. The strength in her steps shocked him. She didn't hesitate, didn't shake. She stepped up beside him, looked straight into Machara's eyes, and spoke. "I'm Laurel. I wish I could say that it's nice to meet you."

Machara gave one short chuckle as her sinister smile grew even wider.

"Ah, I see Raudrich has already tried to poison ye against me. If only we lassies could have spoken first, I doubt ye would have such an ill opinion of me. These men have never been able to understand me, but ye, I think could, if given the chance."

Raudrich could've laughed at the blasé expression on Laurel's face as she paused and pursed her lips. She cocked her head to the side in contemplation, but she knew better than to do anything that might anger Machara.

"I doubt that very much."

"So, tell me, whore, why are ye here? Do ye mean to take my Nicol from me?"

Raudrich watched the exchange with great anticipation. Everything was up to Laurel. How she decided to speak, what she decided to do next, would determine whether or not she was safe inside this castle.

"No. I may not like you, but I am not that sort of woman.

Raudrich watched as Machara's expression softened just the littlest bit, and hope rose within him.

"Who does yer heart belong to then? If it is still yer own, then ye are a threat, for a heart untethered is bound to fall for my Nicol."

Machara was crazy, but Raudrich's heart pounded in his chest as he awaited Laurel's answer. He hoped Laurel understood just how important it was that she give Machara a convincing answer. He hoped the lass was capable of being a better liar now than she had been this morning when trying to convince him that they'd not touched in his bed last night.

Laurel reached for him. Raudrich let out an uneasy breath as he stepped toward her and she wrapped her arm around his waist.

"My heart belongs to Raudrich, Machara. I give you my word as one woman in love to another. I shall never lay a hand on Nicol. My heart is already taken and always shall be."

If he wasn't so worried for Machara's reaction, Raudrich would've swooned at her words. It was convincing even to him.

Machara stayed silent for a long moment as she looked back and forth between them. As she did so, Laurel leaned into him even more, pressing her head into him as her hand came up to gently rub his chest.

When Machara did speak, there was humor in her tone.

"Kiss him, lass. Ye can always tell by the way someone kisses another what precisely is in her heart. Convince me that ye love him. If ye doona succeed, I suggest ye start fearing for yer life. For bound by magic or not, I have ways of ensuring that ye willna be long for this world. Kiss him like yer life depends on it, because trust me, young whore, it does."

Laurel's eyes pleaded with him to cooperate as she turned and reached up toward him. When her lips touched his, he crushed her against him, and together they danced for the damned faerie's pleasure and while he couldn't speak for Laurel, most assuredly his own, as well.

CHAPTER 25

*W*hile fear initiated our performance, I wasn't altogether sure it sustained it. The passion with which Raudrich pulled me against him—the heat and the weight of how he pushed me against the back wall of the dungeon—felt very real. And my response to him was no put-on. It was chemical, completely involuntary. I moaned against his lips as his tongue sought entry into my mouth. As his hands roamed down the side of my body and he backed me into the stones behind us, his lips moved to my neck. I let out a shaky breath in his ear that caused him to growl.

He pressed himself into my stomach, and I could feel how hard and ready he was. It was a familiar sensation, one I remembered all too well from only the night before. His hand cupped at my breast and I closed my eyes from the pleasure of it. I was losing myself— quickly forgetting about the evil faerie standing only a few short feet from us.

Then she spoke, and the reality of our surroundings crashed down on both of us as we awkwardly pulled away, both breathless and weak as Raudrich turned from me to look at her.

"I'll not waste my energy trying to harm ye, lass. Ye are not a threat. If ye are not in love with Raudrich now, ye are well on yer way to being so. My efforts would be better suited to trying to fight my way out of here while The Eight dwindle in number and power."

"Try as ye might, Machara, ye willna succeed as ye hope."

Raudrich's voice was deep and pained. He was still struggling to gain his composure. His response to me had been no performance. I was sure of it.

"Nothing stays buried forever, lad. Each and every one of ye should know that by now. One day I will be free of this cell. When that day comes, ye each shall suffer a fate far worse than Freya's."

Raudrich's left hand clenched at his side. I could see that he was growing angry.

Eager to be away from the smell and the terrifying gaze of such evil, I reached for his arm.

"Let's go. I don't think there's any need for either of us to say anything more."

Without a word, he took my hand and we turned to leave.

I knew I would hear her laughter in my sleep.

———

"*L*ass..."

Raudrich waited until we were far away from Machara —until we stood in the hallway outside his bedchamber— to say a word.

The hallways were dark, the castle quiet, and as he stopped and turned to look at me, all I could hear was his breathing, still ragged and strained.

"Yes?"

My voice shook as I answered him. The energy that passed between us as we stood facing one another, our chests nearly touching with each intake of uneven breath, was palpable in its heat and need. I'd never been so turned on in my life. I'd never been so confused.

This wasn't like me. I didn't do this. I wasn't the sort of person that got swept away with anything. I didn't know this man. How, then, could he make me feel so much?

I felt safe, yet scared—curious, but cautious. I wanted to throw my arms around him. I also wanted to run away as quickly as I could. Too many things stirred inside me as we stood in the darkness and silence together. It couldn't have been more than a few seconds, but the span of time between my breathless "yes" and his answer felt like an eternity.

"Ye lied to me before. Why?"

It was hardly what I expected him to say, and with my thoughts clouded by his closeness, I couldn't recall what he might mean.

"Lie? When did I lie to you?"

He took one step closer and I felt my back bump into the wall behind me. I liked being pinned by him. I liked knowing that I couldn't avoid whatever he might do or say next. It was nerve-wracking in the sexiest way.

He leaned in and whispered in my ear. My whole body shivered as his breath wafted across the exposed skin of my neck. I closed my eyes and leaned back into the wall as he spoke.

"When I apologized for touching ye, ye said that I dinna do so. I know that I did, lass. Why did ye lie?"

"How do you know I was lying? Even if you think you touched me, perhaps it was only a dream."

I enjoyed this dance between us—his gentle prying, my pointless denial—it only served to increase the tension between us. It was so unlike me, but oh, so much fun.

"Because, lass..."

I gasped as he leaned in and cupped my breast in the small hesitation between his words. My breast filled his hands and he groaned.

"Machara's dungeon was not the first time I've held this breast in my hand. I knew how ye felt in my arms before this night. My

525

body remembers it clearly." He removed his hand and stepped away. "I'll ask ye once more. Why did ye lie?"

I reached out and placed both hands lightly on his chest. I wasn't ready for this closeness between us to end. I sighed as I prepared to come clean.

"I was embarrassed, Raudrich. You didn't touch me. I...I turned toward you in the night. You didn't pull me into your arms. I placed myself on your chest. I touched you. I rubbed against you with my leg. It wasn't your fault. None of it was. In my defense, I did believe I was dreaming, but when I woke and realized what I'd done, I was embarrassed."

I couldn't see his smile, but I could feel it in the darkness. He raised his hands and gently cupped my face.

"Embarrassed? Why?"

"I think because I enjoyed it so much. If it was a dream, I was safe in it. Once I knew it was real, I felt embarrassed that I wasn't really the woman I was in my dream—the woman who believed someone like you would want to hold me in such a way."

Only upon saying the words out loud did I realize the truth in them. It wasn't my actions I was embarrassed by. It wasn't guilt at having touched him while he slept.

It was knowing that for me to act in such a way while I slept, my subconscious self must've believed I was desirable enough that there was no threat of rejection in my actions.

I wanted to be that person so very much. But—as many things seemed to be showing me since arriving in this time—my old self-conscious wounds weren't as healed as I thought.

I wasn't that confident go-and-get-what-you-want woman that had rolled over in my sleep and plastered herself against Raudrich as if she were doing him a favor. I was the woman that suspected every man's kind word held a motive. I was the woman that disbelieved every compliment—the woman that pulled away the moment a man got close because I couldn't see how they could possibly be genuine. Why on earth would they want me?

I was the woman that could play confident really well, that could sometimes even convince my mind that I was the confident woman I so desperately wanted to be. But deep inside, in my core, I was still that woman who didn't love herself enough to truly believe that anyone else could love her back.

When I'd woken in Raudrich's arms to find that my dream was real, it had broken my heart. For in real life, no longer free from all my self-loathing talk, all I could think was how much he wouldn't have wanted me if he had known I was there.

CHAPTER 26

*G*od, how he wanted her. He wanted her so badly it stunned him, too badly for him to do as he wished. She wanted him, too. He knew that if he kissed her, they would end up spending the night together. It would be the worst thing he could possibly do for her.

Her admission had made her too vulnerable. If he made love to her now, she would forever wonder if he'd done so out of pity or want. Marcus had been right. This lass, intoxicating as she was, didn't know how to play this game. He knew it all too well. He had an unfair advantage over her. He was older than her and no longer unsure of the man he was or what he wanted. He would wait until the game could be fair. He very much suspected that once she learned to let go and learned to embrace who she really was—once she learned to wield the power she already possessed—the wait would be worth it.

He would have to take things slowly with her. He would have to get to know her mind before he could know her soul, and he would need to know her soul before he allowed himself to taste of her body.

Laurel's fears weren't unusual. He'd known many women in his life that shared such insecurities. What women rarely could see was that men were often riddled even more with such worries.

She'd not known good men as a child, he was almost certain of it. For lassies surrounded by the best sort of men while still children grow up knowing just how lovely and special they are. Too many fathers discount the role they play in their daughter's lives—mayhap an even more important one than that of their sons. Raudrich knew that if he were ever lucky enough to be blessed with a daughter, he would make certain she knew that it was she, and not the men in her life, who had the power to rule the world.

Perhaps, Laurel's time here would show her what good men could be—not that Calder's ignorant and cruel words had helped the situation. He would see to it that the rest of The Eight began to show her the best time of her life. It wouldn't take her long. Just a simple shift in her thinking could unleash her from the cage she kept herself in.

He looked down at Laurel as he held her face in his hands and gently bent to kiss her cheek.

"Lass, I do want to hold ye. I want to do so much more than that, but this night is not meant for us. 'Tis already the wee hours of the morning and ye are nearly asleep on yer feet. Go inside before I talk myself out of showing such restraint. Once ye close the door, I shall spell a lock for ye."

"I am rather tired."

Turning, she opened the door to his room and entered, but he couldn't keep from saying one last thing to her before she closed the door to him.

"Laurel, lass, I believe Morna lied to ye. I doona believe she brought ye here so ye could write a book."

Most nights, they lit their fires by hand so as to reserve their magic, but he didn't trust himself to step inside his bedchamber with her. With a quick flick of his wrist, he brought his room to light and his knees grew weak at the glint in her eye as she leaned into the doorway.

"Oh, yeah? Why do you think she brought me here then?"

"To heal what is broken inside ye and mayhap to find the love ye are so resistant to."

Laurel's brows pulled together and her tone was defiant when she spoke. "I'm not broken, Raudrich."

He wouldn't follow down the road she wished to lead him. He could sense it was one of the ways she so often pushed people away.

"Ye know that is not what I said, lass. Every one of us have broken pieces inside us, but we alone are the only ones that can heal them. Until we do, we canna become the people we are meant to be."

"And you've healed all your broken pieces, have you?"

"'Tis work that never ends, lass, but I shall never stop working to heal whatever may fracture inside me. Growing up here makes one less patient with the pain we cause ourselves. Not when ye know that pain could be brought on by another at any time—pain that ye canna control."

Laurel's eyes were sad and thoughtful as she gently sighed and closed the door between them.

CHAPTER 27

J fell asleep quickly after Raudrich left me. My mind was too full from all I'd seen that night, my body too alive from Raudrich's touch to process all of the things that were running through my mind. Instead, the moment my head hit the pillow, I was out, left to work through all of my thoughts as I slept.

I dreamed of Kate. She sat at the end of the bed and spoke to me as if she knew all that had happened—almost as if she were actually here.

"It's funny, isn't it? How I can tell you the same thing a hundred times and you won't hear it, but the minute you meet a man who calls you on your crap, you can actually see the problem."

Sitting cross-legged across from her, I answered.

"What crap? He didn't call me on any crap."

In my dream, Kate was whole again, unmarred from injury. She crossed her arms and lifted her brows at me. "Oh, really? How exactly did you read that then?"

I'd not had time to read into it at all. I was still processing Nicol and Freya's story, still reeling from the interaction with the wicked-scary faerie. By the time we'd gotten to Raudrich's room, I was so turned on that all I'd been able to think was that I needed to get myself in the bedroom quickly or I was going to rip all of his clothes off.

Then came the whammy of my confession and all of the feelings I realized I didn't even know I was feeling until they came crashing down on me. My mind was too full and weary to read anything into Raudrich's last few words to me.

"I..." I hesitated and shrugged. "I don't know."

Kate shook her head and leaned in close.

"Well, then, let me tell you what he was not actually saying but definitely, totally meant."

I leaned back into the grand, carved headboard and settled in.

"By all means, Kate. Please do."

"That was a man who wants you, Laurel. But unlike most of the men you date, he's not going to let you chew him up and spit him out the moment you get scared or start to doubt your worth or feel a little self-conscious. He can see that you're not ready for him. You're not ready for something that's real, and he's not going to waste his time on anything but that."

There was no doubt my sister was wise, but all this seemed beyond her limited insight into my complicated psyche.

"So what if I'm not ready? Everybody grows in their own time, Kate. It's just not time for me yet."

Kate held up one finger as if she were getting ready to list off a multitude of points.

"First correction: People rarely grow without trying. Change requires effort and you've been at a standstill for quite some time."

As I opened my mouth to argue, she threw up a second finger.

"Second: Don't be stupid, Laurel. Morna could've sent Marcus back here on his own. If she really cared about your writing inspiration, sending you the book and having us stumble across the documentary would've been more than enough. If it wasn't time for something to change in your life, she wouldn't have sent you back here."

"But..."

"No." She held up finger number three. "Three: Even if you don't feel ready, I suggest you get that way real quick. Do you really think that men like Raudrich come around every day? You've been on enough dates lately. You know that they don't. He read you like an open book, Laurel. He was able to get right to the bottom of your issues after spending three hours with you. Issues that you've become an expert on burying."

I knew she was right. I just didn't know what to do about it. I didn't know how to change. I didn't know how to start trying again.

"Okay, Kate, I get it. Something's got to give, but how? What do I do?"

She shrugged and I frowned. I didn't want her to give me some look-inside bullshit, I wanted direction. I needed to know how to make a shift.

"Laurel, I'm no expert either, but just try doing things differently. Don't fall into the same traps you usually do with men. If Raudrich tells you something, believe him. You can see that he likes you. Don't question it so much. Stop doubting how beautiful you are. How about this?"

She hesitated and lifted herself to her knees. She looked beyond excited at whatever revelation had just come to her.

"How do you write your characters, Laurel? They're confident and sassy. They do what they like and say what they want. They don't rail against their own happiness because they believe that they are deserving of it, right? They're different from you, but if you were really honest with yourself, I think you'd find that they're all a part of you, too. I have a theory. I think those characters, those heroines in your stories, they're really just all of the parts of you that you keep locked away. How about, just for a little while, just while you're here, you let them out to play for a bit. Pretend you're them. It may just show you who you really are."

It was an interesting thought, but before I could say so, Kate disappeared. I blinked once and opened my eyes to find that Morna now occupied the same spot Kate had just vanished from.

"I thought perhaps ye might be more open to hearing from Kate since I suspect ye and Marcus are still a wee bit upset with me."

I frowned. Seeing Kate made me miss her. After so many months being around her day and night, I wasn't accustomed to being away from her.

"So all of that was really you? Why am I not surprised? Raudrich was right then? You did lie to me?"

Morna nodded and smiled unapologetically. "Aye, lass. I wasna sure if ye would embark upon the travel back if I told ye the truth. Though, at the time, I dinna know that I was going to have to spell ye back against yer will. I regret how angry Marcus is with me."

I shrugged. I couldn't find it in me to be angry with her. Evil faerie and cursed castle aside, I was enjoying myself. I'd lived more in the last three days than in the past three years.

"Marcus is trying to make the best of it. Although, I have a feeling that after what I tell him tomorrow, that's going to be more difficult for him to do."

Morna sighed and I could see that I was right.

"Aye, he willna take the news well. Not for some time, I expect. Ye must allow him to work through it in his own way. Doona take it personally if he pushes ye away."

That didn't worry me in the least. Marcus wasn't like me. He didn't push people away. He talked things out. He was more of a grown-up than I imagined I would ever be. He wouldn't do to me what I'd done to him after our last trip to Scotland.

"Marcus isn't like that. He'll be upset, but not with me."

"Whatever ye say, lass. I must go now. 'Tis time for ye to wake. Marcus is standing outside yer door. 'Tis time for ye to tell him the truth."

With my next breath, my eyes opened.

Why were my dreams in this castle so flipping weird?

"*L*aurel, are you up? If not, wake up and let me in before everybody else wakes up. I am freaking out. The door's bolted. Let me in."

Slipping back into my dress—I'd dared to sleep naked again—I walked over to the door and unlatched the bolt Raudrich had magically placed there.

"What is it? What's wrong?"

He was covered in sweat.

"Shut the door. I don't want to risk anyone hearing me."

Once the door was shut, he began to pace back and forth across the length of the room.

"Marcus, what happened?"

"I don't know what happened, Laurel. I woke up early and it was freezing in my room. I was laying there with every cover in the room wrapped around me trying to decide if it was worth the effort of uncovering myself to walk across the room and light a fire. Then, out of nowhere, the fire just lit itself."

"It lit itself?"

He nodded. "Yes. And that's not all. I lay there trying to justify it, right? Because otherwise I worried I would go running from this castle screaming. So, I tried to calm myself down by thinking things like *maybe they have the fires set on some sort of timer*, or *maybe there was still a bit of lit kindling in the bottom from before bed and it sparked just right*. But then..." He paused and placed his palm against his forehead as if he still couldn't believe it. "I lay there and began to think, *hmmm...I wonder what time it actually is? I wonder if it's still dark out?* And then, the curtains covering each of the windows on either side of the bed just opened. On their own, Laurel."

He stopped pacing and moved to stand right in front of me.

"Laurel, this castle, these men, they're in my head. They're listening to my thoughts. Someone is doing something to me. I don't like it. I don't like it one bit."

I knew what it was. It wasn't remotely what he thought, and I had no idea how to tell him.

"Marcus, sit down. You look like you've just run five miles."

"I feel like it. My heart is beating fast enough."

I patted the bed and waited until he took a deep breath and moved to join me.

"How are you so calm, Laurel? You don't look surprised at all."

"If you'd seen what I saw last night, you wouldn't be either."

And so it began. I told him everything. I told him where Raudrich had taken me and all about what had happened to Nicol and Freya. I told him about Machara's cell down below the castle and what had happened when Raudrich took me down to see her. I told him about the way Raudrich had held me in his arms while he told me Nicol's story, and the way I felt when I kissed him in front of Machara. I took my time describing the entire night. I was in no hurry to get to the end of the story—to the part where I would have to tell him what he was.

By the time I finished, Marcus' breathing had returned to normal and he appeared much calmer than before.

"He likes you, you know? I could tell he did at dinner last night."

I nodded. I was going to try and take dream-Kate's advice. I wouldn't question what I felt to be true.

"I know, but we don't need to talk about me and Raudrich right now. There's something I have to tell you."

Marcus chuckled, and I sincerely hoped it wouldn't be the last time he would laugh for the foreseeable future.

"Even more happened last night? Geez, Laurel, that was enough to fill up a week."

I could sense it then—as the words formed in my mind—just how much this would hurt him. The news would be bad enough, but once he learned that I'd suspected this even before Morna sent us back here and didn't tell him...I wasn't sure if he would ever be able to forgive me.

"Marcus, this doesn't have to do with last night. This has to do with you. Something happened before we left for Scotland. Something I now know, I really should've told you about before now. I just..." I started to ramble the way I always did when nervous. "If it turned out to be nothing—which I was pretty sure it would—I didn't want to worry you for no reason. But Marcus, it wasn't nothing. It was a really, really big something and I'm so sorry."

He looked confused as I started to cry.

"Laurel, calm down. It can't possibly be as bad as all that. Just tell me."

"I know I told you about the documentary and the book. Those really are the reasons I wanted to come here. Although, as we both know now, they were what Morna used to prep me for where she was sending us."

Marcus reached for my hands and gently rubbed his thumb back and forth across my knuckles. It pained me more than he could know that he was trying to comfort me as I was trying to figure out how to deliver news to him that would change his life forever.

"I know all that, Laurel."

"I know. But there's something I left out. Something I didn't tell you about the book that I found."

He didn't look worried.

"Okay...what didn't you tell me?"

539

"You're going to hate me, Marcus."

He leaned forward and kissed my forehead. It made my heart ache.

"I could never hate you."

I took a deep breath and braced myself.

"There was a portrait in the book. A portrait of The Eight. You were in the portrait."

He didn't seem to understand.

"Well, we are here now, aren't we? Maybe the portrait is painted while we're here."

"No, you weren't next to The Eight. You were *one* of the The Eight."

I took another deep, shaky breath as I watched realization set it.

"I don't think they're inside your head, Marcus. I think your own powers are starting to come to the surface. I think you're destined to be one of The Eight."

*T*he sudden burst of magic throughout the castle startled him from his sleep. The magic of The Eight was connected—each could feel when another used their powers. This magic was different. It belonged to another.

Raudrich rose from bed quickly. As he stepped outside of Calder's room, he could hear the others rousing. Such a change in the energy of the castle wouldn't go unnoticed by any of them.

Ludo, whose room lay next to Calder's, joined him in the hallway.

"What in the name of Brighid was that? It couldna have been Calder, aye? We would've known if it were him."

It wasn't Calder. If Calder had used his powers or tried to sever them from The Eight, it would've been recognizable. This magic was not.

"No, 'twas not Calder."

Quinn appeared at the end of the hallway, and together they moved to meet him.

"Has anyone seen to Machara? Could it be her?"

As if summoned, Nicol entered the castle doors from his place in the garden. While he possessed no powers of his own, he was linked to the castle and all within it. He could feel the use of magic just like the rest of them.

"I shall make certain she is still locked away. Gather everyone else. We must discern what has just happened."

As Raudrich watched Nicol run toward his bedchamber, he turned to look at Ludo and Quinn.

"I doona believe this is Machara's doing. 'Twas not the magic of the fae."

"I agree." Quinn's voice was sure and certain. "There was no malice in it, though it felt strong and somehow uncontrolled."

Raudrich racked his mind for an answer. In truth, there was only one possibility, even as shocking as it was.

"The magic came from within the castle, aye? We can all agree on that?"

Both men nodded in agreement.

"And we know that 'twas not one of us. There is only one other answer, lads. The magic came from one of our guests. Either Marcus is a druid or Laurel a witch."

Was it possible that he'd spent so much time with her and not seen it? Could she have hidden it from him so well?

He had to find out straight away.

Before either man could even respond to him, he took off toward his own bedchamber, calling after Ludo and Quinn as he left.

"Ye two round up the others. I shall go to Nicol to make certain all is well with Machara. Then, I shall collect Laurel and Marcus, and we will get to the bottom of this in the dining hall."

There was no time to gauge Marcus' reaction. The moment I told him my suspicion, the door to the bedchamber flew open and Raudrich stepped inside.

His expression was surprised. If I didn't know any better, I would've said he looked wounded. He looked quickly between me and Marcus and then locked his gaze with mine. He didn't blink as he spoke.

"Is it ye, Laurel? If so, why dinna ye tell me? I trusted ye with everything ye wished to know about this castle without a second thought. It hurts me that ye dinna trust me enough to do the same."

Marcus was silent next to me and his own gaze was turned downward. I could see him wrestling with what I'd just told him. If not for his own experiences before waking me, he would've laughed at my suspicions, but the incident had been enough to make him wonder if it could be true, and he didn't have the slightest idea how to handle it, if it was.

I stood and walked the short distance to Raudrich and gently reached for his arm. He stepped away to prevent me from touching him.

"What are you talking about?"

"The magic, lass. Everyone in the castle felt it. Did Morna even send ye here, or did ye tell me that so I wouldna learn ye were a witch?"

I chuckled.

"Well, I sure didn't feel it. I'm not a witch, Raudrich. I didn't even know true magic existed until a few days ago."

He looked as if he meant to argue with me, but before he could do so, Marcus stood from his seat on the end of the bed.

"Neither did I, but apparently I possess it. It was me. Whatever happened, it was me."

Raudrich's expression softened at Marcus' tone. He could hear the weariness and confusion in it.

"Ye dinna know, did ye, lad?"

Marcus shook his head. I tried to catch his gaze as he walked over to us, but he wouldn't look at me. A knot settled in my stomach. He was going to do exactly as Morna had predicted in my dream. He was going to push me away.

"Of course I didn't know."

"Has anything strange ever happened around ye before?"

"No."

Raudrich reached out and gently clasped Marcus on the shoulder.

"There is much we must discuss with ye. I know ye must have many questions and even more reservations. We are the only ones that can explain any of this to ye. Will ye come with me to the dining hall? The men are gathering there."

Nodding, Marcus stepped toward the doorway. When I reached out to touch his arm, he whirled on me.

"Don't touch me, Laurel, and don't say a word. I know it was me that suggested we come back to Scotland, but I did that for you. I came here for you. And you suspected before we even left this might be my fate, and you didn't care enough about me to tell me that. If I'd known, I never would've come here. You took that from me, Laurel. You took away my choice. You've taken away my life. How can I possibly ever forgive you for that?"

One tear fell down his cheek, and with it, my heart broke completely.

Sobbing, I tried to reason with him.

"Marcus, I'm so sorry. I should've..."

He held up a hand to stop me.

"Don't. You're selfish, Laurel. So damned selfish. I'm done with you. If I'm going to be trapped here forever, I sure as hell don't want you here with me. Start looking for a way to get Morna to send you home. Until you find one, stay out of my sight."

He stormed away as I sobbed. Once Marcus was out of earshot, Raudrich pulled me into a hug.

"Lass, I think it best that ye stay away from the dining hall today. This shan't be easy on the lad, but with time he will see this for what 'tis—his destiny. He will make his peace with it, and when he does, he will see that ye are not the one to blame. I'll seek ye out later, lass."

I stood shaking in the doorway, tears running down my face, for hours.

I'd never felt more ashamed or alone.

CHAPTER 30

Sometime during the middle of the afternoon—long after I'd run out of tears—I began to hear lots of movement in the hallways and throughout the castle. Whatever they were doing, the men seemed to be in a hurry. While my curiosity was killing me, I knew better than to leave Raudrich's room. Marcus didn't want to see me. I wasn't particularly keen to see him either.

So, as the footsteps, hollering, and commotion continued, I knew I needed to find a way to occupy myself. Otherwise, I would lose my mind. First, I set out to light a fire, which to my everlasting surprise, I succeeded in doing. Second, I shamelessly rummaged around Raudrich's room and opened every chest until I found what I was looking for—parchment, ink well, and a quill.

There was only one person I wanted to talk to. One person that could make me feel a little less alone and hated.

It took me a bit of time to get used to the ink and the rough way the tip of the quill scraped against the thickness of the paper, but I was eventually able to write something legible.

Morna,

I'm going to trust that your word was true and try throwing this note

into the fire. If so, send me something, some way that I can speak to my sister.
I miss her and I'm really in need of a talk with her—a real one. Not some
cloaked version of you that you send to me in my dreams.
Laurel

Tearing the parchment just below my small note, I folded it up and tossed it into the fire. All it did was burn. Frustrated, I moved to the windowsill and looked down into the steep slope of forest that cascaded down the hill surrounding the castle. As I stared across the landscape, there was a slight swooshing sound behind me. I turned to see a folded note fly out of the flames, totally untouched by fire, and land gently on the writing desk where I'd just been sitting,

I hurried over to the table, gently touched the note's edge to make certain it wasn't warm and tore it open.

Laurel,

I know that neither of you seem to believe me, but I do only lie when it is absolutely necessary, lass. If I told you that you could reach me this way, I meant it. Walk over to Raudrich's wardrobe and open the door. At the bottom you will find what you need, but for the love of God, lass, keep it hidden. It would never do for something so modern to be discovered in the time you're in.

It seemed like too much to hope for, but I stood and ran over to the wardrobe and nearly tore the handle from the door in my haste to see if it could possibly be true.

It was.

Right at the bottom lay a phone. Beaming, I picked it up and ran back over to the parchment to respond.

I suppose this doesn't actually need service to work, does it? Thank you.

It wasn't a serious question. I knew, of course, that the phone would need no towers or battery to work.

Morna's response was almost instantaneous.

Of course not. Laurel, this phone shall be the last gift I give you and the last time I'll respond to anything you may write, for I know where your questions will lead, and I can't help you with what must come next. History has cast the die over what shall happen with Machara and the men of this castle. In this case, it wouldn't do for me to interfere. There are too many lives destined to take part in this story, too many things that need to fall into place.

I know you must think this very hypocritical of me, and perhaps it is. From reading my own story, you know that I've changed history more than once, but this time, history doesn't need my meddling to work out well in the end. Remember that when it feels like your world is falling apart.

With love and hope, I leave you.

Morna

I stared at the note, reading it over and over again as I tried to process what she might mean. I had a sinking feeling that I already knew.

Despite her warning, I scribbled out another note and threw it into the flames.

Does this mean that I'm stuck here? What about my family? What about Marcus' family? What about our lives back home?

I waited the rest of the day for her answer.

It never came.

And that in and of itself was answer enough.

I would never see Boston again.

*A*t first Raudrich believed it wasn't working. Perhaps, Marcus' magic was still too new. Mayhap, they would have to teach him to wield his new powers before its strength was potent enough for the spell to bind him to The Eight.

But then, slowly, as their chanting continued, Marcus' face distorted in pain as Machara's screeches rose up from her cell beneath them. The room shook around them as the binds took hold.

Marcus was now one of The Eight.

It should've been a relief to all of them, but as Raudrich looked into the eyes of his brethren, he knew the same worry weighed heavily on all of them.

Until Calder was found and his true motive for leaving known, they were no safer today than they'd been the day before.

CHAPTER 31

*I*t wasn't ideal, but it was the only agreement they could come to.

Marcus' magic was now bound, but it would take months for him to learn to harness the powers that were still his own. He would have to be trained as soon as possible.

Marcus wasn't the only pressing matter. Finding Calder was just as important.

So, after much discussion and many an argument, a plan was set.

All would leave the castle, save him. He would stay to keep an eye on Machara and to see that Laurel was safe. They couldn't risk Laurel leaving with the men who would go in search of Calder, and Marcus wouldn't hear of having her near him.

Even Nicol would leave with the other men—something he'd not done in over a decade.

Paton, Quinn, Ludo, and Marcus would leave for the Isle's furthest corner, far away from the castle where they would spend the following fortnight training The Eight's newest member and helping him to adjust to his new life among them. Such training couldn't be done near the castle grounds where Machara could listen in. She would only look for ways to exploit Marcus' weaknesses if they remained close to her.

The others—Harry, Maddock, and Nicol would leave for the Scottish mainland where they would begin to search and inquire into Calder's whereabouts. He couldn't have gotten far in the span of only a few days. Once they found him, they would hold him prisoner until Marcus' training was complete. Then as a group, they would decide what was to be done with him.

If his only trespass had been his thoughtless words about Laurel, forgiveness would've been the only possibility. They all knew just how easily Machara's power could strike fear into their hearts. Fear could make a fool of any man. What was less easily decided was whether his abandonment was enough to cast him out. If so, it would be a heartbreaking decision for them all.

"What should I do while the rest of ye are away? Is there some task undone, some measure I could take to further assure our safety that was neglected while I was gone?"

Raudrich felt rather useless standing there, watching every other man in the castle ready their horses for their journey. Not that he wished to leave. It was clear that someone must stay and tend to the castle, and there was no possibility of him allowing another man to stay here with Laurel alone.

Harry walked over and roughly punched his arm.

"Come now, Raudrich. We all know that even if I were to tell ye something ye could do, ye are unlikely to do it, not with Laurel about. Ye think of nothing else even when we are here. When we are away, it shall only be the two of ye—possibly for some time."

The anticipation of such extended time with her both delighted and filled him with dread. It was important that he tread carefully with the lass even if it was the last thing he wanted to do.

"Aye, I know. I shall be in need of a distraction."

"I'll not be the one to give ye one. Ye must know that every last one of us would gladly take yer place if we could. To have a lassie as lovely as Laurel, one that clearly likes ye, is a gift I'll not let ye waste. This life we lead here has denied each of us happiness that all men should know. If ye have a chance at finding love, lad, take it. Besides." Harry laughed and clasped his arm. "I know we give ye a hard time for leaving us these past two years, but we all know ye dinna have a choice. And I'd reckon ye worked far harder in those two years than the rest of us have in a decade. Think of this time here as a respite for ye. 'Tis likely we've some tough choices ahead, so find some joy in the days ahead while ye can."

If they did decide to remove Calder from The Eight, the decision would weigh on no one as much as Harry. Harry had been like a father to Calder for most of his life. It pained Raudrich to know how difficult all of this must be for him.

"I'm sorry, Harry. I know that all this with Calder has been difficult for ye."

Harry cleared his throat and looked to the ground.

"Aye, and I canna help but bear some responsibility for it. I've known for some time Calder was struggling. I should've paid him more mind. There is no true evil in Calder's heart. I've hope still that if we find him, his reason for this all will be clear. Doona give up on him yet."

Raudrich nodded. Even with the anger he had for Calder, it wasn't an easy thing to give up on family.

"I shan't. Safe travels, friend. May he be safe and well when ye find him."

Harry walked away from him and mounted his horse with ease as the rest of the men waved and took off toward the gate. He called back to him as he took his place at the tail end of the group.

"Enjoy yerself, Raudrich. Doona squander time that the rest of us would cherish. Farewell for now, my friend."

He waited until he could no longer see them before turning toward the castle.

He didn't care for Laurel's tears. The pain in her eyes as Marcus screamed at her had made him hurt all over.

If it was just to be the two of them there for weeks, he would see to it that her smile was returned to her as quickly as possible.

I didn't call Kate right away. I knew that before I spoke to her I needed to gather myself. I needed to reflect on how I felt about being stuck in this time for the rest of my life, and I needed to decide what I would tell her.

What surprised me more than anything was that the panic I expected to set in never did, neither did the heartbreak or fear. The truth was, I wasn't upset about staying here.

It wasn't that I was ignorant. I knew that with time, there would be many things I would miss. But deep down, if Marcus was destined to be here, then I knew I was destined to be here, too. We were family. Neither of us had ever functioned very well without the other. Boston just wouldn't suit me without him. And I knew—even as angry as he was with me now—seventeenth century Scotland wouldn't suit him without me, either.

There was only one person and one ornery cat that I would miss immeasurably—Kate and Mr. Crinkles. But for some reason I couldn't quite explain, Kate's distance didn't overwhelm me with pain. It didn't feel permanent, even though I knew it most likely was. At least, I would be able to speak to her. That was no small blessing.

I didn't hear Raudrich open the unbolted door. I was too busy turning Morna's magical phone over and over in my hands as I tried to decide how to tell Kate that I would never be returning home.

"Come, lass. Ye've been in this room for far too long today. How would ye like to venture out of this castle and meet some of the people of the village?"

As curious as I was to meet even more people from this time, it was the last thing I wanted to do tonight. My mind was much too occupied.

"It's all right, Raudrich. I don't want to run the risk of bumping into Marcus, and I'm exhausted anyway."

He laughed and came to crouch down in front of me as he placed his hands on my knees.

"From what, lass? Sitting by the fire all day? 'Tis not good for anyone to sit all day. And ye needn't worry about crossing paths with yer friend. He's gone."

I started and pulled back in my seat.

"Gone? What do you mean, he's gone?"

"I'll not lie to ye and tell ye he's pleased with any of this, but as we spoke with him and tested his powers, he couldna deny their existence. He agreed to join us. He became one of The Eight this afternoon. He's gone with half the men to train and learn how to use his magic. He willna be back for weeks."

Perhaps, I shouldn't have felt so relieved at Raudrich's news, but I was. Confrontation had never been my thing, and confrontation with those I loved most was definitely something I shied away from. With Marcus gone, I could move about freely without worrying about his angry glances, and I couldn't help but be glad about it.

"Oh. Well, that's good, I suppose. What's everyone else doing? There was so much noise earlier, but it's quiet now."

He smiled rather guiltily.

"They're gone as well, lass—on their way to the mainland to search for Calder. 'Tis only ye and I," he hesitated, "and Machara and poor Freya in all of the castle. While I've much to worry over, I doona wish to do it this night."

He moved his hands from my knees and gathered my hands in his own.

"Do ye know how long it has been since I've had time without duty or obligation, Laurel? I havena had a day to myself in over two years. Please doona make me celebrate this time of freedom all on my own."

His excitement made him look much younger than he was—like

the young boy inside him was finally getting a chance to peek out for the first time in ages. How could I possibly say no?

For the first time all day, I smiled.

"I...I look like a bit of a mess. I've been crying, and I've worn this same dress for days. It smells of horse."

"Not to worry about that, lass. I've laid out four of Freya's gowns for ye. They may be a wee bit short on ye, but no one shall notice that, I assure ye. I've also prepared a bath for ye in Marcus' room."

While I knew Freya had no real use for her dresses anymore, it still seemed rather intrusive for me to wear one of them.

"Is it okay for me to wear one of Freya's dresses? Do you think she would mind?"

He smiled and shook his head.

"No, lass. I asked her. With Nicol gone, I spent some time with her just as soon as the sun went down. I know she will be lonely without him. 'Twas she who suggested it."

What a strange life I was living—to be offered up dresses by a ghost.

"Okay, then. I'll um...I'll meet you downstairs when I'm ready."

I stood and walked toward the hallway when I heard him call after me.

"I canna wait, lass. I hope ye know how to dance. The people of this village havena seen me in years. I suspect they'll throw quite the party in the tavern for me."

I didn't—like, at all. I was far too excited to care.

CHAPTER 32

*R*audrich hadn't lied. While the tavern was nearly empty upon our arrival, it didn't take long for word to spread that Laird Peyton, as he was known here—I still didn't know why— was back. Before long, everyone in the village arrived. Raudrich was met with more greetings and hugs than I could count. Within a few minutes, he was pulled away from me.

I didn't mind. The people of the village were more than accommodating and I wasn't alone for a moment. As the hours went by, I danced, talked, and drank with nearly everyone in the village. By the time Raudrich came to collect me, I was dizzy from dancing, stuffed full of food, and had just enough ale in me to make my cheeks rosy and my tongue a little looser than normal. I was in a better humor than I'd been in ages.

I wished Marcus and Kate were here to see it. I wasn't sure either of them would recognize this version of me.

"There ye are. I promise ye 'twas not my intention to abandon ye here on yer own. I knew my arrival would be a festive occasion, but I dinna know just how many people would wish to speak with me. I am verra sorry, Laurel."

He stood next to me but leaned in close as he spoke.

I reached out and gave his arm a gentle squeeze as I smiled at him.

"It's okay. Really, it is. I had a great time."

He smiled back and surprised me by placing a protective hand on the lower part of my back.

"I can see that, lass, but do ye mind if we leave now? 'Twas ye I wished to spend my time with, and I havena seen ye at all."

"I don't mind at all. I don't think my feet could take anymore dancing anyway."

He smiled and slowly laced his hand with mine. The gesture surprised me. I wouldn't have expected him to want to do anything that gave the impression that I was with him, not when Raudrich and I, while undeniably attracted to one another, were still no more than friendly acquaintances. What surprised me even more was that no one in the tavern seemed surprised in the least.

"Not even with me, lass? I spent the whole night watching ye, and I envied every man that held ye in his arms."

The admission sent an anticipatory thrill down my spine, but I waited until we stepped out into the cool Scottish air to answer him.

"I might have one more dance in me, but if you were watching, you know how bad I am at it. Everyone was so nice, but I know I stepped on every single one of my partners' toes."

The biggest full moon I'd ever seen hung in the sky, making it easy for us to see our way back to Raudrich's horse.

He helped me up first then deftly mounted the beast behind me. I was settled into him even more closely than I'd been on the way down to the village, and I didn't miss how easily he rested his hands on my thighs.

"Raudrich?"

"Hmm?" He leaned his chest into my back as he reached for the reins. His face was pressed against my own, and I thought I felt his lips brush against my cheek for the briefest moment, but I couldn't say for sure.

"Why do they call you Laird Peyton?"

"Ah. I forget that ye still know so little about me, lass. Most of The Eight came from humble families, so they were free to use their true names when they pledged their loyalty to Nicol and this Isle. My family owns a large portion of Northern Scotland. My brother was laird there for many years. If it were ever to be known that I abandoned my familial clan and pledged my loyalty to another, it would've caused many problems for my brother when he was alive, so I took another name when I came here.

"While we dinna know it at the time, 'twas good that I did so. When my brother and his wife were murdered, his land was passed to me. I became laird of Allen territory. 'Twas not truly mine by right, as I broke my vows to my familial clan long ago, but because I hid my true name, it allowed me to see my brother's people settled after his death and to take the time I needed to sign the land over to someone I knew to be trustworthy."

"I'm so sorry, Raudrich."

He sighed and straightened himself just a little.

"Thank ye. I dinna know my brother as well as I wish I had. Though, the loss of him was painful, all the same."

His tone made it clear it wasn't something he liked to speak about. I hurried to change the subject.

"I've realized something, Raudrich. I think it is time that I make my peace with being here. I don't think I'll ever be going home."

He was quiet a long moment. When he did speak, his voice was thoughtful.

"How do ye feel about that? There must be much that ye left behind. It canna be easy."

It was a short ride to the castle gates. I could already see them in front of us.

"Not the way I should feel about it, probably. I'll miss my sister dreadfully, but...I don't know. Would you believe me if I told you that even though I've only been here a few days, I feel as if I'm meant to be here? As if this time was meant to be my real home all along?"

Raudrich pulled on the horse's reins as we reached the gate. He dismounted quickly and turned to offer me his hands. I allowed him to pull me off and into his arms. Our bodies rubbed against one another as he slowly set me to my feet. He didn't step away. He stood there with his hands on either side of my ribs as he looked down into my eyes.

"I told ye last night, lass. 'Tis not only this time I think yer meant for, but this verra castle, as well. I believe ye shall find yer heart here. Mayhap, the love ye've always wished for." Whether it was the tavern ale or my determination to be bold, I didn't know, but for once in my life, I allowed myself to say the exact thing that was on my mind.

"And you think you might be that love?"

He smiled and moved his right hand to the side of my face, cupping it gently as his thumb trailed back and forth across my cheek.

"I doona believe either of us can say that yet, but whomever captures yer heart shall be lucky to have it. If time shows us that I am that man, I shall wake up every blessed day grateful for it."

I was shaking again, and my cheeks were warm from more than just ale.

"Kiss me then, not because you're trying to save me from some jealous faerie, but simply because you want to."

"What makes ye think that I do want to kiss ye, lass?"

There was a test in his question. He wanted my certainty, none of the doubt I'd shown him the night before.

"Oh, you don't, huh?" I smiled at him so he'd know I wasn't upset by his question. "I guess I'll just..." I brushed past him and started to walk away, but he quickly reached for my hand and spun me back toward him.

"There ye are, lass—a woman who doesna doubt what she does to a man. How long have ye kept her locked away?"

I answered honestly. "Forever, I think."

He leaned in until his lips were nearly touching my own.

"Please doona ever lock her away again. Allow me to show ye just how powerful she is."

His kiss was hungry and demanding as he pulled me against him. I reached for his hair as I leaned into him. I cried out into his mouth as he gently nipped at my lip.

"The distance to the castle shall seem like an eternity, lass. Best we get the horse to his stable before I doona have the strength to pull away from ye."

Just as he broke our kiss, the sound of horses approached and a very American voice spoke out through the darkness.

"Raudrich, I am going to freaking kill you. Do you know how long it's taken me to find you?"

CHAPTER 33

Raudrich staggered away from Laurel, his arousal painful in its intensity. Thank God for the darkness. Without it, he would've been unable to shield it from view. Shaking his head, he tried to pull himself together and think clearly as the small group of riders approached. He'd been certain he would never see or hear from Sydney again. How could she possibly have found him? As the group of riders came into view, his confusion only grew.

Pinkie led the group, his wide smile and few teeth making him unmistakable even in the shaded darkness. Next to him rode Sydney —her voice and dark hair the giveaway. The other two riders, he couldn't yet see.

"Sydney, lass, what are ye doing here?" He looked over to Pinkie before his friend even had time to respond. "Pinkie? Do ye know Sydney?"

Pinkie spoke first, quickly dismounting before walking over to shake his hand.

"It seems yer sight has returned. Ach, I am glad of it, Raudrich. To answer yer question, aye, I know Sydney now, though I dinna a few days ago. I was halfway home when I stopped at a small inn and came across these three. When I heard the description of the man they were looking for, I knew 'twas ye. So, I offered them my assistance, for a price, o'course."

He nodded as he shook the man's hand.

"Naturally." He stepped away. He could feel Sydney's anger at a distance. "Excuse me, Pinkie, I believe I've some apologies to make."

"Aye, ye do. I dinna know lassies knew such language. I only thought wives got so angry at men, but she swears she doesna love ye in such a way."

Ignoring Pinkie, Raudrich hesitantly walked over to Sydney's horse and extended her his hand.

"Let me help ye."

She crossed her arms and shook her head.

"No, thank you. I've lived in this bloody time long enough to know how to get myself on and off a damn horse. Open the gate. I see no need to dismount before we actually get to the castle. When we do, though, you and I are having a nice, long talk. Alone. Do you understand?"

He would never say so, but it pleased him that Sydney was angry. It meant she was the true friend he knew her to be.

"Fine, lass, but who is that ye've brought with ye?"

Both riders brought their horses closer as he mentioned them.

"Silva?"

It couldn't be good that the lass who was meant to be tending to Allen territory was here.

"'Ello, Raudrich. Once Sydney is done with ye, 'tis I who needs to speak with ye. I'm not so pleased with ye, either."

He didn't recognize the man next to Silva, but the man spoke up as he looked at him.

"I've no need to speak with ye, so ye can relax yer mind a little. Ye may not know me. It has been some time since we last met. I'm Griffith MacChristy."

Upon hearing his name, Raudrich could see the resemblance the boy bore to his brothers, but the lad was right. The last time he'd seen young Griffith, the lad had been little more than a boy. Now, he was a strapping beast of a man.

"Aye, I do know ye. Ye've grown."

He turned to unlock the gate.

"Come. All of ye. 'Tis too cold for us to continue this outside."

He stood beside the gate allowing the others to ride inside. Understandably, Pinkie hesitated.

"Last I was here, ye dinna know if 'twas safe. Is it now? I care for ye friend, but I doona care for faeries. If I'm at risk, tell me now, and I will bid ye all goodbye."

He smiled and waved the man on through.

"'Tis fine, lad. I promise to keep ye safe."

---

*R*audrich apologized nonstop as we made the short ride up to the castle. It was unneeded. I'd seen the look of surprise on his face at the sound of his friend's voice. He had no idea they were coming.

Eventually, I couldn't bear to listen to him ramble on any further. I reached my hand up behind me to gently cup his face.

"It's okay. She clearly really needs to speak with you, or she wouldn't have come all this way. I'm rather tired anyway. I'll just slip away to your room when we get inside and leave you to them for the evening."

I felt the sharp intake of his breath against my back.

"Do ye...do ye wish me to stay in Calder's room, lass?"

"Definitely not. It's not like it will be our first time sleeping next to one another."

"Ach, thank God, lass. Knowing that I have yer warm arms to look forward to may be all that helps me survive the angry lassies that await me inside the castle. Doona wait up, though. I canna say how long they will keep me."

There was no way I would sleep, but I had no intention of

letting him know just how much I would be anticipating his return to his bed.

"Okay, I won't. Hurry as fast as you can. It's a cold night. I need you to keep me warm."

He groaned and nibbled at my neck as he rode into the stables.

*D*read settling in his gut at the angry expression on Sydney's face, Raudrich carefully closed the door to the sitting room and approached his friend.

"I know ye are angry with me, but at least give me a hug. I've missed ye, lass."

She stood with her arms crossed by the fire and stepped away as he reached for her.

"Don't touch me. Why did you ignore my letters? Why didn't you tell me about any of this? I've been worried about you for months, Raudrich. Do you know what I'm going to have to deal with when I get home? Callum is going to be furious with me. I knew he'd never let me leave to go looking for you if I told him. So I wrote to his brother and snuck off with him. I've made certain that Callum knew we were safe, but still...he won't be pleased. I've put my life on hold for you, and you're not even in danger, are you? You just...you just what? Decided to cut me out of your life? That's not how this works, Raudrich. You don't get to ghost me. We're not dating, you bloody imbecile."

Seeing that she needed to vent, Raudrich calmly took a seat by the fire and listened as she continued to scream at him.

"Is it that woman you were kissing? Is that it? You found yourself a girlfriend and decided you didn't need friends anymore? Is she the one who made you stop responding to my letters? How did I not know you were one of The Eight? Why didn't you tell me?"

The longer she screamed, the less angry she sounded. Slowly, her anger turned to tears. The moment she began to cry, Raudrich stood and moved to wrap his arms around her.

"Ach, Sydney, I'm sorry. I'm so, so sorry. I dinna mean to hurt or worry ye. 'Twas my pride that kept me from writing to ye. I dinna wish for ye to know the truth. I worried it would change how ye saw me, and there is none in the world that have such a high opinion of me as ye do."

She sniffled, and he tried not to grimace as she shamelessly wiped her nose on his shirt.

"What are you talking about?"

"Sit down and let me explain everything to ye."

With some coaxing, Sydney took her seat by the fire. Slowly, he told her everything—the reason he couldn't risk writing to her about The Eight and why he stopped writing to her because of his eyesight. When he finished, he couldn't help but ask her the one question on his mind.

"Why did ye come here, lass? Even if ye were worried, even if ye were mad, it still doesna explain why ye are here. Not when Silva must've told ye some of what she knew when ye arrived in Allen territory."

"You're right. I came here for Silva's sake. Obviously, I understand why you left in such a hurry now that you've explained everything, but you left her with a mess to clean up—one she never asked for. She doesn't want to be laird, Raudrich. She's still grieving the death of her husband. Allen territory wasn't even her home until a few years ago. She's miserable, and you gave her no choice before you left. You're going to fix this for her."

Such news surprised him. Silva was so strong, so capable. Despite the fact that his decision had been made in haste, he'd truly believed it the right one. Had he truly not even asked the lass if she was willing to be laird? If not, he owed her a great apology.

"I dinna know."

Sydney nodded and reached over to pat his hand.

"I know. So, that's what I'm going to tell Callum about why I came all this way, but the real reason is that I just really missed you, Raudrich. I wanted to see you. I wanted to see your home and make sure that you were okay. Are you okay? Are you happy?"

Happy was something he'd never placed much importance on, but for the first time in a very long time, happy did at least seem possible.

"I believe that I could be."

Sydney wiggled her eyebrows knowingly at him, and he laughed at how silly she looked.

"It's the girl, huh? She's very pretty. Although, she's quite shy, isn't she? I haven't heard her say a word."

He'd never seen anything in Laurel that made him believe she was shy.

"None of us gave her a chance to speak, did we? Ye'll like her. She's one of Morna's lassies, same as ye."

"Ah. I thought she looked, I don't know, out of time somehow. So...do you love her?"

"In truth, she's little more than a stranger to me still, but I do think that I could."

Sydney smiled and looked at him knowingly.

"If Morna sent her, you know you don't really have much of a choice right? Her matches always work out. I should know. Might as well not fight it or try to slow it down for manners' sake. If you feel it—which, from that slaphappy smile on your face, you do—just give in. You'll wind up in the same place either way. You may as well make the journey a little easier on yourself."

He suspected that Sydney was right, but he'd not say anything like that to Laurel just yet. The last thing he wanted to do was push her away by coming on too strongly.

"I doona doubt any of that, lass."

"Where's she at now?"

He could scarcely breathe each time he thought of it.

"In my bed."

Sydney's mouth fell open as she jumped up from the chair and moved to pull him to his feet.

"Then, what are you doing sitting around talking to me? We've got the daytime for that mess. Go and tend to your woman. Bed her well. Help her touch the heavens. Rock her world. Make her toes curl. You can totally do it."

Raudrich laughed at Sydney's bawdy remarks.

"Ach, lass, I'm sure that Pinkie dinna know what to do with ye. Ye do say the strangest things."

"It's what we out-of-time lassies do, Raudrich. If I were you, I'd get used to it. I suspect you'll be hearing it for a very long time."

CHAPTER 35

I was still dressed and awake when Raudrich finally made it up to the room. He sighed at the sight of me sitting next to the dwindling fire when he entered.

"Ach, Laurel, ye truly dinna need to stay awake for my sake. I knew 'twas likely to take me some time to calm Sydney down. Ye must be bone-weary, lass. Stand and I'll tuck ye into bed nice and warm then I'll hold ye while ye sleep."

While I appreciated his thoughtfulness, I was still much too aroused from our journey back from the tavern to sleep. Standing, I walked over to him and reached to run my fingers through his hair.

"I do want you to hold me while I sleep, but if it's all well and fine by you, I'd like to do a few other things with you first."

I'd definitely had more ale than I'd realized. Either that or the characters I was trying my best to imitate had straight up decided to possess me. Such bluntness wasn't at all in my nature.

It felt nice, though. Perhaps, I should work on saying what I wanted more often.

And seeing the lift in his expression at my words made me tingle with anticipation. He wanted me too, just as badly—possibly worse —than I wanted him.

"Are ye sure, lass? I'd consider it an honor to simply sleep next to ye. Ye needn't feel any obligation."

"Raudrich..." I stood on my tiptoes to reach him. After kissing him until he began to tremble, I trailed my lips toward his ear where I whispered, "I want you. I've already had you in my dreams, but tonight I want you in real life. I want to see you and taste you and feel you moving inside of me. Undress me and take me to your bed."

His response was immediate as he spun me away from him.

"This dress, lass, it suits ye."

I laughed as I looked down to see my breasts jiggling as he pulled at the laces of Freya's gown.

"It's too tight."

He bent to nip at my neck, his tongue warm against my neck.

"Precisely. Yer breasts barely stayed inside it while ye danced at the tavern. Every time I glanced at ye, all I wanted to do was taste them."

I gasped as his hands slipped inside the opening at the back of the gown and slid around my waist before slowly pushing upwards until he cupped both my breasts in his hands. He pushed outwards with his arms and in one quick sweep, the dress fell to the ground, leaving me naked and exposed to him.

I didn't move to cover myself. Instead, I leaned back into him as his hands roamed over me. He pulled me tight against him, and I could feel his erection pressing into my back as one hand dipped lower and deftly slipped into the warmth between my legs.

"Christ, lass, I have never wanted a woman so much."

I couldn't speak. My breath was coming too quickly. My heart was beating too fast for me to do anything but writhe against him.

He moved his fingers quickly until my knees buckled from pleasure. As I began to tremble, he spun me toward him once again, quickly lifting me in his arms as I wrapped my legs around his waist and he carried me over to the bed.

The moment he lay me backwards, he removed his shirt and I

reached for the tie on his breeches as I greedily slipped my hands inside to pull them downward.

I reached for him, taking his length in my hands as he groaned and bent to crush his mouth to mine.

The heat of his chest pressed against my bare skin only increased my need for him. Moving my hands to either side of his face, I kissed him as I spread my legs wide.

He felt me open myself to him and plunged inside as I screamed into his mouth.

We found our rhythm quickly. He took care to make sure that he matched his pace with my own, and when we both finally did climax, it was together.

It was hands down the best sex of my life, and from his endless exclamations I expected he would say the same come morning.

"Why do ye write about love, lass?"

"Hmm..." I was half asleep when he spoke. We lay in just the same position I'd woken in several nights before. Tenderly, he twirled a lock of my hair with his fingers. "What was that?"

He lifted himself and my head dropped from his chest to the mattress as he propped himself up on his elbow.

"I asked why ye choose to write love stories."

"How do you even know that? I don't remember telling you that's what I wrote."

He smiled and immediately I knew.

"Ye dinna. Marcus told me."

Seeing in his expression that he really did wish to talk, I pushed myself up and moved to sit cross-legged on the bed as I pulled the blanket up with me for warmth.

"Almost everything is a love story at its core. The love story is just more central in the things that I write. It's what life is about, isn't it? We all have the same basic need to connect deeply with another person. I enjoy exploring that. I enjoy writing about all the different ways people can find love."

He was staring at me with great interest, and I could see that another question was right on the tip of his tongue.

"What?"

"Nothing, lass. Ye fascinate me, is all. If ye understand the value and importance of love so well, why then have ye resisted it so fiercely for most of yer life?"

"How do you..." I paused and shook my head. "Marcus again? Man, he was on a tear with you, wasn't he? What didn't he tell you about me?"

Raudrich laughed and leaned forward to kiss me quickly.

"He dinna tell me much, lass. And ye," he pointed at me playfully, "dinna answer the question."

I shrugged.

"I don't know, really. I guess I never found anyone that made the risk of getting hurt worth the possible reward."

He smiled at that.

"But I am?"

"It would seem so, wouldn't it? I've not been very successful at resisting you, at all."

With a flick of his wrist, he extinguished the flames in the fire and reached for me in the darkness. As we came together once more, he whispered into my ear.

"I'll not hurt ye, lass. Not now, nor ever if I can keep from it."

I didn't doubt the honesty in his words for a moment.

That didn't mean that I was safe in the least. But for once in my life, I simply didn't care.

Love with this man was worth it, no matter how risky.

CHAPTER 36

I woke only a few short hours after we fell asleep in each other's arms. While my body was deliciously exhausted, my mind was racing with a million different thoughts. There seemed to be an energy coursing through and around the castle, a foreboding feeling that left me uneasy and unable to rest. I wondered if Raudrich could feel it, as well. Although, from the look of him—arms spread wide across the bed, his mouth hanging open as he slept—he didn't look like it.

Carefully, I rolled away from his grip and rose from the bed as I quietly felt around on the floor for Freya's dress. I would've preferred to put on my own, but it was all the way across the castle in Marcus' room and I wasn't going to risk being spotted in the nude by our other guests.

Yanking the snug dress on, I tied the laces loosely and slipped quietly from the room.

I left the room with no real agenda—I just needed to move, to walk around in the hopes that some exercise might slow the jumble of thoughts inside my mind.

I'd yet to tell Kate what I knew I must. I was worried over Marcus and how he might or might not be adjusting to his new training and life. My thoughts were with Harry and the men who were searching for Calder. Even with my strong dislike for him, I hoped they would find him safe and well. I knew how strongly each of the men loved him.

There were other thoughts, too, happier ones—thoughts of Raudrich and the way I already knew what I felt for him but wouldn't allow myself to say out loud just yet.

His scent still clung to my skin, and the memory of our night spent together had me walking around the dark hallways of the castle with an embarrassingly goofy grin.

As I wandered, I reveled at how utterly quiet the castle was at night. All were asleep, all except Freya, of course.

I hesitated at the thought. I didn't know if Freya would welcome my company, but my curiosity eventually got the better of me as I paced back and forth in front of the castle's main door.

With Nicol away, Raudrich had said himself that Freya would be lonely. Perhaps, she would welcome the company.

I snuck into the nearest empty bedchamber—Paton's—to grab a blanket to wrap myself in while outside and realized right away why Raudrich had believed Paton would see reason to try and steal his room. The room—if one could even call it that—was little more than a closet. It had no real bed to speak of, only a simple sewn mattress and a small table next to the bed.

Laughing as I thought back on that night which now felt ages ago, I pulled the blanket from the bed and made my way outside.

The moon always seemed to be exceptionally bright on the isle and I was able to make my way to the garden path with ease. The crunch of dead leaves and plants crackled beneath my feet. So as not to frighten her, I called out to Freya and tried to hide the nervousness in my voice. I had no idea what to expect. I'd never seen a ghost before, let alone spoken to one.

"Freya, I'm Laurel. I don't know if Nicol mentioned me to you or not. I thought you might like some company. I was having a hard time sleeping."

I still couldn't see her, but she had the sweetest and most tender voice I'd ever heard.

"Aye, o'course, lass. Company doesna come to me easily. I never deny it when it does. Follow the path to yer left up ahead and ye will reach the garden's center. Ye shall see me right away when ye turn the corner."

I relaxed at her welcome and followed her directions with great anticipation. The moment I laid eyes on her, I couldn't help but gasp. Her translucent figure was breathtaking even from the height of Nicol's bedchamber window. In person, she was so beautiful it was almost difficult to look at her.

"Hi."

Freya smiled but didn't move from her seat as she waved me over to her.

"'Ello, lass. I hoped I would have the opportunity to visit with ye soon. Do ye know how long it has been since I've had the chance to visit with a woman?"

"Decades?"

She didn't look sad as she answered me and I was glad for it. It made it easier to be around her. It was heartbreaking anyway. If Freya appeared to be suffering or if she wallowed in despair, I wasn't sure I would've been able to stand it.

"Precisely, lass."

I moved to sit next to her and stared at her with wide eyes until she broke the silence.

"'Tis fine if ye wish to touch me, lass."

I was very curious.

"Will you feel it if I do?"

"No. Yer hand will sweep right through. Try. I promise ye, I doona mind."

Hesitantly, I reached as if I meant to shake her hand. It felt no different than waving it through air, though I could see my fingers pass through her own.

"Wow. I...I'm sorry, Freya. I can't begin to imagine what this is like for you."

She shrugged rather nonchalantly.

"I made my peace with this long ago, not that I willna welcome a release from this place when it comes. I pray for it every day."

"It will. Someday, you'll be free. I truly believe that."

She smiled and leaned in close.

"I agree, which is precisely why I am so verra glad that ye are here. It has restored my hope."

"Why do you say that? I've far less power than the men that surround you here. I can't see how I could possibly make you hope for anything."

She shook her head as she spoke up to disagree.

"Ye are wrong about that, Laurel. Yer presence here has agitated Machara in a way I've not ever felt before."

"That's only because..." I hesitated. I hoped that saying Machara's suspicions out loud wouldn't give Freya any reason to believe them. "Machara worried that I might be here for Nicol. She's very jealous of him."

Freya laughed loudly.

"Lass, Machara is a lying shrew. She no longer cares for Nicol. If she is ever free, she wouldna take him for herself. She would kill him without thought or feeling. This state she's placed me in, it ties me to her. I feel what she feels, and 'twas not jealousy she felt in yer presence. 'Twas fear."

"Why would she be afraid of me? I've no power over her."

"Why do ye think there are far more stories of faeries ruining the lives of men than of women?"

I hadn't the slightest idea.

"I don't know."

"Men would have us believe that we are the emotional ones, but they only tell themselves that to hide from what they know is true. We hold the power, lass. Faeries know this truth. They know that we are too wise to make the same bargains men strike with them all the time. The day Machara is defeated, it willna be at the hands of the men here. It shall be women that defeat her. Even now, with the two lassies that arrived this night, her fear has grown. With each new lass that steps inside the walls of this castle, Machara's chances of survival dwindle."

I liked the idea of that—Freya's certainty that it would be women that would save the day.

"How do you know that?"

"Because Machara does. She rarely permits herself to think on it, but I feel it each time fear flares up within her. It feels to me almost as if it were destined—a prophecy of sorts—one which she is determined to change. I doona believe she will."

"Have you ever mentioned any of this to Nicol?"

She shook her head, and for the first time all night, she looked sad.

"No. Nicol carries enough guilt for all that happened. His hope that one day he will free me is one of the few things that has made these years bearable for him. There's no need for him to know that it willna be him that saves me."

The sun was slowly beginning to peek over the horizon, and I could see in Freya's gaze that her night was almost over.

"Thank you for speaking with me. I'll visit you again."

She smiled and laid her hand on my knee, although I couldn't feel her touch.

"Oh, please do, Laurel. Even when Nicol returns, doona feel like ye canna interrupt him. I see enough of him. I would welcome yer company over his anytime."

She disappeared while laughing. At least even in such a miserable purgatory, she'd found a way to be joyful.

She was a better woman than I ever hoped to be.

CHAPTER 37

*R*audrich was still asleep when I returned to the bedroom. I even went out of my way to wake him up, stomping around the room and flinging the curtains open so the sunrise would stream in. He didn't move. His soft snore just continued on.

Laughing, I moved over and crawled on top of the bed, crouching on my knees as I bent to kiss him.

"Hey you, wake up. I've been awake for hours now. You're going to sleep the whole day away."

He groaned and reached to pull me down toward him, snugly settling me into the space between his arm and chest.

"Laurel, why in God's name are ye already dressed? And what are ye talking about sleeping the day away? The sun is barely up. I must not have done a proper job of tupping ye last night. If I had, ye would wish to sleep until noon, at least."

I laughed as he nuzzled his lips on my ear, his breath tickling me until I started to writhe against him.

"Trust me, you did an excellent job. I'm just wound up. I'm not sure why."

He growled and turned to roll on top of me.

"Well then, lass, allow me to help ye unwind once more. Get out of that bloody dress. Ye look far better out of it. Why is it even on?"

He asked the question as he lifted my bum so that he could untie the laces and loosen them with his fingers. I didn't wish to think about how he must've gotten so deft at it. As my breasts sprang free from the top of the gown, he quickly pulled the dress to my feet.

"I..." I could barely talk as he bent and latched his teeth down on one of my nipples. "I went to speak to Freya."

He quickly glanced up at me before moving his lips downward, kissing the side of my waist between words.

"Freya...why...did...ye...wish...to...speak...with...her?"

I was squirming now. My hips rising of their own volition as my body began to ache for him. I wanted him inside me, wanted to move with him as we'd done only hours before.

"Holy crap, Raudrich. I can't think when your tongue is..." I cried out as he kissed me between my legs. Reaching for his hair, I pulled him up to me and quickly rolled him over so I could straddle him. I needed him. Now.

"Can we talk about Freya later?"

"Fine by me, lass."

I came down on him hard and heavy, and the cry that escaped his lips as I began to move on top of him quickly escalated my own climax. There was nothing slow in our exploration of each other this time. It was rough and needy, and when we finally came apart, I was trembling with exhaustion.

"Do ye wish to sleep now, lass? Please say aye, for I doona think I have the strength to tup ye again just now."

I laughed as my eyelids grew heavy.

"I actually feel like I could sleep. Well done."

He laughed as I turned onto my side and snuggled my bare bum and feet against him.

Just as my eyes began to close, Sydney's annoyingly chipper voice called to us through the door.

"Wake up you two. I'm sure you're tired from all the boom-boom I hope you guys did last night, but I made breakfast, and it's getting cold fast."

---

*S*ydney's meal was by far the best I'd had since arriving in this time, and I found myself feeling quite jealous of the residents of Cagair Castle who had their very own professional chef to cook their meals.

I sat next to her throughout breakfast. While Raudrich visited with Griffith and Silva, we had a chance to talk about some things only those acquainted with Morna could truly relate to.

"So, how'd she send you back? Did she at least ask your permission first?"

I asked the question as I shoveled yet another bite of frittata into my mouth.

"Oh, that's quite a long story. She actually didn't want me to know about the magic. She wasn't sure I could be trusted. So she spelled my coffee with some sort of truth serum and then once she was convinced I wasn't under the command of some evil witch she had history with, she allowed Callum, my husband, to take me through the stairwell."

"Stairwell?" That sounded much more pleasant than being tossed into a pile of hay in a smelly stable.

"Yes. Cagair's time-travel contraption wasn't actually created by Morna, and it's much easier on the body than the way she always goes about it. You can just walk back and forth between this century and our own."

"What?"

I couldn't hide the astonishment and excitement in my voice. It was like hearing that I'd won the lottery and would stay young for the rest of my life at the same time. If Sydney was telling me the truth, it meant I could see Kate again. Whether I wished to go forward, or she back, I didn't have to say goodbye to my sister forever. It also gave Marcus more options for the rest of his life, once the curse was broken.

Sydney's expression as she looked at me was one of concern.

"Did you think you were trapped here, Laurel? Is that what Morna told you?"

In truth, I guess Morna hadn't said those exact words, but her glib farewell through her letter had sure made it seem that way.

"Yes, I did think that. She didn't say that outright, but she did tell me that she was finished communicating with me. I didn't think there was a way to return home without her."

Sydney shook her head and I got the feeling that even if things tended to turn out well for the women Morna sent back, each of them had their own feelings of frustration toward the meddling witch who had so intrusively upended their lives.

"Morna means well. She truly, always does, but sometimes, I don't agree with the way she goes about things. I'm much fonder of her husband, Jerry. I don't care what Morna made you think. The rest of us go forward and back all of the time, and I'll be damned if you don't have the same option that we do. Listen." She paused and reached to grab my hand. I felt like I might cry at the relief that was slowly flooding my entire system. "If you need to go forward or if someone you love needs to come back, just come to Cagair. It's quite a long journey, but you are welcome anytime. I'll walk you through myself. That passageway isn't Morna's. She has no claim on it and no say on how it is used."

I threw my arms around her with no regard for how odd we must look to the rest of the table.

"Are you sure? It...it doesn't put you guys in danger in any way?"

She pulled back just far enough to look at me.

"We keep it well hidden, but any girl that gets pulled into Morna's shenanigans needs some say in her own life. The stairwell is yours—Cagair is yours—anytime you need it."

"Thank you." I pulled her in for another short hug before

quickly pushing myself away from the table to stand. "Thank you so much. I'm sorry to be rude, but there's something I have to take care of right away."

I couldn't sit at the table a moment longer. I had a phone call to make—one that I no longer dreaded.

CHAPTER 38

*K*ate picked up on the second ring. I'd never been so thrilled to hear her voice.

"Hello?"

"Kate, it's me. Step into a room that Mom isn't in, okay?"

I could hear the quick shuffle of her feet followed by the sound of a door closing before she squealed into the phone.

"Oh, my God, Laurel! You're okay? You're safe? Are you really... are you really in the past? How the hell are you calling me?"

Smiling, I slid down to the floor on the other side of Raudrich's bedroom door and leaned against it as I answered her.

"Yes, yes, and yes, to your first three questions. I'm okay. I'm safe. And I'm speaking to you from the year sixteen hundred and fifty-one. As for how I'm calling you...you can thank the same magical witch that sent me to this time for that."

"Oh, I will. Laurel, I have so much to tell you. You know as well as I do that I've got way too much time on my hands." She paused and snickered. "Or, I guess I should really say hand. Anyway, way too much time with nothing to do. From the second you and Marcus left for the airport, all I could think about was where you were going and what you would be seeing, so I decided to do some research. Where are you exactly? Are you at Conall Castle or are you on the Isle of Eight Lairds?"

I smiled into the phone. She sounded more like her old self. It was really good that she was able to make a joke about her injury without crying.

"Wow, Kate. You must either be really bored, or Mom must be driving you up the wall for you to have done research. Which is it?"

I was the bookworm. Kate definitely was not. Kate had read my first novel out of obligation only. Besides that, I wasn't sure she'd picked up a book since college. Not that I would ever complain about her doing research on this time. It was bound to come in handy. Perhaps Kate would be able to provide me with some of the answers Morna had been so unwilling to give.

"Honestly, it's neither. It was just that when you left, I couldn't shake the feeling—even as crazy as it seemed at the time—that this whole thing was actually real. If it was, I knew this had to be something pretty momentous, ya know? So I just started looking up what I could find about both places. So, tell me, where are you?"

"The Isle of Eight Lairds."

Her voice was giddy with excitement. "Oh, good! I learned way more about that place anyway. Laurel, I haven't slept in days. It's going to take me weeks to come down from the amount of caffeine and chocolate I've consumed since you left. I've been working my way through everything I could find on that place like a maniac. Are you sitting down? I have some seriously serious shit to tell you."

"I am." I'd called believing that I would be the one doing most of the talking. I was quickly getting the feeling that I was wrong.

"Okay, good. Let me think about where I should begin. I wasn't really expecting to hear from you, so I'm not prepared. I was actually just planning on telling you in person."

I quickly interrupted her. "In person?"

"Yeah, in person. Do you really think for a second that after all I've learned that I was going to leave you there alone? No way, girlfriend. I already have flights booked for me, Mr. Crinkles, Mom, and Marcus' dad to Edinburgh in three weeks. I would've booked them sooner but David couldn't get off work before then."

My brain couldn't possibly keep up with the totally unexpected news she was dumping on me. "Hang on. You need to slow down. Mom and David know where Marcus and I are? What did you tell them to make them believe you? I can't imagine either of them took that news well. And more than that, how were you going to get back here when you got to Edinburgh?"

Kate took a deep breath. I suspected that she realized she'd started to let herself run away with things in her excitement. When she spoke again, her tone was calm and collected.

"I'm not an idiot, Laurel. I did tell Mom and David where I thought you were, but I obviously didn't tell either one of them that you were chilling hundreds of years in the past. And I figured we'd get back the same way you did. We'd go looking for Morna."

"How did you get them to agree to go with you?"

"That was trickier, but I told them that you guys had decided to stay in Scotland for the rest of the summer and you wanted everyone together to celebrate Marcus' birthday at the end of the month. When I told them that I would foot the bill, they happily agreed."

I nodded, my thoughts suddenly drifting to what a pain in the butt my mother would be while adjusting to this time. I dreaded the thought of her being here, but I also knew that if Kate was planning to join me here, we could hardly just disappear off the face of the earth without telling her. We were her world, and despite her helicopter nature, we both loved her dearly.

"How can you afford that?"

Kate laughed into the phone. "I can't, but what does it matter? I'll not be coming back here, and I doubt they're going to be able to find me to haul me off to debtor's prison in the seventeenth century."

"Kate." Now, I was worried. I wanted to see Kate, but this was too big of a decision for her to make on a whim. "You can't possibly know that you'll want to be here forever. You don't need to do anything that will ruin your life back home."

"Oh, I do know that I'll be there forever. You will, too."

"How can you possibly know that?"

"Laurel, you really should've read that book you found. Marcus wasn't the only one inside it. I'm pretty sure you were, too. And unless there's another one-handed burn victim with a black cat there at the castle with you now, I'm in the book, too."

*I*t took me a good thirty seconds to respond to her. You would think after so many unbelievable things occurring over the past week, I would've been past the point of being surprised. I wasn't.

"Okay, Kate. You're going to need to explain everything you've read from the beginning. I'm just going to sit back and listen. I'm feeling slightly lightheaded."

My sister laughed and as I settled into my spot on the floor, I could hear Mr. Crinkles purr in the background.

"Okay, I can't blame you for that. It's a lot, and some of it's not so great."

"I'm ready." I was anything but.

"So, I read the book first, start to end. You know how history gets twisted throughout time and then you throw in a few ancient legends and things get even worse, so I have no idea how much of what I read is true, but I'll try to explain the gist of it to you."

I nodded as if she could see me. "Okay, shoot."

"The documentary told us about the legend, right—about The Eight and how they were bound to protect the Isle from the darkness that would threaten it if The Eight were ever broken? The book was much more specific. According to this text, the evil the documentary mentioned is a faerie. While she may gain strength, she poses no real threat with just seven men."

I interrupted to give her some context.

"The book is right. It is a faerie."

"All right, then. That makes me even more confident about everything else. Anyway, as I was saying, if The Eight become seven, that's not necessarily good, but nothing too bad will happen. Six is the magic number. Six is what she's aiming for. If The Eight lose two men without replacing another, she can break free from her prison."

I thought of Calder's disappearance. It was a good thing Marcus' powers had revealed themselves when they did. It was possible that Calder could find a way to break his bind to the men at any time. If he'd managed to do that before Marcus had joined them, Machara would've been free.

Kate paused for a moment, and I assumed she was waiting for me to react.

"That coincides with some things that have already happened here. Continue."

"Okay. What's the name of this faerie? Do you know?"

"Yes, I do. I met her. Her name is Machara."

I could hear Kate's smile in her voice.

"This is all just too flipping cool. The book got that right, too. So, the book alludes to a prophecy given to Machara by her father as punishment for something she'd done to anger him. It doesn't say what. He claimed that a time would come in Machara's life when she would be chained by the magic of men, but her life would end at the hands of mortal women."

Freya's prediction came to my mind. "How many women and when?"

Kate sighed. "Nine women, and there is no date listed in the story."

Of course it didn't.

"Okay, does it say anything about these women. Who are they?"

"That's where you come in, Laurel. You're one of them, and I'm pretty sure, so am I."

The hairs on my arms rose, and I was suddenly very cold.

"Explain."

"Your name isn't mentioned specifically. It only refers to a Laird Allen's wife, which is beyond annoying, I know. Women shouldn't be defined by their husbands, but I'm pretty sure this book was written in the sixties, so we'll just have to forgive it and move on."

My heart beat quickly in my chest.

"I'm not Laird Allen's wife."

"Maybe not yet, but if the rest of this book is to be believed, you're going to be. The woman's description matches you exactly."

It was a real struggle to keep from giggling like an idiot. It was too soon for me to dream of such things with Raudrich, but there was some part of me that knew it was inevitable.

"Okay." I tried to keep my tone calm. "For theory's sake, let's say that it is me. What does it say?"

"That you're the first of the nine women who will ultimately destroy Machara, but that each woman will be tested in her own time and in her own way."

Awesome. I'd never been a very good test taker.

"Does it say how I will be tested?"

"This doesn't, but I found something else that I think does."

"Okay, let's finish with the book first. What does it say of the other women? How do you know that you're one of them?"

"It wasn't even in the main text of the book. It doesn't go into detail about the nine women, but there was an author footnote at the bottom of one of the pages. I don't remember the exact wording, but it said something along the lines of *little is known of the women who lifted the castle's curse, though two of the nine were believed to be sisters, both blonde of hair and blue of eyes, though one had suffered much at the hands of a fire.*"

I sat silently for a few seconds.

"That's an oddly specific footnote."

"I know, right?"

And then, at the exact same time, we both said,

"Morna."

Laughing, I continued.

"Exactly. How much do you want to bet that she added that little piece of information just for you?"

"I'd say the chances are pretty good."

"Is that all you learned from the book?"

There was a brief pause as Kate took a deep breath.

"Pretty much, but the article is what you really need to strap in for, sis. I think it involves you. It was an article about the fall of one of The Eight—the only one who is ever believed to have died of something other than natural causes."

A lump rose in my throat. I didn't even want to ask the question, but I knew that I had to. Silently, praying that she wouldn't say Raudrich's name, I spoke. "Does it have the man's name?"

"A Laird Bracht."

I only knew each of them by their first names. At least I knew it wasn't Raudrich.

"Does it describe him?"

"It does. It describes him as being a tall and slender man in his late twenties at the time of his death. He supposedly had raven black hair and piercing blue eyes."

The air left my chest in a whoosh.

"It's Calder. What does it say?"

He was in his late twenties now. If the article was true, Calder didn't have much time left.

"Supposedly, this man of The Eight—Calder, I suppose—was seduced by a faerie he met on the shores of the isle. After sleeping with her, his lust for her became unquenchable, and he thought himself in love. In his desperation to be with her, he went to the faerie with whom his magic was bound—Machara—and begged her to turn him into one of the fae. As faeries so often do, she offered him a deal. In his blind need, he took it without thought."

I shivered and held the phone up to my ear with my shoulder as I wrapped my arms around my knees for warmth.

"What was the deal?"

"She made him promise that he would surrender the first woman to grace the steps of the castle into her care. In exchange, she would make it so that he could be with the woman he loved."

I was the first woman permitted inside the castle in years, but Calder had made no move to bring me to Machara.

"What else does it say?"

"Well, here's the thing you need to know about faeries, Laurel. I've discovered this during my days of researching them. They keep their word, but only to the degree that they must. If there is a way for them to twist it, to turn what you want against you, they will find it. This is what Machara did with this man. She didn't promise him that she would turn him into a faerie. She promised that she would make it so that they could be together.

"The article says that rather than turn Calder fae, she turned the faerie into a human. There is no worse punishment for one of the fae. In her despair, the woman Calder loved threw herself off the isle's tallest cliff, plunging to her death."

Calder's angry disposition suddenly made so much more sense. So did his belief that I was horribly unattractive. I supposed for a man in love with a faerie, I wasn't quite up to par.

"Oh, my gosh, Kate. That's horrible."

"That's not all. In his rage, he confronted Machara and swore to her that he wouldn't keep his word, but she simply laughed. He'd given his oath to her in blood. She told him that she had the power to control him at will, that when a woman did arrive at the castle, he wouldn't be able to ignore the call to bring the woman to Machara."

"That's why he ran." I whispered the words under my breath, as the pieces of the puzzle clicked into place.

"What?"

"Calder ran away from the castle days ago. The men thought he wished to break his bind to them, but he was just trying to protect me. He was trying to escape Machara's power over him before she forced him to bring me to her."

Kate's voice was sad and filled with worry as she spoke.

"Well, for your sake, I hope he stays gone. If he returns, I'm not sure there's much you'll be able to do to stop him from giving you to Machara."

I hoped so, too, but I'd never been very lucky. I didn't expect that would change anytime soon.

"*I* promise ye, Silva. I will think of a solution soon, and when I do, I shall return home to see ye relieved of yer duties as laird. Ye will then be free to leave. I dinna know 'twas so painful for ye to be there."

I stood far back from Raudrich and Silva, but I could still hear his promise to her as he prepared to bid her farewell. The entire group of travelers was leaving today, then Raudrich and I truly would have the castle to ourselves for the next few weeks.

After seeing Silva settled on her horse, Raudrich moved to bid Pinkie and Griffith goodbye. As I stood there watching them, Sydney gently tapped me on the shoulder.

"Hey, come over here a second. I want to talk to you before we leave."

I needed to speak with her, as well. Together, we walked to the edge of Freya's garden, out of earshot and sight of Raudrich.

"I was wanting to speak to you too, actually. It seems that I may be taking you up on your offer of hospitality sooner rather than later, if that's still okay? My sister means to travel back with our Mom and the father of my dearest friend. You haven't met him."

Sydney's face lit up at the news.

"Of course, it's okay. It will give me another excuse to visit you all here. Next time, I'll bring Callum. I will see your sister and family through then Callum and I will escort them here. I'll work on helping them make the adjustment, too. It's never easy—realizing that all of this could be true."

"Thank you so much, Sydney. I'm so happy to have met you. Now, what did you want to talk to me about?"

She fidgeted nervously from foot to foot for a moment before finally straightening herself as if she'd finally worked up the nerve to say what she wished.

"Well, Laurel, I'm not really looking forward to saying anything about this to you, but Raudrich's worth it, so for just a moment I'm going put aside my scruples and pretend I'm Morna for a minute and meddle. Raudrich is one of the most loyal men I've ever known. If he's important to you, there is absolutely nothing he wouldn't do for you. He's all in with you, Laurel, I can tell. But I don't quite get the same read from you. You're happy, sure, but you don't look like a woman who is crazy in love.

"If I've learned anything from my time in this century and with these people, it's this: everything can change in a second. So, if you feel the same for him as he does for you, don't wait to tell him. Don't hold yourself back just because you're scared. As you and I both know, time is a pretty relative concept anyway. Who cares if this happened quickly? That doesn't make it any less right."

I knew Sydney was right. Even as Kate had laid my destiny out before me, I resisted it. I was scared. I was scared that in the end he might change his mind. I was scared that somehow I wouldn't be enough.

It was time for me to get over my fears. It was time for me to grow up.

*L*aurel was restless. From the moment Sydney and the others had left until they sat down for an evening meal, he'd watched as she paced around the castle, straightening things that didn't need to be straightened and dusting things that were entirely free of dust.

She was nervous about something, and he didn't know whether to pry or allow her whatever space she might need.

Eventually, as her fingers drummed over and over against the table while they ate, Raudrich couldn't contain his concern any longer.

"Laurel, lass, ye've not stopped moving once all day. If there is something wrong, I wish ye would tell me."

"Nothing's the matter."

She continued to drum her fingers over and over.

"I doona believe ye. Yer mind is elsewhere. Was it Freya? We never did get an opportunity to speak of what she said to ye. I've always known her to be a kind and friendly sort of woman, but mayhap she was different with ye?"

Laurel's fingers stopped their assault on the table as she looked up at him in surprise.

"Not at all. Freya was great."

It would've surprised him if Laurel had said otherwise, but it was the only thing he could think of. Unless... "Twas Sydney, aye? Ach, what did she say to ye? I am sorry if she was unkind. She is like a sister to me—she can be verra protective."

Laurel's expression remained confused. "Sydney's great, too."

An unusual emotion was starting to build within him. It had been so long since he'd felt it, he almost didn't recognize it —insecurity.

"If 'twas not Freya and 'twas not Sydney, then it must be me, lass. What did I do to upset ye? Do ye not wish to be here? Have ye tired of me already?"

For the first time in hours, Laurel really looked at him. As she smiled, his worries slowly faded away.

She stood from the table with a mischievous gleam in her eye and walked over toward him. He pushed his chair away from the table and stood to greet her as she stepped into his embrace and wrapped her arms around his waist.

"I'm not upset. There's nowhere else in the world I want to be. And with every minute I spend with you, I become more and more sure of the fact that I'll never grow tired of being around you." Laurel paused and lifted her head so that her chin rested against his chest as she looked up at him. He loved the way her blue eyes sparked in the candlelight. "And do you know what else?" She didn't wait for him to respond. "You're kind of cute when you're worried."

"I wasna worried, lass. 'Tis only that I wouldna wish to keep ye here if ye dinna want to stay."

He tried to argue, but he knew his expression had given everything away.

"I do want to stay. And you can deny it all you want, but you were worried just now. I don't want you to worry ever again, Raudrich."

His heart began to hammer painfully in his chest. There were only three words he wished to hear from her, but he didn't know if she had it in her to trust him so completely just yet.

"Aye?"

"You don't have to say anything back. I want you to know that. I know this has all happened very quickly, and if someone had told me a week ago I'd be about to say this to you now, I would've called them crazy..."

He couldn't bear it another moment. Pulling away, he placed one finger across her lips to silence her before reaching to cup her face as he placed his forehead against hers.

"I'm in love with ye, lass. I doona care if I doona know yer last name or yer favorite season. I'll gladly spend the rest of my life learning all that I can about ye. I'm a man who has always known my own heart, lass, and I knew right away that mine belonged to ye. Marry me. Marry me and make this castle yer home for good."

She answered him with a kiss and a squeal. And right there in the empty dining hall, he got the dance he'd been denied the night before.

He'd not known such happiness could exist.

Why then did he feel such dread?

CHAPTER 41

*wo Weeks Later*

audrich and I spent the two weeks following his proposal enjoying every minute of our time alone. We visited, laughed, ate, and made love. We went on regular horseback rides around the isle where Raudrich took his time telling me the history of the isle and its people. I told him all about Morna's phone and Kate's plan to join us here, and we agreed that we should wait until she was here to begin plans for our wedding.

Each evening, I would spend a few hours with Freya. Selfishly, the more time I spent with her, the more I realized how sad I would be when the day finally did come that she was free of Machara's curse.

On the fifteenth day after the men left, Freya made mention of Machara's shift in mood. While Freya could see no reason for it, I had my own suspicions. There was only one thing that I could see that would lift Machara's mood—the men had succeeded in finding Calder and he was already back on the isle.

My suspicion was proven correct the following morning when Harry, Maddock, and Nicol returned to the castle with Calder. They had him bound and gagged. He looked terrible, nothing like himself as he thrashed about and tried to fight his way free.

Harry looked devastated by Calder's state. None of the men could make sense of his behavior.

I understood it perfectly. He wasn't evil underneath, and he was fighting the evil that controlled him with everything he had.

The weeks of relative quiet around the castle left me with plenty of time to think through Calder's story and all the unanswered questions it posed. Why did Machara want me? And if Calder fulfilled his promise to Machara by delivering me to her, what would be the cause of his death?

It was thinking back on that night down in the dungeon that made the answer clear to me. Machara truly had wished to see the depth of my affection for Raudrich and his for me. She'd been too pleased at the obvious attraction between us for her reaction to have been an act. I could see only one reason why she would even care—if Raudrich loved me, he would do anything for me—even sacrifice his own life to save me.

But seven members wouldn't be enough to free Machara from her cell, and that explained why Calder would have to die, too. The men were already bound to Machara through their magic, but Calder's bargain with her allowed her to control him. Killing him would be as easy as giving him the directive to do the job himself.

If she could make Raudrich sacrifice himself to save me, and if she could order Calder to kill himself before their bargain was complete, then The Eight would be six and Machara would be free.

I would never let that happen. I could see no way of saving Calder, but I sure as hell was going to save Raudrich.

I had a plan—a risky one—one that would require the help of every member of The Eight, save two.

"*L*aurel?"

I dropped the quill at the sound of Marcus' voice in the doorway. I was busy writing a letter—one that I hoped Raudrich would never have to see.

Slowly, I turned to him, unsure of what to expect. There was every reason in the world for him to still be angry with me.

He looked good—really good. His stature was tall, his shoulders broad, and his expression seemed relaxed and even, dare I say, happy?

"Marcus." I stood and all but ran to him, but pulled up short before throwing myself into his arms until I saw him open them to me.

When he did, I nearly knocked him down with my enthusiasm.

"Are you still angry? I really am sorry, Marcus."

My cheek was pressed flush against his chest, but I felt him shrug as I held him.

"Yes, a little, but it's okay."

I pulled away just enough to look up at him. "Really?"

He smiled and I relaxed into him once more.

"Really. It's very odd, Laurel. Logically, I know that I shouldn't be okay with this, but the magic has messed with my head. It's shifted who I am. This is right, somehow. This is where I'm supposed to be."

I nodded against him. "Me, too. I have something to tell you."

I pulled him inside the bedroom and closed the door so we could talk. For the rest of the day, we exchanged stories. I told him of my engagement and of Kate and, most importantly, of how his father would be on his way here by the end of the month. He cried at that, and my heart could've just burst right then and there from the joy I felt at seeing his relief that he wouldn't be forever separated from his favorite person in all the world. Marcus' dad outshone even me in Marcus' eyes.

Then he told me all that he'd learned and even showed off his new skills with a few acts of magic he couldn't have been more proud of.

It was a lovely afternoon, but it was all I could do to keep from wondering...

What if this was the last afternoon I would ever spend with him? I couldn't bear to think of it, but I knew there was a good chance it could be true.

I had to go through with my plan tonight. And there was every possibility in the world things wouldn't end well for me.

CHAPTER 42

"*M*addock?"

I found him in the stables tending to the horse I'd developed a fondness for during my first night here.

"Laurel!" He turned toward me at the sound of my voice and quickly dropped the brush he held in his hands to run toward me with open arms, quickly scooping me up into a bear hug of an embrace as he spun me around in a circle. "Congratulations on yer happy news. I canna tell ye how pleased I am that ye will be here with us forever."

For a moment, I was able to forget about what I knew was coming, and I smiled as he returned me to my feet.

"Thank you, Maddock. Listen, I need your help with something. It's urgent."

"Anything, lass. Ye are one of us now. There is not a one of us who wouldna do anything for ye."

"That's what I'm counting on. I need to meet with all of you, but Raudrich and Marcus absolutely cannot be there. Is there a way we can arrange that?"

He looked at me for a long moment, and I suspected he could see the fear in my eyes.

"Aye. I'll have Harry place them both on Calder watch. We canna leave him alone. 'Tis the strangest thing I've ever seen. He is mad with his desire to leave here."

I nodded. "I know. We need to meet as soon as possible."

"After dinner, I'll ask them both to keep watch. We will meet ye in the dining hall then."

---

*T*hey didn't like it, but I could see by their resigned expressions that there were no other options.

Maddock was the least receptive, which didn't surprise me. He and I shared a bond of sorts, one that I'd noticed from the first day we met.

"Lass, I doona care for this. Faeries are too unpredictable. If anything happened to ye, Raudrich would never forgive us. We would never forgive ourselves for agreeing to help ye with this."

"If any of you have another suggestion, I'm open to it."

"I do, lass." Harry spoke up from the end of the table, and I wanted to cry just by looking at him. He looked ill, heartbroken, and weary. "We keep Calder bound. We imprison him until she loses her patience and kills him. We can keep him from ye."

I'd already considered that possibility.

"I'm sorry, but no. The moment Calder hands me over to her, she will kill him. If we prevent him from following her order, she's likely to do something worse. I couldn't live with it if Calder wound up like Freya because of me."

"I'll do as ye bid, lass. I'll make certain that neither Raudrich or Marcus interfere. What say the rest of ye?"

I appreciated Ludo's interjection. There was no sense in debating.

"Thank you, Ludo."

Slowly, one by one, they all agreed, and our plan was set.

Maddock would relieve Raudrich and Marcus of their watch

duty over Calder. I would go to bed like always and slip out as Raudrich slept. We all knew Raudrich would follow as soon as he realized I was gone. The others would be ready to follow him.

I lingered longer than I planned, but leaving Raudrich's bed was the most difficult thing I'd ever had to do. I felt as if my life were just beginning. I sincerely hoped that it wouldn't be over so soon.

Picking up the letter I'd written earlier to give to Maddock, I lifted the quill one last time and wrote Raudrich a note that I left upon his pillow.

> *Don't blame the men. None of them wanted to do this. It will be okay. If it's not, just know that you showed me what I never knew men could be. You've given me the best few weeks of my life. I love you. – Laurel*

With one soft kiss while he slept, I left him.

CHAPTER 43

*H*arry, not Maddock, sat outside the room where they held Calder. His eyes were red. He'd been crying.

"It must be me who sets him free, lass. I need to be the last one he sees. I need him to know that we forgive him, that we love him."

Without a word, I took a seat on the floor next to him and wrapped my arm around his shoulders. He gave me one painful glance and then allowed himself to cry on my shoulder.

We sat like that for a long time. When Harry finally lifted his head from my shoulder, he leaned forward and kissed my cheek.

"I doona care for grief, lass. Promise me that ye will do all that ye can to return to us. Doona make me go through this heartbreak twice."

I swallowed the lump in my throat and tried to keep my voice steady. "I'll find a way out. Don't you worry about that."

Clearing his throat, Harry stood and offered me his hand and pulled me to my feet.

"Laurel, I doona know just how tied Calder is to Machara. I think it best ye doona allow him to know of yer plan in case she can hear his thoughts. Fight him when he comes for ye."

"I will."

He stepped inside the room without another word. I moved to the main stairwell to wait.

"*I*'m sorry, lass. I'm so, so sorry. I doona wish to do this. 'Tis why I tried to get ye to leave. Ye must know that I doona have a choice."

Calder's grip on my arms was rough as I thrashed about. He was as strong as an ox. The more I tugged and pulled, the more I screamed and bit, the rougher his grip on my arms became as he dragged me. I would have bruises all over, but I was committed to my performance.

"Let me go, Calder. Please. I'll leave. I promise. Just let me go."

We were in Nicol's bedchamber now, and I could hear Machara's laughter echoing up from the dungeon.

"'Tis too late for that, lass."

He opened the passageway and down we went. He continued to beg my forgiveness.

"If I could stop this, I would."

I needed Calder to know that I understood. I wanted him to have a little bit of peace before his death. I only hoped that I would be able to tell him quickly enough before Machara took me so she wouldn't hear and understand.

I squeezed his arm and pulled to get his attention. He quickly turned tortured eyes on me.

"It's okay. I know." I mouthed the words to him, and just as we stepped into Machara's view, I could see that he understood. He now knew why Harry had released him.

He nodded and released his grip, throwing me before Machara's cell as he spoke to her.

"Here. Now, let me go, Machara. I've done as ye bid. Take her and release me."

I looked into Machara's icy eyes and shivered. There was no humanity in her gaze.

She quickly jerked her head upward, and I saw the panic settle over Calder's face. I knew that his death was imminent.

Just as Machara uttered the spell that would pull me into the cell with her, Calder—his hands trembling as he tried to resist—lifted his sword and plunged it into his heart.

CHAPTER 44

"Where did ye go, lass? Ye've moved too far away from me and my side has grown cold. Come closer."

Half-asleep, Raudrich reached for Laurel, only to find the space next to him empty.

Concerned, he sat up to look around the room, but Laurel was nowhere inside. The blankets on her side of the bed were still warm. She couldn't have been gone long, but where would she have gone?

The rest of the men were asleep, and with Nicol now back, she'd not have reason to keep Freya company. He didn't often worry, but the air felt unusually heavy this night, as if it held a warning of something he couldn't yet see.

Doing his best to remain calm, Raudrich rose and lit a fire as he began to dress. It was only once the room was illuminated by the glow of fire that he noticed the small piece of parchment on Laurel's pillow.

He read her words with trembling hands as he rattled his mind and tried to make sense of what she could mean.

Panic coursing through him, he ran out into the hallway. Harry stood only a few steps away from his door.

"What is this? Where is she?"

He thrust the note in Harry's face as his lifelong friend began to cry.

"I'm sorry, Raudrich. We had no choice, truly."

He grabbed Harry by the collar of his shirt, yanking him roughly toward him.

"What do ye mean ye dinna have a choice? Tell me what has happened, Harry."

A sudden pain shot through his chest, so sharp and staggering he fell to his knees in agony. Harry did the same, and for a few brief seconds, all either man could do was scream.

The pain disappeared as quickly as it had come. The change in the magic around them was palpable—one of The Eight was dead.

As Harry began to sob, Raudrich knew—Calder.

"Where is he? Where is Laurel?"

"The dungeon, lad. There is nothing ye can do. We canna allow ye to save her."

He pushed himself to his feet and ran toward Nicol's bedchamber as Machara's blood-curdling laughter reverberated up from the floor.

Let her be safe, let her be safe.

The prayer played itself over and over in his mind as he ran. As he pushed open the door to the dungeon, he had to lean against the wall to keep himself steady.

The space below reeked of death and blood, and he could hear nothing save Machara's laughter.

Bracing, he turned the corner to find Calder's lifeless body only a short distance in front of him. He was on his knees, held up by his sword, which ran through him. Calder's head hung painfully forward as blood drained from his chest.

Swallowing the bile rising in his throat, Raudrich raised his gaze from the floor to stare into Machara's cell. She stood in the center of the small space, and Laurel was on her knees in front of her. Machara's hands were around Laurel's throat.

"There ye are, lad. I knew it wouldna take ye long."

He said nothing. He was too busy looking Laurel up and down for a sign of injury. There was no blood or open wound. Despite Machara's grip around her neck, she appeared unharmed. He would have to proceed carefully to ensure that she remained that way.

"Laurel, lass. I'll not..."

Machara squeezed her fingers around Laurel's neck and he stopped short of what he meant to say. As he stopped speaking, she relaxed her grip.

"Doona speak with her, lad. If ye say another word to her, or she to ye, I'll slip this nail deep into her vein, and I'll let her bleed out in front of ye. This mortal is simply a pawn. The bargain must be struck between ye and I."

"What do ye want, Machara?"

"What I've always wanted. My freedom. With Calder dead, only one more death is required to free me. Ye love her. I can see that. But do ye love her more than ye love yerself? More than ye love the men ye are bound to through yer oath?"

Without another thought, he walked over to Calder's body and pulled the sword from his friend's lifeless chest.

Returning to stand directly in front of Machara, he turned the blade toward his own chest.

"This is what ye want, aye? My own death, as well as Calder's? If I do this, do ye swear to me, ye shall let Laurel go?"

"Aye, lad, I swear to ye. If ye run yerself through with that sword, I will leave the lass unharmed."

Just as he pressed the tip of the blade into his chest, the world went dark around him. He fought against the spell. He could hear the chants of the other men in his mind, but their combined magic was too strong for him to fight against it.

The sword flew out of his hands as he collapsed into unconsciousness.

If Laurel was dead when he woke, he would kill every last one of his men.

*M*achara screamed as Raudrich fell. For a moment, I worried she would snap my neck without another thought.

Instead, she whirled on me, quickly pulling me up by my wrists as she threw me against the wall.

"What did ye do?"

I'd not known how The Eight would stop Raudrich, but the moment I saw him fall, I knew what I needed to do. It would require that I put on a play for Machara once again.

I was more terrified than I'd ever been in my life, but I couldn't allow Machara to see that. She wouldn't believe the callous performance I meant to give her if she saw my fear.

Freya was right. The hubris of faeries was their downfall. They didn't believe they could lose, so they never planned for things to go awry. If I could use her frustration to my advantage, I could survive this.

She'd not expected The Eight to stop Raudrich. She had no back-up plan. She was nervous now, off her game, and I was just stepping up to play my own.

"What could I have possibly done? I'm a mortal, remember? I have no powers."

She screamed again and the walls seemed to shake from the power of her voice. I hoped she couldn't see my hands trembling.

"Calder must've warned them of what I would do. Damn him. I knew he couldna be trusted. He was too soft of heart. Too weak."

She stepped forward and placed her sharp, pointy nail against the main artery in my neck.

"Ye are no longer any use to me, lass. Convince me why I should make yer death painless, and perhaps I shall."

"Why would you kill me when I'm the only one left who can help free you?"

She did her best to give nothing away, but I didn't miss the slight twitch of surprise in her brow at my question.

"Free me? As ye just reminded me—ye are a mortal. There is nothing ye can do for me."

I smiled.

"Yes, there is. I don't want to die."

She was understandably skeptical.

"Ye wouldna do it, lass. Ye doona have it in ye to kill him."

"You're right. On my own, I don't have it in me. But I'm a coward, Machara, and no matter how much I care for Raudrich, I really don't want to die."

I hesitated and slowly reached up to push her hand away from my throat.

"But it doesn't matter if I don't have it in me to kill him, does it? Not when you can make sure that I follow through with my word."

When she just stared at me, mistrust in her eyes, I continued.

"Why was it that Calder brought me to you? He didn't want to. He did it because he had no choice. He did it because his oath to you prevented him from doing differently."

A light sparked in her eyes, and I could see the moment she understood.

"Ye wish to strike a bargain with me, lass?"

I nodded as I carefully formed the deal I wished to make in my mind. I couldn't misspeak a single word, and once the bargain was struck, I would have to move quickly.

"Release me from this cell, promise me that you won't harm me once you are free, and I will run Raudrich through with Calder's sword."

Her hand gripped mine in an instant and our deal was sealed.

Her eyes were sparkling with her anticipated victory as she uttered the words that sent me through to the other side of the cell bars in the span of a blink.

I moved without thought, determined to do what I knew I must before Machara had a chance to realize that I would betray her.

I ran over to where the sword had fallen.

Raudrich lay on his back, his arms spread out beside him.

My hands trembled as I lifted Calder's sword and held it above the center of Raudrich's chest.

Just as Marchara began to laugh, I plunged the sword downward with all my might, changing its direction at the last second before it pierced his skin. Rather than his heart, I ran it through his right shoulder.

When the sword's tip hit the stone floor beneath Raudrich, Machara began to scream.

She no longer had any power over me. I'd not said I would kill him. I'd only promised that I would run him through with the sword.

She cursed and wailed, but I could see in her eyes that she knew she'd been beaten.

CHAPTER 45

*T*hree Weeks Later

Dear Morna,

I know that you won't respond to this letter, and that's absolutely fine. I hope it finds you well all the same. This surprises no one more than me, but I just wanted to say thank you.

Thank you for all you didn't do. I can see now why you stayed away.

If you'd given me a way to get home, I might've run before I allowed myself to fall in love.

If you'd stepped in to help me with Machara, I wouldn't have learned my own strength. And if not for the book you placed in my path, Kate wouldn't have done all the research that prompted her to come here.

She's going to like it in this time, I can tell. And if the way Maddock keeps looking at her is any indication, I have a feeling we may have another romance on our hands very soon.

But you already knew that, didn't you?

"*Y*er mother is looking for ye, lass. She wishes to speak to ye before we leave for our honeymoon."

I groaned and set down the quill as Raudrich entered the bedchamber.

"How long until her cottage is finished?" Mom had been the stressed-out terror I'd known she would be from the moment she arrived.

Raudrich laughed and bent to kiss me as I walked over to him.

"A fortnight, at least. She isna so bad, really. Paton rather likes her."

"Paton doesn't like her. He likes irritating her. He gets way too much pleasure from it."

Secretly, so did I.

Raudrich rested his chin on the top of my head as I snuggled into him.

"What are ye doing, lass? Please doona tell me ye've already grown bored of yer husband and have found another man to write love letters to."

"Nothing about you bores me." I smiled and unthinkingly placed my left hand on his shoulder to pull myself up to kiss him. He winced and stepped away from me.

"Careful, lass. 'Tis still quite tender."

"You should've let them heal you with magic like they did last time."

He shook his head.

"I doona wish to be rid of this scar, lass. It reminds me of how much ye care for me. I've never had someone love me enough to stab me straight through." He paused and pointed to the writing table. "Will ye be long? I've the horse packed and ready."

"I can't wait to go away with you. I'll hurry down as fast as I can."

He kissed me until I was breathless. I knew he meant to give me a taste of what was waiting for me once we got away from the castle for our month-long respite together.

Once he was gone, I moved to finish my letter, scribbling much more quickly than before.

Raudrich is waiting for me, so I must hurry. We're about to leave on our honeymoon, but I just wanted to let you know how thankful I am for your interference in my life. I didn't know how much was missing from my life— the joy, love, adventure, and friendship. I wasn't totally sure at first, but you've converted me. I'm a fan. Although he'll never say it out loud, I'm pretty sure Marcus is, too.

Much love,

Laurel

P.S. Speaking of Marcus, can I ask you for a favor on his behalf? Since you can't seem to help yourself when it comes to setting people up, send someone Marcus' way when the time is right. He needs someone, too.

Folding the letter neatly, I sealed it with a kiss and threw it into the flames.

I could scarcely believe how much my life had changed in a matter of months.

All thanks to one meddling witch and a whole lot of love.

EPILOGUE

M̃achara's Dungeon

She could blame no one but herself. Her haste to escape had made her foolish, but she wouldn't make the same mistake again.

It was time to unearth her biggest secret.

One of her children still lived, locked away in the land of the faerie, raised by another far less powerful than she.

It was time to help the boy remember just to whom he belonged.

Soon, she'd have help in escaping.

Once she did, The Eight and all those they loved would die.

It was only a matter of time.

Keep reading for a Sneak Peek of:
Love Beyond Wanting (Book 10 of Morna's Legacy Series).

BOOK 10 OF MORNA'S LEGACY SERIES

LOVE
BEYOND
WANTING

A SCOTTISH, TIME-TRAVELING ROMANCE

USA TODAY BESTSELLING AUTHOR

BETHANY
CLAIRE

PROLOGUE

Many Years Before The Start of Our Story
The Isle of Whispers, Scotland

*M*achara couldn't be trusted. She was the worst sort of fae, but what else did Athdara have to lose? With her son as he was now, he had no life at all. With the body of an old man and the mind of a child, the boy would wither and die long before she would, and whatever time her son had left would be lived in misery. He couldn't speak, could barely feed himself, and rather than be rocked to sleep as a child his age should be, Willy was forced to cry himself to sleep, for he was too large to be held in her arms.

He was just a wee tot when she lost him, barely teetering about and just learning his first words. She'd known the moment he was gone who'd taken him. A week earlier, the baker's son had been lured into the world invisible to mortal eyes by a faerie. While Athdara had warned her young niece—begged her—to keep her son away from the spot where the first lad had disappeared, the girl's curiosity was too strong. Just like the boy before, she was lured into the land of the fae with Athdara's wee son in tow.

The children were only gone a fortnight before the Isle's well-meaning laird struck a devil's bargain with the faerie Machara. But as faeries always do, she found a way to twist her word. Return the children she did, but not as they were before. Their bodies had aged decades in a matter of days, but their minds remained those of children.

"I know ye hate me."

Athdara reared back and spit on the ground near the faerie's feet. "Hate is too kind a word for what I feel for ye, Machara. My son was an innocent. He wasna old enough to be fooled by yer charms. What happened to him was no fault of his own. Ye might as well have killed him. He'd be better off dead."

The faerie's expression didn't change. Athdara knew Machara was incapable of feeling remorse. She knew that for Machara to offer her a bargain, there had to be something in it for her, as well. In order to get what she so desperately wanted, Athdara would have to outwit someone far older and more powerful than she.

"Aye, I know. 'Tis why I've offered ye this and ye alone. I must hide my son from his father, and he canna live amongst the fae. My own father would kill the boy if I brought him into our realm."

The child was no more than four—a wisp of a boy with curly honey-colored hair and shimmering green eyes that showed his half-fae blood more than any of his other features. He looked frightened standing next to his mother, shaking in the cold. Athdara watched as the boy reached for his mother's hand, only to be swatted away by Machara's spindly fingers. The boy's eyes began to fill with tears, and Athdara's heart squeezed.

"Why canna the boy see Nicol? Nicol wouldna harm him."

A lump rose in Athdara's throat as Machara laughed. Her cackle dripped with poison.

"Do ye think I care for the welfare of this child? I wanted a half-fae child so I could use him when it suited me later in life. These children have abilities that others will never know. I may need him if my father's curse comes true. If I gave him to Nicol, the child would grow up poisoned against me, and that willna do for my purposes."

Athdara wanted nothing more than to reach for the young boy and gather him up in her arms. Machara was a fool. The boy was old enough to remember all of this. She could see the child's heart breaking right in front of her. It would take no prompting for the young boy to grow up hating his mother. Machara had already done all the work necessary to plant that seed of hate in his heart.

"And what of yer other children?"

"I returned to Nicol's bed for the pleasure of it, not because I wanted more of his children. Those wretched beings willna be long for this world."

Athdara had to swallow the vomit that threatened to spill from her at Machara's confession. "Doona harm them, Machara. Give them to me, just as ye are doing with this boy, and I will care for them as well."

Machara's brow lifted. "I will use each of my children for a purpose that suits me. Brachan must live. The others must die. If ye speak of them again, I will take my bargain to someone else. 'Tis time for ye to decide, Athdara. Do ye accept my offer or not?"

Carefully, and with a heavy heart, Athdara prepared her words. It was clear to her that she couldn't save Machara's other children. If the faerie wished them dead, she was powerless against the evil fae's will, but perhaps she could spare one of them, and in the process, regain her son.

"If ye will see my Willy returned perfect and whole and to the same age he truly should be now, with no memory of what happened to him, and if ye promise me that ye will never interfere in my life again or look for me or any of my kin or offspring, and ye willna interfere in how I choose to raise yer child, then aye. I shall take the boy in as my own, and I shall leave this isle with him."

Machara smiled and Athdara sent up a silent prayer that she'd left no room for Machara to trick her.

"Then we've reached an agreement."

Before Athdara could move, Machara reached for Willy's wrinkled and twisted hand. As she gripped him, his appearance changed before Athdara's eyes. As her young son returned to the bonny toddler he'd once been, she collapsed on the ground, pulled him into her arms, and wept.

As she held her son, Machara shoved Brachan toward her, and Athdara gathered him in her embrace, as well.

"Leave here now, Machara. Yer need of me is done."

Machara nodded, but didn't leave. "Aye, 'tis. I shall call for my son when 'tis time—when he is grown, not before, as per our bargain."

"How will ye call for him?"

"He will know. There will be an awakening within him that he willna be able to deny. When this happens, ye must tell him who he is and to whom he belongs and return him to me once more. If ye doona do so, I will kill yer son."

Shivering, Athdara gripped each child's hand and rose from the ground. "And what makes ye think that I willna poison Brachan toward ye like ye say Nicol would've? Ye've already sworn that ye willna interfere with how I raise the lad."

Machara laughed, but Athdara could see the faerie's fatal flaw.

"Ye are not his blood. Yer words will have no pull on him. As he grows, he will see ye as little more than the woman who saw him fed and clothed. His loyalty will lie with those whose blood runs through his veins."

Athdara waited until Machara was gone, but once the faerie was out of sight, she laughed. How little Machara knew of humans and love. Blood means little. Family comes from the heart. And this boy —this half-fae rarity—would grow up to be kind and good and brave —nothing like Machara.

He would be her son, and she would love him completely.

———————

READ THE WHOLE SERIES

Love Beyond Time
Love Beyond Reason
A Conall Christmas - A Novella
Love Beyond Hope
Love Beyond Measure
In Due Time – A Novella
Love Beyond Compare
Love Beyond Dreams
Love Beyond Belief
A McMillan Christmas - A Novella
Love Beyond Reach
Morna's Magic & Mistletoe - A Novella
Love Beyond Words
Love Beyond Wanting
Love Beyond Destiny

And More To Follow...

SWEET/CLEAN VERSIONS OF MORNA'S LEGACY SERIES

If you enjoy sweet/clean romances where the love scenes are left behind closed doors or if you know someone else who does, check out the new sweet/clean versions of Morna's Legacy books in the Magical Matchmaker's Legacy.

Morna's Spell

Sweet/Clean Version of *Love Beyond Time*

Morna's Secret

Sweet/Clean Version of *Love Beyond Reason*

The Conalls' Magical Yuletide - A Novella

Sweet/Clean Version of A Conall Christmas

Morna's Magic

Sweet/Clean Version of *Love Beyond Hope*

Morna's Accomplice

Sweet/Clean Version of *Love Beyond Measure*

Jeffrey's Only Wish - A Novella

Sweet/Clean Version of *In Due Time*

Morna's Rogue

Sweet/Clean Version of *Love Beyond Compare*

Morna's Ghost

Sweet/Clean Version of ***Love Beyond Dreams***

Morna's Vow

Sweet/Clean Version of ***Love Beyond Belief***

SUBSCRIBE TO BETHANY'S MAILING LIST

When you sign up for my mailing list, you will be the first to know about new releases, upcoming events, and contests. You will also get sneak peeks into books and have opportunities to participate in special reader groups and occasionally get codes for free books.

Just go to my website (www.bethanyclaire.com) and click the Mailing List link in the header. I can't wait to connect with you there.

ABOUT THE AUTHOR

BETHANY CLAIRE is a USA Today bestselling author of swoon-worthy, Scottish romance and time travel novels. Bethany loves to immerse her readers in worlds filled with lush landscapes, hunky Scots, lots of magic, and happy endings.

She has two ornery fur-babies, plays the piano every day, and loves Disney and yoga pants more than any twenty-something really should. She is most creative after a good night's sleep and the perfect cup of tea. When not writing, Bethany travels as much as she possibly can, and she never leaves home without a good book to keep her company.

If you want to read more about Bethany or if you're curious about when her next book will come out, please visit her website at: www.bethanyclaire.com, where you can sign up to receive email notifications about new releases.

Connect with Bethany on social media, visit her website for lots of book extras, or email her:
www.bethanyclaire.com
bclaire@bethanyclaire.com

Lightning Source UK Ltd.
Milton Keynes UK
UKHW020441070919
349239UK00001B/84/P

9 781947 731783